Reviews of Stephen Benatar's Previous Novels

WISH HER SAFE AT HOME

With this marvellous book, character and poetry return to the English novel . . . Rachel is one of the great English female characters, like the Wife of Bath or Flora Finching: both an individual and a species.

Times Literary Supplement

A remarkably odd and chilling story, the effect of which I found difficult to shake off.

Anthony Thwaite, **Observer**

WHEN I WAS OTHERWISE

The book is remarkably convincing . . . One's first reaction on finishing the novel is "Goodness, how sad!" One's second is "Goodness, how funny!"

Francis King, **Spectator**

An intriguing, funny, sometimes exciting and, finally, sad story; the elegant idiosyncrasy of the author's viewpoint, which made *Wish Her Safe At Home* so enjoyably inventive without discarding a carefully controlled narrative, here creates a moving story from what might at first appear to be the elements of a black farce.

Christopher Hawtree, **Literary Review**

THE MAN ON THE BRIDGE

Handles tricky material with conviction and assurance.

Robert Nye, **Guardian**

Absorbing throughout . . . a haunting book. The subject is treated in depth and is finely characterised.

Pamela Hansford Johnson

Great understanding and depth of feeling.

New Statesman

SUCH MEN ARE DANGEROUS

Extraordinarily powerful. An absorbing read; a novel to make you think.

Times Literary Supplement

Beautifully written . . . a delight . . . a joy to read.

Tribune

FATHER OF THE MAN

Benatar's writing captures the absolute dailiness of real life without being in the least mundane itself, and he is particularly good at capturing life's small lifts and cringing embarrassments. This oddly distinctive and affecting novel . . . intertwines the farcical and tragic.

Sunday Times

Recovery

Stephen Benatar

Welbeck Press

**First Published in Great Britain in 1996
by Welbeck Press**

19 Devonshire Avenue, Beeston, Nottingham NG9 1BS.
Telephone: (0115) 925 1827

Typeset and design by 4 Sheets
52a High Pavement, Nottingham NG1 1HW

Printed by Chas. Goater & Son Ltd
86a North Sherwood Street, Nottingham NG1 4EE

ISBN 0 907123 56 2

THE RETURN OF ETHAN HART

Page 9

RECOVERY

Page 167

THE RETURN
OF ETHAN HART

For Daphne Odin-Pearce

1

Have you ever dreamt that you lived in another time? I did
— just a night or two before my life changed. I dreamt I res-
cued a woman from the Fire of London. She looked a little like
Ginette (Ginette, I mean, when I first knew her) but she certainly wasn't French nor did she have brown hair. She was
called Eliza Frink and was a favourite of the King. Although
it's true I shared a bath with her — a very sexy bath, because
she said she wanted to reward her saviour — in every other
way the dream appeared authentic.

It's not important, though, and I mention it only because a
couple of days later, on March 28th 1992, I was taking a Saturday morning stroll through a nearby cemetery — not in London but in Nottingham — and happened to pass a grave which
bore Eliza Frink's name. I must have done so before, of course,
though without realising. She hadn't been a Restoration
beauty. She may have been an early Victorian one but by the
time she'd lost four infants in as many years I doubt she had
retained much sign of it. As always at such moments I wondered how I could ever dare to feel self-pity.

"Excuse me, sir, you've dropped your watch!"

The young man approaching was tall and well-built; unusu-
ally handsome. He made me think of a commercial for Levi's
that was currently going the rounds. (Even his jeans and
T-shirt looked ready for the cameras — forget the tan, the
gleaming teeth, the thick blond hair.) He also made me think
of my son: by now Philip would have been similarly in his

mid-twenties.

"Obviously my lucky day." For some time I'd been aware my watchstrap was fraying but just hadn't bothered to replace it. Since there was nobody else in sight I wondered what the odds were against anyone having been so providentially on my heels. "Thank you," I said.

I expected him simply to continue on his way. But he saw what I'd been looking at.

"Some people's lives! How did they ever stand it?"

"I'd say they had no choice."

"Yes, that's true, sir. Whatever may be wrong with the present at least we do have choices."

I wasn't sure I appreciated the sir. And I thought fleetingly of Somalia and Bosnia — even of our own inner cities. I thought about the situation I myself was in. Ginette, as well. If I'd expressed it, my own credo would have been that in some way or another most of us were still trapped.

"I'm sorry," he said. "I really wasn't thinking." I found I was impressed.

But I answered only lightly. "Certainly the resourceful young have choices."

(Is it always the case that someone who's outstandingly attractive, whether male or female, can so quickly stir you from your apathy?)

"Well, I'm rather glad of that."

"Now more than ever," I added.

"More than when you ...?"

"Yes, definitely. For one thing, it wasn't the norm in the Fifties to go travelling round the world with a back pack."

"But that's something you'd like to have done?"

I hesitated.

"I know the person I am now would like to have done it — yes."

"What else would he like to have done — the person you are now? I mean, differently?"

"Oh ... What, in a nutshell? Just about everything."

10

He grinned. "No, that was a serious question."

"I know it was. And I gave it a serious answer."

"So are you honestly saying ... if you could live your life again, knowing everything you know now, you would seek to alter ... that much?"

"Undoubtedly I would."

He considered this a moment; then suddenly he held his hand out. "Zach Cornelius," he said.

"Ethan Hart."

He was one of the few who didn't comment on the rareness of my name. I suppose his own was pretty seldom met with. I remembered Zachary Scott: an American film star during my childhood.

I felt quite touched by his courtesy. By his willingness to linger. We left Eliza Frink's grave and followed a path meandering up the hill; on either side the grass was full of dandelions which in the distance made big blurry clumps — cheerfully decorative among the tombstones. When we rounded a bend we saw a row of almshouses, surmounted in the middle by a clock tower, which provided a passage through an archway and thus an exit from the cemetery. "Canning Circus," said the young man, "the crossroads where the suicides used to be buried. Could you fancy a beer?"

We went to the Sir John Borlase Warren ("an admiral at the time of Nelson," replied my knowledgeable informant) and carried our pints through to a back yard, where I took off my sports jacket and tie and we sat at a picnic table under a cherry tree. I offered him a cigarette.

But he didn't smoke.

"I wish I didn't," I said. "But I work in a very boring office and am not sure I could survive without."

He asked the anticipated question.

"Advertising. For my sins. Nowadays it amazes me I could ever have found it even faintly satisfying ... but there it is. What about you?"

"Psychology."

"Ah, then. That explains it. Why I've been unburdening myself so shamelessly to a total stranger."

"I think it's more that we're on the same wavelength. Very occasionally you meet someone with whom you click, right from the word go."

If I'd been a girl, I could easily imagine falling in love with him. It wasn't just his blue eyes and infectious grin. He had strength. Charisma. You wanted to confide in him.

"But do you really feel so trapped?"

"Yes," I said.

"By what?"

"Well." I blew out smoke, deliberately. "A job I don't enjoy. A heavy mortgage. A stupid sense of resentment." I didn't add a sterile marriage; at least I was capable of holding that much back. "Will any of that do — just for starters?"

But I hadn't reckoned on the note of hysteria. I'd kidded myself I could keep it casual. I reached for my glass — and discovered my hand wasn't any steadier than my voice.

"I think we'd better talk of something else."

"Of course." He momentarily touched my shirtsleeve; gave a warm and reassuring smile. "So how about the weather? Or — well, let's see now — what about euthanasia? Or time travel?"

"That's certainly some choice. But on a day like this I feel we ought to pick the weather."

"It's glorious, isn't it?"

"Though do you really think it's going to hold?"

I'd been waiting for him to finish his drink; it was he who'd insisted on buying the first ones.

"Perhaps we can deal with euthanasia," I suggested, "when I return?"

But clearly he didn't want to wait. "Do you approve of it?" he asked. I felt a stirring of bewilderment.

"Well, yes — I suppose so. If the person's desperate and there's honestly no other way." I wittered on for a moment about safeguards. As a form of small talk it seemed a little inappropriate.

"Forgive me," he said. "Yes, you're right — it isn't something one should joke about."

I came back with the fresh beer. "We're disposing of our options pretty fast. It seems we're left with only time travel. What period would *you* choose to return to?" I'd forgotten that time travel, for some, meant the future even more than the past.

"Oh, it's not so easy for me. I'd have to think about it."

"Why wouldn't I?"

"But I assumed you'd already decided. To live your life again with memory intact."

A ladybird landed on my grey trousers.

"Just put the clock back? All right. I feel I could settle for that. 'If youth only knew; if age only could!'"

"Yes — right," he said.

I drew on my cigarette. "Next time round I wouldn't smoke!" And next time round, I thought, I'd perhaps be a little more sportive — swimming, skiing, tennis? I'd have loved, too, to be a really good dancer. I'd also be a traveller, of course. Very much a bon viveur. (Why not a Don Juan? That's something I had definitely missed out on in this present life.) And beyond all that, it rapidly occurred to me, I'd have to be a columnist — or fortune-teller — or inventor: in some way, anyhow, a skilled exploiter of my privileged position. The possibilities were legion; I'd only been considering them the shortest while.

I caught myself up, feeling slightly foolish. Talk about getting carried away, I thought.

He raised his beer glass. "Cheers!"

"Cheers! I find this subject fascinating. There are more things in heaven and earth, Horatio, than are dreamt of in your philosophy."

"Indeed there are. Consult Dr Einstein."

"Or consult Dr Faustus." I watched the ladybird walk across a corner of the table. "But, no, on second thoughts, not *him*.

13

Don't really want to jeopardise my soul."

Zachary laughed.

"Ethan, it wouldn't be required of you. I give my solemn word on that."

2

"Come in — and please forgive the mess." It was Ginette who usually said that but as she wasn't here (she worked in a dress shop in the town and didn't return home for lunch) I found myself now coming out with it — much to my annoyance. There really wasn't any mess. What there was was shabbiness. The carpets for instance had come with the house — had looked worn out even then, four years ago. The curtains had mostly been made over. After four years, too, the walls needed repainting. (I just couldn't be bothered. How long would we remain?) And it certainly didn't help that the sunshine was so bright or that Zach himself somehow seemed so luminous.

But I needn't have worried. He was scarcely in at the front door before he was admiring a framed and blown-up photograph we had on the wall, which showed my grandmother when she was about twenty, taken in the open air with her mother and her siblings. "You've clearly got a strong sense of family."

I agreed.

"You care about your origins," he said.

"They could have been my wife's origins," I pointed out, a shade dryly.

"But they're not, are they? Am I right in believing this one here is your grandmother?"

14

"Why, yes, I'm flattered. Don't you think that she was very beautiful?"

"And this one here her mother?"

"Not so difficult," I smiled.

"I'm showing off. Could we have the light on? Now this sister sitting on her other side . . Mabel?"

I stared at him.

"And this ... Lilian? Julia? Ruth? Madge." He left a pause of some five seconds between each and kept scrutinising my face. His tone grew steadily more certain.

"That's uncanny," I said. "What kind of trick is that?"

"A little gift for telepathy."

"Zach, I'm impressed. But come on. What were the brothers called?"

This time he hardly looked at me. "Frank ... Howard ... Stuart."

That was even more impressive, since then I'd done my best to block him, by trying not to think of my great-uncles' real names and by searching frenziedly for false ones.

"My goodness. I'd say that's not a little gift you have there. God! I shall start thinking things like 'I don't like this man; I wish he'd go away' not because they're in the least bit true but just because I know I mustn't."

He laughed. "Oh, no. I promise you. It's not as bad as that. And even if it were — I'd be extremely understanding."

"Yes, I believe you would." I led him into the kitchen, where I got out a couple of tumblers — I'd bought more bitter on the way home. I began to get some food ready and Zach leant against the worktop, his beer beside him. For the first time — indoors and in the narrow confines of the sunny kitchen — I caught the subtle fragrance on his skin.

"Eternity," he said.

"Smells good."

"I ought to get you a bottle. Happy birthday, by the way. Many happy returns!"

"Is there a single thing I actually needed to tell you this

morning? I mean, that you couldn't have told me?"

"I saw that card on the table on our way through." He smiled, innocently. "Do you mind if I wander a little? That is, if you're really sure I can't help?" The dining room adjoined the kitchen; the sitting room was on the other side of that. He was away for some time. "The things I enjoy looking at are people's books and records and photographs."

"Sorry there aren't more photographs."

"Yes, I was disappointed. So where do you keep them? In an album under the bed?"

"Zach, you're losing your touch. I think it's in the linen chest." I told him I'd fetch it later if he still wanted it — though privately I didn't believe he could be all that interested.

But apparently he was. After we'd eaten he asked again. We sat side by side in deckchairs.

"Ginette is very pretty. You make a handsome couple."

Made.

"Was Philip your only child?" He must have known he was. That time he got the tense right.

Zach had opened the album at random. Now he went back to the beginning: babies — toddlers — on both sides of the Channel. But he seemed less interested in Ginette than in me. "How old were you here?"

I hadn't looked at these photographs in years. It was at best a bitter-sweet experience. At worst it was acutely depressing.

"Eleven." Sloppily, we hadn't always bothered to write captions.

"Primary school?"

"Prep school. It was private."

The snap showed three of us: myself and Johnny Aarons and Gordon Leonard. My mother had taken it. Right outside the school. I didn't realise it immediately: forty-four years ago, to the very day — almost to the very hour.

Oh, God, I thought.

"How well do you remember it — that afternoon?"

"Hardly at all. Only ..." Yet even as I said it I knew that I was wrong.

16

"Watch the birdie," said my mother. "Come on, Ethan —
and you, Johnny — let's have some really nice big smiles ...
Darling, I wish your socks weren't always round your ankles.
Or that you'd sometimes have your cap on straight."

"Mum, do hurry up. We feel silly standing here with everybody watching."

That was a slight exaggeration. A few stragglers were still
emerging from the side entrance, yes, but most of them just
called out a quick goodbye.

It wasn't like it would have been tomorrow. Tomorrow we
were breaking up.

My mother had suggested it: that instead of giving me a
party she would collect me and any two friends I wanted and
take us out to tea. Then we'd all go to the pictures: my father
ran the only cinema in town. Today there was a film with
Bobby Driscoll.

But I hadn't known she meant to bring her camera.

It seemed such ages till the shutter clicked.

"Well, I'm not sure how it will turn out; but let's just hope."
She was busy winding on the spool.

"Mum, can't you do that after? Gordon says he's starving."

"Oh, you liar! When did I say that?"

But anyhow it was too late. We had known any moment
Dickie might see us — and now indeed the front door opened
and he came limping down the steps. "Ah. Mrs Hart. Good
afternoon."

"Good afternoon, Mr Eliot."

"If I may be permitted to say so — how very well you're
looking! What an extremely charming hat!"

And I didn't just remember him saying this; I actually, literally, heard.

For suddenly we weren't sitting in the garden any more. We
were standing on the pavement opposite the school.

*

17

"My God, my God, my God!" And then — weakly and inadequately — after a disbelieving pause: "My God, Zach! Can they see us?"

"They can see you — not me." I must have looked considerably alarmed. "But don't worry. Who's going to recognise you? Twenty years older than your mother. Only five years short of Richard Eliot..." He asked me if I'd like to speak to them.

"No!" I shook my head in panic. Zach seemed disappointed.

"Your mum's been dead for five years; I'd have thought at least you'd want to say hello. You were always very fond of her."

"I was fond of both my parents."

But it was all so incredibly mind-blowing. If I took the brief walk to the Regent, I should now be seventeen years older than my dad. I could no longer blithely taunt him on his first grey hairs.

Zach laughed. "Even if you just stayed put," he pointed out, although I hadn't spoken.

"I think I've changed my mind," I told him. Already starting to take it a little more for granted: this whole fantastic situation.

"Fine. I guessed you would. But don't let anybody sense you're more than just a passer-by. It would only very much confuse and upset them."

I crossed the road — a shade precipitately, before I had a chance to reconsider: to be put off by the racing in my chest. I heard my mother say, "Yes, I like it too when Easter comes a little late. It gives the weather time to pull its socks up." Then she added gaily (and startled me by just the use of my own name): "Do you think Ethan could be made to follow its example?"

She and Mr Eliot laughed; more committedly than the joke appeared to warrant. I remembered my mother had always thought of herself as somewhat scatterbrained and she must have found it reassuring that her son's headmaster should so clearly be smitten. How in the past could I have failed to notice?

The boys — standing silently, impatiently, awkwardly — were the first to become aware that I was hovering.

"Excuse me," I said, "I'm looking for the station."

I addressed myself just to the three of them; left my mother and Mr Eliot to the enjoyment of their mild flirtation, while at the same time I tried to drink in every detail. As much as the hat which Mr Eliot admired — the black felt with the dark blue feathers, iridescent like a blackbird's plumage — I'd completely forgotten her wine-coloured tweed suit and slim black court shoes that laced up near the toe.

Believe it or not, I'd even forgotten she had dimples.

And the boys. While asking for directions I'd looked chiefly at myself (so soft-skinned and bright-eyed and full of possibility! ... this, oddly, was the part of it which really shook me up) but Gordon Leonard very soon took over. I recalled that within ten years he would become a pop star and ten years after that something big in the City. But while we stood there that afternoon in Sycamore Road directing a stranger to the railway station — at that period I thought that he was wonderful; was proud to have him as my best friend. I never dreamt that when success came he would drop me.

The man kept staring at me, kept staring at my mother too, kept staring at everything, as though he was playing that game where you have fifty things upon a tray and try to memorise as many as you can. There was something rather fishy about him — not just the fact he wore no jacket and no hat and that his trousers looked a bit strange. I got the feeling he wasn't even listening properly to what Gordon was telling him and even began to wonder if he was the kind who'd offer you sweets and want to take you on a long walk. But then I realised this was stupid: that sort of person didn't come up to you while you were standing with two friends and your mum and your headmaster. So perhaps he was more interested in the open front door of the school, in casing the joint, as Buck Ryan would have put it. Anyhow. His behaviour was definitely suspicious. He was smarmy, too. He said to my mother:

"May I congratulate you on three such helpful sons? You must be proud of them."

She smiled at me; and although her smile was a bit constrained (was it my manner or appearance or something oddly familiar in my face?) it made me feel so close to her, so much a part of her young womanhood again.

"Thank you, but only one of them is mine. Perhaps it's Mr Eliot you should congratulate. They're all of them his pupils."

"They told you the way to the station? Ask them to do it in Latin and see how helpful they are then."

This time we all laughed. Zach did, too. "Disgraceful lot of sycophants," he said. "If you really want to be sycophantic just turn in my direction."

We were back in the garden. The album lay between our deckchairs.

I felt reproachful. "Why couldn't we have stayed a bit longer?"

"Ethan, you can go back any time you wish."

My readjustment proved quite rapid. "But you do realise, don't you? I not only saw me, I was me — just for a second! It was weird." I gave a sudden whoop. "And wonderful."

"I wanted to convince you it was possible."

"Zach, who are you?"

He smiled. "Not Mephistopheles."

"No, I wouldn't seriously think that for a moment. But ... Oh, God, I can't believe this. I can't believe any of it. And yet at the same time I believe it all. I think that you're an alchemist."

"Sort of."

"What would I have to do in return?"

"Why do you assume anything?"

"Well ..." I shrugged. "Nothing's ever for nothing. Is it?"

"But what I'm going to ask isn't really in the nature of a price tag. I just need to see how fully you're prepared to trust me."

I waited. He slowly closed the photograph album, stood it upright on his knee, seemed to be considering it with some attention. "What, then?" I repeated.

"What we were talking about earlier. A small case of euthanasia."

3

I didn't know if he were serious. "Euthanasia?" I said, feebly.

"Ethan, it's not such a big deal. You told me you approved. So long as it wasn't abused."

"But the taking of someone's life!"

"Mercifully. He's ill. He wants to die. You'd be doing him a service."

"No, I'm not sure."

"What about?"

"Any of it. It's too ..."

"Way-out?"

"More than way-out. Unknown."

"Yes, of course. I can understand that. Anybody could."

Half-mesmerised, I watched a black cat creep along the garden wall towards an unsuspecting sparrow. Zach cried a warning the second before I did. The bird flew off; the cat glared — balefully; it served to break the tension. "Ethan, think it over. I certainly don't want to pressure you." Zach stretched and yawned — reluctantly stood up. "All this sunshine," he grinned. "It must be tiring. I know it couldn't be the beer."

"Do you have to go?"

"Or the good lunch," he added. "Yes, I think it's better. Give you some breathing space."

"When shall I see you?"

"Whenever you like. A week from now? Two weeks? Longer?"

I too had risen. I squatted to pick up the album; heard the click in my knee joint. "I was thinking more of — say — tonight."

"Tonight?"

"Or wouldn't that be possible?"

He thought about it. "But what about Ginette? Wouldn't she expect you to spend Saturday evening here at home — or at least together?"

"No. We often go our own ways." I didn't know why he'd asked. Hadn't he realised?

"Well, if you're sure."

"Back at the pub?"

"No — come to my place."

We went indoors. He wrote down his address. "Zach?" I said. "If I really did decide ... decide to go back ...?"

"Mm?"

"Would I have to look the same?"

"Why? What's the matter with the way you look?"

I shrugged. "I'm not talking of radical changes. Just a bit more handsome, that's all. A bit better built." I watched him playing with an orange, tossing it from hand to hand. "A lot better built," I conceded.

"That's something you can always work at on your own account."

"But I couldn't make myself taller," I said. I smiled. I wasn't in the least bit shy with him. "Or increase the size of my penis."

"You seem to be under the impression you're placing an order at Harrods. What about the size of your brain?"

But then he held his hand up, hastily.

"No, that isn't on offer. I was only pulling your leg. Yet at a pinch I can agree to those other things ... provided you don't

22

add to them."

In any case a higher IQ might change one's personality and I wanted — maybe this was arrogant — to remain essentially myself. It was also a paradox. I felt little love for the man that I'd grown into. I knew I was often small-minded and stingy and old-maidish.

But these too were things which I could work at. And I would work at them — my God, given a clean slate, how I should work at them.

"Hair dark instead of indeterminate?" was the only thing I added. Hopefully.

Before he left I asked what would become of me when I had once more reached my present age. I was told I'd simply go on living until the day appointed for my death.

But after death?

"I repeat, Ethan. Your soul is not in any way at risk as a result of today's meeting."

"And what will happen to Ginette?"

"Ginette? Well, if she never married you she'll clearly have travelled a very different path. She could be anywhere. Let's hope at least she's happier."

"Could hardly fail to be," I said.

I went with him to the corner; stood in the sunshine watching him walk down the hill — he turned and waved just once before a curve concealed him from my view. I felt a huge sense of happiness and energy and quiet excitement; all the more potent for being so unaccustomed. Ironically it was only as I re-entered the comparative gloom of the house that I remembered I had agreed to kill someone.

4

One wall and ceiling in his flat depicted a fiery sunset: crimson, orange, yellow — with whorls of gathering black. Another ceiling conjured up the night sky — deep blue and domelike; myriad tiny stars pricked high above the drifting cloud. In his bedroom, lucent waves lapped round the skirting boards, and stretches of silvery sand were fringed with palm trees. He had done it all himself. I hadn't been prepared for it. I'd walked past the pair of wheely-bins flanking an unimposing entrance, climbed the dreary staircase which served both upper flats, thought how the landlord ought to be obliged to fork out, but then — suddenly —

It wasn't all like that, of course. Zach himself was dressed in black. Shirt, trousers, socks and loafers — tonight he could have been in mourning. And yet, once, when he turned away from me to draw some inky, velvet, floor-length curtains, and his blond hair was all that remained clearly visible for that moment, it made me think of an Olympic torch burning brightly in the darkness.

Showing the way forward.

5

On Monday morning I ran up to her bedroom. She was brushing her hair. She looked round in surprise. Normally I merely shouted from the hall.

"Have a good day, Ginette."

"You too, Ethan. Not that I imagine either of us will — particularly." She turned back to the mirror and continued with the slow and rhythmic strokes.

Perhaps I would never see her again. I tried to feel something. I tried to remember her as she was during the early years of our marriage, when she had still loved me and been passionate; forever thinking up small treats, gastronomic or otherwise; forever thinking up new ways to make me happy. I tried to picture her lying on the floor and helping Philip build Meccano; running back down the shingle, bikini-clad and squeaking, ice cream dripping from the three cones.

But it didn't work. It was all too long ago; something that had happened in another world, to different people; I couldn't remember it as real.

"I'm sorry you have to work at such a boring job."

"Ah, well. That's life. I daresay most people's jobs are boring."

"I'm sorry that things haven't worked out better."

She appeared to have no answer for that; of course, there wasn't any. "Don't stop me or you'll make me late. Besides being late yourself."

"I'll wait if you like and give you a lift. It won't be any fun your having to walk through this." It was raining. Our freak change in climate had come and gone in just one day.

"Good heavens, I won't melt. And I'd only feel hustled and think that you were growing impatient." Her shop — which regarded itself as being exclusive — didn't open until ten. "There. Now you've made me smudge mascara."

What I experienced difficulty in feeling for her I tried to feel for the house. But that was worthless and absurd. The most that could be said for the house was that I'd been four years younger when we first walked into it; and my chances of escape had seemed a little higher. But smiling at people in the street, striking up conversations in the queues at supermarkets or occasionally cruising the pubs, even writing to Lonely Hearts advertisers in the Guardian: all this had come to nothing and — besides — the thought of starting out afresh had sometimes

25

frightened me. At least at home I had the comforts of home.

So all I could manage for my adieu to the house was to speculate a moment on what other family might be living in it shortly — in a sense, maybe, was living in it already — and how different it could all look by tonight, without anyone having rearranged a single ornament, far less picked up a paintbrush or had to mix adhesive in a bucket.

Arriving at work I asked about Brian Douglas.

"Not here yet, Mr Hart." Iris, who operated the switchboard, seemed mildly taken aback by my inquiry.

Zach had told me that in all probability Brian Douglas would not be in today.

I asked again some half-hour later.

"No, he hasn't even rung."

Alone in my office I tried to tie up loose ends, clarify things for my successor ... until I realised how senseless this was. I had no affairs to put in order. I didn't have to make my peace with anyone. I didn't have to send off any cheques. Nothing.

It would have been nice to draw out all my money and rush with it to Oxfam. (All my money? Forty-seven pounds and sixty-three pence.) It would have been nice — but useless. Dishonest. Almost flippant.Though I was doing my best, indeed, to be a little flippant.

Because I was now committed; although the excitement had largely drained away for the moment, been supplanted just by stage fright. Which wasn't because of my new life to come. When I thought of that, in fact, I was immediately sustained. Had the chance been taken from me I'd have felt distraught. No, it wasn't my new life. It was what still had to be done in my present one. The very last thing which had to be done in my present one.

I trusted Zach; trusted him implicitly and only deplored the fact he couldn't look into my innermost feelings deeply enough to recognise this, without my needing to furnish him with proof. When he said it was a fine thing I'd be doing for Brian Douglas I unreservedly believed him.

26

And yet there remained in my mind one insistently perverse association: the questionable connection between euthanasia and murder.

But it wasn't only that, even. It was as much the notion of assisting at a death; of possibly being called upon to be the prime mover. By nature I was squeamish. If injected in the arm I looked the other way. If exposed to violence on TV — or to blood or scalpel — I stared into my lap.

Whether it made the business better or worse that I should know the person was a moot point. It wasn't as though Brian Douglas was a friend or indeed as though I'd ever had a lot to do with him. Apart from the odd good morning on the staircase our paths had seldom crossed and as far as I knew we had little in common: he worked in another department, was thirty years younger than me, and in his natty suits and shirts and ties, his expensive, possibly handmade shoes, I'd always thought of him as something of a yuppie. I suppose that I'd been jealous; had hoped to hide it with a coating of contempt.

But little had I realised. Imagine being bent upon killing yourself at the age of twenty-five.

He had AIDS.

I knew this through Zach — not the office grapevine. Douglas had had the virus for years; only within recent weeks had he learnt he'd got the full-blown disease. All the time that I'd been faintly resenting him the poor man had been dying. Now I admired his coordinated clothing, nice haircuts, attention to discreet sartorial detail. I felt bad that it could only be in retrospect.

And apparently it wasn't the physical decline which he couldn't face. It was the prospect of the suffering of his parents. The other things, of course, were factors — the pain, the pity, the indignity. The fear. But these, said Zach, were purely secondary.

"In any case. Why doesn't he simply overdose on sleeping pills? Or Paracetamol or something?"

27

"I think you'll have to ask him that." I was undecided whether Zach didn't know or was merely disinclined to tell.

Because one's so used to following certain lines of thought — or at any rate because I am — I had planned at first to go to Douglas' home as soon as I had finished work. (Work?) But then it occurred to me: why wait until this evening, why not drive there during the lunch hour? And then it finally arrived: stuff the lunch hour, what's wrong with right now? Get the thing over with; you're never coming back; there could be someone else sitting in your place by this afternoon, with his own name on your door and his own accumulation of junk filling all your desk drawers. So go on. Be decisive. Begin as you mean to continue.

There was nothing I had to take with me: neither my briefcase, nor my raincoat, nor even my umbrella. (Yes, it was still raining but what the hell? Let me get wet, let me get soaked to the skin, let me catch pneumonia. All equally irrelevant.) I felt free — despite my apprehension. I raised my hand, in obligated gesture of farewell, to Iris and the three secretaries who also had their places in the outer office.

"See you," I said.

Yet of course I never would — or if I did, it would only be because something had gone seriously wrong.

With that would-be jaunty little wave I headed on towards the main door. I offered no excuse, no other lies.

"But Mr Hart. The chairman has been asking for you. I was just ringing your number."

I said: "Tough!"

I knew that over the past four years I'd been regarded as a plodder and a yes-man, as predictable as I was prone to be passed over. I decided that I might as well go out in style.

"Tell Mr Walters he's a talentless and exploitative bastard who's only where he is because he has a rich and well-connected wife. Talk to him about the milk of human kindness and getting his priorities in order." Coming from me, of course, that last bit was especially fine.

28

Her reply astonished me.

"But where's your umbrella? Just look out the window. You want to take care of yourself."

"Iris, I make you a present of my umbrella." For the few hours she would have it I hoped it gave her pleasure.

Similarly, for the few hours Mr Walters would have my final instruction to mull over, was it possible it could give him sufficient food for thought to reach out sideways across time? But naturally Iris would never deliver it. Perhaps I should have put it into writing.

"So long, girls. Lead happy lives."

It was pleasant to leave them all so open-mouthed. It was also a little childish but at least it would provide them with diversion on a particularly drab morning.

Brian Douglas lived some miles out of the centre of town but Zach had mentioned the name of the area — Sneinton — and a telephone directory supplied the rest. It took me a quarter of an hour to drive there. I found a terraced house much like twenty others in the same street but this one looked far better cared for; or was that just its window boxes and attractive curtains? I paced up and down for several minutes before I rang. Then I noticed I was arousing the interest of two women chatting on a nearby corner — in spite of the drizzle — and a teenager pumping up his tyres. The door was fairly promptly opened.

It was some time since I'd seen him and the weeks had sharply altered his appearance. Always lean he was now thin; his shoulders bony beneath the open-necked shirt. But he was still nice-looking — in some ascetic way even more so than before; and along with the weight, he had lost that touch of complacency ... which I might only have imagined in the first place. "You got here very quickly," he said.

"You were expecting me?"

"I had a call that you were on your way."

"Who from?"

He gave a shrug.

I suddenly realised he didn't know who I was. "I'm Ethan

Hart, Mr Douglas." Although he nodded I still believed he hadn't recognised me; his handshake was extremely formal. But it seemed insulting to say: I'm from the office, we sometimes pass each other on the stairs. It hadn't been insulting to tell him my name for the simple reason — amongst so large a staff — I might have been anonymous.

He ushered me into his living room.

"What will you have? Tea? Coffee? Or something alcoholic?"

I could have been the first to arrive at some get-together; he sounded like a perfect host. Which struck me as commendable. But grotesque.

"That's very kind but — no, nothing, thank you." It amazed me that either of us could be coherent; let alone mindful of the niceties.

"Of course. No drinking on duty." I detected a hint of mockery. "But I shall have one if you don't mind."

"On second thoughts — I think I'll join you."

"Good. There's beer if you want it but I'm going to have a Scotch."

"I'd like a Scotch as well." He poured two hefty ones. It was Chivas Regal and we took it neat. I don't think I had ever in my life drunk whisky before noon.

We sat on either side of a simulated coal fire.

"Brian," I said.

But I looked at the fire and not at him.

"Are you sure that you want to go through with this?"

"Never been surer of anything."

"But suppose they found a cure tomorrow? Some kind of breakthrough?"

"Oh, cut the crap — please. You'll tell me next that there are books and music; sunshine and friendship. For God's sake. Spare me."

He got up and poured himself another drink — as generous as before. Anger and resolution and whisky; at least, I thought, unangry and irresolute, if the thing really had to be gone through, there could scarcely be a better recipe. He held the bottle out. I followed his example.

"I don't need advice," he said. "What I need is practical assistance." It was probable that two innocent-sounding words had seldom revived such apprehension. "You know this thing has got to look like murder?" He seemed to think I'd been a lot better briefed than I had.

"Murder? But why?" I added unsteadily: "Is it a question of insurance?" I had vague ideas that there were still assurance companies that didn't pay up in cases of suicide.

"No."

"But why should you want a murder hunt ..." I had to clear my throat ... "that would cost possibly tens of thousands of pounds ...?"

"You're right. I'm sorry about those wasted thousands. But in the last resort I care more for my parents than I do for the tax-payer."

I intimated that I didn't follow.

He said, "It's simple. It would almost finish them to realise I was homosexual. But that's not the worst part. They think suicide the greatest sin on earth, a sin that would annihilate my chances of salvation. And they'd just never forgive themselves. Now do you understand?"

"But if they're wrong ... ?"

"Of course they're wrong. But what difference does that make?"

"You're obviously a good son." It may have struck him as banal but at least it was sincere.

"Do you have children?" he asked.

"I had a boy who ... He died when he was twelve." And I hoped he would just leave it at that. I shuddered slightly. If I couldn't bear to think about a loss due to accident how could any parents ever learn to cope with the idea of their child having been murdered?

"What did he die of?"

"Run over."

And yet if I knew I was going to get him back, why then, yes, naturally I could bear to think about it. It was just a matter of determination. Guts. I had the pattern right before me. Brian Douglas wanted to die. I wanted to live; I wanted Philip to live. Surely I too should be capable of summoning up the strength.

"A good son," he repeated.

"Yes."

"It's ironic."

"Why? Because you happened to be gay?" *Are you sure they're really worth it, these bloody parents of yours?*

"No, I don't mean that. I think I have been a fairly good son. Give or take."

"What, then?"

"No, nothing. Just a dream. A rather silly dream." Then he suddenly stood up. "Let's get on with it," he said.

For a moment I was paralysed. He started to push over chairs and tables; to hurl things to the floor. "Pull open those drawers," he commanded. "Tip out the contents." I stumbled when I rose to help him.

But it wasn't drunkenness. Or rather if it was I knew my head would very quickly clear. "And then?" I asked. "What happens then?" The words were barely croaked into existence; I was about to try again.

"You're going to drown me."

I forgot that he was meant to be an example.

"I can't."

"You've got to. You've bloody well got to."

"Drown you?" I had a vivid picture of trying to hold his head down.

I had imagined — although I had done my best not to imagine it — a plastic bag. I could tie in place a plastic bag and then rush headlong from the room. I wouldn't have to watch him die. In fact, I need never return to witness the result. (With his last breath wouldn't there come my own first breath? That was vaguely the way I'd understood it.)

"I want to use a plastic bag," I said.

"Christ — no."

"But drowning ... ?"

"They say it's quite a peaceful way to die. There even comes a point you'd feel reluctant to have someone save you."

"But how long before you reach that point?"

That was vile. It was unspeakable. For the first time his voice betrayed signs of what he must be going through: a terror which even my own terror could only dimly comprehend. "All right. Do you think I don't know? In the open sea ... when you've swum out so far that you're exhausted ... the situation ... could be different." But then he stopped — regained control; all trace of quaver disappeared. "And if it's true you see your whole life pass before you ..." He smiled, albeit a bit twistedly. "Then at least it gives you something else to think about, doesn't it?"

I was forced to have a second go. "Is there no one? Are you sure?"

"Other than my parents? No one who'd honestly give a shit."

I wanted to say I would. But it might have sounded glib. And could I truly have given sufficient of a shit to stay with him through every stage of his disintegration — hardly a case of simply holding onto his hand? I could almost believe yes at that very moment, but that very moment was charged with an emotion that would have made any sacrifice seem easy.

Except the one he really wanted.

"Drowning," he said.

I nodded.

"Well, that should do it." For a second I misunderstood. But he was referring only to the state of the room.

I followed him upstairs. "I'm going to get undressed. You run the bath," he told me.

I removed my jacket and tie, rolled up both sleeves, unfastened the top button, did everything but use my elbow to test the temperature of the water — it might have been Philip I was going to see to, sail his boat with, or yellow plastic duck; then we'd play this-little-piggy-went-to-market while I dried

33

him, repeatedly parting my knees to let him fall through, loving to hear his unremitting squeals of excitement. I could still hear them now — extremely clearly. I did my utmost not to let them go.

Douglas came in wearing a bathrobe but long before there was sufficient water. "It's always slow; I should have thought of doing it earlier." He had been down to the kitchen and collected me an apron — the kind that butchers wore. I took it from him wordlessly but didn't put it on.

He sat down on the edge of the bath. After a moment I did the same thing, at the opposite end, facing him. A picture of domestic harmony. Companionship.

"Ethan? Another drink?"

"Yes."

He brought up two filled glasses; resumed his seat. "Don't worry. They're clean. No chance of your ... of your catching anything."

"Oh, for God's sake!"

I had to turn my head and look the other way. And then I thought: oh what the hell. If I ever knew I was within minutes of my own death I should like to see that somebody was crying for me.

But on one level at least it wasn't of value to him. I noticed his bottom lip tremble. I said abruptly: "Zachary Cornelius. Do you know him?"

"Who's Zachary Cornelius?"

It wasn't a question I could even start to answer. The bath was still not ready. Panic threatened to take hold of me. Again. Philip, I thought. Philip. "Tell me of that dream you mentioned."

"There's nothing much to tell. It's laughable. And yet I've had it several times within the past few weeks. I dreamt I had a son."

I hadn't realised that he'd meant it literally: a dream.

"It was so vivid," he said, "and so very much the same each time — I could have sworn it was prophetic."

34

"Supposing you were right?" I asked. The level appeared now to be rising faster. "Supposing you were going to have a son?"

He shrugged. His shoulders seemed less bony underneath the robe. "I think that it would be a miracle. I have never even once made love to a woman."

"And yet you keep being sent a message. If it's that persistent how can you ignore it?"

"You're not suggesting that a man with AIDS should now go out and procreate?"

"No. But —"

He uttered a harsh laugh.

"Of course, you could always place bets on whether I or the woman or the child died first. That would be interesting."

"Fostering?" I murmured. "Adoption?" I believe I must have been much drunker than I realised; these options truly did sound feasible.

"Mind you," he said, "all that, that would have been the rational part."

The water now was quite high.

"What do you mean?"

"Guess who my son turned out to be."

"Prime Minister?"

He shook his head.

"King?"

"You're getting warm."

The phrase was unfortunate. Sweat was running down my neck. I had to turn off the water. I tried to make the movement seem entirely casual.

"I give up."

"My son," he said, "turned out to be Arthur."

"Arthur?" I repeated, stupidly.

"*King* Arthur," he amended.

"Goodness." I couldn't think of anything more adequate.

"Surely you know the story? That when Britain finds itself on the brink of destruction King Arthur will return to save it?"

35

"Oh. Yes, of course. Isn't he sleeping in a cave somewhere? Glastonbury?"

"What — with his trusty steed alongside? And when we need him he'll simply wake and leap into the saddle and ride hell-for-leather down the motorway?"

"Well, it's only a legend," I replied. I sounded almost sulky.

"Then tell me, why should I have dreamt — repeatedly dreamt — that he was born again and went to school and led a relatively normal childhood — here in Nottingham — and that his birth coincided with my own twenty-seventh birthday ...?"

His voice had actually been rising. It was indescribably dreadful how the words suddenly tailed off and he remembered; how we both remembered. For fully a minute, I think, each of us had forgotten our surroundings — certainly the reason why we sat in them. For fully a minute he had seemed inspired. More than inspired. Elated.

But now he abruptly stood up. He took off his bathrobe.

He looked at me; and shook my hand again.

"Oughtn't we to pray?" I said.

But the few sentences I managed to come up with sounded unnatural, false. He nodded his Amen. We hugged and then he stepped into the bath. "Thank you," were his last words — he raised his knees and let his head slip underneath the water. My sweat and my tears and my concentration on the future (scenes from a life I hadn't lived passed fragmentedly and unconvincingly before me) — my sweat and my tears and the peeing of my pants; almost, but not quite, the shitting of them too — all played their desperate part in the drowning of a man I used to say good morning to upon the stairs, and never greatly liked.

6

So it was done.

So it was done and I was still here.

Zach was a fake.

He was not only a fake. He was evil. He was inwardly as black as he was outwardly beguiling.

I had just spent the most horrific minutes of my life. Killed someone. Held a man's head under water and watched his frenzied splashings for survival, watched the bubbles streaming to the surface with tenacious, terrifying vigour. Been forced to watch because if I'd looked away I should undoubtedly have lost my grip — my God, how he had threshed and seemed to possess a strength belied by his frail body. My God, how it had lasted. And why — why had I done it? I couldn't even feel any longer he had really wanted to die; not after all that flailing — those wild, reverberating thumps. More than once I'd almost stopped. But how could I have stopped, when the worst, or half the worst, or an eighth part of the worst, had had to be over by then; when he was perhaps a split second away from that hoped-for review of his brief time on earth? How could I have raised his head only — it was possible — to have to re-submerge it?

Yet I was scared, scared now that it was over and his eyes gazed up at me quietly through the water, now that the bathroom lino was awash and my shirt and shoes and trousers were all drenched; my socks and underwear as well. Scared that he might have changed his mind. Scared that what had started out as suicide — or even manslaughter — had indeed turned into murder.

But why had Zach wanted him to die?

And how had he achieved it?

This was the twentieth century; almost the end of it. It wasn't the Dark Ages. How could I have believed even for a single moment ... ?

Since my meeting with Zach on Saturday morning (Zach? *Zach?*), no, since my meeting with Cornelius on Saturday morning I had been in a state of trance — of hypnosis — of enchantment; I could see that now. I had not been like a real person living in the real world. I had been a dazzled marionette, bewitched.

Bedevilled.

Spellbound.

I had thought he represented the Enlightenment. Of course, he'd represented nothing of the kind. Despite his denial of it he had surely come from hell.

I sat hunched inside my car, forearms flung across the steering wheel, face pressing into damp flesh. Had the meeting with my mother, then — her half-forgotten dimples, flirtatiousness, Utility wine-coloured suit, blue-feathered hat — had all that been hallucination? Were his powers so strong he could just sweep me back to boyhood without preparation; transport my present body to address an earlier one; escort me there as keeper or control? If so he could almost certainly have mesmerised a person into suicide. Drowning wasn't necessary. Why would Cornelius care about the feelings of the dead man's parents?

But apparently his plan had needed somebody like me. I was a nonentity; had nothing to offer, no special talent. Why should he wish to have myself — or anyone — convicted of this killing?

For beyond a doubt they would convict me. They'd find my jacket in the bathroom. Driving licence, credit cards — the lot. Fingerprints all over. I'd slammed the door as I came running from the house but even if I hadn't … could I really have been bothered to go round trying to wipe away the evidence? Did I really care that much about my future?

I raised my head, dully. The women who had witnessed my arrival were gone, and so was the boy who'd been working on his bike. But there were others who could talk of my departure. I'd almost collided with the postman as I charged onto the street.

So here was one murder hunt that wouldn't cost the public tens of thousands. Only the motive was going to prove a puzzle.

I started the windscreen wipers.

I gazed at them like Bob Hope gazing at a swinging brooch in *Road to Rio*.

Then something occurred to me. I'd always heard that you were safe when orders proved abhorrent to your nature.

So? In that case had part of me actually enjoyed what I'd been doing? Found it fascinating — seductive: the lure of the forbidden, the unique power of the strong. My God! Had it been *excitement* which had helped maintain my pressure on his skull, bone against enamel, while his hair waved between my fingers like black seaweed?

No.

It wasn't true. It was not true.

No pleasure. No fascination. Just the thought of Philip. Of my life ahead, and Philip. Those were the only things which could have made it possible — apart from the victim's own resolve to have it happen. I would swear to it.

I engaged the engine.

I had to see Cornelius.

I had to hope against hope that he'd be home.

I was hardly aware of how I got back into town — but that of course was little different to the outward journey. Presumably I stopped at traffic lights — pedestrian crossings — presumably I got into the right lanes. At any rate no police car gave me chase. It was too early for that.

The road where he lived ran alongside the cemetery where we'd first met. I remembered my lightness of spirit — although not unmixed with trepidation — as I'd approached this house on Saturday; but the memory now evoked only loathing and self-pity, literally a howl of self-pity. I hadn't known when I was well off.

The buzzer sounded without my needing even to identify myself. His party trick. I felt relief — along with, as I climbed

39

the stairs, unusual breathlessness; even, against the odds, a modicum of hope. Now I would get an explanation, possibly a solution — I would know what I must do.

But it was a stranger who awaited me: short and puny, yet sharp-faced — accusatory.

"You're not the Gas Board."

People had always hoped for something that I wasn't.

I had always hoped for something that I wasn't.

I said: "I'm looking for Zachary Cornelius."

"Who?"

I repeated it.

"You've got the wrong house."

"I spent the evening here — night before last."

"This flat's been empty for three weeks."

"No." A note of cunning, even one of fierce triumph, had seeped into my tone. "If I hadn't been here how would I know about the sunset and the beach? The starry sky?"

He began to back away but I got my foot in the door. Shoved him to one side. The flat had two rooms plus kitchen and bath. All walls and ceilings were covered in white. The paint looked somewhat dingy. It didn't have a smell.

Further evidence, of course, that I'd been fantasising. But if I was losing my mind — experiencing some form of mental breakdown — at least I was aware of it; and you weren't truly mad while you could recognise that things were wrong. Or was this as fallacious as that claim about hypnotism? In any case I apologised to the landlord. I returned to my car. Sat back and covered my face with my hands.

Should I go to the police? Send them to Sneinton — give them Cornelius' description — say he worked for an organisation involved with euthanasia? Say that I (a sympathiser) had offered to help out?

Would it matter if they didn't find him?

Was he even there to find?

I took my hands down from my face.

If I had imagined that whole striking use of colour how

much else might then be false? Though the events of these past few hours had been amongst the most vivid of my entire life, I had heard that people sometimes suffered from delusions which they clung to obdurately, in the face of all reason. I was beginning to hope that it could be the same with me; that if I returned to the office I should find my colleague looking just as yuppyish as ever — and just as fit — and say good morning to him on the stairs tomorrow as naturally as if I hadn't drowned him in his bath today. Did I *dare* hope that?

I sat in the car and experienced practically a sense of well-being. I was working the whole thing out so calmly. Step by lucid step. In the end I wouldn't even need to see the police. (Already the notion of what I might have said caused me embarrassment: just for starters how would Brian have felt about the rumour he had AIDS?) For basically there was only one point unexplained. Why was I so very wet? I saw of course that it was raining ... but ...

In time, no doubt, the answer would arrive. In the meanwhile ought I perhaps to drive to hospital and place myself in the hands of some psychiatrist?

(Suppose it was a Dr Zachary Cornelius? The thought even produced a smile — no matter how grim, or wry.)

I switched on the ignition.

But that was the last positive action I took. I was about to move off, of course, but fortunately I didn't. It seems I had a heart attack. I slumped across the wheel. Extraordinarily, I don't remember pain; it was the sort of thing I'd always dreaded and this attack was certainly no small one — long before the ambulance came I was viewing the situation from somewhere above the heads of the people who had gathered and of the policeman who kept asking everyone to stand back please (by then somebody had sat me up in the seat and the pressure on the horn had been released). I was viewing it, moreover, with a remarkable degree of detachment, which meant that either I was close to death or had already died, my spirit not yet able to wrench itself away. I watched the jostling

41

and regrouping of umbrellas and listened to the hushed exchange of anecdote; then the ambulance was there and I saw the two men lift me into it (an experience not unlike that of apparently standing in Sycamore Road in Amersham), check for vital signs, put a blanket over me and give me oxygen. I heard them comment on the state of my clothing and the fact I must have urinated ... and felt glad I hadn't also defecated (as yet); glad for their sakes, I mean, rather than my own — dignity didn't seem an overriding issue any more. At the hospital, they wheeled me inside, still with the oxygen mask held firmly in position, and muzzy scraps of conversation floated in and out of my awareness (none of them connected with myself: one with the forthcoming election and John Major: one, incredibly — but I thought I might have blacked out, had possibly dreamt this — with King George and the forthcoming coronation), scraps of cheerful comment we picked up in the corridors en route to our destination. Our destination came as a surprise. I had expected the emergency department; not a delivery room. My arrival even coincided with a baby's startled bellow as he emerged from cosy shelter into cold electric light and with the midwife's reassuring exclamation, before she deftly cut the cord and wiped the baby clean and wrapped him up and passed him over to my mother.

7

As she would tell me more than once in future years, and had told me more than once in past years too, I arrived early on the morning of Easter Sunday ... "and thereby did me out of my chocolate egg, you devil!"

"Why?"

"Because you made me feel so ill. I got a thrombosis on

account of you!"

("How to pave the way for chronic guilt!" was what I felt like saying. But at the age of three or even thirteen I had to express my sentiments with care, of course, even if only teasing.)

Expressing my sentiments with care wasn't easy. There were endless pitfalls. "What a precocious fellow you are!" my father once observed fondly. "Don't tell me we've a genius on our hands; I don't think I could stand it!" Pitfalls and temptation ... especially when I started school; the urge to show off then was strong.

But it was easier to handle in the playpen. For instance when I heard my mother tell a friend about Errol Flynn's sex appeal in *Mutiny on the Bounty* I may have almost ached to correct her but I knew it wasn't possible. And when on that same afternoon I listened to their optimistic reference to the Munich Pact I wouldn't even have wanted to reveal the truth.

I remembered peace for our time, of course; I remembered such dates as September 3rd 1939 and May 8th 1945. I remembered Hiroshima and Nagasaki. In fact I remembered all the major events of the next half century about as clearly as most people would, except in the rare cases where a warning could have been instrumental in averting catastrophe — hence although I knew that Mahatma Gandhi and Dag Hammarskjöld and John Kennedy and Martin Luther King and President Sadat were all going to be assassinated, and even in what order, I had no idea of the dates or the places. On my fortieth birthday, fifteen years before, I had read that on the previous day two Boeings had collided on the ground at Santa Cruz airport in Tenerife, killing over five hundred passengers, which was one of the few disasters I could normally have dated with exactitude; but now I should have to wait another forty years to read of it again. I knew about the enforced mass suicide of an American religious cult in which nearly a thousand people poisoned themselves or were shot; but I'd forgotten it happened in Guyana in '78 and that the leader of the sect was called Jim Jones. I'd forgotten such unnecessary happenings as the Aberfan slag heap tragedy and the My Lai massacre and the destruction of a Korean Airlines plane in Russian air space; such things as Chernobyl and the Exxon Valdez spill, the Alpha Piper oil rig and the Zeebrugge ferry disaster. I'd forgotten, even roughly, such recent dates as that of the explosion above Lockerby or those on which the two Sicilian magistrates, Falconi and Borsellino, were blown up by the Mafia. I'd forgotten the name of the Yorkshire Ripper. And so on. And so on. I should never be allowed to change the course of history.

I didn't even know any longer that Timothy Evans had been hanged for a murder he didn't commit or the year in which Marilyn Monroe ended her own life or the names of the people taken hostage in Beirut. Although I spent countless hours in trying to pinpoint such pieces of information it was always wholly useless.

"But it's inevitable I shall be changing history," I had said to Zach, in the flat he had apparently never inhabited. "In small ways. Others will work in those offices I won't return to; the jobs I do take, on the other hand, will now be closed to their original holders. And even more than that: because I won't marry the same woman and this time will father a son who doesn't die. Besides — it's possible, isn't it, that I may have other children?"

"Oh, small ways, yes," Zach had conceded. (They didn't seem to me so small; I thought, a little tipsily, I'd rather like to have a large family.) "In time, of course, a descendant of yours could hugely influence the history of the world, but ... nothing before ... what the heck's the date on Monday? ... that's the one unbreakable restraint. We even need to have it correct to the exact minute." He smiled. "After that it's up to you."

"Not merely a restraint," I had said. "An impossibility." I could hardly see myself becoming, say, a scientist and as a brilliantly creative thirty-year-old discovering a cure for heart trouble or cancer or a preventative for AIDS before the disease was even heard of. I didn't yet know, on that warm Saturday evening in Nottingham overlooking the cemetery, that some forty hours later I myself should be coming into such close contact with AIDS and should be stricken down with heart trouble.

My views on Zach — as must be evident from all of this — had once more undergone a change. Not only had he existed and kept his promise. I had glorious proof that he still existed. (Is *still* the proper word?) One afternoon as my mother was pushing my pram through the town — I think she'd paused to look into the corner window of the Bucks Library — there was suddenly a handsome and familiar face gazing down at me and a finger playfully prodding at my tummy. "Who's a pretty baby then?" He was wearing tweed jacket, shirt and tie — despite the fact it was a pleasant day in June — and even a fedora; and I reflected a little dryly, after I'd got over my surprise, though certainly not my pleasure, this must have gone a bit against the grain.

To my mother no amount of admiration could appear way-out, especially if it came from a singularly attractive young man who remembered to ask all the proper questions as though he were genuinely interested to hear the answers. "You obviously like babies," said my mother. "Have you any of your own?"

"I'm not married," Zach replied.

"Do you live in Amersham?" she asked.

"No. Just a flying visit."

"I thought it strange I'd never noticed you." She then inquired, hesitantly, if he were there on business.

"In a manner of speaking."

"A man of mystery," she laughed. "But what a shame!"

How forward she was — what an unobservant child I must have been. "And here you thought," he said, "you might have found yourself a baby-sitter!" I wanted to ask him how many such come-ons he normally received in the course of a day; he heard me, naturally, and gave a surreptitious wink. "You must be very proud of Ethan."

45

"There's never been another baby like him! And that's not just a doting mother speaking — everybody says the same. He's just so happy all the time. He smiles and gurgles and looks at you as though he really understands everything you're telling him. And would you believe this — he never cries! Honestly, he never cries. (Well, only sometimes when his nappy needs changing and it's his only way of telling me, poor little scrap.) And he slept through from the very first day I left the hospital. My friends say he's a miracle."

"Are you a miracle, poor little scrap?"

"Piss off!" I answered, with enjoyment. I gave a winning smile; gurgled delightedly. This wasn't the kind of language which — once — he (or anyone) would have expected.

It should have felt odd: this reversal of our generations.

"I wonder if babies of Ethan's age ever have any real problems," Zach asked.

"Not Ethan," said my mother.

I did my best to clear my mind of static.

"My greatest problem," I told him, "is sheer boredom. Obviously I sleep a lot but when I'm awake I don't find sucking my toes incredibly stimulating, even though I still can't get over my ability to do it and am determined to keep in practice for as long as I can."

Even at the same time he was talking to my mother there was something about the tilt of his head which assured me I had most of his attention.

"My greatest frustration is that I haven't got the strength yet to climb out of my cot and lay my hands on a good book. My greatest regret is that — apart from the toe-sucking — I don't feel much sense of wonder. And also ..."

He glanced round at me, encouragingly.

"Also — I'm a bundle of neuroses. Fifty-five years' worth of phobias and foibles, which is something, Zach, I completely failed to bargain for."

I'm not sure how he managed it but it was as though he asked me to elaborate.

46

"Well, to begin with ... spiders. I never minded them when I was small but I remember we had masses every summer and some of them seemed huge. Now I dread that any minute one could scurry down the wall and head straight towards my cot ... Another thing I've remembered — which may be some years away yet but still worries me a bit — is that when my mother wanted me to wee at bedtime or before we were going out anywhere she would stand in the doorway and go 'Psss ...' But these days I find it impossible to empty either bladder or bowels if anyone's too close at hand." I paused. "Then there are all sorts of silly irritations which make my stomach tighten and give me nervous indigestion. There's indeed the whole question of hypochondria — I know that's totally devoid of sense. There's also the matter of noise. But I think by now you get the general drift. Is there any way that you can help?"

He nodded — ostensibly in reply to something that my mother had been telling him. A feeling of great calm possessed me.

"Won't you come next time when I'm on my own? Then we could have a proper conversation." I didn't doubt that he could make himself invisible.

Zach shook his head, sorrowfully. He said, "You know, this is such a quiet and charming sort of place, I wish I could get to Amersham more often. But sadly all the things one has to see to in this life ...! Ah, well. No rest for the weary."

My mother laughed. "But just in case you ever grow less weary — we live in the flat above the cinema. There ... you can see it from here. It's called the Regent."

"Thank you," he said. He took out a notebook and — to my mother's obvious pleasure — prepared to write it down. "My name's Zach Cornelius, by the way."

"Mine, Sally Hart."

I admired the thoroughness with which he played his part. I told him so. "But what I'd really love to know is who you are when you're not playing a part."

He put away his notebook. I knew I couldn't receive an

47

answer now. I wondered if I ever should.

Yet even as I wondered it — I wouldn't have believed this possible — I fell asleep. Next thing I knew, my mother and I were back at home. I speculated on whether Zach had departed by train or whether he had some other means of transport; and rather more than that on where he might have gone and into which period. In any case, I felt privileged he'd come and hoped that soon he would return. I couldn't seriously believe in Zach of all people having major problems over time.

I also felt quite gratified that my mother had spoken of me as she had. I aimed to be one of the most cheerful and considerate babies ever known to man. Ditto boy and youth. At the same time I must be wary of getting labelled goody-goody or bore. "A fine athlete with an inquiring mind and his heart very much in the right place; with the knack of making people laugh ...": this was more the sort of thing I'd want to hear. There wasn't a single good experience I meant to miss out on — although of course I would; you'd need a hundred lives, not simply two, to do all the things that were worth doing, see all the places, meet all the people, learn all the languages. Even a hundred would be nowhere near enough — and that's what made my present incapacity so particularly frustrating.

So there were certain drawbacks even in those very early days. I hoped especially in those very early days.

On the other hand, in spite of these, I had begun almost from the start trying to live for the moment: something I'd often attempted before but quickly grown discouraged over, perhaps because it had always seemed so late. Now, though, I believed I should be able to develop a habit of mind that could become almost automatic: live fully for the present.

To kick off with, at any rate, I was determined to appreciate my room — the room I had slept in until I was twenty-two, when the Regent had been pulled down to make way for a supermarket. Before, I hadn't come fully to appreciate it much before my middle forties, with a marriage that had disintegrated and a personality that had grown soured and staid through disappointment. (Once I'd been a fighter — or had seemed to be. Even Zach had said on that first Saturday afternoon, in the kitchen in Park Avenue, "I admire the way you're holding out for what you want. I don't know why you couldn't have done that more often in your present life," and I had answered: "Because that wasn't make-believe. I'm still not totally sure that this ... may not be.") The room was small but I hadn't seen its size as any disadvantage — not in retrospect, certainly. Small equalled snug. You could batten down the hatches and then were safe no matter how the ocean heaved or tempest raged. Its two best features, however, weren't even part of it; not integrally. The first was a view of the sky that would remind me now of the wall and ceilings in Cromwell Street to which the landlord had denied all knowledge but which even in my prior existence had constantly provided me with entertainment and an aid to peaceful meditation. (And this time, I thought, I'd maybe save to buy a telescope, through which I could observe the stars.) The second was a thing I'd been at risk of losing, although a neurotic, middle-aged aversion to noise must not, could not, be allowed to take from me something which had always given me such pleasure — be it derived from gunshot blast or lion's roar or the clash of steel on armour or just the raucous laughter of a dumb blonde; I mean the soundtracks which floated up to me six nights a week and which were gaudily woven into the fabric of my youth.

I liked the westerns best — although I was regularly disappointed to find I hadn't managed to stay awake to catch the longed-for retribution overtake the villain. If the picture was a murder mystery Dad would tell me who the culprit was and fill me in on the story as best he could — at most I was allowed actually to see only one programme a week, though I frequently did a trade and saw two second-features, sometimes on a Wednesday and Saturday, so that I could flesh out the work of my imagination (yet this could often prove an anticlimax), sometimes on a Monday and Thursday, so that for the next three nights I was able to have the pleasure of a mental re-run.

I seldom bothered to see the musicals; but even so it was enjoyable to have Bing Crosby or Dan Dailey or Betty Grable softly sing me to sleep.

The room, as a room, was not otherwise extraordinary; but it had been mine, wholly mine, and no other room had ever measured up to it, either in the security it gave or the potential that it promised (at least in hindsight). The reacquisition of my room was something which alone made up for any drawback.

Except one.

The biggest of the lot.

(But how on earth had I not thought to speak of this to Zach when I had spoken to him of spiders and wee-wee and noise and nervous indigestion?)

My memory of Brian Douglas.

That memory gave me nightmares; my mother had forgotten to mention there were times when I woke up screaming (although, it's true, just two of them were known to her — I could immediately contain my horror). If only he had died gently. Zach had asked me to do it and because I trusted Zach I knew it had been necessary. And merciful. And right. But all the same ...

If only he had died gently.

I couldn't regret what I had done; how could I possibly regret it? I felt completely confident there was a heaven and that Brian Douglas would have gone to it — how could I regret it?

And yet. Every single time my mother put me in the bath — some thirty years, for Christ's sake, before he had even been born — I needed to school myself not to resist, not to grow tense, not to cry out in panic ... and this, whether or not she laid my head back to shampoo my hair; whether or not I got water up my nose and in my eyes. My God, I had to pray then — yes, how I had to pray — for me, for Brian, for every living thing on earth; my frantic prayers were not selective. (In fact I also prayed — but this was different — during the times I was alone.)

Yet it always came back to the same thing.

If only he had died more gently.

8

For our first English homework at the grammar Mr Hawk-Genn told us to write a composition.

"On any subject. I just want to gauge the kind of work you're capable of — the range of your interests, the depths of your imaginations."

"Oh, sir! Do we have to?"

"Mine isn't very deep, sir — I can tell you that right now."

"I don't have any interests, sir."

"Couldn't we learn a sonnet, sir? Hickory, dickory, dock ..."

Poor Mr Hawk-Genn. I now realised that he was a poet with a growing reputation — although this was something I'd discovered only many years later, after he'd committed suicide and I happened to see his obituary in the Telegraph. He was about thirty when I first knew him, quite nice-looking in a mildly effeminate way, a slight man of only medium height, whose slicked-down flaxen hair was always neatly parted on the right and who mainly wore a yellow corduroy jacket that stank of cigarettes. He left the school before I did, having banged down a desk lid on top of a boy's head and given him concussion. The boy, a new boy, had been winding him up, by repeatedly opening his desk to have a lengthy rummage.

We ourselves — as new boys — also thought we'd got him sussed within the first week. Whereas with Mr Blackburn and Mr Horwood and Mr Tank you knew you had to toe the line, with Mr Hawk-Genn it was believed that you could get away with anything.

And the pity of it was — he would have been a fine teacher. He longed to enthuse us with his own love of literature. And language.

"He said on any subject. Let's write about rubbing up. Let's all write about rubbing up."

The first time I'd heard it — on this same morning and in this same context — I hadn't understood what the expression meant; hadn't even been aware of the activity it specified.

It had all been something of a shock.

"I know! We'll claim we've done it so much we've gone blind but haven't yet learnt brail!" Gordon Leonard put out his hands and stumbled down the aisle in the unattended class-room, zigzagging drunkenly and helped along his way with pushes. "Alms for the blind! Alms for the blind! Hendrix, you've let off, you filthy beast. Don't try to deny it. You're *disgusting!*"

And I had used to think he was so wonderful: this dashing Gordon Leonard.

"Tell you what, though. We can time ourselves — see who can write the thing in under ten minutes. Say twelve at the most."

Then small, hairy, grey-haired Dr Derry came in and uproar was followed by silence — followed by a dynamic if coldly astonished homily — followed by a squeakily edifying text upon the blackboard: "'Manners maketh man' is the motto of Winchester College and I should like to say how thoroughly I agree with that!": which we were then informed we should have to write a hundred times before tomorrow — followed by more silence which lasted, except for authorised interruption, throughout the whole of that miserable Latin period: our first and possibly least enjoyable.

I didn't know what to do about Mr Hawk-Genn. During those chaotic few minutes between classes I could perhaps have remonstrated, said, "Hey, he's all right, let's give him a chance!", but probably a better way was to try to win over Gordon in private (since Gordon was very much a leader) or hope

52

to influence some of the others at a more conducive time.

Meanwhile, there was the question of the essay.

"Any ideas?" asked Johnny Aarons, as we sauntered home that evening.

"*A visit to the seaside*," I offered. "*The life of a threepenny bit.*"

"Gosh, yes. Thanks, Ethan. Original thinker — ahead of your time."

I smiled. "Talking of which, I reckon I might do the shape of things to come. But not according to H.G. Wells. According to E.S. Hart." It was a subject I'd often been drawn towards at prep school but which I now felt glad I'd saved. "I'd like — if I can — to produce something quite impressive."

"For Hawk-Genn? You'll be in a minority."

"Sounds like it."

"Minority of one."

"What about minority of two?"

"Hah! You know what old Eliot used to say about my English."

"But if I try to help you with it ..." In any case we'd frequently done our homework together — and Johnny's mathematics had always been far in advance of mine. "And why should we just sit back and let Gordon run this show?"

It hadn't been a ploy but it was providential. A spot of rivalry existed. In times past they'd seldom vied for the greater share of my affection. Yet to be better-looking and taller and sturdier had certainly made a difference. Not least, of course, in the matter of my own confidence.

It was strange I'd again picked Gordon for a friend — but perhaps in some ways we were closer than before: in part, I think, simply because I didn't fawn on him as I had used to. And, invariably more thoughtful when away from the crowd, he was by far the best person to go bird-watching with, or bicycling or camping: a trait in him I had never before recognised, let alone appreciated. As it happened, too, we were currently talking about buying a set of weights together, from the proceeds of our paper rounds (and also of a visit from one of Gordon's great-aunts — he was a generous friend), and exercising in his father's garage; and since Johnny was less interested in physical and outdoor pursuits and more into music and the sciences — together, twice now, we had made an effective crystal set which passed between us alternating weeks — they now complemented one another better than when I myself had not been so attracted to such things as long rambles and football and fishing. (Though I still objected unreservedly to shooting.) Gordon's father was a keen huntsman who enjoyed baiting me on the subject of blood sports but nowadays I could answer back whereas previously I'd avoided him or if unable to do so had addressed him assiduously as 'sir'. Previously, however, I had missed out on the tree house he had helped us build in their cherry orchard: the really splendid tree house which Gordon had also missed out on, since the idea for it and even the first rough sketch had originated with me.

So despite the changes that had taken place in myself Johnny and Gordon were still my best friends — and it had felt weird on my eleventh birthday to have my mother snap the three of us in front of our prep school and remember the second occasion on which it had happened, when Zach and I had stood on the opposite pavement and watched her flirt with Mr Eliot. And when the camera had been put away I wouldn't even have been flabbergasted to hear a familiar stranger asking the way to the station: a sly joke, maybe — a wink across the calendar — engineered by Zach. "Ethan, what do you keep looking for over there?" Gordon had asked. ("What? Oh, nothing really. Ghosts!" And he had laughed.)

"Or perhaps I'll write about the building of the tree house," I remarked. Johnny had been invited up to it a lot and though at first he had refused to come the subject was no longer awkward.

"No. That doesn't sound so interesting. Not nearly. The future according to Hart!"

"Okay," I said.

"What sort of thing will you write?"

54

"Thought I might use the Festival of Britain as my framework. Not really sure yet." Instead of getting it done in ten minutes — or even twelve — I could envisage it taking more like ten hours. Or even twelve.

But I was wrong. It took me fifty minutes. It flowed. It flowed as fast as the ink out of my Platignum — faster, in fact, since the nib kept scratching up the paper. It could have been a lesson in dictation; my only task being to get the words down.

Yet it wasn't about the future. Mr Hawk-Genn had asked us to plan what we wrote so that it might build to a satisfying climax or at least to a logical conclusion. Naturally I could see the sense in this but I had started writing with a mind that was practically blank, save for the projected Skylon, save for the exciting Dome of Discovery.

And I found the result to be horrifying.

9

So okay. I hit him. Big deal. He was a weakling. *Messiah*? The man who was going to carry us to victory? You should've seen him. He couldn't even carry his own cross. Stumbling this way — stumbling that. Pitiful. They had to pull a foreigner out of the crowd. To get that bit of wood up the hillside for our self-appointed hero the Romans had to commandeer a wog. That's when I hit him.

And I promise you: that really threw him off his balance all right.

He looked at me. It was supposed to be one of those I-know-you-didn't-mean-it-I-forgive-you looks. Blood, sweat and condescension. Turn the other cheek. So I walloped him again.

And everyone applauded.

All right, not everyone — I'm not a liar. A lot of 'em. But I didn't hang around to milk my sixty seconds' worth of glory. I wanted to get up the hill before he did — *three* crucifixions there were going to be — I didn't want to miss a minute.

And at first it was fun; all but some of the women loved it. (Women of both sexes.) It came to *him* and they rammed that crown of thorns down even tighter. They bowed and spat and laughed and bowed again. They ripped off his clothes and pushed him to the ground. They stretched his arms along the crossbar — and still they joked and chuckled as they did it. They showed him the first nail. Good and thick and long and rusty; perhaps it had been used before. "This'll knock a bit of sense into you, Yer Majesty! Let in the daylight, as it were!" I saw his mother's face.

The stupid bitch.

Oh, God! Was it because the word rhymed? Bitch? Witch? I saw a woman tied to a stake and standing in the midst of fire. Even as I glanced, the flesh was turning to charred meat. I had to close my eyes. Me! Press my hands against my ears. It didn't help. I threw up on the grass.

Then people stared at me and backed away and I realised I'd been dreaming. I felt stupid — ashamed. Went hot, cold. Unsteady at the knees. But, Christ Almighty! It was like the heat of those flames had been licking at my own body. I hardly dared look down. Half thought my garment would be scorched.

I made an effort, however. Huge effort. Controlled myself. Wiped my mouth clean. Cast out my own demons. I wasn't a weakling. I wasn't the kind of man demons should ever think to mix with. My God, I'd show 'em!

The stupid bitch, I said, looking back at his mother. Stupid bugger, I said, looking back at him. And for fully a minute I managed to enjoy his sweaty contortions almost as much as I'd hoped. I remembered the insolence he'd shown towards my master when asked outright: *Are* you King of the Jews?" I bet he was wishing now all right he'd tried to curry favour!

56

But then it happened again!

This time I saw a man on another kind of gibbet; only, this time, he was white-skinned like the burning woman (I think she'd been white-skinned) — like all the strangely garbed spectators struggling now to get a closer view. He was white-skinned and writhing, with a rope around his neck (but not pulled tight, not yet) and there was this ... hangman? executioner? ... playfully pricking out upon his stomach the journey which he meant his knife to take ... Dear Lord! I felt the blade slice into my own gut; turn amidst my own entrails; cause the blood to run between my own fingers.

Yet that was me — safe on Golgotha — thank God, oh thank God: me scraping savagely upon the back of one hand with the crudely pared fingernails of the other. I looked towards Jesus of Nazareth. But again! It wasn't him I saw. It was two street children in Guatemala City (which wasn't any place I'd ever heard of, I'm not an educated man, how could I be, just a slave in the governor's palace) — urchins whose eyes were burnt out by police cigars, their tongues torn from their heads with pliers.

And I cried out.

No more. No more. Please stop.

I wailed.

I don't know what cigars are, or pliers, or police, I don't know any country but this, or any customs but ours, or any times but the times I live in.

I'm not sure who I cried out to but one thing's certain. I didn't expect an answer. When I got one I passed out.

"Cartophilus! You may not know them, but you're going to get to know them: other customs and other countries — yes, and other times. You're going to get to know them, Cartophilus."

10

It was several days before he commented. He had our exercise books piled in two heaps in front of him.

"Shall I give them back, sir?"

"No, Nesbitt. Not yet. Later."

"Oh, go on, sir, let me do it now."

"I said — later."

"Please ..." Nesbitt, already on his feet, clasped his hands in piteous supplication. He looked like Al Jolson about to sink onto one knee before a picture of his mammy.

"Sit down!"

Nesbitt sat down — in the central aisle between the desks. The titters turned to laughter. There came, too, a smattering of applause.

I myself stood up.

"Oh, Andrew, stow it! It isn't funny. We want to hear about our work."

The ensuing hush was one of amazement. At that moment nobody looked on me with favour — not even Mr Hawk-Genn. But I suddenly drew my shoulders back and thought, heck, I'm doing right. Surely I'm doing right. And the reflection steadied me and helped me stand my ground — do so, moreover, with an air of assurance even Gordon might have envied. I felt I was making my bid for top dog in the Mafia.

"Thank you, Hart," said Mr Hawk-Genn. "That's more than good of you, I'm sure."

His irony appeared ungracious but at least if I wanted to be noble the laughter of the class was now with him rather than against him.

"It's interesting it should be you," he said.

"Sir?"

"My saviour."

It occurred to me this had to be a tactical error: the admission that he'd needed saving, had not been in control. But the silence was still absolute — everybody loves a whiff of drama, or at least the unpredictable — and on top of that it seemed blessedly certain, whether or not I was now in the running for Legs Diamond, I was no longer any candidate for Teacher's Pet.

"I just wanted us to get on, sir."

"And that's what I find interesting."

"Why, sir?" I was still standing — and even if puzzled by the sarcasm, still feeling big and assured and competent to handle things.

(But I suddenly wondered why I'd stood up in the first place. Had it been courtesy? Or arrogance?)

"Well, Hart, let me put it this way. There are those who didn't do the work ... and I shall have a thing or two to say to them. Osborne, for instance, Whittaker — are you listening? I hope you've got your explanations ready. Also Simmons, Brown and ..." (he ran his finger down his open markbook) "... ah, yes, Thomas. Why have none of you done the work I asked for?"

The silence lasted while each of them in turn made his pathetic excuse; and though each of them in turn played to the gallery each of them in turn found his material less rib-tickling than he had clearly hoped.

"Well, enough of this. Unless the work is handed in without fail by break tomorrow morning, and unless the work is of a considerably higher standard than most of what I have in front of me, then you make your excuses to the headmaster and that's an end to it. You can sit down again, the five of you. No, Hart, not you. Where's Yardley?"

Yardley stood up.

"Yardley, well done. If we have time I may ask you to read it out. But pay attention to my comments at the bottom."

Yardley smirked a bit and sat down.

"Nesbitt, give him back his book. No — give it; don't throw it."

Nesbitt gave him back his book.

"Fletcher?"

Simon stood up.

"Fletcher, your spelling is appalling and your grammar at times a little strange. But the story was good fun. I enjoyed reading it. Thank you."

Simon was a shy boy and didn't look round for appreciation; I took to him nowadays far more than I'd ever used to.

"Aarons? One or two quite interesting ideas and pleasantly expressed. Try to keep that up. Leonard? May I ask how long you took to do this?"

"I don't know, sir." Now we did get a low ripple of laughter and Gordon glanced behind him quellingly. He had been bragging how he'd scraped in under seven minutes — his father had a stopwatch.

"Half an hour? More than that? Less than that?"

"Maybe a bit less, sir." I think he may actually have blushed.

"Twenty minutes?"

"Don't know, sir."

"I see. Well, Leonard, how about rewriting it for me over this coming weekend? The idea of your tree house — I found that appealing — perhaps because I grew up in the middle of a big city. Will you try to take a lot more care this time and really do yourself some justice?"

Gordon shrugged. Again he glanced round at the rest of us. Whatever — quite — had happened, he found there was no backup.

"If you like, sir." He was permitted to sit down and I was again the only one left standing.

Gordon's book was returned to him as Simon's and Johnny's had been to them and the books of half a dozen others, in no particular order of merit.

"Now, Nesbitt, you can hand back the rest. But while you're doing so I just want to say this to most of you. Don't let it happen again! Do you understand?"

I didn't understand. I had tried — and surely he must have

seen I had tried. (No, that wasn't right. I hadn't tried. But the intention to do so had been there.)

My book wasn't amongst the others.

"Which leaves us merely with our friend here."

If my book had got lost I'd have been singled out with those who hadn't handed in their work. So was it a case, I wondered, just of his being shocked by what I'd written? I myself had been shocked by what I'd written, but not on account of its sensationalism nor because I'd thought it blasphemous (except in its basic premise of divine overreaction); just because I hadn't known where it had come from.

"Tell me something, Hart. Precisely what sort of fool do you take me for?"

"I don't take you for any sort of fool, sir."

"I think you must. I don't know what source you've copied from but rest assured that if you don't tell me I shall find out. You really had the gall to believe you could pass this off as your own work?" He drew my book out from amidst the pages of his register and now waved it contemptuously above his head. "We shall forget — for the moment — its highly dubious content. But I repeat: you must regard me as a fool. And I don't take kindly to plagiarism. Who can tell me what plagiarism means?"

But he was too worked up to allow sufficient of a pause for anyone to tell him anything.

"I'll tell you what it means. It means lifting almost word for word what somebody else has written. In effect, it means lying. Cheating. Taking mean advantage." (Robin Baines — in the middle of the front row — shook his head and tut-tutted.) "Doesn't it, Hart? Isn't that the proper definition? Or have you got a better one?" He stared at me and defied me to produce it.

I was not enjoying this. I said: "I try not to tell lies, sir. I don't believe I ever have." I realised that 'ever' was relative; but reckoned they'd all assume I meant only the past eleven years. "And I don't cheat." (Or was it cheating to have Johnny help me with my maths and try to help him with his English?) I wasn't sure about taking mean advantage. "In any case I'm not a plagiarist."

But that was showing off again and it was showing off which had brought about this present pass. I was assailed by self-disgust.

The silence continued. I faced the master with what I hoped was a total lack of priggishness but just having the fear in my mind had possibly reduced my chances of success. Luckily the bell went. It made me start — maybe most of us. I shouldn't think Mr Hawk-Genn had often seen so much reluctance on the part of his pupils to take themselves off at the end of a lesson. It was the final period of the afternoon.

He had told me, crisply, to remain behind.

"Come over here," he said, when finally the room was empty. "Sit down."

On the teacher's dais he'd placed another chair.

"Please look me in the eye."

I did so.

"Ethan, I shall ask you only once." My full name, of course, was written on the cover of the book, as well as in his register. "Tell me the truth and we won't say any more about it but if you persist in —"

"Sir, I didn't copy so much as a single word. I'll swear it on the Bible if you like. But I really do promise."

He sighed.

There was a fairly long pause.

I hated anyone to think that I told lies.

"I suppose, then, in that case, I really do believe you."

I don't know if it had been the passion in my voice or something that he might have seen in my expression. He smiled — a little bleakly. "I have to add: contrary to every conceivable expectation."

He wiped a hand across his brow. His thin fingers were heavily nicotined.

"But if all this is pure invention ..." He opened the book, ran his eye down its first few pages, didn't seem to gather inspiration. "Then I don't know what to say, apart from the obvious fact it's powerful stuff — practically uncanny coming from a lad of eleven. Do you mind if I smoke?"

He used his matchbox as an ashtray.

"You *are* only eleven?" It was stupid, I didn't even like to nod. But the question was rhetorical. "Ethan, where do you get your vocabulary? The adult way you phrase things?"

"Couldn't it be, sir, just because I've read a lot?" I indicated the essay; added naively, "I'm sorry about calling the Virgin Mary a bitch and Jesus a —"

"Yes. Well, that wasn't you, was it? It was the character you wrote about." He drew lengthily on his Senior Service and gazed for a moment at its burning tip. "What gave you the idea of writing on the Wandering Jew? I gather from Mr Marne that in Scripture at present you're dealing with King David."

"The Wandering Jew?" I said.

"Didn't you even realise who Cartophilus was?"

"No. The whole thing ... you see, the whole thing sort of wrote itself. In a way all I did was hold the pen."

"But obviously you've read about him?"

"I suppose I must have."

"You don't remember?"

"Perhaps I've just heard people speaking of him. The wireless maybe?"

"Your parents talk to you about such things?"

"No."

"And hanging, drawing and quartering ...?"

"I know I've read of that. I almost wish I hadn't."

He lifted a shred of tobacco off his tongue.

"And why on earth Guatemala City?"

I shrugged.

"Ethan, has it happened to you before — anything of this kind?"

"No."

"Did you tell your parents?"

I shook my head.

"And yet you brought the work to school."

I wished more than ever that I hadn't. (Yet found it a comfort that I still heard a whisper in my mind: appreciate the present: sitting here amid the chalk dust and September sunlight: facing a man who's deeply well-intentioned — but ridiculed — and who will have killed himself in less than twenty years.) Why couldn't I simply have produced a replacement? Damn it all, it was only fifty minutes I had lost.

He gave another sigh.

"What worries me is ... where these awful images proceed from. Ethan, are you in any sort of trouble or ... or torment? Do you often think about such things as burnings and crucifixions and torture?"

"No. No, sir. Not more than most."

"I'm not sure at your age you should think of them at all. Ever have bad dreams — anything like that?"

He must have seen me hesitate.

"Do you?"

"Only one," I said. "Occasionally."

"What do you dream?"

"I dream I'm drowning someone."

"My God. Why? Do you know why?"

I bit my lip — but then said, carefully: "I once saw someone drown."

"And is that the person who figures in your dream?"

"Yes."

"Do you feel you were responsible?"

"Partly. But, sir. I'm coping with it. If you told my parents it would only upset them. There's nothing they can do."

He stubbed out the cigarette; we watched its thin, expiring gasp of smoke. He almost took another — then looked at me, decided not to.

"I'll say one thing. You certainly have the air of somebody who is coping. Except for this ..." He tapped the book a few times on his knee.

"And please don't tell Mr Saunders. I've mentioned it to you, sir, because you asked, but if it ever got out — if it ever reached my parents ..."

"Don't worry. If I do talk to the headmaster it will be simply because I think you've got exceptional gifts."

"Sir, you should see my geometry — and science. My French isn't all that hot, either."

He laughed. "Too soon to say about geometry and science and French — you've only just started. But this ..."

" ... is almost certainly a fluke," I said. I didn't have exceptional gifts — other than the obvious one I had received about a dozen years earlier. Neither in this life nor my last had I shown any particular aptitude for writing; nor any inexplicable reaching out of the imagination beyond the boundaries of my own experience. The only card I still had up my sleeve was the shape of things to come — and even then I had no guarantee I'd be able to set it down vividly enough to enthral anyone who didn't know it was a bona fide revelation.

"Well, anyway," he said, "we'll see. Whatever happens you don't need to feel at all pressured."

He stood up and put his smoking materials back in his pocket.

"I suppose you wouldn't like someone to talk to about this other thing — this drowning? You don't think it might help?"

"No, sir."

"Fair enough. But if ever for any reason you want to change your mind ..." Then, oddly, he held out his hand. As I shook it he said: "Sorry about the unpleasantness in class. I hope you'll be able to forgive all that."

I told him with conviction that it hadn't been his fault; and then held open the door for him and we left the room.

If only he had died more gently ... A terrifying notion came to me. In March of 1992 would I be called upon to drown him a second time? I wouldn't. I couldn't. I should just have to make sure I was a very long way from Nottingham during the period surrounding my fifty-fifth birthday.

It was my grandparents' sixty-third wedding anniversary. Three years ago we had had a slap-up celebration at the Golden Hind but today was a somewhat quieter affair — Nana and Gramps, my mother's widowed sister and unmarried brother and our three selves. (My father's parents were both dead.) Also, it was a daytime, not an evening do. The anniversary this year fell on a Sunday.

In fact it was to be just a glorified Sunday dinner — made special by having chicken in place of a joint and wine in place of water. The chickens, two of them, were to be eaten cold, with salad and new potatoes, because it was July and for the past week the weather had been sultry. The four bottles of white wine clinked up against each other in a bucket in the bathroom.

While laying the breakfast my mother was laughing but prepared to panic.

"Do you realise that they'll be here in three hours and I haven't done a thing? I should have got it all ready yesterday."

"But yesterday you made the cakes and trifle — and you and Ethan thoroughly enjoyed your picnic in the woods. You weren't just standing idle."

"Thank you. So I've now got half the pudding prepared and maybe half the tea. Oh, wonderful! What about all those potatoes which need to be scrubbed, the salad which needs to be washed, the chickens which need to be cooked, the table which needs to be laid, the eggs which need to be beaten, the cream which needs to be whipped, the chickens which need to be carved? Now what about all that?"

"You know," said my father solemnly, "I think they could have done with you as Mr Churchill's speech-writer. Have we ever heard such rhetoric?"

"There's also the present to be wrapped; the card to be written. I'd also like to have a bath and wash my hair and spend a little time on getting myself ready. There are probably dozens of other little also's that I've overlooked."

"I don't suppose his trifle would compare with yours, either."

"I wish you'd be serious for a moment."

"You know you'll get through it all just fine." He lightly smacked her bottom as she leant across the table to find space for the Post-Toasties. "You know you have a highly domesticated husband and at times a semi-domesticated son —"

"Yes, I do have a domesticated son, thank God."

"I shall ignore that. And after all it's only your mum and dad and brother and sister. It isn't the King and Queen."

"I happen to believe I should try to treat my family as if they were the King and Queen."

"Now, you know what that means, Ethan. You walk out of the room backwards. And you must bow from the waist."

"It isn't funny," said my mother. "If you hadn't ..." (she glanced in my direction) " ... kept us awake so late last night ... reading ... I'd have been up an hour ago — even two hours — getting on as I had planned. It's all very well for you to make jokes." She herself was half joking; but only half.

Even at fourteen, even with the accumulated experience of — give or take — seventy years, I found it oddly disturbing to

67

know my parents had a sex life. I ought to have been pleased
— and in a way I was — and yet it was by no means as simple
as seventy years should have made it. And I wondered if Dad
saw a little of this in my expression.

"You're very quiet, my son."

"Just thinking."

"That's my boy — and don't I know what you're thinking
about? Why, about how you're going to take over and make
light of all your mother's little problems:" He pinched my
cheek in imitation of Alec Guinness's Fagin. *"Jewel!"* he said.
"Treasure!" he said. *"Angel!"* he said. (Three pinches in total,
though I tried to duck away.) "All you need do is keep your reputation alive for one more morning, little prince — earn yourself half-a-crown or maybe three bob into the bargain — and
let your mum retire to beautify herself, put on her regalia,
practise her curtseys and let me have my own bath in peace
and read the News of the World in time to get the scandalised
look off my face before our royal visitors arrive!"

Unfortunately, his humour today was falling somewhat flat.
Inwardly I railed at the awkwardness of life. I'd had literally
years in which to remember the importance of this date and I
had remembered it listening to the crystal set at five-to-nine
that very morning — in other words, less than half an hour
previously. Why did things invariably have to happen that way
... no matter how far-sighted or backward-looking you tried
religiously to be? And while I'd been listening, of all things, to
the weather forecast!

"Dad. This is rotten. I was just going to tell you both — I've
got to go out."

"Oh, Ethan!" cried my mother — and now the last sign of
her being able to laugh at this situation immediately disappeared. "Oh, no, but you can't! I've been relying on you! Where
have you got to go?"

"Aylesbury."

In other words — about fifteen miles from Amersham. The
train service, even on a Sunday, wasn't too bad but there'd

be several miles to cycle once I reached the other end. Even if things went smoothly I couldn't expect to get home much before our guests.

"Son, you can't," said my father. "That's all there is to it. Who were you going with? Well, whoever it was, just give them a ring and explain your mother needs you."

"I can't."

"Of course you can. Say you're ill if you like."

"I mean, I'm not going with anybody and there's no way I can put it off."

"You're not making much sense."

"Dad, I have to see somebody."

"Who?"

"I don't know. I mean, I don't know her name."

My father looked at my mother.

"No, it isn't like that," I said. "It's —"

"Ethan, frankly I don't care what it's like. Not right now. The thing is — you're not going anyway."

"Dad, I've got to."

"Sorry," he said.

"I shall have to go — whether you let me or not." This was miserable. At fourteen I was already much taller and broader than my father.

"Ethan, be very careful. I feel tired. I'm not in any mood to mess around. If you walk out of here this morning without my permission then you just needn't bother to come back."

"Bethel!" screamed my mother, and then to me: "No, obviously he doesn't mean that. But all the same —"

"I'm sorry. I really am. I'm sorry, Mum. Dad. Look — I'll make a start on the potatoes right now. In twenty minutes I can almost have them done."

My mother looked as if she were about to cry. "No, you haven't eaten any breakfast — not a thing. I want you to at least sit down again and eat your breakfast."

"Yes, sit down and eat your breakfast," said my father, "and while you do so you can tell us perhaps what this is all about."

I didn't sit down again. Now that he was struggling to recover his temper I realised I was fast losing hold of mine. I too was feeling tired; I too had been having orgasms — though merely on my own. (I didn't much like the thought of Zach knowing, or indeed my Granny and Granddad, but the drive at times was just too strong.) I had lost my temper before — by no means the saintlike individual I had hoped and prayed to be — but at least it hadn't happened often and at least I'd always done my best to make amends. And at least, too, I didn't sulk. Not any more. But my voice had a hard and bitter quality which — even now — I hated myself for.

"No, I can't tell you. You've just got to take my word for it that it's important. I'd really have thought by now that you'd have learnt to trust me and realise I'd have put this off, if only I could have!"

I felt relief I didn't actually say, "Sometimes I think you take advantage of me!", although the phrase was in my mind — because I knew my parents depended on me for dozens of things that fourteen-year-olds didn't normally get asked to do (from mending fuses and replacing washers to decorating and cleaning windows and digging the allotment); and I was really glad this was the case — in theory I wanted to be made use of, always and as fully as possible — but I wished that I could just get round things on occasion by telling harmless little lies, the sort that hurt nobody and simply eased away the complications.

"All right! Go off on your little jaunt," said my father.

"It isn't a little jaunt and I can't see why there should be all this fuss anyway. Like you said yourself, it's just family for heaven's sake — and all of them would be only too happy to pitch in if necessary; I honestly know they would. Truly know it."

But by this time my mother was actually crying. On the one hand I was tempted to put my arms about her but on the other I felt it was all so ridiculous; and in any case my father was there to put his arms about her.

He called after me. "Next time someone says how wonderful you are I think we'll have a slightly different answer for them!"

"Like don't let people take advantage of you!" I shouted back. I just had to have the last word.

Already, though, as I was cycling down to the station, teeth uncleaned, hair unbrushed (and this was a day we'd all been looking forward to!), the tears were welling up in my own eyes; and would have been easier to hold back if only they'd been an expression of real and righteous recrimination. But they weren't. Inevitably they'd been brought on by remorse and shame. I should have handled it far better: that whole silly scene which had sprung up out of nothing! If only I had been less tired! I would have liked to turn round then and there and throw my arms about the pair of them and confess I'd spoken wholly out of turn and without having meant a word of it. But I hadn't got the time and what could I have offered, anyway, apart from my apology, that would have made the situation more acceptable? I wished I could have talked to Zach.

I often wished I could have talked to Zach — whom I had seen only once since infancy; and that had been when I was ten.

I'd been wandering on my own round Woolworths — or, more precisely, standing at one of the long counters looking a little aimlessly through photographs of film stars.

"I hope this isn't how you normally spend your time," he'd said, suddenly beside me with a grin. It was as though we saw each other every day; there was absolutely no need for formalities or catching up.

"Why? What should I be doing?" Then I put my arms around his legs for a moment and held my head against his stomach.

"Reading something improving, not looking at pictures of Susan Hayward and Jean Kent."

"I'm always reading something improving," I grumbled — though the grumble was as counterfeit as the reproach it

71

answered.

"Like what — at the moment?"

"*Confessions of St Augustine* and *Just William*. The first one has an Arthur Ransome dust jacket around it."

"And before that?"

"Bertrand Russell — protected by Enid Blyton."

"Where do you find such things as St Augustine and Russell?"

"There's a secondhand bookshop in — ," and then I saw his face and realised he knew perfectly well. "The old man thinks I've got the best-read family in the whole of Bucks — and that there's always one of them having a birthday. He feels sorry for me and lets me take things for practically nothing. *The Brothers Karamazov*, for instance, cost me sixpence."

Being certain that Zach was in some way involved I had wanted to convey my thanks.

"How are you enjoying your childhood in general?"

We were walking slowly round the various counters.

"Oh, it's great!"

"Tell me."

"I don't know how. Do you want a list of things?"

"Why not?"

"Well ..." Where did I begin? A sense of wonder had gradually been restored to me, a boy's-eye view of the world, that noticed as if for the first time the patterning on a snail's shell or the inside of a foxglove. It had been fun being pushed along in one's buggy, being given rides on shoulders, having a teddy bear, tricycle, scooter, roller skates — electric train set — wind-up gramophone. It had been fun staying with grandparents and sleeping in a room with sloping ceiling and a sloping floor and scattering grain for the hens and going mushroom-picking before breakfast. It had been fun being taken to children's plays and circuses and pantomimes — and knowing that this time one had to hang onto everything one could, since it was all so fleeting and unrepeatable and precious. (Essentially unrepeatable.) But it wasn't easy just to

72

pick out in a few minutes and without warning the thousand contributing ingredients. "I honestly can't do it justice."

"But if you don't even try I shall think it very feeble. And be enormously disappointed."

I needed no greater spur; and well he knew it.

"Okay, then. Completely at random. One's first glimpse of the sea — out of a train window. The smell of a grocer's shop. Tobogganing on a tin tray. Riding on a pram base. Running after car tyres. Playing hide-and seek on summer evenings in the dark. I think this all sounds very naff."

Zach smiled.

"It's 1947. I don't know the meaning of that word."

"There's a negative side as well."

He was riffling through some sheet music.

"Like financial dependence and lack of freedom. Like still getting scared of things. Silly things. I had hoped I might get over that."

"Had you? I'm sure I don't know why."

"But anyway. On balance it's been ... phenomenal." Perhaps no other childhood — well certainly not my own — had ever been so rich.

"And what about your looks?"

"My looks? Oh, fine. Yes." But somehow they didn't seem important any longer. Maybe they would come to be so as I grew older and got interested in girls; or maybe it was just a case of wanting what you hadn't got and not reflecting much on all the things you had. But I liked to think of meat and cheese and peanut butter changing into muscle.

"I note you haven't mentioned the halt, the lame and the blind."

"Don't mock," I said. "It may not amount to much — but I do try."

"I wasn't mocking." But undoubtedly he'd parodied the phrase.

"I'm only a little boy of ten. Unfortunately there are limits to what people will accept from little boys of ten."

73

He laughed but then added more seriously:

"Never mind. You'll get older. That's a promise."

"Big-Hearted Arthur," I said.

He turned from his desultory inspection of assorted loose biscuits and looked at me closely. "Why do you say that?"

I was cock-a-hoop.

"Oh, Zach, you surprise me. I thought you knew everything. And you haven't heard of Arthur Askey!"

"Oh. Right. 'Hello, playmates' ... 'Bzz, bzz, bzz, honey bee, honey bee ...'"

"Too late," I said complacently. "Just can't bear to think I caught you out, can you?"

"You jumped-up specimen! Don't break a lance with me!" He smiled as he ruffled my hair.

I hadn't met the expression. "Derived from jousting?"

"Which in turn derives from *jouster*, Old French. To fight on horseback."

"That's something I'd like to take up as soon as I can."

"Jousting?"

"Yes — and fencing — why not? But what I really meant (as I *think* you must have known) happened to be riding."

"I agree. It's an imperative. It's also great fun."

"Along with tennis and squash and boxing and ..." I stopped — aware that, again, my voice had risen in excitement. "Zach? Do you ever get the feeling I've a lot to make up for?"

When I'd said it I had meant lost time but the phrase had hung around in my mind, reverberated, and increasingly taken on a different connotation.

"I've got a lot to make up for," I thought now, as I cycled on towards the station.

Once more, when he had gone, it stuck me that I had spoken largely of inanities (just carried away by the sheer exhilaration of seeing him again — *very* schoolboyish) and still hadn't mentioned the thing which cut to the very heart of my being — my unshakable guilt over Brian Douglas. It seemed there was a temporary malfunction in that part of my memory —

all-too-soon self-regulating. But it also seemed, whether I mentioned it or not, that Zach must already know. Yet why in that case didn't he help, as he was always, in other ways, so very quick to do? God certainly knew — why didn't *he* help? (Was what I was doing, had done, so unforgivable, so wrong, so very much beyond the pale?) The prayer was daily in my thoughts — the prayer for both Brian Douglas and for me — and yet the burden remained intact (the cross I had to carry, as Miss Evers at the library would have phrased it; an expression I abominated with a force that simply wasn't rational and could sometimes make me shudder): the nightmares continued as before, though admittedly not so often, perhaps only twice or thrice a year. It was enough. I didn't have to be asleep to remember its content.

I got to Aylesbury at half-past-ten and then cycled to the village where Major Shipman lived. The Major was one of my father's bosses. He and Mr King owned not only the Regent but — in Chesham — the Embassy and the Astoria, as well as one or two other cinemas in neighbouring towns. I had met him on several occasions, received good presents from him and his wife on each of the past six Christmases, as well as from Mr and Mrs King — Dad had come back from the war in September 1945 and almost at once been taken on as the Regent's manager — but I'd never visited the Shipmans at their home and it wasn't them I'd come to see today. (As a matter of fact, I knew that on the following morning the Major would be calling upon us — and bringing with him a package of his wife's homemade meringues.) Luckily, though, the way to the village had been decently signposted.

I hoped to heaven the Shipmans had only one close set of neighbours; for if there were houses all about and more or less equidistant then my job was made at once more difficult. Even now, merely thinking about it — the embarrassment involved — made me sweat as I busily pedalled and if the land had been hilly my Aertex shirt would have been damper than it was. Just the humidity in the atmosphere made the ride seem strenuous. But that also, the humidity, served as a reminder and a spur.

Apple Tree House was the only dwelling in any direction that could have been called close to Shipman's Farm but my heart was showing no signs of slowing down in gratitude as I pushed open the front gate and walked along the narrow path between rows of neatly planted vegetables that were interspersed with pinks and marigolds and lavender. Perhaps the apple trees — or at least tree — were in the back garden. The house itself was unpretentious: redbrick, small and functional: and looked more in keeping somehow with its vegetables than with the somewhat opulent display of roses around the front door.

A man answered my knock in his shirt and braces and with a crumpled sheet of the Sunday paper dangling from one hand.

I wished him good morning and asked him if his wife were home. I knew I sounded polite and middle-class and stupid.

"No — what do you want her for?" His eyes appeared to narrow. "If you're trying to sell her something, lad ... ?"

I shook my head. But instinct had told me not to deal with anyone other than the woman of the house; not to blunt my message by talking either to the husband or the son. In her absence, however, I wondered if maybe I should in fact talk to the son.

"Not here, either. If you must know, they've gone to church, the pair of them. Another hour, round about." Happily he didn't again ask what I wanted nor offer to take a message. I settled myself on the ground outside their cottage and leant back against the low wall of the garden.

He'd been right about the timing — but wrong about their coming back together. Because she was alone I wasn't sure until the last moment that this was the woman whom I had to talk to.

What was encouraging, she gave me a friendly smile when she drew near. "Tired? You haven't got a puncture?"

I scrambled to my feet.

"Could I ask you something?" I said. I didn't like not knowing what to call her. And 'ask' sounded better than 'tell'.

"A glass of water? Certainly, my love. Might even find a bit of orange squash to put in it. My goodness, it is hot, though." With the screwed-up handkerchief already in her hand she wiped at her forehead. "Real close and muggy. Full of all these horrid gnats and midges." She inspected her handkerchief and maybe saw that she'd put paid to one or two of them.

"There's going to be a storm," I said.

"Good thing. What we need to clear the air." She had turned in at the garden gate. "Mind you, we expected one yesterday — and the day before that, too. Will you come in with me or would you rather wait out here?"

"No, I know there is. Going to be one. In just an hour or so. That's the reason why I've come." I was conscious of not having started very well.

She looked at me uncertainly.

I no longer hesitated.

"There's going to be a storm and your cottage will be hit by lightning. And your son will be killed if he's lying down."

She didn't say anything.

"I'm sorry if I put it bluntly. But I didn't know how else to tell you."

In a moment she recovered her composure. "Listen, love, you can't go about frightening folks like that — making up wild stories — I think you'd better be off without that glass of orangeade, just as a bit of a punishment, mind. You didn't look the type of boy who'd go in for silly pranks like that."

She turned her back on me then and started up the path. I ran after her; caught her by the arm. The warmth and moistness of her flesh was disconcerting.

"You've got to believe what I'm telling you!"

"I think I've got to do nothing of the kind." She shook free of me and stared, furiously. "Now I don't know if this is your own idea or whether you've been put up to it by someone — but I'm not having it, do you hear! You'd better be off, before I

77

get my old man. Or before I call the police, which is more what you deserve. And don't you ever dare to do it again!"

"Please listen. Please! I know what I'm talking about."

"Oh, I haven't got time for this. Already late and if lunch isn't on the table by one o'clock I'll have a sulky husband for the rest of the afternoon. I just can't do with that."

"And if it is on the table by one o'clock," I said, "you'll have a dead son for the rest of your life. Would that please you better?"

"Colin!" she called.

"Listen. How do you think I know that your son always goes to lie on his bed immediately after Sunday lunch?"

"Colin!" And then for the first time since I'd made my revelation she looked at me with more curiosity than annoyance. "How *do* you know it?"

"But it's right, isn't it? He does always go upstairs to lie down after lunch?"

"Are you a friend of Billy's? No, you couldn't be, I've never seen you. Who've you been talking to?"

"Nobody. I promise. But your house is going to be struck by lightning shortly after two and Billy's room is right beneath the point where it will strike. His bed — moments later — will be just a mound of ashes. Whether or not he is on it will be largely up to you."

The front door opened.

"Oh, there you are," the man said. "I thought I heard you call me?" (I said a silent prayer — though by no means the first during the past few minutes; or indeed the past few hours.) "That boy still here? What's he want, for God's sake?"

"Nothing. Nothing. I'll be in in half a jiffy."

(Remembered — as I didn't always — to say thank you.)

"Getting late," the man observed, with faint truculence. "Don't give him any money, if that's what he's after."

He returned inside but left the door open.

"How do you *know*?" she whispered, urgently.

"Just do."

"That's not an answer."

"I mean, I have this ... I sometimes know that things are going to happen."

"Like what?"

"But that's got nothing to — I ... Oh, like the King is going to die next February. Like on the same day Princess Elizabeth is crowned we'll get the news they've conquered Everest. Like, in the year after the Coronation, Roger Bannister is going to run the four-minute-mile ..." Suddenly, I'd felt the need to impress her.

"And like someone who'll never make the headlines is going to be struck by lightning in an unknown village at the back of beyond. Why?" She added in the same near-monotone: "You don't even know our name, do you?"

I shook my head.

"It isn't much I'm asking. Only that you delay your lunch a bit. What have you got to lose?"

"Oh, you don't know my husband!" Yet at least she was smiling. Albeit somewhat tensely. "The name," she said, "is Cooper."

"Thank you, Mrs Cooper."

"And you? What's yours?"

Just then there came a roll of thunder. We instantly looked up.

"So will you make lunch late?" I asked.

She nodded. "I may be as touched as you are; but whether you're touched or not I can see you believe what you're telling me."

"Turn the clocks back, if you have to." I grinned, then picked up my bike from the grass verge. It occurred to me I should have been a recognised authority — on turning the clock back.

"You haven't told me your name," she called.

"But remember. You've promised. And you'll soon thank God you did." I waved as I cycled off. Turned my head just once — and she was still standing there. I gave a final wave. Felt the

79

first big drops of rain.

By the time I got home I was wet through. Nana and Gramps, Aunt Gwen and Uncle Max were all sipping sherry in the front room.

"Ah, there you are, you bad lad," said Nana — invariably more stern than Granny used to be. "You must go and make your peace with your mother. She's highly displeased with you."

"And so's your father," said Gramps, cheerfully.

"And so's your venerated uncle," said Max, "who's absolutely starving. And so's your sadly disreputable aunt — who always kowtows to the winning team. All-round disgrace. I wouldn't be in your shoes, not for nothing."

Gwen hugged me like he had, however — wet or no. "I'll come into the kitchen with you and try to cushion the blows a bit. No guarantee of success, you understand."

"But just bear in mind," said Gramps. "A hundred years hence. What will any of it matter a hundred years hence? In the meanwhile we'll try to save you a glass of sherry."

The only distressing thing about all of this was that I recalled the last time so very clearly. My mother had certainly got up late, just as she'd done this morning, but she'd been singing as we scraped the potatoes together and laid the dining-room table (though I couldn't remember that I'd done much more than that — nor, I think, had Dad). And when everyone had turned up early in Uncle Max's car we'd all stood merrily about in the kitchen, sherry glasses in hand, my mum laughing just as much as anybody at the signs of chaos in the sink and on the scrubbed wooden table. Nana and Max, anyway, had briskly disposed of most of it, with dishcloth and tea towel respectively. Gramps had tried to whisk the cream — but been told he hadn't got the wrist for it. And Gwen had been separating the eggs for the mayonnaise, letting the whites run through her fingers and threatening me (once) with the remaining yolk, instead of pushing protectively in front of me as we went into the kitchen and saying while she did so, "The

80

return of the Prodigal Son ... we've all been beating him soundly ..."

"And just look at you!" exclaimed my mother. "And I'd like to know, what time do you call *this*?"

I glanced at my watch — almost automatically. It was shortly after two.

"I've got a good mind to send you right to bed. You've thoroughly ruined my day. I hope you realise that."

"Yes, the goodness of the Lord!" said Major Shipman the next day, stroking meringue crumbs from his white moustaches and reflectively gazing into his teacup in our front room. "Yes, indeed! ... Don't know why he'd concern himself with Billy Cooper, mind, who's always been a bit of a ne'er-do-well, besides at times not seeming altogether there. Still might mend; might mend. The ways of Providence are often very strange. (And, poor lad, one's only too happy, of course, for his deliverance.) But makes you think, doesn't it? Miracles and all that."

"Who was the boy on the bike?"

"No idea. Vanished into thin air. Could have been a ghost — all sorts of stories going around. Mavis Cooper said she asked him twice but never got an answer."

He paused.

"Apparently the poor old King's going to die next year. And Everest is going to be climbed on the same day as the Coronation. And somebody called something is going to run a mile in ... well, she wasn't quite certain. Still, just have to see, shan't we? You been thinking of running the mile, young-fellow-me-lad?"

Before, it had all been long faces, and condolences by proxy. Today it was mystified speculation, and shaken heads, and giggles. It really made a difference.

13

"I suppose you feel proud of yourself?"

I thought he meant smug. I had smugness on the brain. I knew I showed a tendency towards it, even though I also knew I had no reason to. It made a perennial and insidious enemy. "Rid me of it then," I said. Not that I thought he would — or even at heart wanted him to. I wasn't a puppet. I had autonomy. It was one of those battles I should have to fight for myself.

He'd just got on. There was always a long wait at Rickmansworth while they replaced with a steam one the electric engine which had brought the train from Baker Street. I knew there was no point in asking him what he'd been doing at Rickmansworth.

Apart from me, the carriage had been empty. It was supposedly a non-smoker and yet it still smelled of tobacco — that, or the dustiness of ages, caught up in its grey-green patterned upholstery. My initial exclamation of delight had quickly petrified — along with my grin. He was angry and I hadn't yet seen him angry. The blackness of his expression matched the blackness of his overcoat. Although it was the same period of spring as the one in which I'd met him nineteen years before — even a day or two later — the weather continued wintry, with reports of snow still falling in the Highlands. It was true I'd seen him all in black before but it hadn't been a reflection of his mood. His uncovered blond hair again made me think of a flame but this time he put me in mind not of a beacon but of a black candle at a witches' sabbath.

"Don't be cute," he snarled. 'Snarled' is clearly an exaggeration but in spirit it almost seemed like that. There'd been no smile, no form of greeting: just the staccato delivery of that first question — statement. *I suppose you feel proud of yourself?*

He sat huddled in a corner by the corridor — as far away

from me, it felt, as he could possibly get; for I had been sitting by the window when he came in and had now resettled myself there. He'd even left the carriage door open, as though he couldn't bear to breathe the same air undiluted.

"Why have I made you so angry? What is it I've done?"

"Perhaps you'd like to tell me!" he said.

I held onto the broad leather window strap — gripped it tightly — without even realising I did so.

"I've been getting a bit above myself. I know I can hide it from others; but that isn't quite the point, is it?"

"Don't be a fool. And don't take me for one, either. I'm well aware you're trying to get on top of it."

His acknowledgment of this — under such circumstances — was worth more than he realised. (Except, of course, it wasn't.)

I faltered.

"Is it sex?" I asked.

"No, dammit — it is not sex."

I searched my memory for a sin I hadn't recognised as big enough to provoke this present outburst.

"Zach, I don't know. I'm sorry. Is it lack of charity? Lack of tolerance? Lack of understanding? Is it laziness? Self-absorption? I'd hoped I was improving."

"What about basic dishonesty?" he said.

I stared at him.

"And you don't even know!" he sneered. "To be dishonest and know it is one thing. But when a person's principles are so ... non-existent ... that he doesn't even realise ... ! Oh, yes, go on, cry," he said. "That's bound to answer everything!"

But for once they were indeed tears of anger — in no way of remorse or shame. And I thought that his alluding to them (they hadn't even overflowed) seemed not just unnecessary — but shabby and contemptible.

"All right, Zach. I don't know what I've done. I suppose I've been kidding myself but everybody kids themselves about something. That isn't such a crime."

His look became sardonic.

"And if you want to talk about basic dishonesty — in fact you could say my whole life is basically dishonest."

"Interesting," he said.

"But that's your fault as much as it is mine. I even think in some ways you could be more dishonest than me. It was never any part of our agreement that I shouldn't just go my own way absolutely, lie and cheat and waste my time: if that's what I felt like. It was never a condition I'd behave."

"You wouldn't consider that great gifts carry their own conditions? Their own responsibilities?"

"If they do, it was a bit deceitful not to point that out at the beginning."

"Nonsense. You should have been aware of it."

"No. Any honest businessman automatically shows his customer the small print."

"Unless he prefers him to write his own small print."

"What! Well, then all I can say is — he's expecting a bit much."

"Yes."

"What does *yes* mean?"

"Only that in that case he'll choose his customer with extra care and insight, won't he? Or at least ... will certainly try to." He emphasised these last few words in such a way as to denote, presumably, his own complete and bitter failure.

"My God," I said, "you're a bastard."

I received an icy stare.

"Another birthday hasn't brought a great advance in wisdom, has it?"

"That's rich. I don't know how old — or ancient — you are but it obviously wasn't enormously bright picking on me in the first place. Was it? I'm sorry I've been such a disappointment to you. I'm sorry I've buggered up all your reams of fine old do-it-yourself small print."

I turned my head towards the window — let go of the leather strap almost before I'd been fully aware of holding it; saw the harsh red marks it had made on my palm and fingers.

84

I stared at a poster for Ovaltine across the track — the healthy country life it represented, the rewards of a good day's hard work, the peaceful rosy future. The tears spilled from my eyes and now I let them run.

Idiot! And you had thought your worst problem had been complacency: complacency engendered most recently by two days spent in London distributing largesse — almost the very shirt off your back, why don't you say? (In fact it had been only my padded macintosh.) At the bottom of Villiers Street there was an all-night coffee stand where I'd met a tramp whose teeth had actually been chattering. I hadn't meant to give away my clothes but the relevant shops had all been shut and if I'd handed him just money I felt it might have been spent at an off-licence rather than a secondhand clothes shop or an army surplus store. I'd been able to buy him some food, however (and a bottle of beer and a packet of cigarettes), as I had for several others I'd found stretched out along the Embankment, although it was mainly money I had been planning to distribute. With nearly five hundred pounds in my pocket and a burning desire to be in one of those places where it might do the most good I'd been — and all right — I've already said as much — the glutinous Squire Bountiful bestowing charity and getting a terrific buzz out of doing so (but as much because I wanted genuinely to help as because it made me feel such a good guy) yet wasn't it better to do it even for mixed reasons than not do it at all? My last life had been so completely wasted I didn't regard it as astonishing, given the opportunity, I should try to justify my second, go all out in the attempt. Okay, I was plainly having setbacks, when I'd thought that I was making progress, but —

But right at the moment smugness wasn't my problem. Self-pity was muscling its way in.

The train gave a great jolt which signified that the new coupling had taken place. I was damned if I'd feel self-pity. I blew my nose and wiped my eyes and turned my head back. He seemed hardly to have moved.

85

"All right, Zach. I'm sorry. I don't know where I've gone wrong, I mean not in any vast way, and I can see why this should make you extra angry. All I can say is that if you'll tell me where the trouble lies — and if it isn't too late — I'd like to make a fresh start. Another fresh start."

"No, it's not too late," he said. But the steeliness of his expression didn't change.

"Then tell me how I've been dishonest."

"I said no. I want you to tell me," he insisted.

"You can't be talking of the thousand pounds I won?" (Half of it had gone to charities that dealt with famine in the Third World.)

"Can't I?" he said.

"Well, you never suggested that I shouldn't gamble."

"And am I in fact suggesting it now?"

"But then what ... ?"

Yet, looking at him, suddenly I saw.

"You're saying that of course it wasn't a gamble?"

"And more importantly: what are you saying?"

"No. It wasn't. You're right. But it didn't occur to me that I was doing wrong. In fact, it seemed ... almost a heaven-sent opportunity." I smiled — wanly.

He didn't. He didn't smile at all.

"And should it have occurred to you?"

"Yes. I suppose it should."

"Suppose?"

"I still can't help thinking you're overreacting."

"You've always thought people were overreacting."

"But was it so wrong? All's fair in love and war. And with bookmakers —"

"Don't give me that crap."

"I was merely going to say that with bookmakers —"

"All's fair in love and war."

"Zach, it's only an expression. I wouldn't stand by it."

"You just did."

I bit my lip and while I wondered if I should simply shut up and let him carry on without trying to defend myself any further I looked over at the picture of a mother and toddler bouncing a beach ball at Rhyl: 'Fine sands — bracing air — beautiful scenery.' On the other side of the small central mirror there was a family paddling at Scarborough. I couldn't let him get away with it.

"And anyway, Zach, you'd had almost a year in which to stop me. Surely you knew why I was saving up so hard."

He must have done. Twelve months before, hearing of someone who'd done well on the Grand National, I was suddenly reminded that the following year — when I was working at the Times Bookshop in Wigmore Street, instead of, as now, being on vacation from King's College Cambridge, where I was reading Divinity — that in 1956 I had won a few pounds on a horse called E.S.B. He was practically the only horse whose name I remembered, for he was the only horse on whom I'd ever won. Not as a result of studying form but because a friend and I had once spent a coffee-break inventing middle names for our colleagues: Edward Blick was a lad in the stockroom so po-faced he inevitably became Edward Sunshine Blick. It was an adolescent game but for some reason his initials stuck when nobody else's did. This friend was called Kenneth and as a matter of fact, only that very afternoon, my mission having been completed, I'd called in at the bookshop and chatted with him for fifteen very pleasant minutes, initially of course about books — although I'd found I hadn't got the money to buy anything I wanted — but then about various topics, including the Grand National. (No, unfortunately, he said, he hadn't backed the winner.) It had been very pleasant, yes, but rather melancholy too. I should have liked to speak to Mrs Morton, who had once said when she'd heard me singing from the *Noel Coward Song Book* (there was a copy of it there this very afternoon, I saw it on the central table — could it be the selfsame copy I had leafed through, light-heartedly, before?), said that my tenor voice was charming — she herself, between the wars, had sung in operetta and she had chosen the word with kindness and

87

with care — and who, even as I watched her single out *Gone With the Wind* for her present customer, had already, in a sense, been dead for countless years; should have liked to speak to Mrs Morton and to Jenny Nyman and Anthea and Annette and Caroline and many others. So in the end I felt a little wistful as I walked towards the station, for it had been a good time in my life, full of hope, enjoyed not just in retrospect but even as I lived it. Whilst talking to Kenneth I'd taken in greedily every well-remembered detail, would have loved to find some excuse to get to see again the small canteen, hear the echo of our laughter and our silly conversations (there was one I particularly recollected about men's body hair — sparked off by my own arms and by William Holden's chest) and once more visit the quaint Victorian lavatory with its wooden seat, flowered porcelain and air of cocooned and comfortable solidity. Also whilst talking to him I'd grown conscious, suddenly, of straining to glimpse some spark of bewildered recognition in his eyes; this rank absurdity being heightened by my catching sight of a young salesman who was a complete stranger to me and had presumably taken my own place. Kenneth had sometimes come my way in the evening, travelling on the Met as far as Harrow, but it was too much to hope, of course, that tonight would be one of those times for visiting his grandmother. I thought about returning to the shop before the end of my vacation and after further congenial conversation casually suggesting we should meet. But what would be the point? We had lost touch anyway soon after the folding of the business and when at a later date I'd tried to track him down I hadn't managed it. Perhaps I shouldn't have returned at all. It was one of the few times I'd felt something near regret for my Nottingham decision; and it hardly helped I knew it was illogical.

I experienced much the same uncertainty scarcely an hour later — there in the carriage with Zach. It occurred to me I must be tired. "Surely you knew why I was saving up so hard."

"Of course I did. It was a test. I kept hoping against hope that you were going to pass. Come to your senses."

"It was only —"

"Don't you dare!"

I'd been going to say robbing the rich to feed the poor. I hadn't even thought of it as robbing until a minute earlier.

"If you'd got to me sooner I could at least have given the money back."

He made no answer. It seemed unanswerable. But this didn't dispose me to feel in any way that I had scored.

"Anyhow. Just bear in mind ... that there are tests and tests. It's not the end of everything."

"What do I have to do to be forgiven?"

His tone appeared to be lightening a little. "Well, for one thing — not catch your death of pneumonia. You'd better take this coat; *your* need of it is greater than mine."

The idea of possessing something of Zach's gave me pleasure in itself but the idea of his presenting it to me immediately after such a very low point in our relationship made it especially precious.

"What do I tell them, then, at home?"

"That you were given it. That it was warmer than yours. That you gave your own away."

"Is this another test?" I said.

14

Again ... no mention of Brian Douglas.

But a way of maybe dealing with my guilt was beginning to suggest itself. It was outlandish, the sort of inspired lunacy that always came at night and guaranteed you had no chance to sleep. It certainly brought no other kind of guarantee; nor even a very clear picture of what I would be aiming at. If I spoke of it to anyone except Zach I should either be avoided or sent to a psychiatrist. Yet I knew it to be right (it was as if something had gone click inside my soul) and years before I could even start to put it into practice it was already obsessing me. I believed I had been shown the outline of my life's work — as nebulous as a figure glimpsed through fog but just as certain to take solid shape.

And it was all due to Brian Douglas.

15

And when Abram was ninety years old and nine, the Lord appeared to Abram, and said unto him, walk before me, and be thou perfect, I will make thee exceeding fruitful, and kings shall come out of thee.

At ninety-nine? Not bad. Do you think the Lord might have similar objectives for me? (But all I really ask is that he'll just get off my back.) That's my own age now — ninety-nine — and somebody recently wanted to know when I'd last got it up, the salacious old sot. Of course I wasn't going to tell him I could hardly remember, must be thirty years or more — which is an added grievance — having all this time and still being deprived of a good fuck.

Not that longevity would be all it's cracked up to be even with a rampant cock. Well, not for me. Maybe for Abram.

You get so tired. That's the thing. You've had enough. You want to put an end to it. Rest. It isn't just the aches and pains — and, yes, I really do mean pains — the rheumatism and arthritis; the wheezing; the cataracts and deafness. It's everything. It isn't just seeing your mates drop all around you, in truth I haven't got any. It's the damned monotony, exertion, having to get up in the morning, go to bed at night (though knowing you won't sleep), having to fill the time up in between, find food, rely on people who in no way are reliable — people you'd rather just spit in the eye of anyhow, not have to bow and scrape before: oh, thank you, thank you, thank you. (Thank you for what? Thank you for nothing!) We Jews are supposed to venerate old age but I know there's always someone ready to snicker behind my back, make fun of me, point me out as a freak and an outcast. A leper. I'd rather be a leper — much. You die of leprosy. Your days are numbered. Me, I don't know if even my centuries are numbered. My God, before long I'll be crawling about on my hands and knees, creaks in every joint, agony in every movement, seeing nothing, hearing nothing and stinking to the high heavens. (Well, that at least would serve them right, the high heavens, if my stench could really carry up as far as that, a subtle form of vengeance.) Not that I truly want to stink — it's not the way I was brought up. I do my best but even now ... So it's not even just the tedium and the pain and the exhaustion, it's the endless small humiliations — when you're doomed to eternity how are you meant to trim your toenails?

Too often now I think about my childhood. My parents. I had no time for them when I was young. But I was wrong. I see that more and more. I wish I didn't. It's sentimental, it's disgusting; last night I even had to wipe away the rheum and snot when I allowed myself to reminisce.

I still see my mother as a young woman; tend to forget that she could be a fishwife. Even my father can sometimes seem almost all right. I hate it that my early years — before that bloody man was crucified — should be turning into something sacred. Precious. It wasn't much of a life, even then.

I'll tell you what's really precious about life — I've thought a lot about this: the fact you don't know when it's going to end. It's short, it's fleeting, you want to hang onto it, hang onto it at any cost. Death is the thing that's precious about life.

If you're normal, that is.

Don't think I haven't tried. I've tried by jumping off a cliff; I've tried with knife and rope and poison. And I can break my neck and back and arms and legs and virtually every bone in my body (which accounts for the shape I'm in now, all the twists and the deformities — I'm not just a freak, I'm a monster, beside me Cerberus would sweep the board in any beauty contest — and for the fact, like I said, I can't even sleep at nights, there's no position I can lie in for ten minutes on end that doesn't then become sheer purgatory). So no escape, you see, not even on the rare occasions I manage to scrounge a bit of wine; a whole *amphora* wouldn't help. Scrounge, because I haven't any money — how should I have? Quite often I starve and thereby add to my manifold physical attractions an air of charming emaciation and to my manifold physical discomforts the ache of gnawing hunger; denied not just of food but far more cruelly of the comfort of knowing at least that I shall starve to death. After the clifftop dive you'd have thought I'd had enough; the thing was, then I'd believed that though the chance of survival might be only one in a million, I, wouldn't you know, had been that poor dumb millionth sap. So I drove a knife through my chest. (God, one has to try to black it out — somehow. You need courage to do these things. You need courage to do them and courage to recover from them; or would do if you had the least bit of choice about that.) And yet even now I thought I lived because I'd missed my heart — the physician said I had, anyhow. But in truth it could have been only desperation that permitted me to think it. After I'd hung myself — and swung three feet above the ground for six whole hours, scrabbling and clawing for my breath — I knew finally that there was no way out; though that didn't stop me rushing at the henbane, packing it into my mouth, gulping it down unchewed, in the second I hoped they might be looking the other way — they, my persecutors. And I got the convulsions all right, the sensation of having swallowed shards of heated glass that burned and tore at my gut, but (when I could think at all, in the intervals between the torture) I knew I hadn't

92

caught them by surprise; whatever surprises might be going I was the one who'd always be on the receiving end. The bastards.

Sodding bastards.

Yet — why the plural? I see I keep on doing it. Persecutors, bastards. Why?

Of course there's a lot of nonsense talked now about a father-and-son act and I've heard mention, even, of a Holy Ghost but I really think of this goddam bully boy as the same who buttered up Abram and could obviously be pretty free with the goodies when he thought he was going to get something out of it. I mean! Imagine a fellow of my years still being able to get his leg over and squirt his juices in the right place. Lucky git, I bet he'd done his share of sucking up: "Yes Lord, whatever you say Lord, perfect you want Lord, perfect you'll get Lord, if that's the price these days of your king-sized erections — ha, ha — your erections worthy of begetting kings. You bet. Is it all right if I get up off my face now, Lord?" But the even luckier git: better far than fucking: Then Abraham gave up the ghost, and died in a good old age, an old man, and full of years. *That's* happiness. True happiness. Beats bonking.

Because if I knew that like him I was going to die at a hundred-and-seventy-five — in other words, just another seventy-six years, well over halfway there — I could bear it. Even looking as I do now, even functioning as I do now; not functioning as I do now. I could bear it. Just to know that one day all of this would really come to an end. Seventy-six years. *Finito.*

I thought about the Witch of Endor; don't know what put her in my mind. (My mother had once said she sounded like a nice woman. When Saul had gone to consult her, on the eve of his death, he hadn't eaten all day and his blood sugar was obviously very low — she had quickly rustled up a meal and insisted he stay for it.) Certainly I wasn't thinking of journeying to Endor or travelling back through past centuries; it was enough that I must travel forward through future ones.

Besides, I had a fear of witches now, since I had seen that woman perish in the fire. But the notion remained with me: might witchcraft cure my ills? After all, I could not go on like this, unless they simply put me in a cage and left me there as an interesting though hardly edifying exhibit — a decrepit, floorbound, defecating beast, barely recognisable as human. That voice had told me I would travel not merely through other times but also through other lands, yet how could this be true unless someone, somewhere, in some way, could take pity on me and help?

Someone did take pity. She set down her buckets and her yoke and procured me bread and gave me water and didn't seem to mind she almost had to shout at me on account of my poor hearing. I felt so starved of talk, or normal human intercourse. I would have liked to touch her face but didn't dare request it — my warty fingers, no doubt dirty nails. Besides, it was sentimental again: who cared what she looked like, so long as she delivered?

It was she who told me of the wizard who had recently arrived in Jerusalem. "I could take you to visit him," she offered, "or ..." I pictured her looking first at me and then at the state of my hovel. "Perhaps he would visit you here, if you feel you're ready to receive him."

"Ready? I have been ready these past thirty years!"

He came. He came. He was the kindest man I knew. (The only kind man I knew.) "But how on earth would you recognise kindness?" he asked harshly — it didn't make me change in my regard. "Wouldn't you say it always takes a Jew to recognise a Jew?"

I had no answer.

"However," he said. "I hear you want assistance."

I would have thrown myself onto my knees in gratitude if I had been physically able.

"You can help me die?"

"No. No one can. They tell me it's decreed that you must live until the Second Coming."

I moaned.

"The Second Fiddlesticks! How can you help me then, if not to die?"

"It can be arranged that every hundred years or so you are rejuvenated."

I pondered over this. (It didn't occur to me I was having no difficulty in hearing him.) It sounded so good there just had to be a catch in it.

Probably that he was bluffing.

"No catch in it," he said. "I'm certainly not bluffing."

I was impressed — and even frightened.

"To childhood every time?"

"Yes, Cartophilus."

Constant renewal. That was hardly very frightening. An elixir of life that eliminated drawbacks — well, some at any rate, maybe even most. Eternal life: the thing all mortals hunger for. (I'd always had my doubts about the heaven that is spoken of.) No longer a punishment, indeed. I could hardly believe it.

"Sex?"

"Is that honestly your first question — almost your first question?"

"No. No. Of course it isn't." But then I paused. "Well, yes, it is! If you say honestly." However, my voice was just a mumble.

Yet, oddly, I felt that he was pleased by such an answer, although all he said was, "You'll be a normal child, normal youth, normal adult, with all that normality implies — except —"

"I won't be so normal if I have to live to be a hundred."

"That wasn't what I was about to say."

"Every time? Couldn't you make it fifty?"

"No."

"Seventy-five?"

He said no again but I felt a little more cajolement might accomplish something. "So much compassion," I said. "I can

95

see you don't mean to sound inflexible." I could sense that he was smiling. "All right. Not seventy-five. I accept that. But does it have to be a hundred?"

I knew the smile still lingered. He wavered. "That depends."

"On what — O wise one?"

"On how things go."

But I couldn't get him to elaborate — although I wheedled till he cut me short. I heard my tone grow plaintive.

"I don't want to live so long."

"Great men in the past have often lived as long."

"That's different," I grumbled. Already I was grumbling. I should have been dancing. Tomorrow I'd be dancing.

"A newborn baby finds it hard to dance." (I hadn't said a word.)

"Besides," I pointed out. I wished to demonstrate I was his equal; that he wasn't dealing merely with a fool. "Besides, I shan't know then that I've got any reason to dance. Shall I?"

"Yes," he said.

"What?"

"As I was going to say. You'll be normal in every way — except for memory."

I digested this one, slowly.

"You mean, I shall remember things?"

"Everything."

I didn't want to remember anything. There was weariness of spirit — my God, was there not weariness of spirit — as much as weariness of body.

"Each thousand years," he said. He added, as if with the consciousness of being droll; as if mocking the very essence of negotiation: "Give or take."

"Each thousand years — what?"

"You'll have the slate wiped clean. One lifetime in ten — there won't be any recollection and you'll start again."

"Just one in ten! I shall go mad."

"That's up to you," he said.

I paused. I steadied myself. I took a deep breath.

96

"Couldn't we at least make it one in five?"

"No!" But then he laughed. "I can respect the haggling. It's the grumbling I don't take to."

"You're right. You're right. I wouldn't take to it either. 'What an ingrate!' I would say. 'Doesn't he know when he's well off?'" But still, I thought. It's easy for you. You've never had to walk on my legs; never had to cover even half a mile on *my* legs. Never had to step off a cliff. Never stumbled blindly up the hillside feeling watery with terror ...

But then my mind veered away from that thought very sharply. It made me think of — well, not so much that awful, anguished, windy, hellbound night —

It made me think of other things.

16

I remember the night the Regent closed. At least I was more understanding the second time. About the way my father felt. The end of an era. An era only fourteen years old — for him — but the cinema business was changing: all bingo now — soon to be bowling. For the final week he would have liked to show a selection of classic movies — a fresh double programme for each of the six days — but for some reason it wasn't possible. He ended up with *Carry On Nurse* — I think the second in the series — and an Audie Murphy western. Good popular stuff, of course, but even then the last performance wasn't well attended. As the main movie was approaching its end Dad took up his position in the foyer — just as he'd done for practically every final performance of the day since 1945; only, his demob suit of the first years had been replaced as soon as coupons allowed, first by one dinner jacket, then by another — for purposes of rotation. My father wasn't a handsome man but he looked distinguished in his dinner suit, it gave him an air, and he always seemed a little like the squire — no, there was nothing of condescension in it — more like mine host seeing his guests off the premises at the end of what he trusted had been a highly enjoyable evening. (If someone occasionally told him he thought the programme had been rotten, a total waste of time, it genuinely distressed my dad, even if it didn't altogether surprise him; he always hoped, even with the poorest movies, that some sort of alchemy might be occurring in the darkness and all his patrons would emerge in a glow, feeling that the world was truly a better place. Poor Dad, in some ways it was his whole life, the enjoyment of those groups of people underneath his roof for three or four hours at a time. He felt personally responsible. He hated it whenever the projector broke down, or the heating system. He really worried about what records should be played before the house lights faded.)

The final night was different in one way to all the others: there was a table brought into the lobby set with glasses and bottles of wine, both red and white, and also of American Cream Soda and Tizer. He'd hired two hundred glasses but realised by the time the main feature started that — despite all his posters and a message to his patrons in the local press — he was going to need hardly half that number. In the event he didn't need a quarter. People seemed unexpectedly awkward and in a hurry to get away, like worshippers slipping out of church by the side entrance in order to avoid the vicar. The modest party he'd envisaged (I knew he'd even prepared a short speech) had turned into a sprinkling of embarrassed customers and stilted dialogues and unhappy silences.

That had been the first time. Doris the usherette and Mrs Wilson at the box office had both made excuses — one to do with her own health, one to do with her mother's — and the projectionist was a kind man but rather shy and he too asked if he could possibly cry off. Both the Shipmans and the Kings had said they felt it better not to put in an appearance, since their presence, they claimed, might prove a spot inhibiting. So it fell to my mother and me to help Dad through it all as best we could. Mother got the giggles.

In fact she was almost drunk. Knowing the quantities of wine that wouldn't be required she had slipped downstairs far earlier than was necessary.

She looked very pretty in her red dress and black heels. Always much fairer than my father or me she had recently lightened her hair still more and it suited her. She called it her Grace Kelly look.

The first time I had been as merry as she had and giggled just as much. I had ended the evening by suddenly being sick and not even getting to the lavatory. (And my father, bless him, had never uttered a single word of reproach.) This time I went easy on the wine myself and tried hard to make her do the same. But I proved as unsuccessful in this as I'd been in attempting to dissuade Dad from holding such a function in the first place. My endeavours to keep her entertained upstairs with games of gin rummy and silly impersonations and putting on her favourite records only managed to make the matter worse.

"Oh, Ethan, don't be such a spoilsport! You can see how much of the stuff there is here."

"But it's all on sale or return. We don't have to polish off every last drop unaided."

"My darling, let yourself go a little. I sometimes wish you would. I worry about you, Ethan."

"Why?"

"I don't know that you always get the fun out of life I think you should."

She hadn't said this to me the first time.

"Mum, it's been a wonderful life. I'm the happiest man in the world."

She touched me on the tip of my nose with a forefinger. "You say." She was already on her second glass. "You know what really worries me, my love? I'd hate any son of mine to turn into ..." This time she dipped her finger in her glass and put a drop of wine onto the end of my nose.

"Turn into what, Mum?"

"Oh, you mustn't be offended by this, my love."

"By what?"

"A prig. Just a teensy-weensy bit of a prig — a very little one." She measured it: about an inch high.

It speaks volumes for my advanced development that I was, in fact, considerably offended.

"Just the smallest signs," she said. "Sometimes the way you seem to hold yourself aloof. To be standing a little bit on the outside and just watching the rest of us. As if in judgement. Only sometimes. It isn't serious. But, Ethan — promise. We don't want a prig in the family, do we?"

"I promise we don't want a prig in the family do we." But I couldn't make my voice sound as light as I had aimed for.

"Oh, now I've offended him! Come on, have some wine. Drink my health. Tell me I'm forgiven. Dance a little dance with me."

"Mum!"

For she had now begun to hum it: tell me I'm forgiven, for making you cry ... ; and she had taken my hands and was pulling me back and forth in a grotesque parody of some kind of light fantastic — could it be a quickstep? (But at least she had set down her wineglass, in order to do it.)

"There you are! You see! So stiff. You should unbend. There's nobody watching. You could do a striptease."

None of this had taken place before.

"Come on. Do a striptease! I bet you really strip to advantage. What a long time since I've seen my little boy all bare."

She retrieved her glass and raised it to me, as she swayed in a far more graceful imitation of a dance than when she'd had to propel her lumpish son in front of her.

She winked at me, lewdly.

"Mum, I'll be back. Just a minute or two."

I found my father standing at the rear of the stalls and looking as if he were positively willing his patrons into finding the film funny; assessing the frequency and depth of their laughter in relation to last opportunities. Lost opportunities.

"Dad. Mum's in the foyer getting tight. I think you ought to be there."

"Your mother? Tight? No!"

"Well, no. Not tight. But well on the way."

"Oh, let her be. She enjoys her little glass of wine; doesn't often get the chance. And I ordered far more than we need."

"She won't thank us, though, if we let her make a spectacle of herself."

"Baloney," he said. "It's the last night. It's a celebration. I may well come and get tight with her. You mustn't be a wet blanket."

Spoilsport. Prig. Judgmental. A wet blanket. All within the space of five or ten minutes. Was that really the image I projected? It was such a trivial thing, perhaps, but the happiest man in the world suddenly felt remarkably downcast.

I went upstairs to the flat; bypassed the lobby. I sat on my bed and tried to pray but felt too sulky. Hard done by. Hurt. Prigs and critics and wet blankets: weren't they more the types who'd pray?

I reviewed my university career. (I had stayed on to do an M.A; had come home this weekend especially for my father's big occasion — to see whether, having failed to persuade him not to hold it, I could help make it any better than last time. I had bought *A Pictorial History of the Talkies* to present to him at the end of the evening — or, rather, to leave just casually lying in his chair — in appreciation, partly, of that particular act of forbearance he didn't even know about but which had been one of the many kind things I would chiefly remember him for.) I reviewed my sixth-form days. I reviewed my whole social history. Perhaps I wasn't the life and soul of the party but I had never set out to be. Perhaps I didn't often throw back my head and enjoy a really good laugh — but I just wasn't that type. I smiled at things and softly chuckled. I hoped that I was

101

fun to be with; tried — and on the whole thought I succeeded — to be an entertaining companion. But in spite of my increased self-confidence I still had moments of shyness, was still at times a scaredy-cat, although I thought this probably didn't show. I tended to be serious about life — more so than I had been in the past, more into politics and world affairs and all that sort of thing — but I wasn't a wet blanket.

Or was I?

People sometimes said, "Divinity? What in heaven's name made you choose Divinity?", and I would have to answer lamely that I just found it rather interesting. ("But what are you going to do with it? You're surely not planning to enter the Church?" "No — no — nothing like that. Future very vague.") But Divinity didn't turn you into a wet blanket.

Did it?

And could I really be judgmental? For twenty years I'd tried to echo John Bradford who in 1550 saw some criminals being led away to execution and exclaimed, "But for the grace of God there goes John Bradford!" Besides, I had far too much to remember from my previous existence (as well as having plenty from this one) to be in any position to chuck stones. I truly didn't believe I was judgmental.

But prig? I looked it up in the dictionary. A person who is smugly self-righteous and narrow-minded. (C18: of unknown origin.)

Certainly my life was not developing in quite the way I had imagined. I had pictured myself sowing my wild oats — having a swinging sex life well before the Swinging Sixties — going all out for a stage career. I had always envied actors. (Actors who were constantly in work.) I thought I knew my goal.

But I found it was really just the camaraderie, the laughter, the sense of belonging, of importance, which in fact appealed to me; I had no burning ambition to act and since there were thousands of others who presumably did, was it even fair to try to take up room which someone else would occupy more worthily?

And as for the sex: was it shyness — or the spirit of the times — or an unwillingness for merely casual encounters? Don Juan no longer seemed a character to emulate.

Did all this make of me a prig?

In any case ... you were what you were. You did your damnedest to avoid the pitfalls but when you didn't manage this it was best that you should know. Obviously.

Then you just went on trying.

Full stop.

I returned downstairs.

As I did so, I heard the National Anthem. My father was already — as he would have been on any other evening — waiting and gently rubbing his hands in the foyer. My mother was tapping her foot quite happily in time to a tune that now remained inside her head, but she looked all right; only my father's worried glances suggested otherwise. The vanguard of the audience came dribbling out: mainly comprised of the young ones who'd been sitting in the back row, wondering where they could go now, to continue with the petting. (But it was May and not too cold; it shouldn't be a problem.) My father said, "Good evening; would you like some wine?", and held out a filled glass in either hand. These first arrivals looked at one another and giggled and murmured, "What's this for? — yeah then — don't mind — ta." A card had been screened during the interval announcing there would be wine served afterwards — and why — but presumably they hadn't been looking at the screen. I went and helped my father pass around the drinks. By now the main body of the audience was either slipping out — with heads studiously lowered — or lingering; irresolute. But there were perhaps three or four couples who rose to the occasion. "We're going to miss having a cinema! What a shame about all this!" I said: "Yes, television has a lot to answer for!" I'd prepared a few trite questions to match. "What sort of films do you like best?" "Did you happen to see any of these here at the Regent?" (Dad and I had spent a cheerfully nostalgic morning going through his stock of old posters, picking out many which advertised our favourite movies and then pinning them all up: *Kind Hearts and Coronets, Song of the South, Call Northside 777, Road House, Road to Rio, Picnic, All That Heaven Allows* ... there must have been a hundred.) "Do you think the day will ever come when we can just buy films — or rent them — and play them on our television screens?"

"My father's really choked," I said, "to think this place is going to be demolished." But only two people asked me if he had another job or where we were going to live now. (In fact we weren't yet sure. There was a month or so before we had to move and I was still trying to deter my parents from finally picking on London. They hadn't been happy there before. My father had missed his allotment, the only cinema work he'd obtained had been at the Classic in Baker Street and even that had soon closed down, they hadn't found many friends ... But it was hard to make my reasons sound convincing.) And my list of questions didn't really elicit much response. I had wanted to get Johnny and one or two others to come — Gordon had by then gone off to be a pop star — but Dad had asked me not to, on the grounds that somehow it wouldn't be quite honest, nor yet quite dignified — and the first at least of these arguments had got through to me. But Johnny and Simon and some of Mum's and Dad's own friends would certainly have put a little sparkle into things; even if privately they had found it all a bit pathetic.

My mother did her best as well.

"Would anybody like to dance with me? Poor man's Grace Kelly. Any takers? Roll up!"

She weaved amongst the rest of us and undeniably added some much-needed pizzazz. "'Ten cents a dance — that's all they pay me — oh, how they weigh me down ...'"

Also variety.

"Anyone here do conjuring tricks? ... Juggling? ... Has anybody here got any balls?"

She sang again.

"'Knees up, Mother Brown. Knees up, Mother Brown. Under the table you must go — ee-ay-ee-ay-ee-ay-oh!'"

My father did his utmost, too: to carry on doggedly with his own one-sided conversations; to pretend that nothing was wrong. But people were either standing there, frankly watching Mum, fascinated, or else they were edging steadily towards the doors. It must have been evident to him for sometime now that his little speech of gratitude and regret and best wishes wasn't going to be needed. Poor Dad. It was what I think he'd regarded as the climax of his career — albeit with another fifteen years supposedly to run until retirement.

Mum finished her song and did a little curtsey. Unfortunately, she wobbled — and then fell. She fell with quite a smack; the floor wasn't carpeted. Dad and I rushed across to help. She seemed disorientated — blankly shook her head when asked if she had hurt herself — she stood between us and looked at us in slightly sad surprise.

And then — without a word of warning — she soundlessly, but copiously, threw up. Eight people, excluding Dad and me, had their coats and trousers, shoes and stockings thoroughly splashed. One woman even asked to send her handbag to the cleaners.

17

The following August, my parents having settled in East Finchley, Johnny and I took a furnished flat in Camden Town. ("That's nice," my mother said. "Two good Jewish boys to keep each other company. Don't forget to light the Sabbath candle, Friday nights! Have a mezuzah at your front door!" She'd been a little miffed by my decision to leave home.)

And after we'd been there just a short time — in fact it was only our first Sunday and we were sitting, pyjama-clad, over a celebratory brunch of eggs and bacon, coffee and hot rolls and honey, with the newspapers spread out beside our plates and overflowing onto our laps — Johnny suddenly said, "Let's go to Paris for the New Year!" He was reading an article upon Versailles.

By the New Year he would have completed his first six months at Air France — he worked in their reservations department in New Bond Street — and would then qualify for fantastically reduced travel (though on a strictly stand-by basis) which someone flying with him could also enjoy.

"Great! I'd love it! But how do you know you'll get the New Year off? Doesn't everybody fight tooth and nail in order to grab it?"

But this was just small talk: what I sometimes thought of as keeping up appearances. I knew damned well that he would get the time off. In fact, though not expecting it for a further week or so, I'd been eagerly awaiting his first mention of the subject. But memory plays tricks. I could have sworn it had happened one evening in the Volunteer.

Johnny was fair-haired and of medium height and had the air of a serious-minded student — especially when he wore his glasses — not of someone who had frittered away the past six years in a series of dead-end jobs in the country. Indeed, I'd tried hard to nag him into staying on at school and going to university — reading for a degree in science or in music. But he'd been keen to be out in the world and his parents had supported him in this. Yet when I remembered such things as the crystal set, really far more his achievement than it had ever been mine, I kept being cross at his short-sightedness and the thought of all that he was missing. However, it mightn't be too late. I'd spoken about the fun of my own undergraduate days — the balls and the picnics and the punting, the all-night discussions fuelled by wine and chocolate biscuits, the playing of the drums and saxophone at dawn in misty meadows near the

106

river bank — until he'd asked me please, for the love of Mike, just to put a sock in it. I wasn't sure that this was altogether a bad sign.

"Well, if we're really off to France," I said, "tomorrow I'll enquire about an evening class in French."

"But we're only going for a couple of days! And in Paris you don't even need to speak French."

"It's all right for you. You get practice at work. But, for me, my 'O' levels seem a long time ago — and I don't want to sound a charlie. Anyhow, when I actually scraped through French, old Horwood nearly fainted from the shock of it."

In fact that had been the last time — occasionally I got muddled; this time my pass had been more respectable. (But Johnny no doubt ascribed to modesty what I'd just said.) Modern languages — unlike the classical ones, including, oddly, the small amount of Hebrew which I'd had to study — had never been my forte and even having a French wife hadn't helped me much. Both Ginette and her parents spoke excellent English; by the time Ginette had lived in Britain twenty years most people were surprised to learn she wasn't British. Previously I'd been content not to have to make the effort. Now things would be very different.

"I think you're a nut," said Johnny. "Just two or three days," he repeated.

"This won't be the only time I'll go to France."

"Maybe not, but on that principle you might as well take evening classes in Italian too — throw in Spanish and Greek, why not? — people are getting better-travelled all the time."

It was through Johnny I'd first met Ginette. She had become a colleague of his at Air France. (Some five years hence.) Johnny stayed on there for nearly two decades. He hadn't risen very high, however — too many people chasing after too few openings — and finally had handed in his notice in a fit of pique, before he'd found another job to go to. From then on it had been downhill all the way; our destinies had been remarkably alike — two reasonably bright boys who'd

107

messed around and never fulfilled one tenth of their potential. Yet we hadn't even remained close. I didn't much like his wife from the start but it wasn't until he walked out on her in the late Seventies — as well as on his job — that I lost touch with him entirely; I had a letter returned: 'Moved away, address unknown'. This had been a year or so before Philip died, when Ginette and I had still had ... I am tempted to say a good marriage but it couldn't have been that, a good marriage would have better absorbed the stress, would have survived as something other than a travesty. Ironically, I think my own domestic happiness had been hard for Johnny to accept; and perhaps, too, seeing me could only remind him of his youth and the dreams he'd had of fame as a composer — though, damn it, I don't know how he'd thought he was going to achieve this without the proper grounding. (I remember he'd argued there were successful songwriters who couldn't read a note.) In any case, it was essential to get him away from Air France before he'd been there very long. His marriage had been childless — Sandra wouldn't, rather than couldn't, become pregnant — and she'd been terrified of flying too, so after the first half-dozen years he hadn't even travelled much. Sandra had joined the company a year before Ginette.

Furthermore, it wasn't enough just to get him away from Air France — which was a pretty good experience for a short while: Australia, China, America drew close — he needed to be pushed towards university or towards some satisfying career.

Does all this sound a bit high-handed? Organisational? Perhaps. It certainly sounds like please do as I say and not as I do. For my own future was very far from being mapped out. (At present I was doing some portering in a hospital.) I had made inquiries about openings in jobs as diverse as the charity field and the London fire brigade and even bomb disposal work; despite my protestations, openings in the Church of England, too. (I didn't see the need to mention to my parents — yet — that earlier in the year, in Oxford, I had been both baptised and confirmed. I regarded Christianity not as a new faith but as a logical extension to my old, which I had long been heading towards, during my past life as much as in this present one.) I was wanting to make sure that, this time, I got things absolutely right.

But in the meanwhile — because I wanted to be thorough — there was the question of my learning French; and also — because I wanted to be thorough — there was the question of Ginette. (The order, obviously, is wrong.)

To put it very coldly: I needed Ginette if I wanted Philip.

Philip wasn't due to be conceived until 1966 but it would be nice for Philip to have siblings — as well as nice for us, of course; and some of these siblings could be older just as easily as younger.

To put it less coldly: I remembered Ginette as she was at the time of our meeting and during the first fifteen years of our marriage; and I knew she would never have grown bitter if, firstly, Philip hadn't died (and Philip wasn't going to die) and — secondly — if I had been a better husband (and I was going to be a better husband). And just as when my mother had succumbed in her middle seventies, lined and strained and petulant, it hadn't taken me long to cast off the image of her old age and instinctively picture her again as she had been, during her heyday — so my renewed youth caused me to think of Ginette in the same fashion: laughing and vivacious and full of devilment — and charity. In the end I felt there was nothing cold at all about my decision to woo back my wife.

Previously, as I say, I'd met her in London — but of course I had often visited her parents' home in the Boulevard Beaumarchais, near the Place de la Bastille.

This time, however, I met her again on the eve not simply of a new year but of a new decade. It seemed appropriate.

I'd taken Johnny to a nightclub in the Latin Quarter called Les Enfants du Paradis. I had been there with Ginette on another New Year's Eve and knew it was by no means the first on which she'd celebrated beneath its imitation theatre boxes, gilt cherubs and maroon rococo plushness — its seasonal balloons and streamers. The chances of her coming here tonight seemed roughly even. But I reckoned that if I didn't see her I could just hang about her apartment block the following day — though this would present the problem of what to do with Johnny, and also of what to tell him.

That might be something I should need to sleep on.

We had both brought evening clothes. Me, I'd done remarkably well at a secondhand place just round the corner from where we lived, while Johnny, being about the same build as my father, had borrowed one of Dad's suits and shirts. As with most men, dinner jackets became us. We turned up at the nightclub feeling debonair and elegant and British. We had each drunk a couple of Pernods in the hotel bedroom.

I'd reserved us a table by telephone from London. In return for the air fare I had determined to give Johnny a really memorable New Year's Eve — or try to. My having planned this so far in advance, moreover, had provided a further incentive to work hard at my French: I'd given myself three months and apart from the evening classes had attended conversation circles and bought records and spent an average of at least three hours a night on becoming conversant with the grammar and vocabulary and idiom. I was too single-minded, maybe. But the result was a happy one. When it came to our short break I spoke the language fairly well, which boosted my morale, hugely. Whether Ginette was there or not we were going to have a great evening.

But she was there — although, incredibly, for the first moment I didn't even recognise her. I saw this young woman in a deep blue dress and for the fraction of a second was prepared to be deflected by a total stranger. The impact was as strong, every bit as stunning, as it had been half a century earlier.

"My God!" I said.

Johnny followed the direction of my gaze.

I told him, recklessly: "That's the girl I'm going to marry."

"Oh. Right. Not bad. For myself, I've lined up Audrey Hepburn."

"Just look at her. Oh, just *look* at her! Isn't she everything you ever dreamt of?"

"What about that little matter of the blond guy whose arm she's holding? From the looks of her I'd say he could be everything she ever dreamt of."

"Only because he's just made her laugh at something. In any case — an irrelevance," I smiled. "How do I get to talk to her?"

"Don't they have a Gentleman's Excuse-Me in France? Or what about a nice Paul Jones?"

"No, you don't understand. I'm serious."

"Then why not simply go across and ask her to dance? You're looking sufficiently fetching. Once on the floor you can tell her of your marriage plans."

"Good idea," I said. I stood up.

"Great Scott! Can it really be the lad's not bluffing?" He pushed my wineglass towards me. "Dutch courage."

"I don't need it." But halfway across the floor I decided that I did. I returned to Johnny.

"Her parents are also at the table. I didn't see that."

"But why does that affect things? Besides, they could be his. And at least it will provide him with people to chat with, while you're proposing to his fiancée."

Yet my knowledge of the outcome was no longer enough, suddenly, to furnish the required bravado. The eventual outcome, I reminded myself. Perhaps, after all, I'd have to wait until she joined Air France at the start of her projected year in London.

I sat down again.

"Funk!" he said.

I took a sip of wine; several sips of wine. "Hold on. I've got to work this out."

I crossed my arms and stared down at my pumps. If in the long run I was going to marry her, I had nothing to lose in the short run by possibly making a fool of myself. Five years from now, in London, either she wouldn't recognise me or if she did we would laugh about the incident — by then it might even have acquired an aura of romance. By the same token, though I had nothing to lose, I clearly had much to win: at the very least, several years' worth of consummated love — and companionship — and support — and freedom from impatience; but more than that, the possibility of other lives, the lives of our children, who, if I failed to act, then lost their chance for ever. So. It was my unknown children I heard crying out to me; saw reflected in the glossy surface of my pumps.

And, in that case, when would there ever be a moment any better than this? For if I waited in the Boulevard Beaumarchais tomorrow — and she came out of her block of flats alone — and if I caught her up and said, "Excuse me but didn't I see you at Les Enfants du Paradis last night? ... I don't suppose you'd like to come and have a cup of coffee with me?" — in short, if everything went just as perfectly as I could wish, there would still be the problem of what to tell Johnny. I could hardly tell him the truth. And I wasn't prepared to tell him anything less, not even along the lines of, "Such a coincidence — you're never going to believe this!" While a refusal to tell him anything might have set a severe strain on our friendship and certainly blighted a thoroughly happy New Year.

"Here goes!" I said. Up on my feet again.

"Really? If you do go through with it I'll never cease to speak of you with awe-struck reverence."

"Will you apply to university?" I asked.

"What?"

The words had come to me totally unannounced and made me feel that this was right: this was the path which I was meant to follow.

I repeated my question.

"Hey! You've got a hope. What — just in exchange for your making sheep's eyes at some dolly bird you fancy?"

"But supposing I get her to dance with me — how about that?"

"What do you think I am?"

"I'll let you off needing to speak of me with awe-struck reverence. Remember, you've taken on a lifelong commitment there."

"Nah! I'll just never mention you again."

"Oh, come on, Johnny, be a sport. Bribe me in some way. Say at least you'll think about your 'A' levels if I get her to dance."

I was so earnest about it that almost unknowingly I'd resumed my seat. Maybe he saw this as a second chickening out.

"Tell you what," he compromised. "If you get her not just to dance with you but also to marry you I'll go for my 'A'levels, apply to university *and* speak of you with awe-struck reverence."

"Promise?"

"Promise."

"Even if she turns me down tonight I can redeem that pledge on the day she eventually does marry me?"

He contemplated my outstretched hand for a moment. "Oh, why not? I've decided to be big about this."

We shook on it.

It immediately occurred to me that Zach would speak of the Grand National syndrome — and tell me good intentions didn't alter things. On the other hand, his advice on how to explain away his overcoat had also been dishonest. (Incidentally, I'd told my parents the exact truth: that I'd given my mack away and that someone I'd met on the train had known this and thought that I looked cold and given me his own coat.) While bearing this in mind I silently passed on to Zach what Mr Eliot had always told us about English grammar: when at last we knew the rules, perhaps then we'd be allowed, occasionally, to break them. I hoped Zach would understand.

One of the cabaret spots began: it was half-past-ten. From my own point of view this seemed like bad timing, since it gave my nerves more of a chance to exasperate my bladder. Even

113

the apache dance wasn't riveting; much less so, the preceding songs and little set pieces between this gangster and his girl, pursued by comic *flics*. But at least it did supply me with the opportunity to pray. There was a lot riding on what could happen in the next half-hour or so.

The performers were applauded and bowed their way out of the spotlights. Ginette came onto the dance floor with her blond boyfriend; there was no denying his attractiveness and — stupidly — I felt jealous. Johnny didn't help.

"You know, it isn't going to be that easy. She looks quite cosy in his arms." After the quick violence of the apache dance the band had started up again with something smoochy.

"Stop it!" I said.

He looked at me in some surprise.

"I mean ... ," I amended, sheepishly.

"You mean ... stop it?"

I managed to smile. "That puts it pretty well."

The waltz came to an end. Ginette's parents had also been on the floor — and now there was a change of partners between the two couples. The music continued slow.

"Wish me luck."

I walked onto the floor and tapped Monsieur Tavernier on the shoulder. "Would you permit me, sir, to dance with your daughter? I do have a special reason." Obviously I spoke in French. The couple came to a standstill.

"And what is your special reason?" asked my former (future) father-in-law: so familiar in his discreet smell of expensive cigars and cologne, his compact dynamism, five-o'clock shadow and humorous eyes. I had always got on well with him.

"Next April," I said, impressively, "it will be the fifty-sixth anniversary of the Entente Cordiale — the fifty-sixth, monsieur!"

"My word! I really didn't know! Next April, you say?"

I looked at Ginette and gave a grin. My nerves had settled; I felt immediately at home. "She's also the prettiest woman in

114

the room — but what has that to do with anything?"

Ginette lowered her eyes — demurely. (And deceptively.) "You have an unfair advantage, monsieur: your being alone in a strange country on New Year's Eve. I should be very hard-hearted to refuse. Don't you say so, Papa?"

"I suppose I do, my child. And another thing I would point out. There will be practically nothing left of this dance if we continue to deliberate."

Saying which, he gave me a nod and turned away. The orchestra was playing *Volare*. Ginette had always made of me a far more graceful dancer than any other woman had. For a moment I simply enjoyed the sensation of having her again in my arms and of inhaling again her Mitsouko. But it was potent stuff — the feel of her, I mean, rather than the smell of her. I began to get a hard-on.

I said, a bit abruptly: "My name is Ethan Hart."

She laughed — there seemed no reason for it; unless she'd guessed at the cause of my abruptness, and the relaxation of my hold.

"And mine is Geneviève Tavernier."

Ginette was her second name. I had always called her that because it was less of a mouthful than Geneviève — and because she didn't like abbreviations. Besides, the anglicised pronunciation made people think at once of the veteran racing car from the British film of that title. "Ethan, I am not an old crock," she had pouted, "and I will not be named after one!" I decided on the instant that this time I would call her Geneviève, with the French pronunciation and with no attempt at shortening. It would mark a little difference: a tiny — and unsuspected — break with the past; a further symbol that could have meant nothing to anyone, except to me.

"You speak French very well, monsieur."

"Thank you, mademoiselle. But something tells me you speak English just as well. And probably better."

She looked surprised. "No — no — I keep meaning to make a proper study of it. But I don't suppose I've spoken more than

115

a dozen words since doing my *bac*. My mother is quite fluent, though. Maybe I should fix you up with her?"

"You're very kind. Yet I ought to say that although I let you think I was alone in Paris, that isn't quite true. But the friend I'm with is a man and it might attract attention if I danced with him. So to that extent you were certainly right to take pity on me."

"Perhaps I took pity on you just for being an Englishman," she laughed. "Oh, I'm sorry, that is a mean and silly joke, but I was thinking of you boiling all your meat — and then eating jam on it! I am sorry to make fun of you."

"But that is not true!" I said. "It is a lie, it is a — it is a —" I couldn't find the word for myth. "Like King Arthur and the Knights of the Round Table," I said. "What do you call that sort of story in French?"

"*Légende*."

"Like a legend — a kind of legend — but ... Oh, very well. What you've accused us of is a lie and a legend."

She laughed again. "The Legend of the Boiled Meat and Jam! It has not quite the same ring of romance. I mean, not to a French person. No doubt the English could feel properly romantic about it."

"Oh, if we weren't in a public place ... ," I said. But such talk was dangerous; I had to move a little bit away again.

Then, unhappily, the dance ended.

"Please. Another one. I haven't asked you yet to marry me."

But all the dancers were now beginning to leave the floor. I turned towards the band leader and asked him pleadingly for just one more — now — clasping my hands to him rather like Nesbitt had once done to Hawk-Genn; but though he smiled he shook his head and shrugged as if his players were to blame. "Typically French!" I said to Ginette — to Geneviève. "So practical. So unpoetic. Thinking of nothing but the next Gauloise."

"But even if you're right," she answered, reasonably, "my boyfriend might not like it: your asking me to marry you."

"Dog in the ... something," I said.

We had another spot of bother over that — a little more understandably. (*Il fait l'empêcheur de tourner en rond* as opposed to the word for myth — which happened to be *mythe*.) "You see," I explained, "your boyfriend is never going to ask you to marry him. Take my word for it."

"But he already has," she said. "Several times."

And then I did the unforgivable. It was shocked out of me. I'd suddenly remembered; or suddenly made the connection. I wasn't on my guard.

"My God! That's not Jean-Paul?"

She had often told me that Jean-Paul was the most persistent of her suitors; would never take no for a final answer. Sometimes, she had said, she thought she should have answered yes — and less and less had there been any air of jokiness about the manner of her saying it. Jean-Paul had not only been handsome but he had become rich and had acquired the reputation of being an excellent father to his six children.

Now she had taken a couple of paces back — and was just standing there staring at me.

She asked eventually: "How do you know about Jean-Paul?"

"I ..."

"How do you know?"

"You see, we've met before — you and I — in a previous incarnation."

"No," she said, "seriously."

"And we got married and you were always throwing Jean-Paul up in my face. You told me how he was forever asking you to marry him and how you should have done so because he was very handsome and became rich and besides all that was a wonderful father to his six children. It was a sort of family joke — well, not really such a joke, to be honest. You used to taunt me with it, rather. You see, we weren't very happy."

I spoke quickly but she was still staring — only now, she was again dissolving into laugher. "Oh, what a fool you are. Are lots of English just like you? I always understood the English to be stuffy. No sense of humour."

117

"It's all that jam they have to spread on their boiled meat. Could you do that and retain your sense of humour?"

"No, probably not. But, monsieur, I'm intrigued. If we've been married before — and yet weren't very happy — and I was beastly to you — then why do you want to marry me again?"

"Oh, because this time it will be different. Enormously different. I shall cherish you. You'll never have a single moment's regret."

"I've got to say — I find that rather comforting."

"And you were only beastly to me because I was beastly to you. In fact — I'm sure I was the beastlier."

"You have an unusual way of putting yourself across."

"I can afford to tell the truth. You see, I'm a reformed character. And in future I shall make you a fine husband."

"I don't believe you can ever have been that beastly." Fleetingly she touched my sleeve. "How many children did we have?"

"Only one. That was a sadness. I don't know why we didn't have a dozen. This time, however, we'll make up for it."

The dance floor was deserted; had been, maybe, for some minutes. Suddenly aware of this and suddenly aware that I should take her back to her table and so risk losing her for the present I said something that must have seemed a little out of tune.

"My Geneviève — but we shall be so very happy!"

I immediately tried to give it a lighter touch, but it had come out sounding like what it was: a *cri de coeur*: and for the moment she was disconcerted.

"Don't worry. That wasn't me. It was David Garrick. Impersonating me. An instant of deathless drama — but I'm afraid I forgot to warn you."

"Ah, then were we married in the time of David Garrick too?"

I shrugged. "As to that ... well, who can say with any certainty?" It seemed all right again.

The very next second, though, it wasn't so all right: we had been joined by Jean-Paul. Jean-Paul wasn't happy. His fair skin was suffused by a flush of — at best — impatience. "Ah, *chéri*," said Ginette — Geneviève. "Meet the gentleman from England. Monsieur Gerard, Monsieur Hart. Jean-Paul, Monsieur Hart claims to be my long-lost husband."

He shook my hand and muttered a conventional greeting but he didn't respond to this statement with the least degree of amusement.

"There is some evidence in support of it," Geneviève persisted, wide-eyed and meaning to impress. "He knew your name, Jean-Paul! So how do you account for that?"

"No doubt he overheard someone use it as we made our way to the table."

This was an explanation which suited me extremely well, even if it did carry certain undertones: to wit, I was an opportunist and a spy.

"Oh, Jean-Paul,"she said, "how prosaic you are! Even on New Year's Eve. How unpoetic! How practical! How typically French!"

"Geneviève, you are wanted back at the table. Besides, it seems odd, your continuing to stand here in this way. You are drawing too much attention."

Geneviève gave me her hand. "But we can't help it, can we, Monsieur Hart, if we make such a very handsome couple?" She was obviously annoyed with Jean-Paul, a little unfairly, on account of his failure to enter into the spirit of her game. "Ah, well, monsieur. It has been nice. I shall remember this encounter."

I retained her hand several seconds longer than necessary — or even proper — and looked her in the eyes while I did so. "*Au revoir*, Geneviève. *Bonne année*! *A la prochaine*."

Jean-Paul gave a little *tst* of irritation and took Geneviève's arm and firmly led her away. I myself returned to Johnny.

"Well done," he said. "I watched you both. It looked as though you were really ... I don't know ... getting through to her. Smarmy devil."

He had risen — and clapped me on the back.

"So what happens now?"

"I know her address. Tomorrow I go and sing 'On the street where you live' on the street where she lives."

"You do, do you? So I have to play the abandoned tourist?"

"Johnny, it's for your own good. Remember that. But let's not think about tomorrow. Right now I'm going to order some champagne. This is an occasion which I feel demands it."

"In a place like this champagne is going to knock you back a bob or two."

"So much the better," I said. And actually I meant it. One of my constant little battles was against meanness. When for fifty years or more you've been a bit tight with your money the defect isn't one you can eradicate easily just because you want to.

"Hope you won't regret it when you see your bill! Hope you won't regret it in the morning!"

He obviously didn't intend it but his tone was faintly taunting. The implicit reminder that the crest of the wave descends into the trough was no doubt timely — yet I could have done without it. For some reason it made me think of the last New Year's Eve on which I'd seen Ginette; and suddenly I felt a sharp chill. It was impossible to imagine her as the same woman. Impossible — and yet only too possible as well — to imagine me as the same man. We hadn't even stayed up until midnight. We'd had a glass or two of sherry, yes, watched some television, spoken as little as we usually did, gone upstairs about eleven — upstairs and to our separate rooms. But it wasn't as if we hadn't started out, then too, as lively, decent, well-intentioned people, both of us. It wasn't even as if we hadn't each remained, basically, decent and well-intentioned.

No wonder that I shuddered.

18

We got married — in Paris — in June 1960; and in the following September Johnny enrolled at the City of Westminster
College in Victoria to study three 'A' levels. He passed them all
during the next summer and then was free to go to Durham to
read for a degree in music. He never met Sandra and was never
lucky enough to have Geneviève for a colleague. In fact,
Geneviève never went to Air France. Apart from all else, she
was too busy bringing up babies. Anne came in 1961, Jacqueline a year later. After a two-month honeymoon in France we
returned to live in Lincoln: a rented house in Steep Hill, quite
close to the cathedral. There I studied for three years at the
Theological College — which I could scarcely have done, of
course, if my parents-in-law, bless them, hadn't been helping
out financially. Life was good. Life was terrific. My wife and my
daughters were as lovely as any man's wife and daughters possibly could be. And I had very much chosen a career which
suited me. My studies, moreover, weren't purely academic: far
from it: I spent a lot of the time getting out into the villages
around Lincoln, being inducted into preaching and pastoral
work, hospital-visiting, school-teaching, learning about mental
health and psychiatric care — I mean, learning about them as
much on the job as in the classroom. And then towards the end
of my course the college found me a position in the one city
which I'd been holding out for. At Petertide I was ordained as
deacon in Southwell Minster and having been licensed to St
Andrew's in Nottingham I then began life as a curate. My
curacy and Geneviève's new pregnancy roughly coincided. The
following year I would be twenty-seven. I wanted the baby to
be born on my birthday and I prayed that it would be a boy.

Obviously I knew I must be grateful for whatever God sent,
but to have a son born in Nottingham on my twenty-seventh
birthday had been an overriding ambition since my late teens.
More than an ambition. An absolute necessity.

And he had to be called Arthur.

"*Zut*! What kind of crazy British name is this? In France they would just laugh at it. This isn't Camelot; it's not the Middle Ages." Geneviève ran her finger round my ear, coaxingly — along the nape and round my other ear. "Darling, why can't we have Philipe? Even Philip? I know you like Philip; you've already told me so." I promised her that Philip would be the name of our next son and remained adamant on the choice of Arthur. Since I had wanted Sarah and Rachel, or Rebecca, for the girls, but had, with foresight, given in on both occasions to Geneviève's own preferences, she knew she wasn't justified in denying me the name I wanted now. "*Merde*!" she said. "I hope that it will be a girl!" But her pout turned — as I knew it would — to giggles when I told her that even the crazy British might consider this a touch eccentric: a little girl called Arthur. It also helped that I had deliberately brought the topic up in bed and that I knew her ticklish spots and had most shamelessly exploited my knowledge.

However, I still realised there was something quite unbalanced about the way I felt. I was objective enough to know that if I'd met anyone who had advocated a similar scenario, or smilingly encouraged mine, I should assuredly have given him a very wide berth indeed. And yet the thing was in my blood. I lived it, breathed it, thought about it as I went to sleep, thought about it when I woke. I wondered if it was always a contradiction in terms: to speak about a sane madman.

For Arthur — of course — was to be my means of recompense to Brian Douglas: the son he'd never had, never could have had, yet who was going to make his dream come true — as literally as lay within my grasp and Arthur's own predilections. A senseless vow, maybe, made to myself, not even to the man whom I had so finally, if ambivalently, sinned against (or in any case not made to him directly); senseless and perhaps inordinately presumptuous.

Yet wholly inescapable.

Or so at least it had seemed.

(And wasn't it significant that from the time I'd made my vow I hadn't once been troubled by that regularly recurring nightmare? Okay, this could have been purely psychological. But even so I saw it as a sign. Though again I agree: I was always pretty good at spotting signs.)

In early March 1964 I wrote a letter to my former English master and sent it via his publishers. It was a shortish letter in which I simply told him I had read his poems and how very much some of them had meant to me — and in which I asked if we might meet; possibly in London. I don't know which was dominant — my sadness or my guilt — when I received an answer not from him but from his editor, to the effect that Humphrey Hawk-Genn "had very tragically take his own life on February 29th," barely a fortnight before — "just when he seemed to be getting fully into his stride, potentially a most tremendous loss to the world of English letters." (On a second reading, as though I myself was the poet being discussed, I mildly resented that word *English*.) I was shaken; and castigated myself for days because I hadn't sent off my letter a year earlier — I could have done so easily — what had there been to stop me? But I had felt so entirely certain that, before, I'd come across his obituary in the Telegraph such a long time later, three years at the very least. Still. Since my feelings of shame and inadequacy, which even prayer apparently could do little to eradicate, were obviously of no value to anyone, it was as well that by then my birthday was approaching and that things about the house were hectic: Geneviève was expecting to go into labour almost literally from one moment to the next.

And she did — most wonderfully — at 9pm on March 27th; and our child was born a little under ten hours later. And he was our first boy and when he was merely minutes old Geneviève held him to her with tears in her eyes and whispered, "*Oh, mon petit mignon, que tu es beau! Tu est tellement beau, mon chéri, que je te pardonne immédiatement que tu t'appelle Arthur.*"

123

19

Nottingham in the middle Sixties was a lot pleasanter than in the early Nineties — even though the mystifying vandalism that would tear down acres of fine Georgian housing in order to replace them with unmitigated ugliness was by then well under way. We lived in Forest Road, which was peaceful and tree-lined, in a late-Victorian house that belonged to the Church and was not only about the same age as our old one in Park Avenue, also peaceful and tree-lined, but likewise had three floors and knew all about rattling window frames and irrepressible, frequently icy, draughts. (And here we had no central heating.) St Andrew's was roughly equidistant from the two. Sometimes I used to cycle up the hill expressly to have a look at No 17 — which was now let out to students — and to remind myself of how extraordinarily blest I was; and that I should never, ever, start to take for granted a life so cram-full of miracles. Park Avenue represented deadness; or, at best, limbo. Forest Road, on the other hand, seemed practically in paradise.

20

Arthur grew up against a background of classical music. I'd put a record player in his nursery and from the very start kept it softly on the go — or as much as was feasible; at least it had an autochanger. But oh, I thought, for a tape deck complete with autoreverse or an eight-track cartridge player! Or what about — just possibly — an endless loop? (Anyhow, I was doing my best to be inventive in that region, and, more practically, to inspire Johnny to be inventive in it too.) At all events, Arthur, when awake, was seldom without good music for any appreciable length of time; and even when asleep wasn't some part of his brain — or soul — conceivably receptive to it? Both the girls had been breast-fed and at first I was disappointed that on this occasion Geneviève had dried up but in one respect I came to look upon it as a blessing: that I myself could spend time with him during the night, either for one feed or for two, and so provide not just more music but poetry as well — including passages from Shakespeare and Chaucer — whilst my son sucked, pausingly, upon his gently sloshing Cow & Gate. Under this general heading of poetry there also figured occasional readings from the King James Bible. Both Testaments.

All right, you can laugh, of course. I admit: on one level ludicrous — the idea of a month-old, six-month-old, nine-month-old baby being subjected to Middle English before he had even properly managed Mamma or Dadda. But on the other hand what harm could it do him? There weren't going to be any end-of-term tests; I would fight against unacceptable pressures of any kind being placed upon him by a too demanding and fanatical father. At the worst, perhaps, he could get a little muddled; but if he started speaking in Tennysonian verse or soaring biblical cadences when asking for his potty or demanding Marmite on his bread and butter, all this could be sorted out when it happened. Surely, it was worth an element of risk.

Geneviève didn't know at first about our son's early exposure to literature; for although she wasn't disapproving of the music — well, not exactly — there was one aspect of it that worried her.

"Why now? It may be good, it may be ... *inutile*, but why didn't you do any of this with Anne or Jacqueline?" Hairbrush poised, she watched me in the mirror.

"I should have done. I didn't think."

I should have done. I hadn't thought.

"Then why didn't you think? Experiments are fine but — do

125

the girls mean less to you than Arthur?"

"No, of course not." Nor did they — considered purely as persons and personalities. "Surely you know how much I love them. Have I ever left you in any doubt of that?"

"Not until now."

"Sweetheart, I can only say I had my studies to contend with when the girls were Arthur's age — so much was going on — everything, everything, was new to me ..." I spread my hands and hoped for understanding. We both watched my reflection.

"It isn't, then, just because they were girls — but now you have the boy you always wanted? Everything had to be so just right from the very first minute you knew I was pregnant. Even the name ..."

"And didn't everything have to be so just right from the minute I knew you were pregnant with Anne — and then with Jacqueline? Didn't it?"

"Yes. But not quite in the same way. And you were never so concerned before with — oh, I don't know — whether they were warm enough ... or too quiet ... or lying in the right position ... You never once mentioned *ce cauchemar effroyable*, this thing you call the cot death."

I should surely have foreseen all this.

"So I say again: it isn't because, deep down, you think that girls are somehow less important than boys?"

"Darling ... I swear it."

"You're sure?"

"I promise you. I couldn't be more sure." At times like this I got glimpses of the woman I had left at her dressing table just a mile away from the dressing table where she now sat. Such glimpses were both a little frightening and heart-warmingly reassuring.

She allowed herself to be convinced. And in the circumstances I decided not to pick her up on that statement she had just made: 'the boy you always wanted.' It was a complete misreading of the case. If we had to speak in those terms at all, then Philip was the boy I'd always wanted. It was partly for Philip — very much for Philip — that I had gone through all of this in the first place. If it hadn't been for Philip there was a strong chance that Arthur wouldn't even be here. Nor Anne. Nor Jacqueline.

Denying it, though, would have been fusspotty; and too much fraught with complexity.

The situation developed one night when Geneviève, happening to wake and go out to the loo whilst I was feeding Arthur, heard me reciting to him:

"'Where the bee sucks, there suck I

In a cowslip's bell I lie ...'"

"Oh, darling!" she remonstrated. "What are you doing to him? My poor little pet! *The Tempest*? He's barely five months old!"

Irrelevantly, I was impressed she knew it was *The Tempest*. But then of course I remembered: we'd seen a production of it at the Theatre Royal the previous year. I felt the need to make a joke.

"You're lucky it wasn't *Titus Andronicus*."

She regarded me angrily. "*Assez de faux-fuyants!*" She came and gathered up into her own arms our little son in his Babygro suit and took the bottle from me and the wooden chair. Arthur looked surprised and interested. Geneviève kissed him on the neck and made him chuckle. "*Ah, ton coquin papa! Que fait-il? Mon petit chou, mon pauvre petit! Where the bee sucks, there suck I*, indeed!"

Arthur chuckled.

I'd felt tempted to say that I was merely entertaining myself — not him; but the pause had given me time to realise that I mustn't.

"You go back to bed," she told me in a hard tone — I was clearly in disgrace; Arthur hadn't saved me. "If you must feed him poetry, what's wrong with Jack and Jill went up the hill or ba-ba black sheep?" (What indeed? In my zeal I had wholly overlooked the nursery rhymes — perhaps on the assumption that he would soon get to know those anyway. And as Geneviève now pointed out: I had told them often enough to his sisters.) "And why must it always be Mozart or Vivaldi or Purcell? What's wrong with Charles Trenet or Aznavour or Brel? And turn off that machine please, whoever it is. I am going to sing my son a lullaby — in French. I am going to have a whole long conversation with him — about silly, unimportant things — in French. So there."

I laughed and put my arms about her shoulders and kissed the crown of her head. "Oh, I'm all in favour of his learning French! You know I am."

Then I went back to bed grinning — having given Arthur, too, a kiss on the crown of his head — but, no longer sleepy, read as I waited for Geneviève's return, so that I could make sure the day (or at least the dawn) didn't go down on her disapproval.

Yet following this confrontation over Arthur there was something which now niggled at me. It wasn't that I believed Geneviève capable of sabotage — she wasn't at all, not on a conscious level — but she was a person who very much went to extremes and I could imagine her thinking that if Arthur had to be force-fed on music he needed to know about Gershwin and Kern and *Oklahoma!* and *My Fair Lady*. Again, I had no real quarrel with this but only thought he didn't need a *grounding* in it. So I took to popping home throughout the day a little more often than I had ever done before and began to worry lest my parish duties might suffer on account of it. For the first time it occurred to me that if I wanted to take a more active part in my son's upbringing — in my children's upbringing — I might have to think eventually about giving up church work, at least temporarily, and looking for some sort of evening job or even night position.

About nine months later there arose a further contretemps. I had offered to take the girls to a local swimming pool — Geneviève herself didn't care for swimming — and I automatically assumed that I'd be taking Arthur too.

"What! Are you crazy? What would you do with him?"

"How do you mean?"

"Clearly you can't have him with you in the water."

"Why on earth not?"

"Why not? Because he's still a baby. Because he can't even walk yet. Or perhaps you hadn't noticed?"

"It's catching on in America that babies should be taught to swim long before they can walk. In fact, they hardly need any teaching; it comes to them so naturally."

"Ethan, I don't care about America. You are not taking Arthur to the swimming pool."

"I only wanted him to get used to the feel of water; to realise how much fun it can be."

"He can do that in his bath, thank you very much."

"I wasn't going to say, 'Go on — swim three lengths.'"

"I wouldn't put it past you. With that poor little baby I wouldn't put anything past you."

"Oh, Geneviève!"

"Sometimes I think you're not safe to leave him with."

"This is ridiculous."

"And what about your daughters? You have daughters. Three- and four-years-old — and a lot of fun they're going to have with their daddy if you're taken up all the time with the baby in your arms. A fat lot of help with their swimming *they're* going to get!"

"Dammit, they've got water-wings. They only need a hand under the chin. I could give them that just as easily with Arthur in my other arm as I could without him."

"Oh — *treats*! What little girl ever wants to splash and race and ride upon the shoulders? But you can still do all of that, of course, with Arthur in one arm. Or have you perhaps left him by this time — how do you say it — to sink or swim? Sent him off on his three lengths?"

"All right; let's forget it. It obviously wasn't a good idea. I'm sorry."

"And suppose that one of the girls got into difficulties —

what then? You make me sound unreasonable but I wouldn't have a minute's peace. I didn't raise my children to let them all be drowned." She was beginning to cry. "Not by you or anybody else."

I walked out of the room. It was the first time I'd really lost my temper with her. I was angrier than I'd been in years — maybe since childhood. If I'd stayed I think I might have hit her.

Of course, we were fairly soon reconciled, and I took Anne and Jacqueline to the pool, and it was fine — Geneviève was right: Arthur *would* have been in the way. But our quarrel secretly left me miserable. For many days I kept returning to it in my thoughts, wasting time and energy by wishing I'd avoided it, wishing I hadn't lost control, wishing I'd stayed to comfort her when she broke down. The way I had behaved seriously dented my image — for the first time — of the perfect husband I was trying to be. (Perhaps this should have happened sooner.) The only clearly positive things which resulted from it, apart from the relief and pleasure of our making up, was that it reminded me how careful I would have to be — over everything — which surely I shouldn't have needed reminding of; and that when a month or so later I asked if I could take Arthur on his own to the pool, Geneviève agreed without any fuss, even though he still couldn't walk yet, the lazy brat.

At fifteen months my unconcerned son may have been a lazy brat; at twenty-eight and a quarter years his deeply concerned father was getting ever more industrious. Once Arthur was finally sleeping through I began to get up two hours earlier every morning and go down to the kitchen, where it was warmest, and make myself a pot of strong black coffee and spread my books and papers all over the table and start to study. I studied history — mainly British to begin with but not entirely so — world politics, world religion, world mythology, world geography. I rotated and integrated and imposed upon myself no deadlines (as I had in the first instance with my

130

French) because on all such subjects it was clearly absurd to set limits. Gradually I would try to add at least the rudiments of all the major ideas and beliefs which people had held at various points in history, as well as the rudiments of philosophy and psychology and astronomy, physics, chemistry, biology ... well, in short I wanted to become as well-informed as it was possible for an ordinary layman to be, not for the sake of my own education but for the sake of my son's. I wanted to be knowledgeable about sport and architecture and antiques and wine-making and horticulture and ... oh, do I really need to go on? *But don't let me pontificate* was a prayer I added to my many other prayers. I want to teach — but don't let it appear like teaching. Let me be lively and stimulating and funny and relaxed. Please save me from solemnity.

And let me be patient.

Endlessly tolerant — and patient.

I began my course of studies, appropriately enough, by reading up about King Arthur; both the Celtic warrior *and* the creator of the Knights of the Round Table. It was strange I hadn't thought about doing this before. Right at the beginning I didn't even know which of them was spoken of as being the one who would return. The Once and Future King.

21

"Death to the infidels!" ... "Enemies of Christ!" ... "Child killers!"

Oh, how they hated us. They borrowed money off us — and often didn't pay it back, so we had to take them to the assizes — and I don't know how they'd have got on without us, a lot of them, but oh how they hated us, these solid citizens of York.

Often they spat on us in passing or even assaulted us — sometimes, for a great joke, cornered one of us and forced him to eat pork; sometimes beat us up so cruelly our blood seeped between the cobblestones and we were left for dead. Somehow those robes of ours seemed always an affront. We tried to make them look less costly and occasionally risked taking off our yellow badges, too. But our swarthy skins and Semitic features invariably betrayed us and so invited trouble; and there'd have been fines to pay, perhaps imprisonment, if the papal authorities had ever got to hear of it. Besides, it seemed to most of us dishonourable: we aimed to wear our badges with distinction. With pride.

A lot of it had to do with the crusades. A priest from the Christian Pope had come to the marketplace on a recruiting drive to get men to join the armies in the Holy Land and take up arms against the infidels. "But what about the infidels in York?" the crowd had shouted. "All Jews are infidels." It seemed there was just as much anti-Jewish as anti-Moslem hysteria sweeping through the city. (Even the Pope himself had warned the English to beware of us: we exerted a 'corrupting influence on Christian souls,' he'd written.) That priest was a demagogue who hardly cared in what direction the passions of the mob would flow.

It hadn't always been like this. Intermittently we'd been allowed to exist in peace — especially while King Henry ruled; he'd treated us well and it was largely due to him that when we had to take defaulters into court we usually won our case — although, as payment for this, we'd had to send the king a tenth of whatever money we got back. Throughout his reign — well, by and large — York wasn't such an awful place to live.

I'd started off in Lincoln; I spent nearly the whole of my last life in Lincoln. Until I was very old, however (or more accurately, I suppose, until I was very young), I didn't think in terms of last life — this life — next life; it was a passing stranger in our tiny synagogue who drew me on one side and acquainted me with how things stood. He told me that a thousand years ago I'd struck Jesus Christ when he was on his way to crucifixion. I couldn't believe I'd done that; I still can't believe it. And yet ...

I mean, I'm not a saint or anything. (My God, you should have asked my wife — Rebekah.) I'm not even a reasonably good man, I never kid myself about this, no patience that's my trouble, I *do* sometimes hit out wildly, not physically, I mean, not any longer, I haven't got the strength, but with a vicious, irrepressible tongue, *intolerant*, though at least these days I always feel ashamed and seek forgiveness. But what I'm saying is — I may not be a good man but I can't believe I'd hit someone when he's down, even someone I'd felt disappointed in, scornful of, like him, like Jesus Christ. You see, I know too well what it's like to be down, to be the underdog.

But if I didn't know it then, and if I really did strike him — as I suppose I must have done — well, at least I've got to be improving. This travelling wise man (I don't know what to call him) acknowledged that much — grudgingly; well, half grudgingly, half encouragingly, it seemed like an odd mix. And though, like I say, I didn't believe him at the time — how could he even be a Jew, with a countenance and hair as fair as that? — I was obliged to stop and listen on account of some magnetic power he had, magical maybe (since, later, no one could remember seeing him), and I was also obliged to believe him afterwards, just by the fact of living to such an old age ... and coming back.

So I'm improving — I believe that too, and if there's hope for me there must be hope for anyone, even for the vilest of the curs that persecute us.

Improving ... and the knowledge you're improving makes you want to improve more, like when you've first got a bit of money saved and you're determined to do everything you can to see the balance grow.

Improving.

But at what a cost.

Because I've got to tell you.

I've spilt human blood. I've spilt a lot of human blood.

Spring, 1190 — and I myself am older than the century. There's this man called Malebisse — Richard Malebisse — who's the arch-conspirator against us Jews.

Some months back he borrowed heavily from one of my neighbours, Benjamin of York, but afterwards denied that he had done so. The case was about to come to court; Malebisse would almost certainly have had to cough up. But one stormy night in mid-March he and a band of his henchmen broke into Benjamin's house, killed him, killed everybody, then set the place on fire and carried off what treasure they could find. I heard the screams and smelt the smoke but thought at first these were just part of some dreadful dream; I believed that Benjamin had fortified his windows and his doors and his courtyard doors, just as we all had, and had servants always on the watch, just as we all did. So by the time I'd struggled up from sleep and managed to get downstairs and out into the street the murdering cowards had made their getaway. But I knew that it was Malebisse because my own two servants saw him; and anyway, later on, before he fled to Scotland, he even bragged about it. Drunkenly. Claimed recognition as 'the man who gave the signal for the massacre'.

That's right. Massacre.

For by the middle of the next day the narrow streets were all but jammed with looters on the rampage, looters and murderers who cried out for vengeance. Vengeance for what? I ask you. For the fact that our forefathers had come to England with nothing and by sheer hard work as much as native wit had turned that nothing into something? For the fact that a year ago two hundred Christians had died in York from a plague which hadn't killed a single Jew there? For the fact that three 'boy martyrs' had recently been canonised in England because *we* allegedly had killed them — ritually and horribly — by crucifixion?

Or was it vengeance for those most terrible crimes of not sharing in their beliefs, of being more thorough in our ablutions, more particular about our diets; of wanting to teach our sons — and having the kind of close-knit family life which many might have envied?

Anyhow.

By now the whole of the Jewish population had been smoked out and was running for its life — or I, for my unmutilated limbs. There were fewer than two hundred of *us*; of *them* there were many thousands. We thought about hiding in one or other of the city's forty churches or in the crypt of the cathedral; but that rabble would no more have respected the sanctuary of their own places of worship than they would of ours. (The houses of God! It was impossible to think these animals acknowledged any god — ever — anywhere — but I suppose at times you could say the same of anyone, myself included; myself very much included.) So we decided to make for the castle.

We made for it by the back alleys and even, the more nimble ones, over rooftops; and prayed we wouldn't be anticipated. Behind the thickness of castle walls we might be safe; or certainly as safe as anywhere. The Royal Constable would have to let us in, since we went in fear of our lives and were as much the subjects of the king as were those who'd do us harm. In a day or two, we thought, the situation must have been defused — either by the authorities or by the elements: it was very wet and very windy. Disappointed of their sport and lacking the stamina, please God, for any lengthy siege, the crowds would eventually drift home, in search of sustenance, dry clothing and of sleep. Besides — didn't they have their livelihoods to reckon with?

Getting to the castle was the hardest part — or so at least it then seemed. We did it in little groups of two and three and mainly — though often heart-in-mouth — we were able to slip through successfully; only nine of us were seen and chased and caught and killed. (Or in fact three of these were merely bludgeoned senseless but those of us who got through assumed at the time that death was inescapable at the hands of such a

135

mob: inescapable and maybe even preferable, so long as it were speedy.) I was one of the lucky ones, if lucky is a word that can be used, in having two stalwart young men to lend me their support, half lifting me between them as they ran, for otherwise my infirmities must certainly have meant my falling prey to our pursuers. We got there, however, sliding along the base of walls as if we aped our shadows, pressing into doorways, disturbing sleeping cats, which — stepped on in the gloom — sprang into screeching life; hearing more than once the clamour of the crowd grow closer and reverberate all round us, seeing the blaze of several torches lighting up the brickwork only yards from where we cowered, feeling almost irresistibly drawn to show ourselves and so cut short the agonising uncertainty ... yes, in the end we got there, to the castle, fighting for breath and with the sweat of fear making our robes seem even damper and more weighty, the sweat of effort too, they must have doubted that I'd ever make it, those two young men, doubted my heart could possibly withstand the strain. (But I could have told them that although I'd suffered more than one heart attack over the past two centuries none was as yet likely to prove fatal.) We got there and the Constable had been prevailed upon to admit us and safety seemed — perhaps — within our grasp.

Yet there were those who didn't trust the Constable and infused the rest of us with their suspicions. Finally we locked the man out of his own castle. It proved a wretched move. The Constable appealed to the Sheriff of Yorkshire; and the Sheriff decided to use his soldiers to eject us.

The soldiers joined the mob, who now waited jubilant beneath the battlements. The people cheered wildly at their arrival. They believed the presence of the troops symbolised the new king's sanction for the way they felt about the situation; it was a kind of royal warrant. A white-robed monk, parading back and forth along the walls, whipped them up into a frenzy. The soldiers had a battering ram with which they stormed the gate.

By then — in spite of our more confident predictions — the seige had lasted several days: several days of prayer and fasting and of trying to keep our spirits up; days of darkness and hunger and coldness and fear. The screaming of babies, the sobbing of children. Acts of kindness and sacrifice. Confessions in the dark. In conditions such as those ... you learn about your fellow beings.

But this was the end. There remained only the one course open to us if we wished — if they wished — to avoid a lingering death.

Yet we Jews only very exceptionally commit the sin of suicide. So it was agreed the men should first cut the throats of their children and their wives; then kill each other. Which was how it started. But the rising consternation as the children realised what was happening, the stifled sobs and hysteria of the mothers, the final terror in the eyes of dearly loved ones: all this led inevitably to a weakening of resolve. Strong men, hardened men, world-weary men — they found they couldn't do it.

And so it was that with the regular and terrifying thud of that battering ram shaking the very floor beneath us even in the castle keep I felt obliged to offer my services. Oh, God! Dear God! I dispatched maybe sixty lives in the space of just ten or fifteen minutes. It didn't get easier after the first. "Peace — and may the Lord receive you," fifty or sixty times over (some of these people were my friends, had done me many kindnesses, all of them were known to me; this was a kindness I was giving in return but the thought did nothing to bolster me — possibly the two most difficult throats to cut were those of the strong young men who had recently supported me saying, "Are you all right, old Solomon, rest a moment, have no fear that we'll desert you ..."); only fifteen minutes, yes, but undoubtedly the most debilitating of my life — lives. When I was the only living thing left in that foul-smelling room — apart from the rats — where even the very walls seemed to be weeping for us, I sank down on my knees through sheer

137

exhaustion and slumped red-handed and **wet-robed** across the
nearest pile of still-warm corpses — still very much the loner;
the outsider who could never ever belong. And not a minute too
soon, either, for already they were battering at the dungeon
door and the hinges were about to give. And, oh, you should
have heard them shouting at us, telling us to come out and be
killed, asking if we had crucified any little boys recently,
describing the terrible things they were going to do to us as
soon as they had broken through. I lay there stiff and cramped
and aching and with my nostrils filled with the stench of dead
humanity but knew I couldn't fool them into thinking that I
too was dead: uncontrollable breathing — shudders — tear
ducts. I prayed. God, in your infinite mercy, take me forward
to my next life. Don't let me fall into the hands of these bar-
barians. Forgive me my sins. Show pity. Take me.

But in truth I had no faith that his mercy was infinite; or
that he hadn't simply left me to the devil.

22

We were having problems which we hadn't had before.
Down-and-outs. Charitable appeals. Flag days.
But mainly down-and-outs.
Although in Birmingham (where we now were) there
weren't as many as there would be later, not nearly, there was
still, unhappily, a large number. I felt a need to give. To give
substantially. I knew I might sometimes be duped but this
seemed unimportant. "For I was an hungred, and ye gave me
meat ... Inasmuch as ye have done it unto one of the least of
these my brethren, ye have done it unto me." I wanted — no,
felt driven — to act out the teachings of Jesus as fully as I

138

could. I didn't wait to have hands held out to me in want; I searched for those who looked as though they needed help. But I simply couldn't stop myself — no special virtue. In fact, in some ways I felt it was far from being a virtue: witness the dissension it provoked at home.

"But this is madness. We are getting into debt." She was always accusing me of madness, in one form or another: in prison-visiting 'when you can't even find the time to visit your own parents'; in helping out in missions 'until you're practically sleep-walking and no doubt thoroughly in the way of the people who are *trained* to do this work'; in giving shelter to derelicts 'who might steal everything we have, or be sick on our Persian rug, or even murder us while we sleep — though on these occasions, as you know very well, I never do sleep; not that you ever care about *that*, obviously!' "Steeply into debt," she added. "What sort of example do you think that you'll be setting for your children?"

She was speaking, of course, about financial management but inadvertently had gone straight to the nub of it. When I was out with my children (and despite her taunts about not visiting my parents — which I didn't believe justified — I was out with my children just as often as I could be, more so indeed than with my wife and children, though that was never of my own choosing, not in the slightest) I neither repressed this urge towards giving nor encouraged or exaggerated it merely for show. The children put it down to 'Daddy being in one of his crazy moods,' a phrase they had possibly picked up from their mother — but whereas Anne and Philip spoke about it with me and themselves would shyly hold out a half-crown (or 12½p: we were just then on the cusp) to the 'poor people who just aren't lucky like we are', Jacqueline and Arthur were often visibly ill-at-ease. Of the four, unfortunately, Arthur was the most embarrassed. "Don't! Daddy — don't! It makes us look so silly. And besides — Mummy says they only drink it." Later I heard Philip say to him, "If they have to drink money they really are very poor people!", and out of the corner of my eye saw the

139

six-year-old Arthur — having first decided, erroneously, that my attention was otherwise engaged — give him a pretty vicious pinch.

Philip was three. He was our youngest and our last; Geneviève had put her foot down, very firmly, about having any more — and indeed I had even had an unexpected fight to secure Philip. I wasn't sure what I'd have done if she had continued to hold out against him; his life had been even more important to me than Arthur's — though of course in a different way. He was precisely the same Philip as before: good-humoured, generous, funny, endlessly endearing. We enjoyed a rapport, he and I, which I knew was missing from my relationships with all my other children but which I didn't feel in any way guilty about. Clearly, I tried to keep it secret.

We had other problems; again related to money — or partly so. Partly related to prestige. Not all that much related to education.

"Geneviève. How would you feel about our keeping the children at home and educating them ourselves?"

I'd realised this would be a bombshell; but hadn't known how to lead up to it in easy stages. It wasn't as though the three who were already at school were at all unhappy there — bullied or repressed or friendless. It wasn't even as though they weren't doing reasonably well and getting fine reports. They just weren't doing as well as if they'd had more individual attention: i.e., teachers who were burningly committed to them alone. "Wouldn't you like the thought," I said, "of being able to shoulder full responsibility for the way our children develop academically?"

"No. I should hate it. I should find it terrifying."

"One person on his own maybe. But the two of us together. In partnership. And think how it would draw us closer."

"Why, don't you feel we're close, then?"

"What I mean is — it would be yet another bond between us."

"You don't feel we're as close as we should be, do you?"

140

"Geneviève, I love you. Very much. You know I do."

"Pooh! You love everybody."

"You're talking nonsense. But don't let's get distracted. We were speaking about the children."

"No. You were speaking about Arthur."

"Darling, all our children. I haven't got a particular preference for Arthur — except in some ways. I have particular preferences for all our children — in some ways."

"What about Anne, for instance?"

"The way she buys us presents for no special reason; the way she's always wanting to give us small surprises. A dozen things. But —"

"Jacqueline?"

"Oh — Jacqueline. They way she looks like you; the way she walks about in your shoes, little coquette, and looks so very pleased with herself ... so *mignonne* and adorable. The way she's so determined and will stand up to anything: large dogs, angry parents; but will suddenly, too, get very shy ..." My grin broadened. "Why do I get the feeling that you're testing me? And why won't you please stick to the subject under discussion?"

"Ethan, you're not really serious about it? You can't be." She stirred her coffee for the umpteenth time. "In any case. A partnership, you said. But you meant you, didn't you? Basically you meant you. But how could you ever stay at home to give the full-time education that you speak of?"

"Which brings us to my next point," I said — wishing I had a little more of my second daughter's fearlessness.

My next point involved leaving the Church. Leaving the Church involved moving to rented property probably much inferior to that which we'd been used to. I had already been making casual telephone inquiries about possible night work in hospices and hostels and old people's homes. Geneviève would also need to take a job. None of this, of course, was easy. But I hadn't envisaged it as being impossible.

"No, I refuse to talk about it. I just refuse to talk about it.

141

Now you really have taken leave of your senses."

"Geneviève, this means a lot to me. Right or wrong, you can't dismiss it out of hand."

"We're nearly at the end of your second curacy. Nearly there. Your being a vicar means a lot to *me* — if that's of any interest to you whatsoever."

"You know it is, but —"

"All those years of study. Which my father paid for. All those platitudes. All these expressions of ...?"

"Piety?" I offered the word grimly.

"Pretensions of caring."

"I do care. I care very much but there are other curates — other vicars — our children have only one father and I genuinely believe that I've a duty to them which —"

"And what about your duty to me?"

I looked down at my own *demitasse*.

"Just look around you," she said. "We're surrounded by people with young families. But the fathers are just normal, loving fathers who want the best for their children, like we all do, but without expecting their wives to give up everything, go out to work, have no fun, never see their husbands ..." (Since we now lived very close to a large housing estate where there was much poverty and drunkenness and wife-battering — in stark contrast to the parish in which we'd started out in Nottingham — I felt her picture was not a fully impartial one, any more than was her subsequent comment.) "They'd be amazed to hear a young man talking of anything so menial. So immature; so irresponsible. Working like a porter — or a caretaker — or a cleaner! What would you suggest for me? To be one of those women who look after a public convenience?"

This was quite a diatribe and there were sometimes disadvantages to Geneviève's having so quickly acquired such very proficient English.

So I let the subject drop, and continued to pray about it and (try to) be thankful in all things, but Geneviève remained inflexible. I couldn't believe that God wanted my marriage

142

ruined for the sake of a unilateral decision that could be in any case highly questionable. And why had he encouraged me to go into the ministry in the first place if I was only going to let down so many people who'd been relying on me? Certainly my children hadn't been relying on me — not for their education.

So that same September — September 1970 — I became a fully-fledged vicar; my first incumbency as such in Dorset. Geneviève was happy and busy and radiant and full of common-sense supportiveness; there was no question but that I'd done the right thing. Friends from both Nottingham and Birmingham came for the induction, and Geneviève's parents from Paris, and from London Johnny brought not only Mary, his wife of six months, but Gordon too, whom he had bumped into one day in Selfridges — Gordon, on hearing of the event, had thought it would be fun to join in and had got in touch with me again that very night. (In fact, to be absolutely accurate about it, it was Gordon who brought Johnny and Mary — in his new Porsche.) And it *would* have been fun, too — well, to an extent it was fun — all of us making do together in our grand new vicarage; but my father had just died from lung cancer (his funeral had been only eight days earlier) and though Mum came to Bridport, driven there by Max, with Gwen in the back seat, still, the fact my dad couldn't be there with us, my dad whom I had loved so much, inevitably cast something of a blight, as far at least as she and I were concerned. ("He was so proud of you at Southwell and later at your priesting," said my mum. "Just think how he'd have felt if he'd been here with us tonight." I told her that I thought he had been there with us tonight — and tried hard to believe it.) Anne, too, said that it wasn't the same without Granddad, and Jacqueline agreed, and Philip climbed up on my mother's lap and put his arms about her neck and looked into her eyes and said, "I *loved* my granddad!" I said, "Yes, I know, we all did — didn't we, Arthur?" and Arthur said, "What? 'My daddy said ... *his* daddy's dead.' Granny, I want to be a poet when I'm a man — did you know that? — and that's a poem I've only just made

143

up." I found I had to restrain myself, the vicar not half an hour returned from his induction and from the small party thrown after it in his honour, at which he'd spoken a few soft-tongued words to every member of his parish then present in the church hall; had to restrain myself from giving him a fair old clip round the ear.

23

I plodded on, regardless. As Arthur grew older it seemed to me he became less and less the sort of person I had hoped for — and yet, I often wondered, who on earth was I to be the judge of that? He was a nice enough boy in many ways; there were moments when he surprised me by his thoughtfulness. (I suppose the fact that I was surprised was in itself indicative.) But he was naturally — or so it appeared — very right-wing in most of his attitudes, very chauvinistic, quite demanding. Where the others would all help willingly — or more or less willingly — with chores about the house Arthur took a great deal of persuasion and would often only do what he'd been asked with a rather poor grace. He insisted on rosters — which was fine — but if the rosters got snarled up, as for one reason or another they inevitably did, he wasn't flexible, he just got angry and refused to step in; unless, that is, Geneviève bribed him — which she knew I didn't approve of and which I usually, therefore, didn't get to hear about until after the event. (She would even look innocent and lie if questioned outright.) He didn't seem to profit from example, either; in fact I think he probably reacted against it. (The right-wing business might have been a pose — although on second thoughts his mother also sometimes showed some right-wing tendencies.) He glowered more often than he smiled. He was far more inclined than any of the others to indulge in tantrums and to sulk and to hit out with apparently minimal provocation. Perhaps his namesake had been this kind of fellow too; perhaps it was appropriate for a king, certainly a sixth-century king, to be arrogant and aggressive, chauvinistic and unbending. But Arthur — my Arthur — didn't appear to exhibit those qualities of leadership which might have excused, or explained, those other facets of his character. One sensed an underlying weakness, rather than a strength.

Philip was far more (was exactly) the kind of material I had hoped for, and expected. But Philip was not Arthur. He had neither been born in Nottingham nor on my twenty-seventh birthday; he hadn't ever been the subject of a dying man's recurring dream. It contravened the rules to attempt to give to Philip the place that had been designed for Arthur. For surely it *had* been designed for Arthur?

But I plodded on, regardless. What else was there to do? I'd got into the habit of preparing my son for kingship and — as I say — who was I to know what changes the years were going to bring, or what groundwork should have been laid by the time those changes had occurred? And if Arthur didn't seem responsive, certainly Philip did — and, to a lesser extent, the girls. So, to put it at its very lowest, at least they were likely to benefit from the kind of education, and example, with which I tried to supplement their more conventional schooling.

There was a date engraved upon my mind: November 23rd 1980. I felt tempted on that day not to let Philip out of the house — not for a moment — but clearly this was paranoid. Before, we had been living in London; Philip had been attending a comprehensive school in West Hampstead. The car he hadn't seen until too late, hidden from his view because of a parked van, would still presumably be speeding along that same stretch of the Finchley Road at 4.25pm — and the van would still be stationed in that selfsame position — but nobody would step out from behind it at 4.25; assuredly not Philip,

145

who'd be three hundred miles away. Poor Mrs Bancroft's life — along of course with mine and Geneviève's — wasn't again about to be ruined; supposing that it ever had been; I hadn't felt inclined then to call her *poor* Mrs Bancroft — although undoubtedly she must have suffered. We never saw or heard from her, however, after the inquest. (What had I expected: a Christmas card each year: *so sorry, know that you'll be missing him?*) But even so — absurdly — I felt scared. The closer drew the day the more apprehensive I became. Prayer seemed powerless to help. I decided the only way to cope with it had to be through taking action.

"Geneviève, I shall be going down to London tomorrow." After Bridport I'd been sent to Newcastle.

"Oh, yes. Why?"

"Just something I've got to see to." There was a funeral arranged for that afternoon which my curate would have to handle; otherwise, providentially, there was nothing that couldn't be rescheduled, not even, for once, a meeting of any kind.

"I thought we were supposed to be having a quiet evening at home tomorrow night." On such occasions she often planned something special — and celebratory — for our dinner.

I said: "I can be home by eight, or thereabouts."

"What can you possibly have to see to in London at such short notice?"

"Ah ... secrets!" I tried to make it sound as if I might be going to buy her Christmas present; though what I could get in London that I couldn't get in Newcastle, or what might be worth all those hours spent in travelling, was going to prove a little problematic. "But look — why don't you come too? Make it a day out? I'd only have to desert you for an hour or so."

"Oh, it may be all right for vicars to go swanning off at just a moment's notice. It's obviously much harder for the vicars' wives."

Nowadays, Geneviève had mixed feelings about the role of vicar's wife. She still thought it carried a certain cachet; and

146

even enjoyed the element of exposure — was happy to think it would be noticed when she put on a new dress or styled her hair a little differently. Always charming and lively and popular she liked to believe she was fairly much at the centre of things, had her finger on the pulse. But on the other hand she resented it that a vicar's wife was so often considered an extension of her husband, an unpaid worker who was available at any time to come to coffee mornings, sort out grievances, open fetes, answer the door to hard-up strangers. "I'm spied on, I'm spied on!" she had sometimes said. "I can't do anything without the whole world knowing. I haven't got a life of my own! I'm not a person in my own right!"

I'd suggested she should take a job — "I mean, just to escape the claustrophobia."

"A job! I'm not trained. Selling in a sweet shop?"

"Why not train for something?"

"Perhaps I shall. Perhaps I shall one of these days. When Philip is a little older."

The two girls had already started at university. Geneviève often spoke about studying for a degree herself. I didn't believe she ever would.

In the meantime, perversely, she didn't really mind serving on committees and being greatly in demand. She felt just as pleased as she did disgruntled that she couldn't 'go swanning off at just a moment's notice', although if truth be told she very often had.

I emerged from Finchley Road underground in very good time. When I reached the spot where the accident had taken place — and I had visited that spot many times before, though never in this current life (passed it, yes, but never 'visited') — there wasn't any van parked there as yet. However, I knew that it must come. There was a space just waiting for it — and no reason on earth why that space should not be filled. And come it did: at twenty-one minutes and several seconds past the hour. The driver climbed down and took out of the back two large boxes containing packets of matzos to deliver to a nearby delicatessen.

I thought I'd forgotten what he looked like but I recognised him immediately; believed I would have recognised him even in Oxford Street or Newcastle. He gave me a cheery smile, just as if he recognised me too, and fifty-five years ago I should never have imagined myself being capable of responding. I wondered if Philip had once been the recipient of that same cheery smile.

I stationed myself in the gap between the van and the vehicle on its left, blocked the way to any schoolchild who might be in a hurry to get home, and stayed there, not just until I'd seen Mrs Bancroft drive past, searching for something in her handbag ("Why, that bloody bitch!" I thought), but until the delivery man had returned and with a further pleasant nod driven out into the traffic. For this I had rescheduled my whole timetable and paid to travel all these miles. But at least it had given me a purpose to help get me through the day; had provided time for me to read, and put me in the way of an old vagrant I should never otherwise have met. (Well, more than one, but one I thought of in particular.) Had placed a hatbox in my hand that came from Bond Street and that had something inside it which — I felt confident — could rival, saucily, even Parisian chic.

When I got home there was a note from Geneviève.

"Philip hurt in accident. Serious. We're with him at the hospital. Come as quickly as you can."

There was a duck, half taken from its wrappings, also on the table.

I couldn't understand it. Why had they allowed Billy Cooper to live? Why had they allowed Anne and Jacqueline — and Arthur — to be born? (Whom did I mean by 'they'? The Fates — God — Zach — whom?) Had there been something in Philip's future life which overstepped the bounds of acceptability? Some accident or atrocity that one of his children or descendants might have caused, bringing destruction to those who simply weren't expendable? All questions such as these I only asked myself a long time after. For the moment I went off the rails — at least inside my head — even if, on the outside, I might appear to be able to cope. People were kind; sympathetic; supportive. The girls came home and stayed until the following term. Arthur, who was normally quite undemonstrative, kept giving me hugs for no apparent reason. I suspected that he cried even more than his sisters did: I often noticed his red rims and twice found him washing his face at unusual times of day. I began to feel that during all these years I might totally have misjudged Arthur — never known him — failed to appreciate him.

I was equally surprised by the lorry driver; I mean, my attitude towards the lorry driver. (Especially in view of how I'd recently reacted to Mrs Bancroft.) Geneviève beat at him with both her fists and had to be, quite literally, pulled off by bystanders, but I felt no animosity at all. If it hadn't been him it would have been someone else. In fact, I just felt sorry for the man: why him — why should this pleasant-faced stranger need to bear on his conscience the killing of a boy? If Philip had had to go, why couldn't he have fallen out of a tree or something ... perhaps died quickly from some heart condition, totally undiagnosed? I didn't understand the ways of God. I told myself that was his loss, not mine. I couldn't give a fuck about the ways of God.

It was God, indeed, for whom I saved my animosity. God and Zach. I hadn't seen Zach in over twenty years. He had clearly altogether washed his hands of me. A little thing like the loss of a favourite son was too unimportant, of course, to merit the time-consuming inconvenience of a visit.

Fuck Zach.

People said that I was wonderful. How did I manage to remain so calm, so active, so forgiving? Mixed in with their admiration — if indeed any of it was genuine — was undoubtedly a deep vein of criticism. The subtext read: how can you be so cold, so distanced, so inhuman?

I didn't give a fig for the subtext.

Geneviève certainly felt no admiration. "Who are you? What

149

are you? Why don't you rail and cry and beat your breast? You always told him that you loved him. What hypocrisy! The only one you ever loved was you. You're the only one you ever will love. You see — I know you now."

She pushed me away when I tried to comfort her; tried to take her in my arms and let her howl. "Oh yes — I know — you like to feel superior!" I saw history repeat itself before my very eyes — and would never have believed that it could happen. When her parents came to take her back to France for Christmas (they'd been travelling in Australia at the time of the accident, impossible to get hold of) I didn't know what she had told them on the car ride from the airport — or had written to them in her letter — but they were untypically cool towards me for the few days they remained. When Geneviève and the children returned from Paris (all three of them had just paid lip service to the idea of staying behind with me; Philip would never have done that) I guessed our marriage would be over, in everything but name. I wasn't even too sure that Geneviève would return — or not for any length of time.

But she did. And our marriage was over — in everything but name. Never once did we make love again.

My friendship with her parents surprisingly revived.

My friendship with my wife just couldn't make it.

Perhaps it never had the chance.

When Gordon Leonard returned from wheeling-and-dealing in Los Angeles the following February he heard from Johnny what had befallen us; and came posthaste to Newcastle — by air. Ironically, that week of his arrival, I happened to be on a retreat, in a monastery in Norfolk: trying to find some pattern to my life, some plan, some meaning; to gather strength; to make my peace with God; to learn from him the way I must proceed. With Geneviève. With Arthur. With everyone.

With everything.

I returned on the Friday evening to find the vicarage empty. There was a light on in the hall and my supper in the oven and a note once more upon the kitchen table. This time, however, in an envelope — sealed. Normally the only envelopes she employed in her communications with myself were used ones which she wrote upon the back of: see you at about ten, make sure you heat the meat through properly.

The first time she had met Gordon had been at my induction in Dorset. They had hit if off immediately — anyone could see that. Part of the chemistry had obviously been sexual. But for ten years (so I was told under the harsh fluorescent light and with a tap dripping in the background) they had fought against doing anything about it. Yet now, she asked, where was the point? She and I clearly had nothing to offer one another any longer; she felt that she could make a new start with Gordon. The clothes she had left behind could be given to Oxfam. We should be in touch about details of the divorce. Arthur liked the idea of living in London and of completing his 'A' level course at a technical college down there. Naturally I could see him whenever I wanted.

End of twenty-year marriage. I'd walked back from the station planning to take her in my arms, override her protestations, romance her, ply her with pretty things; with bottles of champagne and candlelit dinners and weekends well away from the parish; yes, to start again, make a third beginning, renew all those resolves I'd made at the commencement of the second. When once determined on some course of action I was usually able to carry it through.

But why in God's name had Gordon come back from the States during that particular week?

What made it worse: there was a retreat a fortnight earlier I could have gone upon. I remembered praying about it. Shouldn't I have been given some glimmer of a premonition? The faintest stirring of a merciful sixth sense?

I didn't even believe they had always fought very hard against temptation. There'd been frequent shopping and theatre expeditions which she'd made to London when I couldn't get away — her bubbliness at such times had been a little suspect even when I'd supposed that basically we were still happy

151

together. I hadn't formulated such suspicions then. Yet had this been only because I'd felt it was unworthy? Or more because my stupid male pride couldn't accept the fact she wasn't satisfied at home?

Oh hell! Oh hell, oh hell, oh hell!

I took the train to London early the following morning: resolute to win her back and confident that in the long term I could surely make her as happy as Gordon, whose tastes up till now had always seemed to run to very much younger women. I was prepared to do battle; and I trusted in my ability to be persuasive. But the porter at Gordon's Knightsbridge block informed me that Mr Leonard had left about two hours earlier for the south of France, accompanied by a ladyfriend and a young gentleman — they would be gone for several days.

At first I felt tempted to follow them: they would be easy to find, I thought, staying at one of the best hotels in Nice or Cannes or Monte Carlo. It would have been a fairly dashing line to pursue, one that would have been likely to appeal to Geneviève. But I had my responsibilities: a sermon to be preached the next morning, a heavy week ahead — with my curate and his wife departing this evening for a holiday (plus family wedding) on the Algarve. The timing of it all continued to amaze me.

I rang my mother; met her for lunch and told her what had happened. Her sympathies were mainly with Geneviève — I wasn't surprised. She had once warned me she thought I was neglecting my wife in favour of my children. While she was talking, it occurred to me that Geneviève had never spoken of Jean-Paul, not this time round, as being an excellent father. Indeed, she had hardly ever spoken of him at all. But in our last life there hadn't been Gordon Leonard, had there, resplendent on his dashing white charger? (Or in his Porsche? His Jaguar? His Lamborghini?)

My own days of excellent fatherhood were over; would-be excellent fatherhood. I felt I'd now discharged my duties to Arthur — my duties to Brian Douglas. The fact that I had failed in what I'd set out to do was unfortunate but irrelevant. Let Arthur make of himself what he would. Now my duties lay primarily with my wife, my mother and my parish.

But over the next few days I changed my mind about the nature of my duties towards my wife. Who knew? Maybe Gordon would indeed prove to be the person who could make her happiest. If this were so, then I should clearly serve her best by standing down. If, on the other hand, things didn't work out for them she would at least have got him out of her system and *that* perhaps would be the best time for a new start. I felt that a new start then might reanimate our love and give it the strength which it had seemed to have in the beginning; but then, of course, I had felt this before and life had just got in the way. There was no guarantee, I supposed, that life wouldn't always just get in the way. I still hoped — not very nobly — one day I'd be able to find out.

Slowly, too (very slowly: it took about a year), I changed my mind about the nature of my duties towards my parish — or, rather, towards the cloth. It wasn't that I saw myself as being played out. It was simply that I thought I could perhaps be more useful somewhere else. I had no family commitments now. A man without family commitments was a relatively free agent. And as I had felt over a decade before: there was no shortage of good vicars.

I had to try to be of maximum service.

That was now my one reason for living.

To leave the church wasn't all that simple — there were many attempts at dissuasion — but at last I was working out my notice. While I did so I took a crash course in nursing and first-aid. It was my idea to do some voluntary work abroad, most probably in Africa, and see what opportunities suggested themselves while I was out there. But then, in 1983, practically upon the eve of my departure — to Tanzania — there was that earthquake in Turkey in which the death toll eventually rose to two thousand. On the day the news reached Britain I booked my flight; and three days after that was slowly making my way by train towards the devastated areas. And there I didn't any longer need to wonder how I could best make myself useful. Any able-bodied man who was anxious to help would have been welcome but one who had nursing skills was greeted with additional enthusiasm. I thought I'd found my niche; had soon learnt enough of the language to be able to communicate quite well — if ungrammatically; had been prepared to stay on indefinitely to help rebuild broken communities — even literally rebuild, for I was happy to turn my hand to anything.

But then, a year later, there was the famine in Ethiopia ... and the year after that the cyclone and tidal wave which hit the Bay of Bengal and as a result of which the numbers of dead and missing went as high as fifteen thousand — and where, again, to bring succour and comfort to those suffering people felt like the most important work anywhere on earth.

In any of these places I could cheerfully have stayed put but somehow, when news reached me of the next famine or natural disaster or even, once, of the next war, the urge to move on was always so strong as to prove irresistible: Lee Marvin's *wand'ring star* seemed nothing as compared to mine. I was drawn, too, to areas of oppression.

I had meant to return to England in 1990 — not simply to recharge my batteries but to learn about Geneviève and Gordon and to see my children — but was stopped by a further earthquake, this time in Iran, where apart from the thirty-six thousand dead there were a hundred thousand injured; and then in '91 there was the famine in the Sudan. I had flown back very briefly in 1987 when Gwen had written to say that my mother was in hospital — and thank God she had, for Mum had died just two days after I'd got there. She had been lucid, for the most part — and loving — and cantankerous — and had seen Geneviève fairly often, it appeared, though Geneviève had just then been in Florence, spending practically a year there towards her degree in European Studies. ("Happy? I suppose so. But I never liked *him* all that much — not even when he was a boy — too glib, too plausible, too pleased with himself

154

— not a patch on Johnny." But she hadn't said that on the day I'd gone to her from Knightsbridge, so I wondered what, if anything, this change of view might indicate. Paradoxically, though, it made me remember chiefly how generous he had been: when finally we had sold our weights, for instance, he'd insisted I take half the proceeds. It had been good to have him as a friend.) I had returned to Guatemala City immediately after the funeral. In early 1992 I knew Somalia was going to be the place I should go to next — either there or Bosnia and Hercegovina, where the situation seemed so grave some said it could be hatching an apocalypse — but I wanted (no, not wanted, just felt compelled) to be in England for my birthday. Not just in England, either; Nottingham. I believed this part of my life had to be sloughed off *officially* and that my birthday — or, more properly, the second day that followed it — would be the time when this would happen. After that I would be ... well, mortal again. No longer the bearer of a charmed existence. But was I bothered? During the past nine years or so I had been totally absorbed in what I did and knew that I had been of use: which, of course, was happiness — of a kind; but I wasn't sure when I'd last been happy. *Happy*-happy. Possibly not since my arrival back in Newcastle on the day of Philip's death; certainly not since my arrival back in Newcastle on the day of Geneviève's departure.

Not *happy*-happy.

My return, then, to Nottingham was one I felt I had no choice about — I was being led there, hypnotically — despite the freedom of choice I'd known in every other way. I thought it was intended I should meet Brian Douglas. This second real encounter would undoubtedly mark my final break with the past; the bit of ceremony which was somehow required. (I no longer had any hope of seeing Zach; for far too many years now I had needed to get by without him.) In my worst moments, of course, I had feared I might even have to drown him again — Brian — that it would be a nightmare that recurred, regularly, every fifty-five years, a nightmare from which there was

155

absolutely no escape, my debt for having presumed to hope that I could get things right, when from the start I should have realised I was doomed. But even during those worst moments I had also tried to reason with myself: that no matter the degree of mesmerism involved, or hopeful illusion, or promises held out, nothing could persuade me a second time to help him go through any form of suicide.

24

So ... Monday 30th March 1992 ... and naturally it was raining. Steadily. I got to the office at about ten. Even now, even towards the end of the phenomenon, I was still surprised at how things remained just as I remembered them. (Yet perversely I was more surprised when they didn't: small details present I'd forgotten; small details absent I must either have imagined or transposed. For I doubted — maybe arrogantly — that others were also leading the sort of double life which could affect these things.) I'd have liked to see the name on my own door, but here, from the reception area, it wasn't quite possible. Iris finished putting through a call to Mr Walters.

She looked up at me with her usual friendly smile. "May I help you?"

Although I'd stood and watched for a few minutes in the Sixties while this office block was being erected, it was ridiculous to think I hadn't actually set foot inside it, or exchanged pleasantries with any of these four young women, for well over half a century. It felt more as if I'd been on just my annual break.

"I'm here to see Brian Douglas."

"Mr Douglas? Oh — do you have an appointment, sir?"

"No. But I believe he'll want to see me; may even be expecting me. The name is Hart — Ethan Hart."

"I don't think he's come in yet."

"You mean, he's sick?"

"Well, it's not like him to be late, so — yes — he could be. I'll check with his secretary."

"No, I was wondering in general. Does he have ... problems with his health?"

She laughed. "Not unless you include the odd hangover!" (That laugh. So very well remembered. From someone who would be nearly eighty now.) Then: "Oh, Debbie, there's a Mr Ethan Hart in reception asking for Brian ... What? Yes, I thought I hadn't seen him. No, he hasn't called in ... Just a tick." She looked back at me. "Is it something that his secretary can deal with?"

"No, thanks. That's all right. I know where he lives."

I'd have liked to stop and chat. But I couldn't think of anything. It suddenly struck me: it was a long time since I'd tried to savour my surroundings. I nodded goodbye to Iris and her colleagues with regret.

I travelled to Sneinton by bus. The bus was crowded; whoever had sat previously in the seat which I now occupied was either standing or sitting somewhere else. I wondered if he or she could be getting into conversation with their new neighbour, and whether they had once got into conversation with their old one — a young woman with a baby on her lap and a wet umbrella she couldn't find a place for. I spoke to her myself, took charge of the umbrella and was sorry when she finally got up. Hearing about her life with Jason — and even the continuing disapproval of her parents — was preferable to merely sitting and becoming nervous; although otherwise I would have tried to pray. After she and Jason had gone my prayer in fact began with them (when she wasn't aware of it I had slipped a ten-pound note into the pocket of her anorak but now I felt annoyed I hadn't made it more) and then widened to include everyone inside the bus. I nearly overshot my stop.

In the street where Brian lived there weren't any women talking on the corner, nor was there any young lad pumping up his tyres. I guessed I was a little earlier than before. The rain had not yet turned to drizzle.

But the door was opened just as swiftly; no chance for me to wonder whether after all there might be no one home and what I should then have to do. It was the scariest repetition of my life: a face last seen when it was under water; eyes last met when they were staring up at me with such emotions as would spawn my dreams. The minutes we had shared had been more intimate than any I had shared ever afterwards. I'd wondered if Brian, out of all the other people I had come across (though always with the exception of Zach), might be the one person who was going to recognise me. Despite the change in my appearance.

There was a change in his appearance, too. It wasn't simply that he wore a suit this time: one that I might — or might not — have seen at the office. His body underneath it looked more solid.

"Ethan Hart?"

"Yes."

"Come in, sir, I was expecting you."

He didn't sound the same, either. This wasn't a man who was dying, or was wanting to die.

After he'd taken my umbrella and my coat we went into his living room. That certainly remained the same. I turned and faced him squarely. "I don't know why I'm here. Can you put me in the picture?"

"First let me get you a drink."

It was Chivas Regal again — possibly the same bottle. This time I sipped it more appreciatively. I was beginning to relax.

Before he sat he lifted his own glass. "And may I congratulate you, sir?"

"On what?"

"On coming through."

"You may with pleasure. But it seems to me I had no choice.

158

Being invulnerable." I didn't know how much he knew but I suspected it was plenty.

"On coming through, I mean, with such distinction."

I pulled a face and shook my head. "But anyway — thank you." I offered him my hand.

I was reminded of our last handshake. The handshake in the bathroom. That was a room I had no wish to see again.

I felt that it required some comment, though — if only for the sake of peace of mind.

"I'm sorry I was forced to do — no, that I chose to do — what I —"

He waited. He didn't help me out.

"What I did."

"What did you do?" he asked.

I stared at him. "You have no memory of it?"

"None."

I stalled. "Do you remember speaking of a recurring dream you had?"

"Yes, sir. I dreamt of Britain in its hour of need."

A pause.

"Britain?" I said.

I felt a moment's detachment from reality. My surroundings seemed to draw back and disconnect from me. A muffle of stillness and silence settled like a heavy snow that stretched as far as the horizon.

"Yes," he repeated. "Britain's hour of need." He said it without emphasis. "That's what I dreamt of."

Of course it was. I shouldn't have been traumatised to hear it.

But the sudden awareness of a misconception spread across an entire lifetime ... *that* was traumatic. Somehow, through all the stress and steam and sadness emanating from that terrible and terrifying bathroom, *Britain's hour of need* had become so garbled it had left a vapour trail proclaiming the whole world's hour of need, had written a far less parochial phrase across the ceiling, or the sky.

Old Chaos.

Old Chaos. The bottomless pit towards which — in theory — all of civilisation was almost irresistibly and irreversibly being drawn.

"Britain's hour of need," I said again. Slowly. Stupidly. How many more times could we bear the repetition?

"And when I spoke about King Arthur," he said "you mentioned Glastonbury. I asked if you imagined he'd have his trusty steed beside him and just leap into the saddle and tear off down the motorway ..." He looked at me a little sheepishly. "I'm sorry, sir. That wasn't very respectful. I didn't realise."

I murmured absently: "All this respect. I'm not sure I can stand it. What didn't you realise?"

"About the dream."

"What about the dream?"

"That you were the one whom it involved."

"You mean, because I tried — so misguidedly — to take it over? I feel ashamed that I couldn't make it work."

"But you did! It is working. It's working perfectly."

"I don't understand." I shook my head. "I'm sorry but I just don't understand."

"You think you merely attempted to take it over? No. Good heavens, no. You were the subject of it."

It was nonsense to suppose the whisky had affected me.

"You don't know what you're saying."

I felt nauseous — giddy — faint.

"Somewhere you've made a mistake," I said. I tried to say it reasonably. "The most colossal mistake imaginable. Blasphemous if you but knew."

"Why do you think that?"

"Why? I'll tell you why." I swallowed; cleared my throat; still couldn't get it right. "You talk of crisis and disruption. You talk of the return of Arthur. And you talk about these things —" At first I couldn't even say it. I forced myself to say it. "And you talk about these things to the benighted oaf who struck the Saviour on his way to execution."

160

Brian Douglas didn't flinch. His tone was as reasonable as mine had aimed to be.

"And who five centuries later," he said, "found his way over here to Britain."

"Oh, yes." My laugh was bitter; brutal; full of self-loathing. "Didn't you always know that Arthur was a Jew? Not just a Jew. A disgrace to every decent Jew who ever lived?"

He shrugged. "Well, to be honest," he smiled, "I never heard it mentioned, one way or the other."

25

Other memories came: flashes from a past life of the kind Brian Douglas had once hoped he'd get in his bath — although now, presumably, he didn't remember whether he'd had them or not. I saw a hermit living in his shack in the woods at St Albans and looked after in his dotage by the monks — that was during the thirteenth century; a beggar travelling throughout Germany, ragged and hirsute, during the sixteenth; a gambler in Italy the century after. I had a glimpse of him in 1772 sitting for his portrait in Belgium. God knows how I knew it was 1772. There wasn't any calendar.

And — yes — I saw him too in sixth-century Britain. Chieftain of a warring people.

Although these were simply glimpses, I felt an affinity towards the man, maybe not a liking but an interest in his welfare and an instant acceptance; the empathy I felt for such as Isaac Laquedem in Brussels, Solomon in York, Arthur at Tintagel and even Cartophilus in Jerusalem was so strong, so instinctive, it could only have been inspired by direct knowledge. I sat there with my glass in my hand; feeling no longer

161

nauseous but dazed; and it seemed that every time I lifted the glass I saw reflected in the depths of that golden liquid a further facet of my own personality.

26

Zach came in. Brian went out. (He gave a smile and a salute.) It was thirty-six years since I'd seen Zach but the moment I'd heard that he was nearby all the resentment I'd ever felt towards him dissipated. He told me his apparent withdrawal had been the final test. "I had to know that you could make it on your own."

I had no idea now what he had in store for me; what the world might have in store for me. Yet whatever it was — at the moment it seemed irrelevant. I felt honoured and numbed and undeserving. Perhaps the fact of feeling numbed prevented me from feeling frightened. But though I knew that fear might come I also knew that I could deal with it. Anything. Whatever there was in the future could never be worse than some of those things in the past. And I'd come through. I had come through. Thanks to Zach. And whatever befell me — Zach would be there. That was why I knew that I could cope; or certainly a good part of it.

"Zach, why did you pick on me?"

'Pick on', however, had a pejorative connotation and I wanted to change it. But of course that wasn't necessary — I'd almost forgotten that Zach knew me better than I knew myself. I changed it, anyway. "What made you take a chance on me? Such an obviously lost cause?"

"The harshness of your punishment," he answered. "I had a fellow feeling. We were both lost causes." He added: "That

162

sense of fellow feeling was probably the very thing which they'd been banking on. They're enormously devious." He said it with a smile.

"I'm not with you."

"Look. You wanted to make amends. I wanted to make amends. I knew of course atonement was wholly out of the question for myself — I hadn't got a chance in hell — but I wanted to be the means of *your* being able to atone. At least I could do that much: show that I still knew how to be selfless; that the goodness which I'd once possessed hadn't been entirely lost. Why should it have been?"

I said: "Is it totally impossible for you to atone?"

"Yes. To atone sufficiently," he replied. He gave me what he thought were reasons. From now on there was nothing I felt I couldn't handle.

"But listen. If God represents forgiveness — and mercy — and if you're genuinely repentant ...?" I couldn't bear the thought of myself having been saved largely through Zach's faithful supervision of me over two thousand years; me going forward into light and him still relegated to the outer darkness. "Just because you were ambitious; just because you were tempted, succumbed to your temptations ... Just because you spearheaded a rebellion ... Zach, when I die, if they won't have you back into heaven I don't want any part of it either. I'd rather be with you."

"I don't think they could ever have reckoned on such loyalty," he said.

He made light of it; but I could see that he was deeply moved.

"Ethan, let me get this straight. What scared you most at the beginning was that I'd try to claim your soul. Now you're actually offering it. But have you considered? You know how I react to temptation. Very strong temptation."

"Which makes me think you need me all the more. Somewhere I'll be perfectly placed to keep an eye on you."

"You aim to infiltrate the underworld?"

163

"Something like that. But did the G-men generally discuss it with the gangland bosses first?"

He looked thoughtfully across the gulf which separated our two chairs. "The idea has a certain irresistible charm. The Wandering Jew keeping an eye on Lucifer. Am I my brother's keeper?"

"No — Arthur keeping his eye on the Bearer of Light," I said. "Strategically positioned to be the first to know when trouble's brewing. Plus, attempting to repay an almost unpayable debt. And yes. I am my brother's keeper. We can argue this until the Second Coming but I think you're stuck with me. You always were stuck with me. From the moment I hit Christ, Zach, I think your days were numbered."

RECOVERY

For Jaffa Abram

1

Okay. Don't panic. This isn't going to last. In a minute
you'll remember.

And your reflection in a shop window tells you quite a lot.

Male. Youngish. Dark blond hair.

Jeans; tee shirt; loafers.

Your pockets tell you less. Just a tissue and a silver hip
flask (empty - but so well-handled that the chasing's pretty
worn) plus the snapshot of a woman who's at present unfamiliar. Nothing else. No billfold. No credit cards. Not even
any change. You guess you must have lost your jacket.

Left it behind you someplace.

But... just try to think now. Where exactly are you?

Exactly you're outside a narrow building in Foley Street
W1 (since you've now moved back from gazing in the window of the barbershop); there's a street sign if you turn
your head, *City of Westminster* printed at the bottom.

London, then.

The front door of the building is open. The door is white
and dingy. Beyond it you see pale blue walls, blue lino, blue
banisters. The occupiers are a textiles company, a school of
fashion and... yes, you look back at the plate a little nervously, to check you're not hallucinating... a private detective.

Yet none of these things stirs any memories.

You walk inside. Up the steep, blue-linoed staircase. The
detective's name is Merrill. "Good evening," you say, when
he opens his office door — your watch has told you that it's

nearly six. "I know this is going to sound a little crazy..."
And then you stop.

For the first time you realise. You're American.

The detective could be forty or forty-five; a very youthful
forty-five; tall, lean, dark. Grey-suited, smart. You're
patently a stranger to him.

His office breaks with the general theme of blue. Cream
walls, grey carpet and green drapes. There are plants on the
window-sill; a David Hockney print. The obviously more
functional aspects include filing cabinets, a computer, reference books, a Cona coffee-maker —

My God. I'm an American.

I sit across the desk from him.

I guess that on my way up I'd been hoping he would say
I'd only just left him — and that he'd been on the point of
chasing after me with my jacket.

"Have you tried the floors below?" he asks.

I shake my head. "Textiles... a fashion school... They
don't sound much like me."

"How do you know what sounds much like you? Maybe
you've been doing a spot of modelling. You're working your
way through Europe."

"Oh, yes, sure." I watch him fiddle with a paperclip.
We've dismissed the possibility of my having been
assaulted. That would have accounted perhaps for the
amnesia but on the other hand I haven't any bruises; nor
did I need to pick myself up off the sidewalk; nor would any
mugger have left me with my watch. "Anyhow," I say. "At
least it was providential that if I had to lose my marbles it
should've been outside the office of a private dick."

He concentrates for a moment on the pulling open of his
paperclip. "Mightn't it have seemed more providential if it
had happened outside a hospital? You see, I can't help
thinking it's a doctor you require — or even just a good
night's rest. Not a detective."

He has a kind face. Attractive manner.

Yet rejection is still rejection, however pleasantly it's
wrapped up.

"Even if you're right, then... where do I get that good night's rest?"

"That's why I said a hospital. I could have said the embassy. But there's also the question of whether or not you'd be better off sedated."

Slowly, I get to my feet. "There's something one doesn't forget, even with amnesia. Everybody likes to be paid. But I thought that once I'd found my jacket... Or have you forgotten: this watch is a Rolex?" I say it with a mixture of sarcasm and swank. "Yellow gold; eighteen-carat. Costs upwards of nine thousand dollars." I sound like a salesman.

He looks a bit nonplussed. Suddenly he grins.

"How do you know all that?"

This reaction is a tad disarming; I even remove my hand from the doorknob. "I know. It's weird, isn't it?"

"You don't remember buying it?"

"No, nothing like that. Clearly I'm just very well-informed."

He laughs. There is a slight pause.

"I'm sorry," he says then. "You know, it wasn't the money I was thinking of."

I don't make any answer.

"No, that isn't wholly true. But what is true is that I was also worried about my not being the person best qualified to help."

"And I had this hunch you might be. The person best qualified to help."

"Well, as a detective I too am a great respecter of hunches." He holds out his hand and with a rueful smile indicates the empty chair. He says, "I have a flat in Golders Green and you'd be welcome to its spare room."

So naturally I sit down again and he makes us both a cup of coffee. Oddly, even before I taste it, I realise that I don't take sugar; in the same way that I've not forgotten, say, the year we're in is 1990. "So what are we going to call you?" he asks. "My own first name is Tom."

"How about X?"

"No way. How about Tex?"

169

"Do you really see me as a singing cowboy? Anyway. My accent isn't Texan."

"You're a purist... Let's see that snapshot which you mentioned."

I produce it from my back pocket. He studies it for several seconds.

"Hasn't anything occurred to you about this?"

"Yes. It looks old." The photograph is dog-eared. It's in black-and-white.

"No, but I mean the hairstyle. The line of the dress. This is more nineteen-forties than nineteen-nineties."

I stare at him.

"Which would be crazy. Why would I be carrying around the picture of some girl who by now must be an old woman?"

"Your mother possibly?"

"Oh, come on. What normal guy carries a pin-up of his mother? Or practically a pin-up?"

He regards me, consideringly.

"I'd reckon you're in your middle twenties. Right?" I've already told him I've caught up on my reflection.

"Something like that."

"So. If you were born some twenty years after the war why do you have a wartime snapshot in your pocket; either wartime or immediately postwar? And the likelihood is too — because of the church behind her — that she's British. How does that tie in with the fact of your not being?"

I gaze again at the woman's picture as though the answer to his questions can be determined in her face. I get suddenly distracted by some quality about her which is surely more than mere prettiness or charm; and find myself wondering, with strange irrelevance in view of all my problems, what she was thinking about at the moment when the photograph was taken.

2

"Trixie, why not save your film for something special? This is sheer waste."

"Oh, bollocks, Roz — don't hold yourself so cheap. Just smile. Say cheese."

That's rich. Me hold myself cheap. I know damned well how she got hold of that film. I've seen the chap who gave it to her. Preferable, if you ask me, to pay the price on the black market. Or better — far better — to use that ex-RAF stuff, even if they do say that half the time it doesn't work.

Anyhow, being the soul of obedience, I smile like the Bile Beans girl and although I don't say cheese I snatch up one side of my frock, strike what I hope is an alluring pose and for a moment imagine an interesting new me on the cover of Picture Post.

"Oh, that's nice, hold it," she cries; and then, picture taken, with quick change of emphasis: "Yes, that's nice! Right in front of the church! Suppose the vicar saw? He'd think Betty Grable'd come to Suffolk."

"Well, if he'd really think that, let's go in and offer him a second chance."

To go in is the whole purpose of the exercise. I've wanted to do this ever since the first weekend she and I came here, which was nearly two years ago, in the summer of '43, but both on that occasion and the one which followed (Trix being a Philistine) we just never got around to it. I hadn't learned to be assertive.

So now it could be something of an anticlimax.

But it isn't.

I think the first thing that strikes me is the radiance. Except for the west window the stained glass has all been blown out by enemy action and — as if deliberately to compensate — the light just floods in now through the wholly clear replacements, emphasising the loftiness of the nave, the slenderness of the pillars, the fine proportions of the roof. I wish I knew all the names; for someone who enjoys looking round old churches I'm pretty unversed in the terminology. I suppose I'm just a dabbler who likes the inscriptions and the pews and the paving stones: the glamour of past lives. Along with the stillness and the sense of awe. The splendour.

There's a magnificent and brightly coloured pulpit. There's also a wonderfully elaborate organ case and a tall painted screen celebrating some of the saints and angels. It's sixteenth-century but was touched up in Victorian times. A typed card charmingly informs us that St. Jude — as restored — became very like the rector.

I'm just admiring this delightful screen when I hear Trixie talking to someone. This turns out to be an American airman, burly, bull-necked and at that moment lifting a stick of gum towards his mouth.

"Excuse me for butting in," she's saying, "but I couldn't help overhearing — sounds like you and me are in the same boat. Being dragged around to get a bit of culture by our educated friends!" I feel I'd like to slosh her.

"Our *boring*, educated friends!" returns the airman. "That is — no, gee, lady, I'm sorry — I certainly don't mean yours; I'm just referring to that egghead over there."

The fellow whom he indicates smiles vaguely at Trixie but continues to give his main attention to a small wooden man in armour who apparently strikes a bell on every hour. "Say, Walt, come here a minute. This little guy is getting all set to do his stuff. Any second now."

"Hey, Roz," shouts Trixie, "you don't want to miss this."

I cross over to where the three of them are grouped; there's no one else in sight but even so I tell myself crabbily that the church is much too full.

"Come on — hurry! This is Roz," says Trixie, while I'm still ten feet away. "And I'm Trix."

"Pleased to know you," says her big, good-humoured friend. "I'm Walt. And my buddy here is Matt. Just help yourself to gum, ladies."

The little man in armour makes his interruption.

And the egghead laughs.

As he does so my churlishness begins to fade. His pleasure is infectious. Besides — it occurs to me I would have missed out but for him.

"Cute," says Walt. "And you'd always know this guy was English."

"Why?" asks Trixie, so willing to enjoy the joke she's already started to giggle.

"Reminding us it's teatime. And there's a nice place for tea we noticed while coming here to be religious. Would you ladies care to join us?"

I'm about to decline but Trixie says, "We'd love to!", and glares at me no less meaningfully than if my careless talk were costing lives.

She and I know the Sugar Loaf Tearooms. Their bread and carrot cake and soda scones are all delicious and the bread doesn't even have that greyish tinge. We're obliged to queue for a table. The teashop has a holiday atmosphere — not unexpected in a seaside resort on the first warm Saturday of spring. It's the twenty-first of April. The noise level is high — and becomes even higher, breaks into cheering and applause, when a waitress, poor woman, drops a tray. (Tearooms for the moment have lost all their gentility — thank God.) The building is one of the few in Southwold that survived the fire of 1659 and the timber beams speak of precisely that: survival. Indomitable spirit. It's a good place; and even without the Americans is probably the one where we'd have ended up.

When at last we get our table, conversation becomes less superficial. We already know they're stationed at Halesworth, some eight miles away, but now we hear more of the detail: that they're members of the 5th Emergency Rescue Squadron: specialise in air-sea rescue work. Walt talks with enthusiasm about their lifeboat-carrying B-17s, their CA-10 Catalina amphibians and in particular their P-47 Thunderbolts. For a minute I wonder if he should be telling us all this but then I realise that at this stage in the war it can hardly matter much. He also tells us — probably sensing the need to recapture Trixie's interest — about the time last August when Glen Miller came to Boxted. (They had moved the short distance to Halesworth only this January.) Trixie wants a run-down on every piece of music that was played and descriptions not simply of the late major — no one still believes, unhappily, that after all these months he can be referred to any longer just as 'missing' — but of almost every member of the band. While Walt does his best to satisfy her I take the opportunity, surreptitiously, to have a good look at his friend.

Matt's full name is Matthew Cassidy. Before, in the church, it hadn't occurred to me he was especially handsome; only that I liked something about his face. But now I must have got my eye in, for handsome he undoubtedly is. Coarse fair hair — though not as short as you'd expect an English officer to wear his; blue eyes, straight nose, firm jawline. For what I think must be the first time I really know what 'clean-cut' means; even his hands seem to exemplify it. I like looking at his wrists and hands: not just for their shape but the fine coating of hair, the cared-for fingernails. I am twenty-four and probably have never felt so stirred by just the way a man is put together.

Or am I allowed to dignify this and say that of course his whole personality must have contributed? That I'm speaking of the full package?

Walt exhausts the charms of August 6th and of the sweet strains flooding through the main hangar on that golden Sunday afternoon. "We were sitting on the wing of a B-24 being serviced — you remember, Matt? And, ladies, I don't mind telling you: it was swell but it sure made us feel a little homesick."

"Yes, I'll bet!" I say. "But at least you'll soon be getting back there, won't you? Though do you realise: you haven't told us yet where home is?"

"For him, Connecticut," says Walt. "For me, San Francisco."

"Oh, then you must know that song!" cries Trixie. She starts to sing it. "'San Francisco... open your golden gate...'" Heads turn towards our table and she giggles and feigns bashfulness. "I remember Jeanette MacDonald singing it in that film with Clark Gable and Spencer Tracy and the earthquake. I suppose the song's called 'San Francisco'. I can't remember what the film is."

"*San Francisco*," supplies Walt, and we all laugh. I get the passing thought that it was calculated (Trixie is by no means the dumb blonde she pretends, any more than I'm the brainy brunette she also claims) but it's still quite funny.

"And I once read *A Connecticut Yankee in King Arthur's Court*," I say to Matt. "So I'm well up on where you come from, too."

This time it's just him and me who laugh. Trixie is too busy saying to Walt, "I liked that film; I found it ever so inspiring. Spencer Tracy's in the one we're going to see tonight. It's called *Without Love*."

"Well, is that right? We've been wanting to catch up on that movie for months. Didn't you say so just the other day, Matt?"

"What?"

Walt has to repeat to him what he had said so emphatically just the other day.

"Oh, sure. I've been talking about nothing else since... well, really since I can't remember when."

We arrive at the cinema in time for the full programme — and by-pass the longest queues by going in the dearest seats and needing to stand on the staircase for only a few minutes. The full programme comprises a second-feature and the news and Food Flashes and trailers and a Pete Smith Speciality and a medley of tunes on the theatre organ... I'm always pleased to get my money's worth, and so, I now find out, is Matt, "even down to your God Save the King," he shamelessly confesses. But Trixie and Walt decide not to see the end of the big picture (so that we'll have longer in the pub); and Matt and I fall in obligingly.

"You don't mind?" he asks, as we walk together a short way behind the other two — who proceed first arm-in-arm and then, soon after, arm-round-waist.

I shake my head. "But I'm not the one who's been so frantic to catch up with it."

"In fact I have an admission." He already knows — from the little he's drawn out of me — that he isn't really spoiling my enjoyment. "I found it talkative and dull."

"Oh, what a letdown! I really am sorry."

"And irritating! All those 'by gum!'s which were clearly meant to be so full of charm!"

"I know! You sat there almost waiting for the next! And what about her proud and tearful memory of her dying husband — who 'grinned that grin of his'? I think I'd even have traded that for a couple of extra 'by gum!'s."

"Careful! Two extra might have brought us to our screaming point."

So in a way (although the film undoubtedly had entertaining moments — which we conscientiously acknowledge) we have more fun pulling it to pieces than we had perhaps while actually watching it.

"Anyhow, despite all that, it was a good night out at the pictures. A very good night," I add on impulse.

"For me too. Though I'd have to say not wholly on account of the movie. I don't know if you gathered that."

"Thank you for treating me," I laugh.

Then we talk about how wonderful it is that the last blackout restrictions have been lifted and that the streetlights are on again; no more being obliged to carry torches which can only be directed at our feet. No more need, even, for headlamps to wear a covering — although admittedly there isn't much traffic now except for bikes. It's like a glimpse of El Dorado to see the light from the pub spilling out upon the pavement.

Through the open door there comes the welcome of a singsong.

'Yes, we have no bananas,

We have no bananas today...'

Which suggests that dealings in contraband must be at a low ebb, since a bent old seaman with a beard and runny nose tells me while we wait for Matt and Walt to do battle at the bar — well, he tells Trixie too but she plainly isn't listening — that the Lord Nelson has a dormer window on its seaward side from which signals could be flashed to smugglers coming in below the cliff; and that there's many a whispered tale of blocked-up passages which once led from the cliff into the cellars. Matt gives the man one of the two tankards he has brought and heroically returns to fetch himself another. By the time he comes back Walt and Trixie have been able to muscle their way onto a crowded bench — she sitting on his lap — and the seaman has swallowed his drink and has moved off in search of some other sucker (Matt's phrase). "The artful old lush — well, good luck to him," he says.

We then decide to join the group around the piano; yet just as we reach it, it disbands. So we finally manage to edge into a corner, holding our glasses up high, apologising as we go and meeting with smiling reassurance. We could, of course, have taken our drinks outside and sat on a railing overlooking the sea but despite the cardigan I'm now wearing the night feels chilly. Besides — it's exciting to be part of a good-natured crowd that's soaked up the warmth of the day; even if at times it's a little difficult to hear what each of us is saying. He asks where Trixie and I are putting up in Southwold; and I tell him about Mrs Herbert's guest house.

"It's simple but seems luxurious compared to our farm-worker's cottage — where the plumbing is so primitive it's sometimes hard going getting rid of the day's caking of mud."

"No wonder you need to escape."

"But it's a good life: being a land girl."

"Will you be here next Saturday?"

His question takes me by surprise. "Well, usually we only get away about once every —"

"I wish you would," he says. "Perhaps we might meet earlier in the day, go for a picnic, fit in a swim. I think I could maybe wangle us a jeep."

"It sounds fun. I —"

"And I'll take care of the picnic. Yes, I mean it. No argu-

177

ments." He looks round briefly. "I guess Walt is probably making similar but independent plans with Trixie." I glance round too; we both laugh. "But Rosalind?" Suddenly he seems embarrassed.

"Yes?"

"I don't know how to put this, without sounding big-headed. Back home, you see... well, back home I'm engaged to be married."

A slight dip of disappointment — silly, I suppose, on the strength of merely a six-hour acquaintance. Come to that — not such a very slight dip, either.

"Congratulations, Matt."

"You'll still come out next Saturday? Maybe even Sunday as well?"

"I'd like to."

"I damn well wish I was free tomorrow. You're just about the nicest person I've met so far in England — and that's not to say England isn't full of nice people."

"Thanks. And you must tell me about your family and your fiancée and we'll keep our fingers crossed that the weather next weekend is half as good as today's." I laugh. "Especially if you're serious about that swim."

3

The detective takes the snapshot from my hand. "I think it's time we shut up shop," he says.

"I can't help wondering who she is."

"Naturally you can't."

His apartment is on Finchley Road, over a store called Grodzinski's. "I like this area," he tells me. "Bus conductors cry, 'Get out your passports, we're coming to Golders Green!' but that's what's good about it. Jewish. Cosmopolitan. Lively."

"Maybe. But my trouble is — can I really believe in any private eye who doesn't come from Southern California?"

"I know. I sometimes have the same problem."

I ask about his average day.

"It may not inspire you with confidence."

"But I can't take my custom anyplace else. Can I? Especially when you've just bought me a toothbrush and washcloth."

So he mentions process-serving. Debt-collecting. Surveillance work. Investigating cases of pilfering for a company which doesn't want to call in the police. Carrying out a lot of grindingly tedious research. "I'm not sure what's average. Certainly not becoming involved with missing heiresses and stumbling upon fraud and ancient unsuspected murder. Probably just sitting in the office and hoping for business."

"Like this afternoon?"

"Like this afternoon. Your timing was impeccable."

I ask him other things. In a way I wish I hadn't. His wife died fifteen months ago. Of leukaemia. She was thirty-eight. He shows me a picture which he fetches from his bedroom. She is dark, curly-haired, looks radiant and warm-eyed. "Lucy," he says.

I inquire if there's anybody else.

Too late I worry this may not be tactful. But he just shakes his head and answers no. Quite matter-of-factly.

Following a pause he adds one further word. Never.

We listen to Mussorgsky and drink Scotch while waiting for the supper to be done: he has put the contents of two packets of Lean Cuisine into the oven — fillets of cod with broccoli in a light white sauce — and a bottle of German riesling into the fridge.

After supper we watch television and then I have an early night.

It's almost a mistake. For the first time in several hours I'm alone with myself and all the haunting speculation. Just what is it exactly I'm so anxious to forget?

179

Perhaps it's this, perhaps it's that. Perhaps I'm a guy with a broken marriage, a failed ambition, a smashed career, a terminal illness, a kidnapped child, a dead wife. Perhaps I'm wanted by the police. Wanted on a charge of tax evasion, drunken driving, manslaughter, murder...

Surprisingly, I sleep.

Tom wakes me with a cup of tea.

"And... ?" He sounds too eager. "Has anything come back?"

"You mean — anything apart from 'I tort I taw a puddy-tat' or 'I know a bank whereon the wild thyme blows'?" I find it hard, quite suddenly, to hide the note of bitterness.

But he just smiles. "Do you want to shower before or after breakfast? And how do you like your eggs?"

While we're eating he says:

"About that snapshot. During the night I had a thought. Suppose your father was over here in the war. Long before he thought of marrying your mother he met this English girl. The war ended and they lost touch. But when he heard that you were coming to London he asked you to try and trace her."

"Why?"

"I don't know... Nostalgia?"

"Yes — but I mean if he cared that much why didn't he come himself? The guy's had some forty-five years to find his little sweetiepie."

"What I'm saying is, suddenly he has this strong desire to take stock; to come to terms with his past."

"And this is the sort of thing you'd get your son to do for you?"

"Depends," says Tom. "Whenever he's here he probably has your mother with him. And maybe it's something you could speak of to your son a bit more easily."

"Well, I don't know... I don't know if I buy that."

"It's just a theory."

After a moment, though, I give a shrug. "And I suppose that it's the only one we have. Okay, then. *Cherchez la femme*. Why not?"

Tom stirs his coffee. "In fact I'm hoping there could be another *femme*. Slightly more contemporary."

"Meaning a wife?"

"Wife or lover. Anyone who might have raised the alarm by this time."

I pause in the act of spreading toast. My God, I'm a bastard. (And perhaps that's why I've got amnesia: simple self-disgust.) Oh, yes, I've certainly wondered what sort of wife I may have left behind; but up to now I haven't thought there could be someone not so very far away who's maybe feeling frantic. And apart from having a missing husband she's perhaps unsure of herself in a strange country — worried about funds — encumbered by a child, or children... Oh, Christ! I find it's only me that I've been thinking of.

My possible wife, child, children, parents — presumably I have parents, who at some stage will need to be notified? All these begin to acquire... not faces, not personalities... but at least some sort of real and suffering existence. No longer merely adjuncts.

I also start to wonder about my father and that girl.

4

It's now Sunday morning. O hell, I was being far too optimistic hoping to wangle two Saturdays off in a row. Quite late into yesterday evening I was still busy with my milking, after what would undoubtedly have been a dreary day of weeding and hoeing and muck-raking if I hadn't had this morning to anticipate — plus the bliss of a soak in the Crawfórds' own bathtub (just forget the regulation five inches) to wash away not only the grime but the smell: muck-raking is a chore which permeates! At any rate he'd been easy to contact at Halesworth and very understanding about the necessary change in plan; we must have talked for over half an hour, which in itself made up a little for the lost day. Even after half an hour, though, I'd found it difficult to say goodbye; but had cycled away from the box in the village singing at the top of my voice and speeding down hills — well, slopes! — with my feet off the pedals and my hands off the handlebars.

His voice had sounded just so nice; and his conversation had been so easy and so civilised. (We'd even spoken briefly about Shakespeare's birthday, which had fallen on the previous Monday. And there, as Trixie would have said, *there* was culture for you!)

Because although I like the people I mix with — they're kind and helpful and I learn from them some fascinating lore — their talk is never what you'd call relaxing, mainly on account of the dialect; and with our German prisoner-of-war it's not merely the dialect, it's the whole wretched language barrier — we smile and nod and mime (and the mime often makes us giggle) but it's not a conversation. Trixie of course is usually full of chat, yet recently she's been moody because she too had planned on getting off on Saturday and not all her wheedling could accomplish it. ("I'll do a bunk," she'd said; "to hell with them!" But her 'bunk' didn't take place till nearly nine o'clock last night, when she was perfectly free to go anyway. However, she ran out waving her crimson-painted fingernails — not so much in farewell as just to get them dry — and it was the bounciest I'd seen her since last Sunday. "Now don't do anything I wouldn't do, Roz!" Followed, naturally, by its inseparable and very boring rider.)

And now I'm waiting in the lane feeling pretty bouncy myself and savouring the smell arising from the earth, the gossamer on grass and hedges, the stillness which surrounds me: a stillness only deepened by the gentle cry of a winged plover — or is it perhaps a stone curlew? Savouring, too, the sheer pleasure of my yellow coat.

This — a Christmas present from my mother — is fastened with a tie belt and single button at the neck and has

182

a jaunty swing to it. Because I haven't worn it very much it still feels special. With my leather gloves and classic black shoes, my Jacqmar headscarf and my painted legs (it was Amy Crawford who drew the line down the back for me, taking a lot more trouble than Trixie ever does), I feel today that Vogue is more my spiritual home than Picture Post. I wonder if that will instantly occur to Matt. Will he draw up, jump down, give a deeply felt whistle and sigh for his disloyal abandonment of Rita Hayworth? Poor Rita Hayworth.

Amazingly, he doesn't. He jumps down from the jeep all right but forgets to give that whistle. And although he tells me I look nice he adds far too soon for someone genuinely dumbfounded that he hopes he hasn't kept me waiting.

"No, you're very punctual. You had no trouble finding us?" It's been a journey of some twenty-five miles.

He shakes his head... a bit absently? (Certainly he doesn't appear to be dumbfounded; but is it merely wishful thinking that makes me see a look that might be construed — loosely — as appreciative?) "All I had to do was follow your excellent instructions."

"And your more excellent Ordnance Survey?"

He grins. "Well, that helped a bit."

"I hear they're talking about starting to replace the signposts."

"Oh, where's their spirit of adventure?"

I observe drily that I'd better call him Marco Polo — or Dr. Livingstone if he'd prefer it. He glances at the sky. Pulls up the collar of his raincoat.

"Better call me Scott of the Antarctic! What happened to that warmth we had a week ago?"

"And just now you sounded so courageous; don't let me think that after all they breed them soft in Connecticut! Oh, but talking of which ..."

We are going to spend the day in Cambridge; yet first I wonder if he'd be interested in seeing Groton. John Winthrop, the man who became an early governor of Connecticut, was born in Groton.

"I've been doing my homework for you. Sailed to North

America, 1630, on board the *Arabella;* seven hundred Puritans, two hundred cows, sixty horses. But when they landed in Massachusetts Bay two hundred of the immigrants had died at sea — well, either at sea or shortly after landing. Then another hundred decided to return to England."

We are still standing in the lane — a lane that's twisting and leafy, full of cowpats and deep hardened ruts.

"*Those*, I'd say, were definitely the soft ones!" He smiles.

"You think so? After the voyage out I'm not so sure they mightn't have been called the braver element... no matter how base. And, by the way, seventy of the animals had died as well."

"Thank you for doing your homework. Yes, you're right, I'd sure be glad to see it. There's a town called Groton in New London County which was named after Winthrop's birthplace. But I didn't realise he came from just round here." He adds after a moment: "Come to think of that, how did you?"

I tell him that when he'd spoken of Connecticut last Saturday something had stirred at the back of my mind. But I hadn't been able to pinpoint it.

"Gee, I'm impressed."

"Gee, I'm pleased that you're impressed. Actually I'm impressed as well. Let's face it: it's impressive."

Yet first — before Groton and before Cambridge — I also want to show him Polstead.

So we get in the jeep (which is fun — I've never ridden in a jeep before — though later it will prove a little cold) and off we drive to Polstead. There I show him the pond where witches used to undergo their trial by ordeal and into which — allegedly spellbound — someone once drove a coach and four horses. The place must have been a bit jinxed: by the early nineteenth century there were so many ghosts roaming around, it had become somewhat desirable to exorcise them. But poor Reverend Whitmore could have been a forbear of Will Hay: after death he was himself seen driving a horse and trap along the lane to the rectory — and presumably not a man to be outdone by anyone, it was claimed that he was headless.

"Headless?" he cries. "My God. But why?"

"Obviously an arch-bungler."

"Then how was he identified? Did he have his head sitting there on the seat beside him? Wasn't there a danger that it might roll off?"

"I think you have a gruesome streak."

"What tosh." (More British than the British but I don't at this point comment.)

"And if you have" — I give a kindly smile — "in Polstead we can pander to it."

"That's nice." He asks if I believe in ghosts.

We have left the jeep at the bottom of the hill and are now walking up a pleasant footpath to the top of it, from where I want him to see what must be one of the prettiest village greens in England.

"I don't know. I certainly believe in an after-life — in the survival of the spirit — if that's of any help."

He says it isn't much but as I feel that way and as it's Sunday oughtn't I to be in church?

"Well, it doesn't follow; though I'd be happy to go if you would."

"Yes," he says, "I'd enjoy it."

But since the morning service isn't due to start for half an hour we wander round the green.

Facing the green is the Cock, with its attractive inn sign.

"Will it be open when the service ends?"

"Straight out of church and into the pub — tch, tch, Lieutenant Cassidy! Do I approve?"

"I think you've got the emphasis wrong, Miss Farr. You mean... oh, boy, do I approve! I saw you knocking back your Adnam's the other night. And the word, moreover, happens to be Lootenant."

I tell him he's in England now: land of village greens and fine old pubs and men who answer to *Left*enant. Land of Maria Marten and the Red Barn.

He stares at me in some perplexity — just as he was meant to.

185

"Come. I shall lead you now down Marten Lane for the terrifying climax to this fleeting interlude of Grand Guignol. Not for the faint-hearted."

I take him by the hand. It seems so natural that I'm almost unaware of doing so. His own hand closes around mine; and from then on continues to hold it. Firmly.

It needs only a few minutes to reach the thatched cottage where Maria Marten used to live. The red barn is there no longer, having been destroyed by fire.

"Maria was a mole-catcher's daughter," I tell him; "William Corder a rich farmer's son. One night he lured her to the barn with promises; and indeed wrote to her father announcing they were married — married and very happy. But Maria's mother kept having dreams about the barn... Finally she persuaded her husband to go out and excavate. And then, of course, Maria's body came to light. Are you bearing up quite manfully?"

"Gee, I don't know, it's tough."

"Well, anyway, Corder was discovered near London, in a place called Brentford, where — thanks to an advertisement — he had found himself a rich wife. And guess what: they were running a seminary for young ladies! But in August 1828 he was hanged at Bury St. Edmunds — in front of a crowd of ten thousand. The hangman sold the gallows rope at a guinea an inch, and a book about the trial was bound in Corder's skin, which the prison doctor had far-sightedly removed for that very purpose. What do you have to say to this, Lootenant?"

"Enterprising. Though I guess it was a fairly limited edition."

"Just one copy; still on display in Bury Museum. Like to go and see it?"

"Any chance we'd be allowed to fondle it?"

"Oh, don't!"

We begin to retrace our steps. But something impels me to stop again and look back at the cottage. "Actually we make light of it, we turn it into melodrama, we pull out all the stops. But this is a real person we're talking about, silly perhaps but hopeful and trusting and frightened. Poor soul. We ought to say a prayer for her when we're in church."

"Mightn't some people interpret that as being a little late?" He smiles at me, then adds: "The idiots."

"That's right. What idiots."

"After all," he says, "how much do any of us really know about the complexities of time?"

I regard him suspiciously; but his expression appears guileless.

"And in any case," he continues, "supposing that time is indeed just linear, God himself is outside time and had knowledge even on the day she died of the prayer you'll say this morning for Maria Marten; and so if you believe in prayer you must believe it may have eased the pain for her, it may have helped her die more peacefully."

He pauses. "I'm saying all this as though you weren't perfectly aware of it already. Forgive me."

So we make our intercessions for the murdered girl; and I throw in one for William Corder, on the principle of judge not, lest ye be judged...

The service, which began at eleven, is only sparsely attended. The church is Norman, primitive and simple. In the nave arcades, the arches are of brick; the clerestory also. Since the Normans are not supposed to have used brick (we are later informed by the vicar) these are thought to be the earliest bricks made in England since Roman times; earlier than Coggeshall. He is clearly proud of his church: a gaunt old man with snowy white hair, a shuffling gait, a soft voice, some difficulty in hearing. His sermon too was gentle and not very inspiring but at least the hymns were mostly ones I like — and played in a key that was comfortable.

At the end of the service the vicar is of course standing by the door but as there are so few for him to say goodbye to, Matt and I talk to him about the church and the weather and the redecoration of the church hall (we have been invited across to it for a cup of coffee and a biscuit but have made excuses; I already know that neither Camp Coffee nor Bev is the thing which Matt most appreciates about England — and, anyway, by now the Cock will probably be open). But the vicar has just asked where his home is. And when at last the old man hears the answer he suddenly exclaims that some thirty years ago he himself spent time in New Haven, with a family called the Taylors, who lived in... he struggles to remember the name of the district, even the road, and Matt, equally pleased and almost equally frustrated, struggles to assist his recollection. Professor Taylor taught History at Southern Connecticut State College...

And then, by one of those wonderful coincidences, Matt knows exactly whom he means, because the college mentioned is his own Alma Mater. And although he himself didn't study under Professor Taylor he's not only spoken to him on several occasions but once came close to dating his youngest daughter: Jo — Meg — Beth?... he's sure it's something out of *Little Women* ...

"Meg! Yes! You're right! Oh, just a baby at the time. Of all the most extraordinary things... now who would ever have believed ...?"

The two of them stand beaming at one another and I reflect that Matt may shortly change his mind about the coffee but he doesn't and he's right: after that initial explosion of excitement there's disappointingly little to sustain it. The talk deteriorates into stilted references to the rivalries between Yale, also in New Haven, and its lesser-known competitors nearby; to the fact that the Winchester repeating rifle ('the gun that tamed the West!') and Samuel Colt's improved repeating revolver were both developed in New Haven...could that say anything significant one wonders — ahem — about the law-abiding nature of its inhabitants; or possible lack of it? And remind me now: what is the name of the river on which the town is built? (The Quinnipiac, sir... which used to be what the city itself was called.) Ah, yes, and it's all even more highly industrialised these days I feel sure. And are your people — er — in industry? (Yes, sir; my family's in the meat-packing trade.)

I sympathise with Mr. Farlingham. What kind of comment runs trippingly off the tongue, regarding a family which is in the meat-packing trade?

"Ah, yes. How interesting! Meat-packing, you say...?"

There's a pause.

"Well, it's been great meeting you, sir, and we certainly enjoyed the service. Daresay we'll be here again before too long."

Pure courtesy, of course. Nothing but the most basic form of politeness; the Americans are famed for it.

But, even so, my heart leaps up — rejoicing.

5

"Come on, Tex, watch the birdie. Say cheese."

"I might say a number of things — cheese wouldn't be amongst them."

"All right, say up yours; but just keep still whilst doing it."

Tom pulls the film out and waits for the picture to materialise. "Here comes the glamour boy."

His idiocy does what cheese had failed to. "Is this how you normally speak to clients — or only those without money?"

"Let's go in," he says.

The police station is on Savile Row; near Piccadilly. Tom has a friend there, someone whom he got to know during his own time on the force. Sergeant Poke is powerfully built, gap-toothed, beady-eyed. He's certainly no beauty.

"Jim, this is Tex."

"Ritter?" the sergeant asks, shaking my hand.

"Who knows?" I match his own dryness. "That's why we're here."

"Looks pretty good for such an old man, doesn't he?" Then Tom explains.

"Too bad," observes his buddy, "I was hoping for a chorus of that thing from *High Noon*. 'Do Not Forsake Me Oh My Darling.' Might have enlivened a bleak Tuesday."

I can understand why the two of them should aim to keep the tone cheerful but I have a fleeting image of a female face, strained, heavy-eyed with fatigue; and again am shocked at the ease with which I'm able to forget about the pain of others. (I now feel certain that there must be others.) It makes no difference if the face belongs only to that woman in the snapshot.

Do not forsake me oh my darling.

The sergeant checks the computer for anyone of my description recently fed into it.

We watch without speaking. I realise I'm drumming my fingers on the table by my chair.

The computer gives us nothing.

"Okay, then," says the sergeant. "The card index at the Yard. I'll phone and have them do a run-through." He hesitates; it's as though he's apologising in advance. "You see, Tex, missing persons only get priority if it's known they may be ill or vulnerable in some way... people can go walkabout for weeks. Or months." He shrugs and looks to Tom, wryly, for confirmation. "Years."

But I'm the one who answers.

"Vulnerable? I suppose mere amnesia doesn't count then?"

The sergeant says, "Yet who would know you've got it? Apart from us?"

"I can't remember." This also was intended to sound bitter but they think that I'm being funny; and reluctantly I end up smiling too. "Surely you mean — apart from us, a textiles company, a school of fashion, a barbershop, a sandwich bar... and the dental practice opposite?"

"Opposite?"

"I mean Tom's office."

Tom, again, explains all this. "We were trying to find out what Tex was doing in Foley Street."

"A dentist, for God's sake?" says the sergeant, as if a

190

fashion school were quite to be expected.

"We knew he hadn't just received treatment but it could have been a check-up."

"Americans on holiday have check-ups?"

"We're not even sure that Tex is on holiday. He might be working over here. And yes — before you say it — the embassy is most certainly one of our next ports of call."

"Oh, he's incredibly thorough, your friend Tom." Again I think I intend only irony but there's a note of pride there too. "We even went into a pub, several shops, whatever offices were still open, a café-cum-patisserie, a Spanish restaurant —"

"Okay! Okay! Stop!" The sergeant holds up his palms as if to ward off blows. "I'm convinced of it. Half of London knows you've got amnesia. But it still hasn't got you onto the computer — not yet at any rate."

"And I just don't understand it. If I've left my jacket behind, with my money and passport and traveller's cheques in it, surely my wife... or my parents... or others on the same tour... I mean if I am just on vacation... surely someone must have realised by now that something's wrong?"

But nothing can alter the fact I don't figure on that damned computer.

Nor in that damned card index at the Yard. (The sergeant's call was speedily returned.)

He tips back in his seat. "Don't worry, though. I'll keep my eyes peeled for anything that comes in."

Tom produces the picture he took earlier — "in case you can't get hold of us and with any luck are called upon to put someone out of their suspense. We shan't be at the office; a message on the machine at home will probably reach us faster." He jots down details to do with nationality and appearance. "How are Bridget and the girls?"

"Bridget'll want to know when you're next coming to supper."

The sergeant shakes my hand again.

"Just relax, Tex. Think how in time you'll laugh at all of

this and even see it had a purpose — that's what my granny used to say. And she was always right, my granny."

It's rather a sweet thought: great big Sergeant Poke learning at his wise old granny's knee.

On the sidewalk Tom takes more photographs.

"But why? You say all the hotels would get in touch with the police anyway."

"Yes — but if you're over here on your own it could take them time to realise you were missing. The chambermaid would see your bed hadn't been slept in but might assume you'd spent the night in someone else's or that you'd gone out of London for a while. And reception staff, of course, only work in shifts. So therefore..."

"So therefore I can stop belly-aching about expenses; is that what you're trying to say?"

"Yep. You read me like a book. And each hotel will have to have one."

I frown slightly — but not at the price of photographs. "How many hotels?"

"Oh, hundreds... especially if your Rolex is misleading us and we need to lower our sights to the bed-and-breakfasts."

Despite his smile, 'hundreds' proves to be no overstatement. During the next eight or nine hours, dealing with the desk clerks at only the plusher establishments, we hand across forty-four photographs — as well as forty-four of Tom's printed cards — and know we haven't yet covered a quarter of the ground. (And the prospect of the bed-and-breakfasts is truly terrifying — even if mostly we'll only have to telephone.)

"I don't know how you can stand this sort of grind day after day. The monotony; the disappointment."

"I don't do it day after day. In any case it's simple. That old thing about hoping for the best while expecting the worst."

"Merrill the philosopher," I say. "Merrill the philanthropist."

"You also learn to ignore the jibes."

"But clearly not how to recognise a compliment. Sincere

192

compliment."

"Sincere but half-witted. When we've eaten I'll take you to the hospital."

"Right. Only thank God we're going to eat."

He nods. "I think we've earned ourselves a good dinner. My treat, though, not yours. Are you exhausted?"

We go to Rules in Maiden Lane. Steak and kidney pudding, home-made raspberry ice cream, Stilton cheese... undoing all the benefits of last night's Lean Cuisine, if either of us were actually needing to lose weight.

We drive back to Golders Green along Tottenham Court Road. Suddenly Tom makes a right turn and pulls up outside a hospital. University College. Accidents and Out Patients.

"My God, he means it!"

He smiles at my expression. "No, it's just that I know someone who works here. Let's see if he's around."

He knows damned well that he's around. Dr. Ramtullah, who isn't much older than me and who's one of the gangliest creatures I would think I had encountered, gives Tom a hug as though he would wrap his arms about him twice, and fills his small office like a loose-limbed spider with an Oxford accent.

After he's questioned me quite lengthily he spends several minutes parting my hair with his fingers, running his hands across my neck, feeling my temples; forehead, nose, jaw. He looks inside my mouth; shines a torch into my eyes. He seems very conscientious but apparently discovers nothing. He returns to his chair.

"So what's the treatment?" inquires Tom.

"Wonder-drugs, you mean? There aren't any. Contrary to popular belief there is no drug yet invented which can restore a lost or failing memory."

"Hypnosis?" Tom asks.

The doctor gives a shrug. "Personally I would recommend you to wait until the amnesiac state has ended naturally."

"Why?"

"Because a hypnotist will tell you that hypnosis can take care of anything. I myself am sceptical; I believe there are still areas that remain outside its province. Even if I'm wrong it would undoubtedly take time: several sessions at the least. My own feeling is that left to itself" — he inclines his head in my direction — "your memory will return within a week."

"And if it doesn't?"

"And if it doesn't... well, then by all means think about hypnosis; I should be happy to refer you. Yet be prepared for disappointment." He adds: "In any case I would still favour the more natural method. If you are subconsciously blocking out some memory which is painful I should prefer that it come back at a speed which you can cope with."

Dr. Ramtullah unwinds himself. He stands up. We all do.

"Well, Tom, why don't you bring him back next Tuesday? In the meantime," he says to me, "rest as much as you can. Try not to worry. And be patient."

"Ranjit's a good chap," says Tom, while we descend in the elevator. "Did you find him reassuring?"

"Not especially. I found him patronising."

"I'm sorry. That's only his manner. He doesn't at all mean —"

"And what about you? Do you at all mean...?" I draw a breath. "It's nearly ten o'clock. We weren't seen just by luck. You must have telephoned at some point... since we all realise that you're so very thorough."

He admits that he did.

"Then why didn't you tell me?"

He sighs. "I suppose I thought you'd make a fuss."

"Well, I'm damned well making one now. I resent being treated like a ten-year-old."

"So would I — who wouldn't?"

"Yes. Please remember that." And during the silent ride to Golders Green I refuse to let my knowledge of his good intentions start to mitigate the offence.

When we get home he offers me a whisky. I decline. I leave him in the sitting room with just the curtest of good-

194

nights and a closing of the door which is practically a slam.

After twenty minutes in the shower, however, I return in penitence. He is sitting with his feet up — listening to a tape and with a tumbler in his hand.

"Sorry about that."

"Tex, I apologise as well."

"Won't let it happen again," I smile.

"And even if it does I reckon we might manage to survive it. Come and have that drink."

The tape he's listening to is *Chanson de Matin* by Elgar. Is it the music itself or merely the title of it which seems to convey to me a message of hope?

Or is it simply that I've made my peace with Tom?

6

Because of the weather Matt had thought it better not to bring a picnic: "I guessed we might feel snugger in a country pub." ("Wot — no swimming!" I inquire.) Sitting in the Cock I tell him of the Fox and Hounds — equally attractive — so, sight unseen, he decides we'll lunch at Groton, as soon as we arrive.

A good decision. We feel well-fed and much warmer by the time we're looking at the Winthrop birthplace... which is really quite ordinary: a white two-storey building with a tiled roof, small-paned sash windows, gable at either end. But we stand there loyally for several minutes and try to think of things to comment on.

Then we go back to the jeep.

"Full steam ahead for Cambridge!" he decrees, slapping his hands together briskly. "And wouldn't it be swell if we could also take in Grantchester?"

"In Connecticut they breed them ambitious," I declare.

"No — simply wanting to make up for lost time."

"But why haven't you seen these places before this?"

"Who knows? Laziness? Lack of opportunity? Lack of the proper person to see them with?"

"Oh well," I agree airily. "Reason enough."

Groton lies amid some of the most beautiful scenery in the county; this is the edge of Constable country. From time to time we even see a windmill. Matt compares the twisting Suffolk lanes to that strip of Roman road which runs out of Halesworth... and of course to the detriment of the latter... but we hadn't yet met a large car coming in the opposite direction when he'd happened to voice that particular opinion.

"Oh, yes, *naturally* it still holds. Do you see me, then, as someone who lacks constancy?"

It's about half-past-three when we arrive in Cambridge. We park the jeep and wander through the town and look inside the courts of several of the colleges. ("Matt, just listen to those blackbirds sing!") I feel the rightness of the day compounded when we enter Trinity through the Great Gate and a nice old boy with red complexion, thin silvery hair and a grubby pullover engages us in conversation, discovers Matt comes from New England and reveals that John Winthrop was a student here. But in the end he has less to say about Winthrop, who apparently wasn't an object of scandal, than about Lord Byron, who was. Our guide turns out to be one of the masters of the college. He leads us across to the magnificent Franciscan fountain in which it is said that Byron used to disport himself naked.

The old man chuckles. "He's also alleged to have climbed onto the roof of the library and added certain... embellishments... to the statues up there."

As we walk out of Trinity, Matt echoes my own feeling.

"I had a hunch today was going to be special."

"That kind of hunch is very often fatal."

"Agreed. However, today I had a kind of hunch it wouldn't be."

We're now strolling along the Backs, hand-in-hand. We sit down on the river bank and watch a soldier skilfully propel a punt. His companion is leaning back upon a bed of cushions and although the weather is still a long way from being warm, the fitful late-afternoon sunshine (impressively forecast by one of the farmhands) makes it look inviting.

"Maybe," suggests Matt, "we could do that?"

"I think it's not as easy as it looks."

"You can't have forgotten you're talking to one of those courageous men whose forefathers survived the *Arabella*?"

The woman in the punt has red hair. Casually I ask: "What's the colour of your fiancée's hair?"

He answers less casually. "Not a lot different to yours."

"Mousy? Poor girl. Do you have a snapshot?"

He takes out his wallet and passes me a photograph. "Meet Marjorie."

"My goodness! The face and figure of a film star!"

"In fact that's what she wants to be. She's done a bit of summer stock." Is there an element of dryness there? He adds neutrally: "And her father hobnobs with some of the best-known names in Hollywood."

"Where did you meet her?"

"She was engaged to my brother."

I hadn't even known he had a brother.

Now I discover that he hasn't. "Rick died of bone cancer. Three years back."

"Oh, God, how awful. I'm so sorry."

"Yes."

He gives a shrug. "Well, anyway..."

There's still a longish pause.

"Marjorie was left desolate. She may look... But the truth is she's intensely vulnerable and if you'd seen the way she pined for Rick... It fell to me to try to get her over it, make her forget; and gradually, before either of us had realised..."

"She was enormously lucky, then, that Rick had a brother like you." I recognize a certain amount of dryness in my own tone — which I do my level best to eradicate.

197

Matt returns the snapshot to his wallet.

"No, I was the lucky one, to have a brother like Rick. Marjorie would have been all right, anyway. She's the kind of girl who brings out the protective urge in almost any man she meets. Even a guy like me."

"Why do you add that?"

"Oh, I don't know. Wasn't thinking, I guess." He picks a blade of grass and starts to chew on it; lying back and leaning on one elbow. "I guess I used to see myself as being a little weak."

"Weak!" The surprise is genuine.

"Thank you for that — but yes I often used to think so. Before my brother died; before I realised that Marjorie could ever see me as any kind of... well, any kind of a replacement. And in a way that's why this stint in England has been so very good for me. I know that sounds selfish. But it's shown me... shown me I can cope. The same as anyone."

"But what made you think that you were weak?"

He rolls over on his back; throws away the blade of grass. "Well... for one thing, I suppose... I find my father a bit formidable. My mother's also got a forceful personality. I'm fond of them both and missed them like hell when I first arrived in England but —" He laughs. "Which is another thing, of course. Homesickness is hardly the great sign of strength."

"What an idiotic remark... for an egghead."

"I've no idea," he says, "why I'm telling you all this. Well, yes, I have. From the start I've found you very comfortable to talk to."

"I'm glad." I wish I could have met him earlier; during that period when he missed his home.

But suddenly I get a consolation prize (and almost wonder if he might be telepathic).

"You know, Rosalind," he says, "I really found you at the right time. I'd been feeling pretty low... what with Roosevelt's death; the discoveries at Buchenwald... Well, of course, everybody had; I'm not claiming any special sensi-

198

bility, don't get me wrong. But that Jack o' the Clock was the first thing to make me smile in days. I very nearly told Walt to find someone else to go with him to Southwold. In fact I did but he was quite insistent."

"Good old Walt. And you did more than smile. You really laughed."

"I know. It was a true release."

I lie back, feeling happy.

"And see, too," he says, " how you've taken me out of myself today. John Winthrop — Maria Marten — Meg Taylor — Lord Byron..."

We decide to take a punt to Grantchester. Yes, at first he gets the pole caught but then he quickly grows proficient and his movements become a joy to watch.

"'Oh! there the chestnuts, summer through,

Beside the river make for you

A tunnel of green gloom...'"

Also he recites the whole of *The Soldier*; at Southern Connecticut State College he majored in Literature — and is word-perfect. It's a memorable experience: drifting along a lovely river on a fine spring evening (and the sky has at last got rid of all its cloud) and listening to a stirring poem well spoken against the very setting which inspired it.

We tie up the punt and for an enchanted half-hour we ourselves roam her ways and love her flowers and feel we have hearts very much at peace under an English heaven. Is war still raging in the Pacific? Bloodshed, pain, anguish, bereavement — even boredom, muddle, apathy? We poke our heads round the gateway of the Old Vicarage and try to put the clock back forty years or so (forty years ago the poet would have been eighteen) — try to imagine him running across the lawn, sitting on that wrought-iron seat, walking upon the very spot where we ourselves now stand. 1905. It's easy to imagine — here — we could be lingering in that sunlit, safe, Edwardian world. We admire the exterior of the church; we look for his name on the village war memorial (there it is — Brooke — after Baker, Blogg and Bolton) and think a little, too, about those other names inscribed on it.

Then we eat a proper English tea in a proper English cottage with a sign outside its door; and somehow not quite of this world, wandering in a carefree, timeless zone, yet touched with just sufficient melancholy to sharpen our appreciation, we wend our way back to the punt and give a shilling to the boy who's cheerfully been looking after it.

However, once we're in the jeep returning to the farm, tranquillity soon disappears. And how! Pity all the life of field and hedgerow. 'You're in the Army, Mr. Brown'... 'The Lambeth Walk'... 'She'll Be Coming Round the Mountain When She Comes'... 'It's a Grand Night for Singing'...

But then he must have seen me shiver (the weather has again turned cold) for with his free hand he pulls me towards him and I lay my head on his shoulder and we drive along less boisterously for the remainder of the way.

As we get closer to home I tell him he must come in and meet Fred and Amy and have a mug of tea and a sandwich. The Crawfords stand to some extent *in loco parentis* and I would vaguely feel I had to do this anyway even without the urge to show him off and give him something hot and let him see the farm by moonlight; for the house is moated and therefore old as well as picturesque. I could have shown it to him in the morning but had felt then that this was the better way to do it. Another time — and I was now fairly certain there was going to be another time — he could look at it by day.

I can see he's making an impression on Amy and Fred; I've never heard them talk so animatedly to someone they don't know. They even turn down the wireless: Albert Sandler and his Palm Court Orchestra! The lamp, as usual, has the faint aroma of paraffin about it; but its light sheds a soft glow upon the kitchen, and the range gives out the same style of homeliness — with the sukey starting to boil again and whistling on the hob. Fred, stringy, weather-beaten, with slightly protuberant eyes, talks about the execution of Mussolini, the supposed cerebral haemorrhage of Hitler and the dropping of food bombs on Holland. Amy, mending towels, the typical farmer's wife, rosy-cheeked, round, comfortable, talks about the children and the difficulties of making do. ("I have eighteen people to feed; two gallons of broth to prepare each evening!") Then Matt asks about the moat and Fred's well away: protection against peasant uprisings, wolves and winter floods and cattle thieves — well, that's only the start of it. Fred is an authority.

So it's well after eleven when Matt stands up to take his leave — fairly late when you consider we all have to be up early (although as yet there's not been any sound of Trixie). He hesitates about whether to give me a goodnight kiss; then does so, on the cheek, which is exactly right.

In bed in my small room with its sloping floor and sloping ceiling I drunkenly review the day; and suddenly I'm aware of a tremendous sense of loss, an awful ache of longing in the abdomen.

Already.

I don't want to lose him! Can't bear the thought I'll have to lose him!

7

We get to the embassy at half-past-nine; discover it's been open for an hour. We're directed to the Upper Brook Street entrance. A man in front of us has his attaché case looked into, but we're okay, neither of us carries anything. Oh, yes, Tom has a key ring in his trouser pocket. So momentarily he has to hand it over and pass again through the metal-detector. Parking the car has taken all the coins he had; and the money he's lent me wasn't in change.

American Citizen Services is to the right and up some stairs. A marine security guard watches as we go inside. The young woman who greets us from behind her counter sounds Irish rather than American. I explain I've lost my passport. ("Start easy," Tom had advised. "Don't throw it at them all at once.") Totally unfazed, therefore, she hands me a form and asks us if we'd like to sit while I complete it. We go a little further in and the place opens up to resemble a vast modern bank: airy and pleasant: all the walls, desktops and partitions either cream-coloured or grey, the carpet adding a bluish tinge. Typewriters, computers and printers introduce a lighter shade of grey. There are anomalies, of course: a vase of flowers, a large and leafy plant; the U.S. flag drooping from a staff surmounted by an eagle painted gold.

We sit on plastic chairs and glance through the form: Application for Passport Registration. Initially there doesn't seem a lot I can fill in. It starts with name, date and place of birth — social security number. But then I find the next six questions to be simple. For my mailing address I give Tom's. I tell them my gender; that my height is six foot; the colour of my hair, light brown; of my eyes, blue. Again, for my home telephone number, they get Tom's. (They get his business phone as well — that makes a seventh portion not left blank.) After that it's permanent address and occupation. Father's name, father's birthplace, father's date of birth. Is or was father a U.S. citizen? Then comes my mother's maiden name; requests for the same details. Now back to me. Have I ever been issued with a U.S. passport? (If yes, passport number, issue date and disposition.) Have I ever been married? (If yes, date of most recent marriage.) And so on. In other words, not without problems for people like myself. Tom points out one of the notes on the reverse side: if no birth record exists a circumcision certificate might help to prove identity. "Oh, yes, extremely funny," I reply.

"Or family Bible records. I find that almost as endearing."

I put the form into a tray on another counter: more in an attempt to show willing than because I think it's of the slightest use to anyone. In the space for the first answer I have finally written — heaven help me — Tex Merrill. (It should have been John Doe but that's even worse.) As Tom indicates, they must at least have something to call me when they summon me to interview.

Which happens surprisingly soon. An athletic black youth at the counter tells me my form appears to be lacking in many essential details. I reply that I am faced with certain difficulties which I would like to explain to somebody. He glances at the five or six people waiting, and conceding that the matter may be complicated decides to pass me on to a superior. This lady, he informs us, is the supervisor in charge of passport citizen operations. What is equally impressive, she, like the clerk, doesn't keep us hanging about: no more than three minutes before we're on our feet again.

She's an angular woman with greying hair piled high and spectacles dangling from a golden chain. She is British. She means to interview me over the counter but Tom asks if it couldn't be done in an office.

And it could. We pass through a door whose lock is worked by pressing the right combination of studs and she leads us to a room with grey Venetian blinds, the same grey-blue carpeting and again, next to her typewriter, a striking vase of gladioli.

We all sit. She gazes at us from across her desk with an air of solicitous refinement.

"Well, Mr. Merrill, as I was just saying, this form, I'm afraid, requires —"

"I'm not Mr. Merrill. I'm sorry but it's a good deal less simple. You see..."

And I put her in the picture. Tom contributes the odd sentence.

"Oh, you poor young man!" Mrs. Bradley puts on her glasses and picks up my form again; finds nothing more on it than she had found before; replaces it on her desk; takes off her glasses and sucks the bit that hooks behind one ear. Leans forward eagerly. "I don't believe we've ever experienced quite this problem before — although strangely we did recently have occasion to assist an amnesia victim once he had recovered most of his memory." She holds this out to me, almost tangibly, as a solid inducement to hope. "But tell me: have you seen a doctor?"

I assure her that I have.

Tom makes a suggestion.

"Oh, I'm afraid not," she says regretfully. "You see, there must be millions of passports issued yearly in the U.S. and even if we could transmit a picture to every passport office in all the fifty-two states it would be nearly impossible to match it up."

She smiles at me and pulls a face of deep apology.

"And supposing that your passport were issued in 1983, when the renewal period was made longer? Your photo would now be seven years old and, who knows, seven years ago you might have been just eighteen or nineteen... with spots and a crew-cut...?" She shrugs — eloquently.

This is dispiriting. "You speak of all the fifty-two states," I say. "But doesn't my accent pin me down to someplace on the East Coast?"

A short pause. "Oh, dear," she says. "I must confess you've set me a conundrum. I'm a little out of my depth. If you wouldn't mind waiting here a minute..."

It turns out to be more like fifteen. She sends us a Mr. Herb Kramer who is about forty, big, sandy-haired, blue-suited. He comes in alone and shakes our hands with warmth. Mr. Kramer is the vice-consul.

"I believe I've been made thoroughly conversant with your plight. I have to say a case like this puts us in a difficult position."

"Not half so difficult as the one it puts me in."

"No, I'm sure." He laughs, genially. "You see, our problem is we can only provide assistance to someone we know to be an American citizen. You'll realise that given your memory loss this becomes a little awkward."

"But my accent?"

"Yes, your accent. Yet people do sometimes come to us with the most authentic-sounding..." He looks at me intently; looks at Tom; looks back at me. "Oh, hell. At a guess I'd say you come from New England. I'm a New England man myself."

"That's what I'd have said." (On both counts.)

"However, I doubt whether there'd be much value in communicating with the New England passport offices; there's no way to systematically search their records. But I'll tell you what we can do. We can send a cable to the State Department on the chance that someone might have started an inquiry."

He's perched on the edge of Mrs Bradley's desk, thoughtfully stroking his moustache.

"What's tantalising is to think we could've received a cable from them already; from them or from some other post. Or that a caller might actually have been right here inquiring about you. Every last detail could be sitting there waiting for us. But without a name to enter into the lookout check..." He spreads his hands. "So we have to fall back on nothing but the memories of our staff. Just now Mrs Bradley and I were questioning all those on duty today. Unhappily without the least success."

"Thank you, anyhow."

"Well, it's our job, of course. Your accent leads us to believe you're an American — we shall therefore assume you are." He says this in a fairly businesslike way; but then he smiles. "Unless we happen to unearth something to the contrary."

"Like what, for instance? That I'm just a natural born mimic who's spent time in New England?"

"And believe me — it happens! I notice, by the way, you're not totally uninfluenced by British rhythms of speech."

This doesn't strike me as being at all loaded but I do reply that seeing it from his point of view my claim could very easily be a hoax. "Nice work if you can get it."

"Exactly. Oh, you'd be surprised at some of the tricks people try to pull. Also you'd be surprised at some of the talent that goes into them."

"Do they — well, so far as you know — do they ever man-

205

age to get away with it?"

"I'd doubt it. Our tests are extremely stringent. We look for very special responses."

"Such as?"

They both laugh.

"And even apart from those tests," says Herb Kramer, "one somehow very quickly develops a sixth sense."

Although I acknowledge that the answer will be meaningless: "And your sixth sense regarding me?"

"That you're genuine. May I put a somewhat personal question? You have no credit cards nor traveller's cheques. What's your financial situation?"

"A real pain."

Again he laughs. "Sure thing; it must be. But the reason I ask — it's always possible, you know, we could provide assistance to get you back to the U.S. We'd make contact with the Department of Health and Human Services and they if necessary would help you find a place to stay."

I like this man; he seems to come from almost the same category of human being as Tom. I like his attitude of innocent till proven guilty. I like his tact as well: the way he doesn't actually ask what I'm managing to live on. To say that Tom is keeping me would be likely to convey a seriously misleading impression; especially to a man who — however well-disposed — is trained in part to be cynical. Even considering it *en passant* makes me realise all over again how exceptional Tom is and how incredibly blest I was to come across him. Unthinkingly, I flash him an affectionate smile — which possibly confirms whatever suspicions my compatriot may have.

Herb Kramer takes my form and scribbles down some notes. Tom gives him a couple of photographs. The vice-consul promises he will do all in his power to speed up the inquiries.

He escorts us to the entrance (Mrs Bradley waves cheerily from a far corner and mouths the words *good luck*) and we leave the building in a fairly optimistic frame of mind.

We need all the optimistic frame of mind on offer. We have another day ahead of visiting hotels.

8

We'd had a date for the following Sunday.

This time it's Matt who has to change the plan. He phones on Saturday. I run into the kitchen without taking off my wellies. They're caked in mud. Already I can see wet chunks strewn across the red tiles.

"Rosalind, I really am sorry. What about next Tuesday?"

"Next Tuesday?"

"V.E.Day."

"But are you sure, Matt? I listened to the lunchtime news. They claimed it was still only rumour."

"Oh, Miss Farr," he says.

"I see. Privileged information, Lootenant? A tip-off from Uncle Sam?"

"A tip-off from Donald Duck. And Donald Duck tells me you'll get Wednesday off as well." Yes, the wireless had spoken about two days' national holiday; just hadn't been able to say when. "He also wants you to know Walt and I will be driving down to London to be right in the thick of it — and looking for two brave girls who might be interested to join us."

"Well, I admit I've always had rather a soft spot for Donald Duck."

"Must be reciprocal," he says. "He's got you some nylons: no more cold legs in jeeps." (And no more aggravation, either, with the tan cream and the eyebrow pencil!) Matt adds that if he puts them in the mail tomorrow they ought to get to me on Monday. His thoughtfulness has to be exceptional.

Therefore it's hardly fair to take advantage. "I know this is going to sound stuffy. But you wouldn't consider, I suppose...? I mean, before we leave for London...?"

The wireless had also spoken about arrangements being made by the government for a morning thanksgiving service to be held in towns and villages across the country.

"I guess I know what's in your mind."

"You do?"

"But I was thinking of after we'd gotten there, not before we left."

And it's absurd: why should my eyes begin to water?

"Yet you're right," he continues. "St Paul's will be too crowded — and maybe even a bit too grand? Besides, God knows what time we'd have to set out. So how about our old friend Mr. Farlingham? After all, it's nearly a week since we said we'd look him up and I reckon by now he must be missing us."

"Oh, bless you, Matt. I imagine you're aware you must be psychic?" The church at Polstead is nicer than the one nearer home, where the party from the farm is going. Trixie and I find St Leonard's a little too austere — even at Christmas or on Easter Sunday. "Just so long as you can square it with Walt?" I mention, smiling.

They get to us at half-past-nine. (And Donald Duck was right: V.E.Day! — and the war in Europe most wonderfully and most beautifully brought to a glorious end.) They were supposed to be having a guided tour of the farm by daylight; but after the violent storm of a few hours back the place is far too muddy. Never mind, at least they can see the moat and the farmyard — which are the pretty-pretty bits — and say "Wow!" and "Gee!" and "Golly!" in satisfactory style.

Then we take them into the kitchen. Today there are about a dozen gathered there — still! at this hour! — mostly with braces dangling and collars attached only by a back stud; they're drinking strong tea, half-listening to the radio, not openly excited but companiable, content, smoking their Woodbines or the cigarettes they roll themselves. Werner sits there with the rest: in no way ostracised but understandably subdued. I make the introductions. Nods; handshakes; pleasantries (for the most part unintelligible?). Matt goes to chat with Fred, while Walt helps Amy carry off her three hitherto protesting sons to get them smartened up. Then Trixie and I start packing into baskets the picnic things we'd been preparing when Matt and Walt arrived. We haven't told them yet and no doubt they both confidently expect (being men and being American) to march at any time into any restaurant and have their pick of whatever's printed on the menu; but with all the millions prophesied to be in London today the reality will quite assuredly be different. We weren't girl guides for nothing.

We leave the farm at roughly ten-fifteen. The children, with their scrubbed knees, grey flannel suits and shirts, school ties and caps — and smitten patently with hero worship — have begged to be allowed to come to Polstead. They climb onto our laps: mine and Matt's and Trixie's ("Though if you kick and snag my nylons I'll bloody well strangle you with one of 'em!"): and spend their journey first enjoying the novelty of the transport and after that the novelty of the decorations in the village. (The novelty of air-sea rescue work has finally — and mercifully — been exhausted.) Masses of bunting. Prams, cycles, cars all bear their flags — then why not ours, Matt and Walt get asked, reproachfully. The Crawfords point pathetically to other children carrying flags. So what, says Trixie — other women wear rosettes. I try to cause a diversion by pointing to a Scottie trotting beside its owner with a rosette at its neck and a coat which also matches hers strapped round its proud and perky body.

The church is really crowded — how different to nine days ago. But Mr. Farlingham is just as shuffling and unflustered. Before long he'll surely have to stand down for one of the younger men returning to civvy street but today he has a helper, someone no less decrepit than him.

The service, so we're told from the printed sheet, is to follow a set line: Thanksgiving for Victory. Maybe most of us could have predicted the choice of psalm: 'O give thanks unto the Lord, for He is gracious', but possibly it has seldom been said *en masse* with so much heartfelt sincerity. Mr. Farlingham chooses a passage from another psalm for his text — 'When the Lord turned again the captivity of Zion' — and after a shaky start his sermon this time, by the grace of God, manages to rise to the occasion. The whole service is as uplifting as the church bells which are now being heard again throughout the land; I imagine we shall really appreciate the peal of bells from now on, and still feel grateful that never once in all the long years of silence (silence, except for that one November Sunday when we celebrated Monty's victory at El Alamein) did they need to warn us of invasion!

On our leaving the church Mr. Farlingham doesn't at first appear to recognise us. "Professor Taylor," Matt reminds him, with a grin. "New Haven, Connecticut."

"Why, yes, of course," says the old man. "My nice young couple from some weeks ago!" And, to me: "I think you said that you were Meg. God bless you, my children. God bless you. And a very happy peace!"

"The same to you, Mr. Farlingham."

There are tears in his eyes. He calls after us: "And to your father and the family! Oh, if only your fine president had been alive to see this day!"

We don't immediately return to the jeep. Matt wants to find a shop where he can still buy flags. I tell him that he doesn't stand a chance. But marvellously — ten minutes later — he's earned the right to shake his head at me indulgently: "O ye of little faith!" The children are ecstatic; our stockings run an even greater risk. The jeep now sports a flag as well.

We drive the young Crawfords back to the farm. One of them (Matt's, thank heaven!) is complaining; sulky. In a way I feel tempted to plead his cause — their cause. But I can see that it's impractical — and know it's not for me to be magnanimous. "We'll bring you back a souvenir! Something nice for each of you." Yet the moment I've said it I'm conscious I've been rash.

And then — after we've waved goodbye (poor Dick refuses to respond) — phase two of this auspicious day begins.

It's inaugurated by Walt — who's still the driver. "Right! London! Here we come!"

And he makes excellent time, despite a last-minute detour, unnecessary and delaying: by ten-past-two we're driving round Trafalgar Square. ("But are you sure this can

210

be London, folks? There isn't any fog!") I haven't seen so much traffic in years — where have people found the petrol? But, anyway, we're lucky with the parking: Northumberland Avenue, near the river. We walk along the Embankment to Westminster and mingle with the crowds streaming in across the bridge, all making for the Ministry of Works. Whitehall's packed but not impenetrable and thanks to the size of Matt and Walt — their shamelessness as well (but they defend themselves by saying that they were only doing it for our sakes) — we end up in a very good position.

Hardly have we reached it, moreover, when Big Ben strikes. Three o'clock... all eyes directed to the balcony. Mr. Churchill's on his way.

And then he's there: that rotund figure in the dark suit and bow tie, watch-chain stretched across the waistcoat, white handkerchief showing at his breast pocket. A tumultuous cheer bursts out. Replaced by a silence equally amazing.

It now becomes official: the Channel Islands have been liberated — Norway, too — hostilities will end at one minute past midnight.

Tears mix with laughter. The name of Eisenhower and mention of 'our Russian comrades' provoke a further storm of clapping.

"Advance, Britannia! Long live the cause of freedom! God save the King!"

The buglers of the Scots Guards sound the ceremonial cease-fire. The band strikes up the National Anthem.

Eventually we let him go. Next stop the palace. Again the four of us do well. The central balcony is hung with gold and scarlet. At about a quarter-past-four there's a frenzy of cheering as the King himself walks onto it.

He's in naval dress but bareheaded. He stands alone for a few seconds, waving to us with his nice yet serious smile, and then the Queen comes out. She's wearing powder blue. She raises her hand and joins him in acknowledging the

211

roar of cheers. "Jesus but she's swell," exclaims Walt.

The two princesses make their appearance. Princess Elizabeth, in her A.T.S. uniform — also bareheaded — stands at the side of the Queen, while Princess Margaret, in blue, stands next to her father.

People wave their flags and hats and scarves like crazy. When the royal party returns inside, the crowd sings 'For they are jolly good fellows', and although many hundreds leave the forefront of the palace most of us remain; scarcely another five minutes have passed before voices are shouting "We want the King!" and this refrain is taken up in every quarter. It's interspersed with another chant. "We want Winston! W-I-N-S-T-O-N!" While we wait an Australian soldier climbs the gates of the palace, waves his flag like a baton and leads us in community singing.

Roughly an hour later Mr Churchill does indeed join the royal family on the balcony — following his arrival in an open car, when, to a rapturous reception, he stood and waved his hat and mounted policemen had the heck of a job clearing him a pathway. Now he stands between the King and Queen and flourishes his cigar in greeting to us all. Being last to leave the balcony he gets a special round of cheering and applause.

When we at length turn our backs on the palace we go back to the jeep to eat our picnic. Afterwards, in Piccadilly Circus, we see a British sailor, a GI and a Pole perform a striptease; they get plenty of encouragement. (Trixie exhorts Walt and Matt to join in and is almost set to have a go herself.) An American paratrooper whose face is covered in lipstick is asking all the women in his path to add to his collection. From Trixie he gets perhaps more than he had bargained for — a real smacker on the lips — and from me a laughing peck upon the cheek.

"Here!" says Matt. "These blasted Yanks! What nerve! It's time that I got in on this!"

I brush my lips against his cheek in similar friendly fashion. He looks at me ... and then returns this gesture with a close embrace and with a proper kiss.

I'm aware of his erection.

Aware, as well, of my own arousal.

Disorientating.

The next hours pass in a blur. I know that Walt and Trixie decide to leave us. I know that at some point we find ourselves in the blessed tranquillity of Westminster Abbey, where people's heads are bowed in thanksgiving and where the pilgrimage to the tomb of the Unknown Warrior appears unending. I know that at some point we're standing beside the lake in St James's Park. I feel quite sorry when it's time to hear the King's speech.

We infiltrate a small hotel near Piccadilly, with probably a hundred others, to listen on the radio.

We've arranged to meet Walt and Trixie outside Rainbow Corner, in Coventry Street, where the American Red Cross have two or three years back set up a club for GIs. Pushing our way through we find all faces turned towards a lamp-post outside the London Pavilion as an RAF officer and a red-bereted airborne officer compete to climb to the top with a Union Jack.

Ten minutes later the Stars and Stripes is fastened next to it — and then the Russian flag as well: the three Great Powers fluttering alongside.

Even women are trying to climb the lampposts. A bit further on, a girl in a red coat earns the crowd's approval. I can imagine the swirl of colour from up there: the carnival caps, the uniforms, the women in their prettiest frocks. The sashes of bunting. The flowers and ribbons of red and white and blue: pinned either in the hair or on the clothing. Viewed from the lamppost it must be quite impressive.

Tonight nothing is unsuitable. Evening garments saved from pre-war days; full skirts, hobble skirts, backless dresses; long-sleeved day dresses; strangely you don't see many pairs of slacks.

We get to Rainbow Corner.

"Isn't this great!" Walt greets us. "Who said the British never let their hair down?"

"Well, who, indeed?" I ask. A little drily.

213

"But, listen, you kids. We've managed to get two rooms in a hotel in some place called Bayswater."

People are trying to get enough stuff together to start a bonfire in the middle of the street; there's even a hawker's barrow to which a strip of card is still attached (*Flags of all the Allies*). "Some bloody profiteer trying to charge five quid for a single Union Jack!" self-justifies the swaggerer who's commandeered and overturned it. There's much aggressive laughter. I say to Matt: "I thought that we were driving back tonight."

"Me, too. Walt! What is all this?"

"Don't be a schmuck. Me and Trix managed to pull a few strings." He puts that phrase into quotation marks, as though it's quaint. "In fact, we just about had to move heaven and earth — didn't we, babe? 'Cos who in their right mind wants to drive back to camp through half the night? Oh, for Chrissake! This is Victory-in-Europe Day! Hasn't anybody told you yet?"

Trixie takes my arm, imploringly. "Come on, Roz. Don't be a spoilsport. You know how much you like the lad."

She adds, in what's supposed to be a whisper: "And, you know, we've been and got some ... well, you-know-whats."

Oh, Trix. She'll maybe never guess indeed just how much I do like the lad; nor how truly tempted I could feel in many ways. But it wouldn't be right; I know it wouldn't be right. And I don't mean just because of Marjorie or because of morals. It's all much vaguer than that. More the thought of some seedy jumped-up boarding house in Bayswater probably charging the most extortionate prices ... with maybe every available nook and cranny let out to servicemen and their girls and some oily little clerk glancing with a knowing smirk at what we've written in the register ... I shake my head and Matt says: "No. You two take the jeep. I guess it won't be any problem getting rid of that second room." He suggests we all meet up again at noon the following day.

I slip my hand into his — and squeeze — and hope this pressure will tell him it's in no way a rejection of Matt Cas-

214

sidy, only of Bayswater. But after all I remind myself — isn't he the Great Clairvoyant? The Great Telepathetic Cassidy? Surely he already knows.

"Then what you gonna do?" asks Walt. "Wander round the streets all night?"

"Why not? There'll be more than enough going on. It's all part of history and we don't aim to let one single moment of it pass us by."

"That's right," I say. "And even if we do change our minds I know my mother would be glad to put us up." I'd like to ring her anyway if I get the opportunity — simply to say, hello, isn't this great, just listen to London. "Chesham's only about twenty-five miles away."

Matthew grins. "In other words, we could take the jeep and these two can walk or thumb a lift."

I agree, cheerfully. "Plenty of trams about, too. Pity about the taxis."

Trixie looks at Walt and gives a tolerant shrug.

"The pair of them are loony but so far as I'm concerned they're welcome to the jeep — eh, sweetheart?"

9

Thursday. I spend an aimless day on my own, am unable to concentrate on books or newspapers or television; go for a walk on Hampstead Heath, do a small amount of marketing; even a bit of vacuuming; can't stop worrying about my future. Or my past.

I now look back almost with fondness on our hours of trekking round hotels.

Cooking the evening meal is the only thing which affords me any true escape. All that cutting up of meat and bacon into cubes, peeling of shallots, slicing of mushrooms and onion, foraging for garlic and bay leaves and thyme, searing and browning and sprinkling and stirring. The pouring in of cider. The sauce is rich, the chuck steak tender. By halving the quantities I've cooked enough — allegedly — for three. Tom and I dispose of it with ease. He even wipes some bread around his plate; then round the cooking pot. "Perhaps," he says, "we shouldn't have gone to reception to ask about missing guests. We should have marched right into the kitchens to ask about missing chefs."

"It would certainly have got us just as far."

He tells me he's employed a firm to phone the bed-and-breakfast places.

"I've also been faxing off copies of that snapshot to various contacts round the country."

"Why?"

"To try to identify the church. With a magnifying glass one can make out a fair amount of detail. I spent an hour at the R.I.B.A.; hoped Pevsner or some other authority might come up with the answer."

"I don't see that it's important. She was only a day-tripper."

"Any pudding?" he asks.

"Cheesecake." I start to clear the dishes and Tom gets up to help. "No, I'll do it!" — my tone sounds testy.

"Why just you?"

"Pay my way."

"Balls." He continues to help. He says after a minute, "No, I agree with you. About the photo. It does have an air of holiday. But at the moment it's all we've got."

He hesitates.

"And if we locate that church it will at least give us an area to home in on. Maybe we could even publish the picture in the local press."

"In the hope that doing so will provide the name of my father?"

"It could do."

"I'd have thought he'd soon provide his own name — if he were missing me."

216

Tom bites his lip. He doesn't answer.

"Oh, sure. Not that anyone does appear to be missing me." There's certainly been no message from Sergeant Poke. Nothing from Herb Kramer.

"No ... Well, I'd say it now looks increasingly as though you came to London on your own."

"No loving wife? No family?"

"Not here at all events."

"Nor anyplace, I guess. I was hardly dressed for business."

"Perhaps you were taking the day off."

"I can't continue to impose on you like this."

"That's a dazzlingly logical progression." He grins that grin of his — the one that had stopped me leaving his office within the very first ten minutes.

This time it doesn't work so well.

"Having everything bought for me: tee shirts, socks, shorts. Even needing to accept pocket money. Couldn't I maybe get a job in a snack bar? Some sort of casual labour? Find myself a room?"

"If that's what you want. It isn't what I want."

"I don't know." I'm spooning coffee into filter.

"What don't you know?"

"Your friend said amnesia could sometimes last for years."

"He thought it more likely to last a week."

"But supposing he's wrong? If I had a job I could at least be starting to pay you back."

"Ranjit said you needed rest. Not that I think the shopping — cleaning — cooking — constitutes a rest. Frankly, I'm not all that worried about your paying me back. The thing that does worry me ..."

"What?"

"You sound so negative."

"Negative? Because I feel you're trying too hard to trace some woman who ... who ... well, even if she turns out to be still alive ...?"

"Yes?"

217

"I just don't see the point, that's all. You've already told me I could get my memory back within a week."

He looks at the two pieces of cheesecake which he's now transferring from their box. I expect some comment on my change of tune. I reckon I should've known better.

"When you put it that way I'm not honestly sure I see the point myself."

Maybe I have a slightly sheepish look. I shrug. "I guess you just want to make me feel we're getting someplace."

"No, I think you'll have to put it down to more than that. Let's call it instinct."

"Instinct?"

"Gut feeling. Something that's hounding me on. I just believe you've got to find this woman."

10

And then the lights come on!

The lights come on! And some of London's most historic buildings are seen floodlit for the first time since the coronation. We don't mean to miss a single one!

St Paul's ...

A.T.S. girls are lighting up St Paul's. Two sections have brought their mobile searchlights to Ludgate Hill and turned their beams upon the cathedral, while a third picks out the dome and surmounting cross from a bombed site lower down the hill.

In the precincts people sit on the protective coverings to the cellars, relics of the many attacks from the air; or else, like us, stand in groups around the searchlights, watching the girls in charge.

One of the girls talks to Matt and me. She's blonde and pretty and wears a lot of shiny scarlet lipstick. "They never could get it, could they? Don't you think that's sort of symbolic?"

Sort of miraculous, too. This splendid old structure stands triumphant in the midst of desolation, having watched over London through all the fires and explosions of hundreds of raids; is surely more imposing than at any time during the past century or so.

Isolated.

Inspirational.

Plenty of other buildings are adding to the glow which hangs above the city. From the top of the hill we can see the brightly lit newspaper offices in Fleet Street; also the lofty tower of the Shell-Mex building, illumined by flares which every few minutes change from colour to colour. All this is the more impressive since we've again been without any form of street lighting for a week (it wasn't restored to us for very long!) and shall have to be without it for a further ten; it's only for tonight and tomorrow, such beneficence.

Walking back along the Strand we find dozens of men and women sitting on the kerb, raising tankards and toasting the victory. (All the pubs tonight are open until twelve.) We have to stand aside for sailors marching six abreast with linked arms and singing 'Tipperary' — a song more of the last war than of this. However, it makes a change from the equally dated 'Over There', which even Matt, good American though he is, feels we've had quite enough of for the time being. Anyway, me, I much prefer 'Yankee Doodle Dandy' to either of them. That's another song we're hearing pretty frequently.

We get back to Buckingham Palace just before ten-thirty and at precisely the appointed minute all the floodlights and lamps above the gates are switched on to bathe the great grey building in pools of soft white light. As this happens, cheer upon cheer bursts from the delighted crowd. Word goes round that the two princesses, escorted by Guards' officers, are now walking amongst us. We hope to catch a glimpse of them close to — until a quarter of an hour later they appear with their parents on the balcony again; and after that we reckon it's time to see Big Ben and the Houses of Parliament while we still have the chance. People say the lighting will go off at twelve.

But we get detained in Whitehall. The Grenadier Guards are playing 'Land of Hope and Glory' to a crowd which is uncannily hushed until, little by little, the people themselves start to sing the words. Tears mist my eyes. Then we have a further view of Mr Churchill — this time in his siren suit and black homburg — taking over as conductor.

We'd like to stay in Whitehall but there's still something we've been told we shouldn't miss. The view from Waterloo Bridge is panoramic. St Paul's in one direction, Parliament in the other. Ever-shifting searchlights making tracks into the sky. Many of the wharves lit up. Lamps shining on the bridges and Embankment. The magnificence of County Hall. Trains moving slowly in or out of Charing Cross. All mirrored in the water. Magical. Even when we pull ourselves away we have to keep stopping to look back. Matt bemoans the fact we have no camera. I ask what justice he thinks we could possibly have done with one.

Afterwards we make again for Piccadilly Circus, the true vulgar heart of the West End, the place which always calls you back. (Whereas we find we couldn't now return to Waterloo Bridge, for fear of disappointment.) A floodlight plays across the site of Eros, although Eros himself is hidden behind tiers of seating. But when the floodlight gets turned off a universal groan bursts out. It isn't even midnight.

However, searchlight beams soon swing across the sky. A column of men and women forms at once — each person with both hands upon the shoulders of the reveller in front — and goes marching off down Coventry Street with a drummer beating a tin box.

Then the floodlight is switched on again. The crowd had earlier shown signs of dispersing but now begins to be drawn back.

The underground's still open. Police are marshalling people in and out. Near one exit a woman faints. The night's grown sultry; we've seen ambulance after ambulance. Despite their clanging bells these seem to make progress only with bobbies walking in front or riding on their running-boards. A U.S. military police van slowly forcing its way across the Circus is brought to a prolonged standstill. Before it finally disappears down Piccadilly maybe half a dozen men are sitting on its roof. I agree with a fellow in a dinner jacket and an older woman in a veiled and wispy hat this certainly shows a fair degree of insouciance.

So, perhaps, does a small family party inching its way from the opposite direction in a flag-bedecked governess cart. But what about the pony? ... a bonfire is already blazing — complete with effigy of Hitler; airmen are letting off fireworks. (Not that the pony seems in any way disturbed.) Little groups gyrate around the flames or else form into crazy, jigging circles. Crocodiles of dancing civilians — many wearing grotesque fancy dress, with masks and streamers — keep pushing their way through. Flashes of news photographers. Shouting, singing, laughter. Din of rattles, bells, whistles, bangers, rockets. Trumpets, too. Champagne corks. (Champagne flows; we see dozens drinking straight from the bottle — nearest us, a little party of Norwegian airmen and sailors, flourishing a huge Norwegian flag.) It's a night of noise and brilliance. Suddenly we turn to one another ... and know we've had enough.

"Maybe we're hungry," says Matt.

It isn't something which I've thought about but now I realise that it's true. The restaurants and hotels with doors fronting on the Circus have closed those doors (and Swan & Edgar's and other shops have barred all their windows) but anyway I suddenly remember the nearby Trocadero, which years ago I used to think so smart. In fact it goes with its location — it's a bit vulgar: lots of elaborate decoration and variegated marble in the neo-classical style. But it's large and there's only a short queue waiting for tables and people do seem to be leaving.

Here, too, the champagne flows. There appears to be no rationing of it whatsoever ... unless the fact they're charging six pounds a bottle can be seen as rationing. (And obviously it can't. "Rosalind, it's only money; and that looks like nectar they're giving in exchange. So please. Quit worrying." I do — to the extent we eventually work our way through two bottles. It's a thirst-making kind of night, we now realise.)

Matt also orders scrambled egg, which goes surprisingly well with champagne, considering it's made with powder and sits so solidly upon the toast. It resembles a moist yellow cake, fun to cut in slices.

We then have castle puddings with jam sauce — a far cry from the *crêpes suzettes* I'd eaten here before the war with a young man I had thought the very acme of sophistication. But I feel tonight I wouldn't change dried egg and castle puddings for any amount of roast duck or sophistication or balanced menu planning.

At the Troc, moreover, I find a nice lavatory — not such an easy undertaking in London at the moment — and a nice telephone, not only working but actually unqueued-for, on which I ring my mother. Matt then pays our bill — leaves an extraordinary tip for the waiter (it must be a good night for waiters, porters and the like) — and we return, feeling fortified, to face the hubbub.

Before two-thirty, however, we are back in Northumberland Avenue; and by this time the crowds have definitely diminished. Matt has little trouble in getting to Baker Street and from then on our way is clear. We should arrive in Chesham by four.

"We might just beat the milkman! Are you sure your mother's going to greet us with such squeals of joy?"

"Of course I am. She said she'd make up our beds and leave us out a snack. If she's awake she may get up and say hello; if not she'll meet you in the morning."

"To which she's looking forward."

"To which she's looking forward."

"I think you must be drunk. You've already told me all of this."

"Well, if I'm drunk you must be drunk. Which is far more dangerous. In my opinion." And I put my hand on his: to offer him assistance with the steering.

"No. Women have a lower toleration of alcohol." He smiles at me, smugly.

"Are you sure?"

"Utterly."

"Life isn't fair. Why do men have all the fun? What nice hands you have."

"Thank you. You have nice hands, too."

"One of the first things I noticed. So strong. And nice. And ... nice." I caress the hand with my forefinger, stroking the hairs on his wrist the wrong way and causing them to bristle.

"That's nice as well," he says.

"Everything's nice. It's a nice night. It's a nice drive. It'll be nice to introduce you to my mother."

But in fact I don't introduce them. They meet the following morning (no, the same morning, of course, just further along in it) when she knocks on his bedroom door and takes him in a pot of tea. I am by then wallowing in my bath — mercifully free of hangover — and have told her he'll enjoy being pampered. Apparently she means only to extend a simple word of welcome but finishes by staying while he drinks three cups of tea. She hears a lot about his life at home.

And yet she doesn't hear about Marjorie. I discover this while the pair of us are preparing breakfast; and the omission strikes me as significant. I know I mustn't get my hopes up. But I can't help wondering why he hasn't even made a passing reference.

I surmise he learned comparatively little about my mother, not because he isn't a sympathetic listener — which, heaven knows, he is — but because her life now is basically so awful she doesn't like to talk about it, not even with me. She was a widow for three years; remarried when I was sixteen. And how my stepfather changed! Though I'd always thought the generous and attentive suitor very suspect, even I was unprepared for the mean, lazy, tyrannical brute he turned into; and the sheer rapidity of the transformation made one question one's own sanity almost as much as his. I wanted her to divorce. She spoke about the need to honour your vows whatever the enormity of your mistake. Later on I could have added to her knowledge of that enormity. On a night three years ago, while she was at a meeting of the Women's Institute, he tried to rape me. Stupidly I wasn't able to tell her and he made out my avoidance of him from then on was solely due to jealousy.

If I hadn't known that he was currently in hospital I could never have contemplated even this short visit. I see my mother very seldom — only on snatched meetings in London. It is a wretched situation.

Though Matt has heard all this from me — except for the final cause of my departure, which I'd attributed wholly to the fact I wanted to feel more involved in the war effort (up to then I'd been working in a canteen) — the man hasn't been mentioned by the time we start on breakfast. We're given eggs and bacon. Shell-eggs and two rashers of bacon! I have no scruples about knowing we are doing the husband out of his but I wish my mother wasn't making such a sacrifice — especially since Matt and I, he at his air base, I on my farm, in general do quite well. She says she finds fatty things too rich at the moment; fresh eggs make her liverish; people just aren't used to them.

The time goes by too quickly.

"I suppose, though, you two have to get to your appointment and I must go to see your father in the hospital." She had spent most of the preceding day there, which seems to Matt and me — although of course we don't tell her so — a wholly shameful waste of what Mr Churchill has called 'the greatest day in all our long history'. But she assures us the nurses did everything they could to bring an air of celebration into the wards and that she listened to the wireless a good deal, which was all extremely moving. I gaze at her and think, Oh God, just forty-seven and her life is over.

"I wish we could have stayed longer." The front door comes between a branch of the Home & Colonial and the small Astoria cinema.

"Well ... it's been real nice, ma'am. You're everything that Rosalind said."

"And more," I add, "much more. But please go to the doctor — get that checkup; and I'll ring you in a few days to hear what he says."

"Oh — what a nag! Goodbye, my darling. God bless you. Remember me to Trixie." She gives me a hug. "Goodbye, Matthew. This has been such a pleasure. God bless you. Good luck." She gives him first a handshake; that too becomes a hug. "You're going to be so late." Another hug for me — this time an especially long one, as though she really can't bear to let us go. "But no — it doesn't matter if you're late — just so long as you get there in the end."

Then Matt hands me into the jeep; and she remains on the pavement, waving, until we've turned the corner by the Food Office.

11

For this evening's supper I have prepared only salad but Tom comes in brandishing a bottle. "Southwold," he says.

"Well, fine — is that better than Bordeaux?"

"Oh, most amusing. How would you fancy a day out in Suffolk?'

Over supper he elaborates. "And here's something else. I went to school with a bloke who hosts a TV show on Anglia; every Saturday; and though of course it's pre-recorded, what's a mere thirty-second insert, in the name of helping out a friend?"

To my astonishment it turns out he's actually referring to tomorrow's show.

We get to Southwold at about twelve. From the moment we cross the causeway over Buss Creek and Tom tells me

225

'buss' means a square-rigged herring smack — he's clearly done his homework — the last of my reservations has gone. I love the Georgian houses and the colour-washed dwellings of the fishermen; the long sandy beach and little harbour. The town is built on a clifftop and its views take in bracken, heath and marshes, as well as sea. Side streets widen into large green spaces: one of which contains six cannon, another a white lighthouse. Outside an inn, barrels of ale are being lifted from a dray. The drayhorse responds with endearing nuzzles to my overtures of friendship.

I tell him I'll bring him sugar from the bar. Before we get there Tom asks about overnight accommodation — and we're lucky — they do have one remaining room. Anywhere else must have been a letdown: the Red Lion dates from 1623, when it began life as a hostel for mariners.

Following lunch we visit the fifteenth-century church — which must be one of the great ones, Tom says, even for Suffolk. We look at the spot where long ago she posed for a photograph: the woman who's the cause now of our being here. I feel suddenly ashamed at having put up such resistance.

What on earth was I afraid of?

There's a little wooden man in armour: an unusual, fascinating timekeeper. While I'm admiring him and just about to call across to Tom, something strange takes place.

"Tom! Hey! Tom!"

He's been gazing at the brightly painted pulpit; looks round inquiringly.

But now I feel a tad foolish.

"Oh, nothing. It's just that suddenly I thought I must have been here before. Sorry."

Afterwards we go to a men's outfitter's where I choose a pair of trunks; Tom has brought his. We walk down to the beach, which at a closer view turns out to be less sand than shingle. The water's cold but lovely. I feel free — cleansed — weightless; relieved of worry. Drying off, Tom stretches out to sunbathe. I prefer to sit and let my gaze wander. My eyes rest for a moment on the rather ugly pier.

And abruptly I get a second sample of that feeling I'd experienced earlier. "That feeling of ... well, of having been here before," I say.

Tom sits up; clasps his hands beneath his thighs.

"Well ... could you have been here before, I wonder?"

I look at him — and wait.

"I mean, just supposing," he says slowly, "just supposing you've been on the trail of our mystery woman in the past ...? Why should we necessarily assume that this is the first time? Suppose in the past you even found her?"

There's a pause.

"Well, it's an intriguing possibility," he announces finally. "But unfortunately it doesn't get us anywhere."

I feel disproportionately let down. I have a stubborn need to pursue this line of speculation further.

"And I suppose there's no reason, come to that, why I shouldn't just have been here on vacation."

"Oh hell," he says. "Let's take another dip. Then we can visit the local fortune-teller and have her clear up all such piffling question marks."

I laugh. "I haven't been to a fortune-teller since —"

Tom jerks his head round. Stares at me.

"No, it's gone. Damn it."

His tone is thoughtful. "But perhaps now we really are getting somewhere. Tell you what: let's do it, let's actually do it — go to a fortune-teller."

So we make inquiries. And come up with Madam Sonia.

Madam Sonia has her consulting room above a baker's in the High Street. Her appearance, like her setting, has little of the exotic, little of the fairground booth. Despite soft golden hair and unlined skin she must be in her seventies. Good carriage, careful enunciation, a pleasant face. She wears a simple blue and white dress, short sleeves; blue necklace, bracelet, earrings.

Tom sees her first. I sit waiting beside a table with a yucca on it and some magazines. On the wall there's a picture of a girl with flowing hair and gauzy dress gazing at her image in a lake. It originates from the twenties, at a guess; is entitled *Fair Reflections*. My own fair reflections have to occupy me nearly half an hour.

"Sorry to be so long." As I go in she gives me a warm smile. Directs me to sit on the other side of the baize-covered table.

"Have we ever met?" God knows why I should ask her that. She doesn't look familiar. No further flash of *déjà vu*. At least, not of the same order as before.

"I don't believe so, dear. I could be wrong."

"I could be crazy."

"Oh, don't say that!" She smiles again; grows serious. "I wonder what was on your mind to make you think we had."

I answer slowly:

"Mence Smith. Gypsy costume. Golden earrings." I listen to what seems like the echo of someone else's words.

My own take repossession.

"Your surname," I say, "isn't by any chance Mence-Smith?"

"No, dear, it's Wheeler."

"I told you I was going crazy. Let's make a start, though, shall we?" She'd informed us that she mainly read palms; used tarot cards.

She's giving me an odd look. Not greatly to be wondered at.

"You know, when I began in this line, I used to wear Gypsy costume. Golden earrings, too. Felt it was expected of me. A splash of flamboyance to brighten up the drabness of the war years."

"You and Paulette Goddard, both. Not to mention Marlene Dietrich."

"I suppose it's still the same. At the pictures. People don't want to see their fortune-tellers dressed by C & A. What colour was this costume, dear?"

"Red. Studded with stars and moons." Well, it would almost have to be, wouldn't it? Choice between red and mauve and orange; one chance in three. I open my eyes again. "Shawl was black and gold."

She nods. "If it was here I'd show it to you. But I don't

228

live on these premises any longer, although I've always worked from them. There used to be an ironmonger's below. The name of it was Mence Smith."

Curiously, I'm not all that surprised.

"There's a woman," I say. "I don't recall having met her and yet some sort of link exists between us." I take out the snapshot. She gives her spectacles a polish. Up to now they've just been sitting on the table.

"Who is she, dear?"

"I don't know. But I think she must have come to see you. I feel her presence here ..."

She gives me back the photo. "I wish I could say that I remembered her."

I lay first one hand, then the other, palm upward, on the green baize. Her bent head is sometimes less than a foot away; her finger tickles as it runs along the lines.

After that she unwraps a deck of cards from a piece of silk and asks me if I'd like to shuffle it.

Thirdly — "and at no extra charge" — she brings across her crystal ball.

But finally she opens her purse and takes from it two folded five-pound bills. She hands me one of them. "Please return this to your friend. I'm sorry. Your past seems wrapped up in a shroud. I just don't understand."

I should like to tell her to keep the money; certainly she's worked for it. She may be a phony — but at least she's an honest phony. And I divine more than mere bewilderment; I hear silent calls of deep distress. When I tell her about my amnesia I sense an instant rush of warm relief.

"Ah, well, dear. Yes. That would explain it."

Our positions then become reversed: she ends up by trying to give me comfort. "... so very frightening. But just regard it as a test. Hold onto your faith, dear." (Have I any faith?) "Hold onto it fast." She tells me she will pray for me; then after a decent interval asks if Tom and I can find our own way out. She suddenly feels tired.

On the faded wallpaper inside the entrance there's a framed photograph of this corner of the High Street —

taken, it says, in 1942. I hadn't been consciously aware of it but the name of the hardware store is clearly legible. Mence Smith & Son. It's undeniable I have this gift of picking up on things. And fast.

I give Tom back his five pounds but don't mention the Gypsy costume nor the hardware store. It doesn't seem worth it. Also, I don't want to give him the idea I could just be making cheap claims.

The woman wasn't such a phony. She'd told Tom that he worked to uphold the law in some way; thought first he was a customs officer — amended it to policeman. She'd told him he was born in Cornwall (and he swears he doesn't have a trace of accent), that he's a widower, his mother used to be a concert pianist and that two of his brothers are hoteliers. His sister has a mongol child, whom Tom is fond of. (Also godfather to — although she didn't tell him that.)

"So I was impressed. She said nothing much about my future but I began to think she might help us a good deal with your past."

"Some hope. She didn't even comment upon my being an American." But that's an ungracious remark. I immediately feel remorseful — and say so.

"Anyhow." Tom glances at his watch. "All part of our jolly jinks at the seaside. Right? If we go straight back to the Red Lion we'll have time for a drink before the programme. What's more, I think we're going to need one."

The TV lounge is empty; and the show we've come all this way to see is abysmal. Even hefty double Scotches can't improve it.

Tom runs a hand through his hair. "But who am I to criticise? If Simon and I should ever compare bank statements ..."

"And now for something a little different," this banker's pet announces. "Before in these programmes, sometimes with great success, we've often set out to trace a long-lost brother or sister or cousin or friend. This evening we're looking for an unknown woman; and here she is, ladies and gentlemen. This picture was obviously taken in wartime.

Look at it long and hard and it's just possible that one of you may be saying to yourself right this minute, 'Why! Isn't that old Edna or Rita or May ... ?' Well, if you are, there's a Mr Tom Merrill staying at the Red Lion Inn in Southwold who would dearly love to hear from you. He's only there for tonight, so if you've got even a hint of a whisper nagging away inside you, do a nice man a good turn and make another of Simon's friends feel very happy. The number you must ring is ..."

Then, after he has given it twice, Simon, in a very smooth transition, asks the studio audience please to put its hands together for a Mrs Jan Thistleton who has waited half a life-time to see her wildest and most cherished dream come true ... Tom switches off the set, with an apology both to Simon and to Mrs Thistleton, and we inform the desk clerk that we're going upstairs in case anyone should need us. I remove my loafers and throw myself down on one of the beds. Tom paces restlessly between the window and the telephone.

"Why doesn't the damned thing ring?"

And then the damned thing does ring.

"Merrill here ..." (Now I'm sitting up but after a moment Tom pulls a face at me.) "Oh, Simon ... yes. It was great. I really owe you one ... No, there hasn't been, not yet ..." They don't speak very long.

"It really doesn't matter," I say, when Tom replaces the receiver.

"No, of course it doesn't. Were going to get the answer anyway. And if we don't have it by Tuesday we'll think about hypnosis." But he sounds dispirited and I actually pray for the telephone to ring.

It doesn't.

Instead there comes a tap upon the door.

Again the atmosphere grows tense.

Again there follows anticlimax.

On the threshold stands a chambermaid.

Tom bids her good evening but has a job concealing his impatience. "If you're here to turn the beds down thank you

231

but don't bother. We can see to it ourselves."

"No, I'm here because I saw that programme on the telly."

A moment of stillness. Of suspension.

"I couldn't get away quicker because I ... wanted to wash my hands and tidy up a bit. Try and make myself look beautiful." She gives a nervous snicker. "I hope I didn't keep you."

She's an elderly rawboned woman with bleached hair and too much lipstick, too much eye shadow, too much mascara. They don't go with her uniform. They don't go with her attitude. Even now — when she's surely on her best behaviour — her expression indicates that life has been a disappointment.

"Then did that snapshot seem familiar?"

She gives him a coquettish glance. Maybe she thinks she looks about thirty years younger than she does.

"I'd be surprised if it didn't," she answers. "Seeing as I'm the one what took it."

12

During our return to East Anglia we decide to make a short detour; the weather has stayed warm and it's only late afternoon. Back to Southwold then — "to see if they've put up a plaque yet to commemorate our meeting?" suggests Matt.

From the back of the jeep Trixie answers him lugubriously: "It'll probably just say how they met ... and parted." It's been growing more and more obvious that following all our recent excitement a reaction has set in.

"Oh, come on, babe, that's just the Monday morning blues. Catching up with you on Wednesday." Walt sounds uncomfortable and Trixie's reply doesn't exactly reassure him.

"Monday morning blues?" she exclaims, bitterly. "Rest-of-my-life blues, more like."

"Nah, don't say that. And, anyhow, it's still possible we've got a surprise up our sleeve. Eh, Matt?"

"Surprise?" Already a picking up of interest.

"Oh, nothing much. Just a dance at the camp next Saturday. Even if people do say it's going to be a dilly."

"Dance! Next Saturday?" Trixie has the maybe enviable ability to coast along breezily from one highlight to another and not look much beyond the next in line — just so long as there actually is a next in line. "But why didn't you tell us sooner, screwball? The idea of it! Of keeping something like that all to yourselves!"

"We only heard about it Monday."

"So? And today's —"

"And we decided," puts in Matt, overriding her, "that we wouldn't mention it until tonight. In case things felt a tad flat when we'd gotten back from London." There's not a trace of irony but he looks at me a little worriedly. "Rosalind? You'll come to it, won't you?"

"Of course she'll come!" cries Trixie. "Think she's barmy or something? You try to stop her, that's all! Eh, Roz?"

"Truly we weren't just taking the pair of you for granted."

But he's misread my hesitation. *It's a farewell dance, isn't it?* That's really what I want to say.

But instead: "You bet I'll come. It will be wonderful."

Walt is wholly at his ease again. "You and the rest-of-your-life blues!" he teases. "We ought to go and see that woman we noticed the other day — her signboard, you remember — Madam Something-or-Other."

"Oh, yes, let's! That would be a giggle. I'd forgotten her."

"But what makes you think that she'll be there?" The shops round Leicester Square were certainly open — Matt and I went looking for those souvenirs I'd promised the young Crawfords; but suddenly I feel perverse. It seems to me Walt's being insensitive. It's just too easy to fob Trixie off with a dance and with having her palm read.

Yet on the other hand, I suppose, if he can't respond to her cri-de-coeur in the only way she'd wish, there's not much else that he *can* do.

"Oh, pooh!" says Trixie. "The seaside! It'll be just like August Bank Holiday — like how it used to be. Course she'll be open. Everywhere will."

"Madam Trix ...!" says Walt, proudly, even proprietorially; and indeed she turns out to be right — if 'everywhere' doesn't include places like the ironmongery in the High Street, over which Madam Sonia has her premises.

"And what about us? Rosalind, would you like to have your fortune told?"

"I don't know. Do you think she might come up with a tall dark stranger and travels to a distant shore?"

"Bound to."

"Well, I don't mind lashing out five bob for that. What I couldn't stand is spending hard-earned cash and hearing just the truth."

It's providential that when we get there Madam Sonia doesn't have a client. She suggests she see Trixie first, that Walt sit in the waiting room, and that Matt and I return in an hour.

So we again go searching for some presents for the children and this time we're lucky: we find old Dinky Toy models of a red double-decker bus, a tram and taxi. "And heaven forbid anyone should mention," smiles Matt, "that there wasn't a single taxi on the streets of London yesterday!" He attempts to pay for these three purchases himself — I don't see why he should pay for even one — but eventually settles for our going halves. Then we saunter back through the town — which is really very busy. But from a distance we see that the pier is even more crowded. (Red, white and blue are still the colours of the day.) It's not an especially appealing pier; in fact we both think Southwold deserves better. Leaning against some railings for a while we study the coastline — which is a lot more rewarding, despite the quantities of barbed wire.

We arrive at the fortune-teller's about a minute after Trixie and Walt have left; there's a message to meet them at the tearooms.

Madam Sonia looks about thirty. Apart from her shawl and earrings and supposedly Gypsy dress, the two most striking things are her voice and the flawlessness of her complexion. Her voice is loud yet melodious, each word so carefully enunciated you might imagine she taught elocution.

I go in first and when she's finished sit waiting for Matt and abstractedly staring at the sentimental picture of a pre-Raphaelite beauty gazing at her image in a lake. It's called *Fair Reflections*. I rather wish someone would come along and give her a hearty shove.

Later, en route to the tearooms, we compare notes.

"She's not bad, is she?"

"What did she say?" he asks. Am I imagining it or does he seem a little moody?

"Well, not so much about the future. Quite a lot about the present and the past."

"Same here — but we already know about the present and the past."

"For instance, she told me I was working on the land — which, if it was a guess, was reasonably inspired. There isn't any straw behind my ears, is there? You can break it to me gently."

"Not behind yours," he answers. "I don't know about Trixie's."

"Well, that's a point, of course. But then she spoke about my home situation. Was there a stranger in the house? Was one of my parents dead? It struck me that she really has a gift."

He nods — though only after hesitation. "What else? What about ... well, what about the shape of things to come?"

I laugh and shrug and hold on tightly to his arm. "Oh, just the usual sort of stuff."

"What's the usual sort of stuff?"

"Uncertainty about the course one's life is going to take — which surely must apply to just about everyone at present."

Besides, she'd already seen Matt and knew he was American; had probably sensed how much I cared for him.

"She also prophesied a change of job — well, naturally. A change of scenery — well, again, I'd never have guessed that, would you? As I say, she was far less good about the future." (And I certainly don't want to burden him with her predictions of approaching hardship — approaching yet undefined.) "Oh, look, we're nearly there and you haven't given me a hint of what she said to you."

"Nothing of any interest."

He kicks a pebble into the gutter.

"Oh, she was okay about the past. Strained relations with my dad. Death of someone very close." The need to be fair gradually wins out over his humour to be grudging. "Better than okay in fact. She even told me that I come from a town where she could see a large university and lots of water and — yes, listen to this — a theatre I often attend which she thought was named after a well-known composer."

"And?"

"I guess she meant the Shubert."

However, with a slightly lopsided smile, he then tells me, "But it wasn't named after the composer. It was named after the Shubert Brothers. There's a chain of such theatres all across the States."

"That's uncanny," I say, despite the woman's error — surely understandable in someone unconversant with life in America. I try to remember if in London (or anywhere else I know) there's a theatre which sounds as if it might have been commemorating a composer.

"So why," he asks, "if she's so hot on the past can't she be a bit more specific about the future?"

"They never are," I say. "Damn them."

Suddenly he grins; gives my arm a squeeze. "Yes, that's

the ticket. Damn them all to hell."

But already I've had second thoughts; I rapidly recant. "No. It's like I said before. What sane person would seriously want to know the truth about their future? I mean, if they were powerless to change it?"

Why not admit it? I don't even want to know the truth about next Saturday. Not any more. Is the dance really a prelude to departure; is the date all settled for the pulling out of the entire squadron? Earlier — if only in my thoughts — I may have been patronising about Trixie not looking much beyond the next highlight. If so, I apologise. Now I decide I'll follow her example.

13

As Tom stares at the chambermaid she takes a picture from her pocket.

"Look. I been carrying this around for close on forty-five blinking years."

Tom misunderstands her.

"No, I don't mean always in my overall. I live here, you see. Got a tiny bedroom on the top floor."

"Well — good God — this is great! I don't know where to start."

He smiles.

"Oh, first by asking you to sit down — obviously. My name is Merrill, Tom Merrill. And this is ... well, this young man is a good friend of mine who may have some connection to the lady in the photograph ..." I nod at the chambermaid, who by now is seated, a little stiffly, in a small armchair with a striped cover. "It's all a bit complicated but ... Well, now then, you are Ms —?"

"Morris. You can call me Trixie if you like." She folds her

arms; unfolds them. She lets her hands rest limply on her lap. They look stringy and uncared for.

"Right, Trixie. And the name of your friend there?" The photograph is safely back in Trixie's pocket. "At least I take it she's your friend?"

"Oh, yes, we used to be — quite close we were — you see, we both worked on the land. Land girls. That's where we met."

"And her name?"

"Rosalind. Sounds fancy, doesn't it? Rosalind Farr. We called her Roz, though, and she didn't mind — she was never stuck-up or anything." But then a touch of asperity enters a tone that in any case is slightly shrill. "Though probably the Farr bit got changed to Cassidy — and that's what I hope it still is, of course." She adds: "Well, naturally."

"Then you've lost touch with her?" I can hear Tom's disappointment.

"And that's putting it mildly! Haven't seen her since 1945. There were a couple of letters after that, but she'd even stopped writing by early '46. I suppose she went off to America; forgot about her old friends."

"America?" Tom gives me a meaningful glance.

"There was this Yank she was in love with."

Trixie pauses and seems to be struck by the undercurrent of disapproval she catches in her own voice.

"Well, I don't know if I ought to say this — not to strangers — but I suppose it can't do no harm; water under the bridge and all that. She got herself knocked up. And so I thought ... well, maybe you're too young to know about it but there was this American war brides scheme ..."

Tom nods. He bites his lip. "And the American's name, you say, was Cassidy?"

"That's right. Lieutenant, he was. Lieutenant Matt Cassidy."

"Matt? Matthew ..." Tom repeats the name in full,

238

slowly. He looks at me with hopeful eyebrow raised.

I only shrug and shake my head.

Trixie also looks at me. It's the first time she's given me her close attention. "Are you a Yank?"

I haven't spoken up till now; I suddenly become aware of this. "What made you guess?"

"Because you all seem to have that special sort of look. I can always tell. You and him, now. If it wasn't for the differences in clothes and hairstyles and the like ... yes, I'm not being daft ... the pair of you could almost be related." (Tom, behind her, raises his arms in a boxer's gesture of victory.) "I'm right, you know. And I can prove it to you. I got another photo."

After a minute she gets up to fetch it. Tom says: "And by some miracle you haven't saved those letters which you mentioned? But no. No one could be that far-sighted!"

On her return she carries a battered-looking album. The three of us stand in the centre of the room, under the main light, Tom and I on either side of her, while she importantly turns its pages.

"There," she says. "That one at the bottom."

And we all look at the likeness.

*

It's after midnight and we're in our beds.

"Well — back to the embassy on Monday. There may be hundreds of Matthew Cassidys living in the States but there can't be too many who hail from New Haven in Connecticut ... and whose families worked in the meat-packing industry. You'll see: only a matter of days now."

Then why don't I feel more optimistic?

Why indeed do I have the jitters?

I try my best to fight them down.

"Tom, tell me something. Do you think I ought to go to that address?"

"Yes — why not? If you want to. Though after so very long I don't suppose there'll be anyone to remember her.

Your mother," he amends, as though it's impolite to use the pronoun.

Want to? No, *want to* isn't quite the phrase that I'd have chosen. "You don't think you're leaping at conclusions?"

"Why?"

"I just don't get the feeling she's my mother. No flash of recognition like I got when I saw that picture of my dad."

"But that's different. You were recognising yourself, not him."

"Even so." I'm lying on my back, hands clasped behind my head, staring at the branches of a horse chestnut as if they might be going to tap me out a message. "You know what I think? That my father's just died and my mother, knowing about this woman in England, knowing about ... Rosalind, sent me here to try to trace her. It might have been a promise she made him. Or one that I did. Or could have been to do with something in his will."

In the semi-darkness I turn my head in Tom's direction with a slow smile.

"In other words, you crazy dick, it's pretty much as you said it was last Tuesday. But I still don't feel I'd have been carrying round a pin-up picture of my own mother ... which was definitely one of your less good notions, I submit. With respect."

"Okay. What you say does sound ... well, I suppose it does sound feasible."

"In which case we'd better go to Hampstead. Or I had. You're probably right about there not being a great deal of point but ..."

"Why just you?"

"Because we've found out who I am. Like you say, it's only a matter of time now: we'll soon have the name of the hotel where I was putting up in London — my identity, my money, my documents. I can't go on forever keeping you from getting on with your work."

"Yet there's still something that worries me ... How you came to be wandering about a capital city without even a coin in your pocket — let alone a credit card."

"Perhaps I'm naturally extravagant. Perhaps this time I'd simply gone out for a stroll; been determined not to spend a red cent."

"Perhaps." But he doesn't sound convinced. Any more than I do.

In the morning we find a message from Trixie slipped beneath the door. Folded around an enclosure.

"I told some fibs last night. I loved Roz but I was jealous. It just didn't seem fair. I told you how she got pregnant. I didn't say how she'd already had the baby by the time I stopped hearing and how full of it she was. That's why I pretended I couldn't find this second letter — don't really know now why I kept it. It was me who didn't stay in touch. You see, I never answered her, not either of these letters, just couldn't face the thought of it. And also — what was mean — I never reminded her I had that picture of her boyfriend. But I didn't for one second think he'd gone and left her — not like she did — knowing old Roz it was probably just some silly hiccup, not that other woman that she talked about, and nothing like my own case where I knew I had no chance. Anyhow I thought I'd got over all this long before last night. But I can't pretend as how I managed to get much sleep ..."

There's a bit more but then the letter finishes by saying it's a good job she's not at work either today or tomorrow and that she's off to Yorkshire for a short break; and by asking us to give Roz all her love when we do finally succeed in catching up with her.

"If," I say.

I'm pretty sure Tom is about to contradict me — go for *when*; but in fact he surprises me. Stays silent.

"Shall we leave Trixie flowers? Chocolates? Wine? I mean, as well as a bit of cash, naturally." I feel happier now about suggesting further outlay.

Anyway, he'd certainly have come up with that same suggestion. "Yes, good idea — we'll leave something with the originals of your father's snapshot and the letters." He wants to get these three things photocopied.

"Photocopying on a Sunday?"

241

"No, but I was wondering. If the room's not taken tonight why don't we stay over? Just like Trixie, we could probably do with a bit of a break ..." But here his voice tails off; his attention is elsewhere. He has now opened Rosalind Farr's second letter — which I for some reason had fought shy of.

"This one," he says, "is dated March 5th, 1946."

As Trixie had implied — though in fact I had forgotten — it's a happy letter. But the penultimate sentence has acquired a poignancy that leaves us silent for a moment.

"'It will be wonderful to see you and we'll have tremendous fun — just make it soon.'"

I've been standing at the window, staring into the branches of the horse chestnut. "Oh, hell," I say.

"Well, it wasn't your doing."

"No. Then why do I feel as though it were?"

"Because you've got a name like Cassidy. Which probably means you're a Catholic. Which probably means you've got a Catholic conscience."

He laughs.

"Which probably means — in short — that everything is your doing."

14

I wish I could have stunned him with a new dress. I wish I could have stunned him with a carefree bit of jitterbug. I wish I could have just enjoyed myself.

Everything's laid on for our enjoyment.

The dancing takes place in the main hangar which is festooned with crepe paper. Balloons are hung at the entrance to the base and Chinese lanterns brighten several pathways. The refreshments are extraordinary — not just the profusion but the variety. Naturally I exclaim as much as anyone and hope that once I've tasted them I may even start to feel hungry.

Fat chance.

I'm not the only one without an appetite. You see them everywhere: the couples who are either clinging in undisguised desperation or else putting on an act. I too am putting on an act.

I hate it.

And I resent Matt for appearing so very much as normal.

We walk out of the hangar into fresh air. From somewhere comes the unmistakable scent of wallflowers. Can someone on the base have made a little garden?

He's not aware of it, he says, but that isn't to say it hasn't happened. "You're not cold, are you?"

I shake my head.

"Yet after that great heat in there ..." He offers me his jacket. "Wiser not to risk a chill."

Who cares about a chill, I want to ask. Who cares about being wise? He puts the jacket round my shoulders. I don't trust myself to thank him. The last thing I want right now is kindness.

We stroll a little way in silence. Not holding hands. Not linking arms. Nothing.

"Rosalind?" he says. "I am going to see you again, aren't I?"

"On Monday, you mean, when your train leaves? Oh, yes, I'm pretty sure they'll let me get away. And if not ... I'll come anyhow." But the smile I give doesn't in the least diminish my briskness.

"You know that isn't what I meant."

"What, then?"

"I don't know." He shrugs — and suddenly I see that, after all, he too has been pretending. "I've got to try to work things out."

"Why? What is there to work out? You don't owe me anything. You're engaged to a nice girl back in Connecticut and I knew that all along. It's been fun; I'm glad to have known

243

you, Matt; we'll have to write to one another and — who knows? — someday you and your family may come to London or I and mine may come to New York and —"

"Honey. Please don't."

"Don't what?"

"Listen. Just answer me one thing. Will you miss me when I'm gone?"

"Oh, Matt." My tone quavers, treacherously.

"No, but what I mean is — just how much will you miss me?"

"Darling, this is pointless. Let's go back and dance."

"No, it isn't pointless ... Because ... Well, you see ..."

I give up every effort to be bright and brittle and to hold him at a distance.

"You know how much I'm going to miss you. But do you really want to make me spell it out and have myself in tears? That would be a fine way to finish on a night we're all meant to be having so much fun. You almost have to laugh: the band playing 'The sun has got his hat on' while nearly everywhere you look ..."

"I love you, Rosalind."

"There! Now see what you've done." I fumble for my hanky.

He doesn't let me — pushes my evening purse aside. I mumble that his shoulder will get wet; he doesn't seem to care. Eventually I have to pull away, however: it would hardly be romantic to wipe my nose against his shirt.

"But, Matt, just be sure that what you decide is what you really want. We've known each other for three short weeks. Heightened atmosphere of wartime — of wartime coming to an end. It's two years since you've seen Marjorie. Maybe one can forget a bit in two years but the minute you set eyes on her again —"

"You make it sound — what we feel for one another — you make it sound just like some holiday romance."

"I only want to be sensible. I only want to be fair." But how fair is it to come out with the following? "I shall love you, Matt Cassidy, until the day I die — and beyond that,

244

too, if I have any say in the matter, but —"

I don't get any further. Suddenly he whirls me round. "No! No buts! That's all I wanted to hear. Don't say another word." He kisses me; ecstatically. "And *now* we shall go in and dance!"

What's more, I perform one or two pretty deft pieces of jitterbug in the shortish time remaining; I'm only surprised that no one clears a circle to give us space to show off our agility. They always do in films.

"Oh, you'll love America!"

We're on our own again; and once more riding in a jeep. I can't think how he's pulled it off, considering the number of men there are at Halesworth.

"You might also get to care for Britain," I remind him.

"I already do. Though I still can't say a whole lot for your coffee." There's hardly any alteration in his tone. "You spoke earlier about a fine way to finish off things — wasn't that the way you put it? — on a night we're all meant to be having so much fun."

I look at him. And very slowly smile.

At that, he takes my hand and lifts it to his lips. He has avoided touching me till now; is evidently much fairer than I am. "Have you ever been to the Red Lion? In Southwold?"

"Yes; Trix and I have had a drink there a couple of times." I laugh as I remember Trixie queening it at the bar and adopting an ultra-refined accent in which to order pink champagne — she hadn't made herself very popular. Not with me any more than with the bar staff. I'd felt reluctant to return.

When I tell him that, he laughs as well. (Though I'm aware my own laughter is probably occasioned as much by nervousness as amusement.) Then he completes what he was saying.

"The desk clerk may be having forty winks but if I tip him generously I'm sure he won't mind losing just a few of them."

"Oh, you Yanks. You think mere money can accomplish anything."

"No. If I thought that, I'd book for tomorrow night as well."

But suddenly he has to brake, to avoid something which dashes straight in front of us. We think it was a fox.

"I'm sure it was a fox," I say. "It had to be. An unmistakable case of like calling out to like."

15

"Where did Trixie say he came from?"

"New Haven."

"No, over here," I say. "Which U.S. base?"

"Oh. Halesworth."

"Yes, Halesworth. Would it be much off our route?"

He looks it up in the guidebook. "Airfield built in 1942–43, intended as a bomber station," he reads. "Only eight miles from Suffolk coast; ideally placed for escort fighter operations."

"Why?"

"Range, I suppose."

As we approach Holton, the village near which the base was built (two miles out of Halesworth), I find it a moving experience to be driving through this flat East-Anglian countryside where so many of my compatriots served during the war. I think of all those young men who flew up into the skies nearly half a century ago.

"But please don't imagine you're going to absorb the flavour of an airfield," warns Tom. "I gather that most of the land has returned to agriculture; that a good portion's given over to turkey farming."

We discover there's one omission in the guidebook: part of the perimeter has provided the council with a special course for learner lorry drivers.

And, yes, of course it's just sentimental — but there's somehow a sadness in seeing the destruction of any place where life's been lived intensely. Possibly it's worse when you can still distinguish outlines. An employee of the turkey farm, a stocky and grizzled man with bow legs, leads us to those spots where the main runway would have been, and the control tower and the hangars.

"Two thousand yards long," he says, pointing to the runway — you can just make out the traces. "And then, of course, the Nissen huts ... funny to remember there was accommodation here for some three thousand."

He's made quite a study of it; points out where the T2 hangars would have been. "Did you know Glen Miller came to Halesworth? August 6th 1944. A Sunday. But a busy day for Major Miller: Boxted before he came on here."

We're standing maybe at the very point where he had played; it isn't hard, for a moment, to hear 'Moonlight Serenade' or 'String of Pearls' flooding that main hangar, drifting out across the airfield.

But then you remember that you're now on a turkey farm and that facing you is a pool of evil-smelling effluent.

We leave the hangar site and start walking towards what was once the Admin block — though, frankly, I've lost interest. The sooner we return to London the better. I make a last attempt to feel my way back into my father's shoes — this stranger's shoes; to experience just one more fleeting second of what he himself might have experienced. I close my eyes and try to will something to come to me out of the past. But no. Nothing. I open them and find I've trodden on some wallflowers. Wild — incongruous — defiant: even in competition with the effluent they give off a warm and spicy scent. I meet Tom's amused, inquiring glance and shrug self-mockingly. "Okay, you're right. I should have had more sense. But I bet you anything he brought her here at some point. And probably to hear Glen Miller." Unexpectedly, the notion gives me pleasure.

*

In the car I think about the half-brother whom I've never met. I wonder on which side of the Atlantic he may now be roaming.

16

In the garden and just outside our window there's a pink-blossomed horse chestnut. I lie in bed on Monday morning and gaze into its branches and at the sky beyond ... and think why can't the sky be gloomy. The time's just after six and Matt is still asleep; and looking peaceful. It's a pity to wake him but selfishly I want to. I trace his brow with my forefinger. Yet he only stirs and smiles and turns over and I haven't the heart to persevere. I'm not sure what I do have the heart for: certainly not the drive back to Halesworth — the chaos at the railway station — the journey home with Trixie — the greetings, the questions, the commiserations. I don't know how I'm going to get through any of that — not the next few hours, nor even the next few days. (Or next few months? ... But getting back to the farm will somehow be the worst: the place where they collected us on Saturday and where I sang as I got ready; the last time I saw all those familiar objects at the farm I was still — well, relatively and in retrospect — feeling happy and stouthearted.)

But at least we made the most of what we had.

Well, we did until the previous evening. At dinner. And then it suddenly hit me.

In fourteen hours he will be gone.

True, we still had the night ahead of us. But I wanted a whole lifetime of days and nights and I wanted it now. Suppose anything should happen to him? After six years of war one was attuned to the possibility of accidents; of people never coming back.

I knew last night that Matt was feeling just as miserable as me but at least for him there are all the distractions of homecoming to palliate the misery. I almost wish there weren't. In my heart I want him to feel every bit as lost as I do.

Not a very noble sentiment — and in fact I only admit to it as I gaze blindly into the branches of the horse chestnut.

Then I really do wake him; we ought to be out of bed in half an hour.

Breakfast isn't much fun. Indeed it's pretty awful. I dread the thought of having to leave somewhere which has meant so very much to me. Will I ever be able to set foot in it again, I wonder, if I'm on my own — or with anyone but him?

But we've hardly started back to Halesworth when the engine of the jeep begins to cough. Though it requires only a minor adjustment it reminds Matt he's forgotten water. Rather than return to the Red Lion he requests some from a charlady who's opening up a shop. Afterwards he takes the empty jug inside the shop but pauses on his way out. The woman must have gone to fetch her boss because an elderly man comes from the back and smilingly unlocks the glass top of a table — evidently a showcase. In spite of my depression I wonder what I may be missing and quickly get down from the jeep.

"Go away," says Matt. "You're spoiling the surprise."

"Ah? The young lady in question?" Cadaverous, stooped and ginger-haired, the owner doesn't appear to recognise me, although I've been here twice with Trixie. It's a fascinating place, full of secondhand trinkets and pictures and family photographs; books, cutlery, gramophone records, ewers, basins, wireless sets; all sorts of things from threepence to ten pounds. It's this incredible price range which makes you feel you could unearth huge bargains. You only need to scavenge.

Matt, however, hasn't had the time to scavenge. And even as he shoos me away I still can't see what's drawn his attention.

But then he says, "Oh well, since you're here, you may as well help. This gentleman has been kind enough to interrupt his breakfast..." And he reveals to me the object he's been looking at.

Companionably, by my side, the charlady sounds wistful. "Never saw another which was half so nice!"

It's a ring I'm being shown: one that's studded with pearls and turquoise, and is certainly attractive. "I think it dates from about 1875," the man tells us.

But then Matt says: "Honey, this one here was actually what caught my eye." And now he picks up another ring, again Victorian, also gold but this time far from delicate: black-enamelled, with a heart-shape at the front that has a flower and leaves etched on it, the leaf motif continuing on round the band, and the gold tracery, which stands out very strikingly, lightening the effect of the black.

"Oh, sweetheart, this one!" Brazen hussy; no question of Matt-oh-but-you-shouldn't-you-can't-possibly-afford-it. "This one — *please!*"

"You're sure? Try them both on. You're not being swayed by just the price?"

The enamelled ring is cheaper — though of course still closer to ten pounds than to threepence. Much closer.

It has engraving on the inside. If there'd been any doubt in my mind this would have dispelled it. 'Always, Emily and Robert. May 1, 1840.' I instantly form a picture of Emily and Robert — and who cares a jot it it's impossibly idealised? What matters is the sense of strong connection with the past. The date, the passion, the commitment. 'Always.'

The owner of the shop stays neutral. His charlady can't manage it.

"Oh, it's dismal. Would soon bring on the willies. You take the other one, my pet." She tucks a wisp of greying hair back under her beige rayon scarf as through scared too much exposure may start to turn it white.

"Is it dismal?" asks Matt, gently — not specifically of her. "Why should a mourning ring be more dismal or more spooky than any other that's antique? Obviously when any ring's that old whoever wore it first must now be dead."

Stupidly, it hadn't even occurred to me that it's a mourning ring.

"And, pet, it's much too big for you. It's really meant to be worn by a gent."

But Robert must have been slim-fingered. It is too big, admittedly, but it doesn't look ridiculous; a clip will hold it firm.

I try on the turquoise ring as well. "Ah ...," says the charlady, on a sustained and dreamy note.

I smile at her.

"It's no good. I'm sorry. You're right — this is exquisite. But it's the other that I want."

"I hoped it would be," says Matt.

I reach up and kiss him on the cheek.

"Well, anyhow, my pet, we really wish you joy of it."

"Most certainly we do. Now I wonder if I can find you a small box ..."

"I don't suppose you'd have one of those tiny clip things which my ... my fiancée mentioned just a while back?" It's the first time he's ever used that word, in connection with myself.

I wish there were something I could buy for him. A candlestick? A warming pan? A cigarette case? (Why are the two of us just about the only people I know who don't smoke?) A lighter with which to light the cigarettes of others?

Actually I'd thought about buying him something before — a thank-you gift for all his generosity; but I'd been too worried about making him feel under any kind of obligation.

This omission, however, doesn't impinge too much upon the glory of the moment. I shall mail him something; take my time and choose the really perfect gift. In the meanwhile he can have my precious stone, salvaged from the stream in which we paddled yesterday.

Mr Wilton doesn't have a clip; says we'll need to find a proper jeweller's. But in any case he recommends I shouldn't bother with a clip (it would probably cost three bob and fairly soon wear out) when for about the same price I could get the ring cut down and soldered. I say I'll act on his advice. He hasn't got a small box, either. He just wraps the ring in tissue paper — but he knocks ten shillings off the cost of it, "with all our congratulations and good wishes and as a small engagement gift."

"I hoped that bit would come in useful," Matt tells me later, with a smile.

"I don't blame you. It could also serve as a handy sort of prelude to proposal."

"But I thought we'd covered all that. How else ... the sort of plans which we've been making ... ?" He pulls into the side of the road.

"Even so it would be nice to have it actually confirmed in words."

"I'll confirm it in writing if you like."

The echo of this undertaking remains with me. Afterwards I say: "You really will write as often as you can?"

"At least six times a day."

"No, I'm being serious."

"I'll be back to get you very soon. The first minute I'm out of this crazy uniform —"

"Oh, Matt, how long ... how long do you think ... ? There's really no chance of your being sent to the Pacific?" Oh, God, I couldn't stand it if he were.

"No, none at all."

He swears he isn't humouring me.

"By gum! You can see I'm not grinning that grin of mine!" He grins.

Back on the road, a little reassured, I say, "But there's no need for you to come over to collect me. More romantic — yes; but not so practical. On my own I could probably get on a liberty ship much more easily. Even on a Constellation, maybe ... Besides, it would be cheaper."

"The money isn't really so important," he says. "You're marrying into ... But, anyway, I'll fill you in on all that boring kind of detail when I write."

Then he laughs — self-consciously. "No — what an affectation! Money isn't in the least bit boring."

Matt has to drop me at the railway station; no girlfriends would be welcome on the base — not this morning. The train is due to leave at ten: in just over an hour. The Americans will start to embark some fifteen minutes earlier.

I'd vaguely thought of wandering round the town — or more probably of taking a brief stroll outside it; my instincts are all to be alone. But of course I should have realised! The station is already filling up. There are people approaching from every direction — most of them young women. Some are carrying babies; some accompanied by mums. What even looks like whole families have come to make farewells; the Yanks have found a lot of friends in the neighbourhood and life is going to be extremely dull without them.

The station is a small one — not built for all these milling crowds. It's no kind of junction where expresses roar through to more important destinations, leaving a legacy of soot and smoke and grime. It's a place with flowerbeds and a rockery; hanging baskets, wooden benches. Fields and hedges stretching out beyond. You could refer to it as sleepy.

But not today. Today it sounds more like a football stadium before the match — or even like the Mall on V.E. Day (not yet a week ago — oh, God!) except there aren't any fireworks and there's absolutely no cheering and absolutely no singing.

There's a great resounding cry, however, when the Americans begin to arrive; and that's when the real pushing starts. If you don't catch sight of your man before he boards the train he may be lost to you forever. Women are jumping up, straining on tiptoe, standing on benches, crying out for Jack or Joe or Bill, even climbing onto one another's shoulders. Their babies, many of them bawling and red-faced, are held above their heads. One woman holds up a placard — "I love you, Rob, please marry me" — while two others, less pathetic, share a banner which reads,

"Don't forget us, lads, you're welcome back at any time."

Then I spot him — and I wave my arm like mad while calling out his name.

"I was afraid I wouldn't find you."

"Me, too," he says. "I never expected anything like this."

I cling to him. "Matt, will you slip my ring upon your finger for an instant? So I'll know that I'm wearing something which ..."

It fits him well. I see an expression cross his face which looks like a mirrored image of everything I feel myself.

"Don't, my darling," he says. "Remember, if you cry I cry. Please don't do that to me."

He hands me back the ring. An instruction comes over the loudspeaker: all airmen to get on board the train. The instruction has to be repeated. Several times.

"Oh, Christ, I haven't got a photograph!"

"Photographs!" I exclaim. It seems so ludicrous; such an improbable oversight. "I haven't got a photograph of you!"

"I'll send you one," he promises. "You send me one, as well."

I nod. I can't get out the words. But then I remember something; start to scrabble frantically inside my silly purse; not so easy in this fearful crush. All the Yanks have now embarked — though Matt is one of the lucky ones who's ended up with space beside a window. "I've got a snap that Trixie took! Just minutes before we met! She only collected it on Saturday — I meant to let you see!"

The whistle blows. I find the snap — it's caught up behind torn lining and is difficult to extricate. Like in a panic dream. The train's already moving as I thrust it in his hand. There's time for only one botched kiss before the engine picks up speed.

"There'll never be anybody else! Never! Never! Never!" I don't know if he hears.

I stand there blowing kisses — everybody does — until the heads, the hands, the waving arms, have lost all individuality. The final carriage rounds a bend. Only a plume of smoke remains.

Gradually, the people on both platforms turn away. Drift aimlessly towards the exits.

At least half of us are crying. Some of us howling.

I lean against enamelled metal on the wall — advertisement for Mazawattee — and feel first faint, then sick.

It's there that Trixie finds me.

"I never said goodbye to Walt," I tell her, tonelessly.

We walk a short way from the station. By now the crowds have practically dispersed. "Oh, Trixie, isn't this awful!" We hold each other's hand; the tears are pouring down our faces.

We go and have a cup of tea — no, several cups of tea. But every time we think we've got ourselves under control a fresh bout of sobbing starts. The waitress stares at us indifferently.

Trixie gets the giggles; they're close to being hysteria. "Look at the two of us sitting here in our posh dresses and laddered nylons. And both with these soppy little evening bags. No wonder that the fat cow stares!"

Our own train leaves in about an hour. While we're waiting for it — not wanting to return to the station before we have to — we search somewhat listlessly for a jeweller's. But I've decided to ignore Mr Wilton's advice; I don't trust the soldering not to damage the inscription.

Besides. It would no longer be totally the same ring which Matt had handled and then worn.

Moreover, I might need to leave it and have it posted back to me. I couldn't do that. I want to wear it immediately.

Immediately — and forever.

A clip will be just fine.

17

Herb Kramer is impressed — as he damned well ought to be. With so much information on my father, and even a photograph, he's confident he'll soon have news. "And didn't we just prophesy you came from that part of the world?" Again he escorts us to the door.

We pause a minute on the sidewalk. "Half-past-one," Tom says. "Time to feed the inner man."

But, no, I tell him, I'd rather be getting things over with.

"Then why don't I come with you?"

"No point."

He hesitates. "All right. So don't forget: Central Line to Tottenham Court Road — Northern Line from there to Hampstead."

He directs me to the nearest tube; the car is parked the other way, maybe half a mile from where we stand.

"Good luck, Tex. I reckon I'll stay at the office till around seven."

When I've crossed the road I glance back. Tom raises his hand; smiles. "And don't forget you haven't eaten!" Old fuss-budget ... I don't know, I guess I feel this huge affection for the guy ... I buy myself a sandwich at Bond Street, yet have to hold back after just one bite from simply binning it.

I get to Hampstead some thirty minutes later; ask at least six times for Worsley Road. One old man with outsized Adam's apple scratches his head and keeps on telling me, "That sounds familiar, son ... now if only I could put my finger on it ... where was it you said?" There's a post office nearby but I'd maybe have to stand in line ten minutes. In a bookstore I ask to look at street guides. A Worsley Road is listed in E11 and a Worsley Bridge Road in SE26. Worsley Road in NW3 just doesn't exist.

Not in the early nineties, that is; but it sure as hell existed in the mid-forties. I need to check at the town hall.

Going there I pass a police station. The desk sergeant is about fifty. He remembers that Worsley Road is now called

Pilgrim's Lane although it used to be a continuation of it. It's reasonably close by.

I walk the length of Pilgrim's Lane; feel a spurt of satisfaction on seeing faint remnants of the *ley*: an altered street sign at the further end. House numbers have been changed. But in her first letter to Trixie, Rosalind had spoken of a bomb site being next door. There's only one three-storey house adjacent to something that's comparatively modern. I walk slowly up the front steps; scan the names beside a row of bells; choose for starters the apartment on the lowest floor.

I realise, of course, that at 2.30pm on a Monday the whole house is likely to be empty. But I wait for maybe thirty seconds — am about to apply my finger to the next bell up — when I hear the opening of an inside door and then find an old lady eyeing me with interest through a chain-restricted aperture.

"If you're a Jehovah's Witness or a Mormon ... if you're selling double glazing or encyclopedias ... I'm sorry but the answer's no."

"Nothing like that, ma'am. I'm trying to trace somebody who lived in this house immediately after the war."

"I lived in this house immediately after the war."

"You did?"

"Immediately before it too. Which war are we talking of: the first or the second?"

"The second one, ma'am."

She's quick, though. She sees my disappointment. "No, I haven't gone senile, young man. I'm almost ninety years of age and I have a memory just as sharp as yours. I was born in this house — I was married from this house — and God willing I shall die in it, too. I think you'd better come in."

She conducts me to her sitting room: the first door on the left off the hallway. She looks trim in a black pants-suit, green rollneck and red sneakers. She moves with agility.

"Put Henry on the floor," she says. It's a choice between that or disposing of two leaning piles of books which occupy another chair. "I trust you aren't allergic to these things?"

"No, ma'am. On the whole I'd say I like them."

"I approve of your reservation. To say you like cats would be as foolish as to say you like children — or people. Some cats have characters that just aren't likable. And I apologise for the smell. Who is it that you're trying to trace?"

"A young woman called Rosalind Farr. Well, at the time we're speaking of she was a young woman."

"And a very lovely one."

"What?"

She smiles at me, enjoying my surprise. "I told you: I've lived here, on and off, for nearly ninety years."

"But I can't believe that it should be so easy." It doesn't seem quite real.

And yet there's nothing unreal about *her*: this amazing old lady whose pants-suit is covered in cats' hairs and whose anklets and underclothes — along with a blouse and a night robe and some dishtowels — are airing in front of an unlit and antiquated gas fire. "Yes, I remember her vividly. And it wasn't just the niceness of the creature; it was the circumstances which attended her stay here. May I ask the reason for your interest?"

"She was a friend of my father's."

"Your father?" She stares at me intently; stops stroking the large gingery animal in her lap. "And by any chance then ... can your name be Cassidy?"

For a moment I stare back at her. "But how ... ? How on earth ...?"

"Mine by the way is Farnsworth. Jane Farnsworth. It's just that you're American and your father was a figure of some importance in Rosalind's life. So for as long as I retain my faculties it's not a name I'm very likely to forget. Matthew Cassidy."

"That's it, ma'am. Matthew — or Matt — Cassidy."

"Alias the sod."

I can't believe I've heard her right.

"Excuse me, ma'am?"

"Young man. Don't say that I've managed to shock you! How much has your father ever told you about Rosalind?"

"Not a great deal," I reply — carefully. "But at the same time ..." The thing is, I don't want to put him in a worse light than I have to, and speaking about the baby and possible desertion may not even turn out to be necessary. I suppose I could just tell her the truth regarding the condition I'm now in but I feel reluctant to sidetrack her. In any case, my answer seems to do.

She gets to her feet, puts the cat back in the chair, offers me a drink.

"A cup of tea if you want it; but we could always pretend the sun is over the yardarm. At this stage in my career I'm seldom short of a drop of gin."

"That would be great," I say.

"Well, at least I see he taught you manners." (I guess she's referring to the fact I've also risen.) "Or perhaps it was your mother. Would you like to be the barman? You'll find all you need in that cupboard over there — except the ice. Oh, and you Americans are always so mad-keen about the ice!"

"Not me, ma'am. Bad for the digestion. Never touch the stuff."

"May God forgive you. And I don't mean for the lie; I mean for being a nauseating charmer like your father ... And don't be stingy with that gin or *I* won't forgive you — far more to the point. You can be as stingy as you like with the tonic."

While I fix the drinks (trying to ignore the smeary appearance of both tumblers) Mrs Farnsworth moves across to a glass-fronted cabinet in one corner, full of porcelain and knickknacks, and flanked by two tall plants in saucers on the floor. "Here's something which I think might interest you."

I can't see what it is but when I've put the glass into one hand she stretches out the other and uncurls her swollen and arthritic fingers.

I let out a startled exclamation.

In her palm lies a black-enamelled ring.

"Then evidently this is something which he did tell you

about?" Yes. Evidently. My memory — albeit in fits and starts — is unquestionably returning.

"But why so shaken?" she asks, with china doll eyes, wide and blue and scarcely even faded.

"I'm not quite sure, ma'am. Disappointment?"

"Disappointment? And at what, may one inquire?"

"That finally it meant so little to her."

"Oh, stuff! Your father jilted her, of course."

Her hand is still held out to me; she now extends it further. She repeats: "I thought you might be interested." I have to steel myself to take the object from her.

"It's a mourning ring, isn't it?" 'Always, Emily and Robert. May 1, 1840.' Somehow I'd foreseen that I'd find an inscription.

She sips her drink and goes back to her chair. Even with just the one hand she picks up the cat so deftly I barely have time to think about assisting her.

"Do you know something?" Reflectively, she holds up her tumbler to the light. "The very first occasion I saw Rosalind. It could have been out of this selfsame glass — out of these selfsame glasses — we drank our gin and tonic then."

She laughs; adds some comment about how rarely she ever breaks things, despite the clutter she unfailingly creates around her. But although I hear her voice I gradually lose track of what it is she's saying. She's left me in possession of the ring.

I return to my chair, nearly falling over Henry, the disposed and wheezing, still contented tabby, set my glass beside me on the floor and place the ring upon my finger. I do this impulsively. The fit seems well-nigh perfect.

"Then surely it must have been too loose for her?"

But did I actually say that or just think it? Suddenly I feel confused. I don't know where I am.

Not only where I am but who I am.

I tell myself I mustn't panic.

This isn't going to last, I say. In a minute you'll remember.

Just try to concentrate.

You're in a room. There's a voice. A woman's voice.
Talking about ice.

Ice?

I make a real effort. I do concentrate. I struggle.

I whisper to myself:

"Rosalind ... ?"

Then I try it again but this time there's a lot more
strength behind it. It's almost like a shout.

A shout of recognition.

"Rosalind ...!"

18

"I'm sorry? What was that?" My mind had wandered for
a moment; suddenly I'd thought I heard my name being
called — but from a distance. Maybe it was a father, or a
brother, summoning home one of those girls who'd been
bouncing a rubber ball against the side wall of the house
(there's a gap, caused by bomb damage). As I came along
they'd been chanting tirelessly, in time to every bounce,
"Deanna — Durbin — wore a — turban — of red — and
white — and blue." But it would be quite some coincidence
if one of the girls happened to be called Rosalind. I must've
imagined it.

"Only that if I had a fridge," she repeats, "I could offer
you some ice. But I haven't; so I can't. And who needs ice.
anyway?"

She passes me my gin.

"Thank you. What a treat!"

"Question of priorities," she says. "And contacts."

From her appearance you'd never suppose she had that
kind of contact; nor, indeed, that kind of priority. Although
she must be in her middle forties she looks too delicate; too

261

childlike. It's only her voice — a bit gravelly — which somehow prepares you for this more vigorous note.

Certainly the kitten doesn't. Under one arm she carries a Siamese. Sometimes, when she's dispensing gin or lighting cigarettes for instance, he climbs up on her shoulder. "Can you believe it? I thought I didn't like cats! But then along came Rex." Often she raises one of his front paws to place a quick kiss on its pad.

"Cheers! And to the length and happiness of your stay here!"

"Cheers! Thank you." Rex watches with interest the death throes of a bluebottle trapped on the flypaper above; his hind legs are planted in her lap. "But, Mrs Farnsworth, I don't want to mislead you. I'm not really sure how long —"

"Not Mrs Farnsworth. Jane."

"Rosalind."

"Ah. 'From the east to western Ind, there is no jewel like Rosalind ...'" A misquote but she recites it with a flourish; although when she waves her tumbler she has the sense to do it carefully. "Well, anyway, at least we can drink to the *happiness* of your stay here."

"There is one other thing," I remark, slowly. I'd been hoping for a few more sips of the gin before I had to bring it up; but I suppose if I'd been strictly honourable I'd have broached it before accepting the gin in the first place. This is the one point on which I don't ever intend to be even remotely underhand. "You see ... well, the fact is ..." I laugh. This is ridiculous. "The fact is: well, I'm pregnant."

"My congratulations." Although I've taken off my gloves and she's admired my black Victorian ring it's possibly escaped her notice that I'm not wearing any other. "When's the baby due?"

"In February — early February."

"About five-and-a-half months." She extracts a further cigarette from the open packet of Passing Cloud on the arm of her chair. "But these days, with the housing shortage, it takes a long time, you know, to get settled. You mustn't

262

worry that anybody here will mind having a baby on the premises."

Tactfully, she doesn't ask about a husband. "You're very kind," I say, "but before it's born I hope to have joined his father in the States. Matt's an American, you see."

Soon afterwards my landlady conducts me upstairs. The journey may inspire some reservations — a passing glance at the lavatory and bathroom proves a bit depressing and the stair-carpet could do with a good brush — but the room itself isn't bad. I've been lucky. I came to Hampstead on the merest whim. But when I'd started walking down the hill I saw a board on which this room was advertised; the only room on it and at just thirty-five shillings a week. The newsagent told me that he'd put the card there less than forty-five minutes earlier.

So after Jane leaves me I stretch out on the divan, doing nothing much but count my blessings. Then eventually I get up to inspect drawer linings, wardrobe space, number of hangers provided, exciting things like that — unpack my suitcases. This done, I carry the rickety table from the centre of the room, set it under the window and bring across a chair. Later I shall go out to explore a bit, start to stock up; maybe buy myself some flowers. But for the moment I want to finish the letter which I began this morning on the train.

To Matt, of course.

I haven't told him yet about the baby. For one thing, I have only just found out myself — well, had my suspicions officially confirmed. (Suspicions? Certainties.) Partly, maybe, I feel a little nervous; my own initial reaction — already a good two months ago — wasn't by any means unmixed. And obviously I want to do it in the right way, not just throw it at him. But today the first priority is to send my new address. Maybe I'll give it some more thought after I've got this current letter posted. I feel it's never too soon to start upon the next.

I wish he felt the same. But with the best will in the world some people are simply lousy correspondents. At least six times a day, indeed! Did I hear that right, Lootenant?

263

I must write to Amy, too, to let her know I'm settled and apologise for being peevish — I'd been so hoping to have another letter before I left; also, of course, I want to tell her where I am in case there's anything to send on (pray God). My peevishness found outlet in something of a diatribe over the raw deal we land girls have received from the government. It's particularly unfair when compared to the way the women in the armed forces are being treated. People like Trixie and me have been demobbed with practically nothing. You should have heard Trixie going on about it a few days back — while cheerful philosophic me was shrugging it off in a way that must have been infuriating! Poor Trixie. I must write to her, as well. She's now working in a restaurant run by an aunt of hers in Norwich.

But what letters I do receive from Matt are ... well, this goes without saying ... delightful. Quantity — no; quality — and how! Yet I wish he'd get a move on. I'd like to know what arrangements for my transport he considers best. The other day there was a demonstration outside the London hotel where Mrs Roosevelt is staying. U.S war brides who'd marched there to petition her had paraded up and down carrying their babies — a mute proclamation (not so mute) more eloquent than the traditional type of placard: "We want our daddies!" I envied them the opportunity of being able to do even that much.

I suck the top of my mottled pen cap. Nextdoor the girls are still playing on the bomb site but have now combined with a gang of boys to play tag. I start another paragraph. "I'm sitting by the window, which overlooks a strip of horribly neglected garden. Tomorrow I'd probably be out there furtively digging this up for vegetables if I didn't have to be out finding myself a job instead. Something totally frivolous and undemanding. I shall ask to spend my days just spinning daydreams (All I do, the whole day through, is dream of you) and thinking up excuses to work you into every conversation and patiently waiting for the photograph which I'm beginning to think you *never* mean to send (!!) ...."

*

"In the whole course of my life I've never written to anyone so frequently as this — and as I can't guarantee to keep it up (particularly with so signal a lack of response!) just make the most of it, my darling, while you have the opportunity. On a bus this morning I actually heard some fellow say to his mate there's no such thing as love — only lust — and you can imagine how superior and pitying I felt as I sat there straining to hear more ... I was on the bus en route to find that job I spoke about yesterday — and find it I most incredibly did. You remember Oxford Street, the bit of it between Tottenham Court Road and Oxford Circus which we mistakenly drove along with Walt and Trix when we first got to London? Well, there's a large store there called Bourne & Hollingsworth which just so happened to have a vacancy for a smart girl like me in its perfumery department. I wrote of course that I would go for something frivolous — yet little did I know how splendidly I prophesied! From muck-raking to attar of roses in one fell swoop! Can anybody stop this girl? I start on Monday. The money isn't much but neither thankfully is the rent I'm paying here and the members of the staff I met today all seem extremely pleasant. What's more there are the perks of the trade — perhaps from now on these *billets doux* will be discreetly scented. What about your own *billets doux* — although I don't insist they be discreetly scented? Already, even if I know it doesn't make sense, I look wistfully at the table in the hall each time I pass and half-expect a miracle. I know what will happen the moment I see an airmail envelope addressed to me — my pulse will start to race as though you'd just walked through the door, my throat will go all dry, I think I'll even begin to get these symptoms as I leave my room each morning and start running down the stairs ...."

*

265

I still haven't told him about the baby. What is it I think? That for some reason he'll be so upset he won't want anything more to do with me?

Oh, yes. Sure thing. That's my Matt.

That's the boy I fell in love with.

19

The next day there could be something for me. If a letter had been waiting at the farm Amy would have readdressed it at once.

Nothing in the first post.

There's always the second, though.

And the final one — mid-afternoon.

But if it doesn't come by then it may not come for ages. Matt knew the date when I'd be leaving Suffolk; he also knows how long a letter takes to get to England. Well — roughly. So if I don't hear today it must mean he's waiting for my new address — which he won't receive until next Monday at the very earliest. Oh God; dear God.

So my first full day of exploration is marred by constant fretting — although it's a good day by and large and I keep having bursts of sanity when I realise how I'm getting worked up over nothing: one tardy letter in the context of a whole life? And possibly, too, he'll turn out to be blameless: mail can get held up even in peacetime; I suppose it can get lost as well — which would be upsetting, of course, but scarcely a tragedy. And Hampstead with its intimate, Bohemian atmosphere, its network of irregular back streets, its charm and history and interesting shop windows (yes, even now); not to mention its acres and acres of rolling, wooded countryside; Hampstead is enough to offer consolation.

Or anyway — distraction.

Nevertheless, when I return to Worsley Road and find that the hall table holds nothing for me, I put in a trunk call to the farm.

And after Amy's surprised, enthusiastic greeting I explain I thought she'd like to know about my job. "And how are Fred and the children? And is everybody missing me most dreadfully?" But what I really want to hear, of course, is something very different. *Oh, by the way, Roz, Matt's letter has arrived.*

When it seems there's nothing left to say I ask if there's been any mail.

Before I phoned I told myself I'd rather have certainty than suspense. Now I wish I'd stayed with the suspense.

After a supper of Welsh rabbit, a meal I generally enjoy but this evening find hard to finish (and even getting down my sweet and sticky orange juice seems difficult), I decide to make another call.

"Oh, hello, my darling." Thank God, it's usually my mother who answers; if not, I just put down the phone. "I'd been hoping you might ring."

"You'll get a letter in the morning. But having told you all my news in that" (Dearest Mummy, your daughter's pregnant ...) "I suddenly thought wouldn't it be nice if we could spend the day together ... I mean tomorrow, because I've found a job that starts on Monday. I've got a room near Hampstead Heath, so if I meet the train at Finchley Road ..."

"Oh, my sweetheart, I'd love to. But this weekend — it's really such short notice ..."

I suggest that, even if he can't manage for himself, she could surely leave him a sandwich, or something cold, or something he could warm up.

"No, darling, it isn't that. Truth be told, I'm feeling a bit tired and you mustn't be offended but ..."

I'm not offended. Just disappointed. And sulky. (Even though it's probably better she should have the time to assimilate my bombshell.) She asks about my job — and the

267

room — but doesn't want me, she says, just to repeat what I've written and make the phone call needlessly expensive. "Anyway, the main thing is you're well. And Matthew? How are things with him?"

"God knows. Not heard a word. I feel cross."

"Oh, please don't, my darling. I remember when your father and I were engaged and then he suddenly had to go away. Only for a month, but I wrote him fifteen letters, would you believe! I got just four in return. There was nearly a divorce before there was a marriage."

I laugh and find it helpful being reminded. But even so my moodiness persists; I mention very pettishly that he hasn't even thanked me for a silver hip flask which I sent; I recognise I too am tired. (Besides, I'm pregnant; pregnant women are allowed to be a little difficult.) Earlier in the day I'd been planning to spend my evening telling him about the baby. But now I think — well, no, I don't feel like it. Four letters in exchange for fifteen still seems about the going rate. So maybe two can play at that game, Mr Cassidy. Two can start to agitate and wonder.

It's a decision which I fairly soon regret. Of course it's not in any way binding and yet I discover that I'm obstinate. I make a compromise: I'll go on writing but won't actually post what I write until I have received his next letter.

I write about five sides a day; my letter reaches thirty — forty — fifty — sides. But then my average starts to fall. Dramatically. By then it's hard retaining even a semblance of good cheer.

And every morning, yes ... the closing of my door, the running downstairs, the sifting through the pile on the hall table, the philosophic shrug. Continual disappointment; continual slowing of that optimistic heartbeat. The same thing every evening. Over the weeks, disappointment turning to deep anger — to disbelief — to desperation.

My attitude at work begins to change. At first my job enabled me to think of other things; to chat with colleagues, learn about the stock, try to be of service to my customers.

But women who are buying perfume — and, even more, men who are buying it for them — are usually in a carefree mood. They haven't heard about austerity. You see a lot of adoration.

One morning I set out as normal, having largely given up on hope, when suddenly I spot an envelope like the ones Matt used to send. I give an excited exclamation, rush forward — and find it's from Australia. A convulsive sob bursts out of me, just as Jane, in dressing gown and carrying Rex, emerges from her bedroom.

"Oh, Rosalind, my dear, whatever's the matter?"

"Nothing. Just late. Must dash. Goodbye."

"Look in again one evening and have a little drink. I'd enjoy that."

"Yes — all right." At present I only want escape.

What follows is a time of nightmare. It's the day I finally face up to things. I say to myself: He isn't going to write again. He's going to marry Marjorie.

But hasn't got the guts to tell me.

Or maybe not the callousness; the cruelty. He knows I'll get the message. It could be less upsetting. Perhaps that's how he figures it.

In any case it's over. I shall never see him again.

The whole day has a weird feeling of unbalance. Nothing seems quite real; I observe things at a distance, hear even my own voice as though it comes from someone else's mouth. (You'd think that this might dull the pain.) Reality is only restored, briefly, when the afternoon culminates in a dropped bottle of scent, glass shattering as it hits the ground about my feet. After that I faint. Thank God at least I don't throw up.

*

"Four ounces of *My Sin*. I felt it slip; it happened in slow motion. We'll reek of it for weeks."

"But did they make you pay?"

"No, they're very good about those things."

"Well, you've been there for two months. They must know by now you're not cack-handed." The inevitable fumbling for a fresh cigarette. "Why were you crying that morning when you left?"

"I wasn't crying. I was only —"

"And you don't look half so bonny as you did. I know I'm being inquisitive again ... but has something happened? Between you and Matt, I mean?"

I hesitate — and shrug — and force a smile.

"I suppose you could say so. Something? Nothing? Either would be accurate."

"And?"

"And ...? And it's all over."

She pauses. "And you sure?"

"Yes, I'm sure."

"Then he's a fool. Here — let me fill your glass. And you'll be better off without him." I've never asked about her ex- ; wonder suddenly if she's going to speak about him now . "But does the bastard know you're pregnant?"

She's aware, however, this isn't a good line to pursue. I refuse to become one of those girls a man feels it's incumbent upon him to save.

So she contents herself with remarking that at least she sees I now wear a wedding ring.

"Oh, well," I say. "Life's always full of compromise."

My tone encourages her. "Anyhow, who wants a man ... when they can have a dear sweet precious pussycat? Isn't that right, my pretty little darling? What went wrong?" she asks, seeing me smile.

"Oh ... It was just like some holiday romance. At first I thought that it was more."

"More? My perfect dream: one holiday romance per year. From which you'd run like mad if it threatened to get serious."

"Well, anyway — as I think I told you last time — I realised from the start he was engaged. So by letting me down (if you want to call it that; I'm not sure if I do) at least he hasn't let down the girl who had the earlier claim.

You have to give him that."

"No. I have to give him nothing. You mustn't be a nauseating saint."

"Oh, I didn't say I don't resent her. And I resent the fact it was Matt's brother whom she loved — I mean, if she loved anyone. Her transfer to Matt seemed just a matter of convenience. That's what really gets me down. I promise you I'm not a saint."

"Still, love, it isn't just her, is it? It's —"

"Anyway, let's leave it, shall we? I swear to you I'm over him."

Her look is plainly sceptical but at least she doesn't challenge me. "You may not believe this," she says, "but in the end you'll find it's far better to be self-reliant."

A little to her surprise I acquiesce. "Looking back I hate the way that everything I felt depended so entirely on one person."

"Let's drink a toast, then." She smiles. "Confusion to the fellow! He had no right to make you look so peaky."

I also raise my glass. "And may he think about me now and then and experience a short instant of regret! I wouldn't wish him more than that — just the occasional pang."

But Jane gives a gasp of annoyance.

"Sweet Lord. Let me interpret. What was his second name?"

"Cassidy."

She lifts her glass again; pauses, to indicate that here is the really serious toast, the truly definitive version.

"Sod Matthew Cassidy!" she says.

20

That's all very well but as I stand looking from the window of my room I think, Sod you? — no, not quite. And is it really true I'm over you?

But all the same. I'm certainly not going to mourn you — not any longer. We'll make out. Tom and I. And in a way it'll be a comfort just to know that somewhere over there you're still around; it isn't quite as though you're dead. But I only wish I had a photograph; I'm afraid that I'll forget your face. And a faceless blur would not be of much comfort.

Oh ... who needs comfort, anyway? Go to hell. We'll be okay. We'll be okay — won't we, Thomas? The human race hasn't survived this long just feeling sorry for itself. Agreed, my love?

I often talk to him like this. I don't mean Matt; I mean to the baby inside me — the baby who sometimes kicks quite hard now and who is very much a presence; at five months I've become gratifyingly large. I'm aware that perhaps it's not so different to Jane and her Siamese cat but already I see him as a confidant, a boon companion.

The following Sunday, for instance, I'm on Hampstead Heath, sitting on a bench watching a young woman go past with a pram. An older woman who is almost certainly her mother is walking alongside. I fold my hands complacently across my stomach.

"This time next year, my darling, that could be us: you and me and your gran. Your gran is going to be so proud. She's already knitted you some blankets. So from the start, my lad, only the very best. And definitely no stigma. People will say, 'There goes that smashing boy Tom Cassidy; pity he never knew his dad — who died in the Pacific.'" (I'd told my colleagues I'd reverted to my maiden name and taken off my wedding ring simply because I couldn't bear to talk about it; luckily, even during my earliest days, despite the poetic licence of that letter, I'd hugged Matt to myself.) "It's a shame, Tom, but it isn't the end of the world. Especially not when you remember this. A boy's best friend is always his mother."

The two women with the pram pass my bench on their way back; the older woman smiles at me.

"Just like a girl's is."

*

A girl's best friend is her mother ... As a child, the churchyard in Chesham was always one of my favourite haunts. Not only was it pretty — and peaceful — and private, but I liked the old man who tended the graves, and the flowers that people left on them, and above all the names and the dates and the inscriptions. It was a place where I used to read my Violet Needhams and Daphne du Mauriers, find sunshine and security, set off on wild adventures ... from the age of, say, nine or ten until the time my father died ... when following his funeral I never wanted to return. But now on this cold and grey November afternoon more than a decade later it isn't my father who is chiefly in my thoughts — though he is certainly there and at one point I remember him, on the evenings when I met him from the train, hurrying forward with his warm and eager grin, dropping his briefcase on the platform and lifting me high and then tossing me yet higher. When we got home his greeting to his wife was more sedate but just as loving. "Hello, my Sylvia ..." I can still catch that precise inflection. "Hello, my Duncan," she would say.

"Rosalind, your mother was one of the kindest people I ever met." Mrs Morley walks beside me as we leave the graveyard.

"Yes. Thank you."

"And how pleased she must have been to know that she was going to have a grandchild."

"Yes."

"If it's a little girl will you be naming it after her?"

"Yes." I can only bring myself to speak in monosyllables. My handkerchief is crumpled in my hand.

273

Her husband — I mean my mother's — moves up purposefully to join us. After a moment, to my dismay, Mrs Morley, believing she's being tactful, wanders off to leave the two of us together.

He's tall and rangy, with a severe, not unattractive, face. "Well, then, I've been hoping to get you on your own. Perhaps now your mother's gone we could try to be friends again, Roz. Like we were in the beginning."

No; we were never friends.

"I can appreciate you should have been upset about it at the time — about that little incident when I'd been drinking more than was good for me and I didn't know what I was doing. But it was all such a terrible misunderstanding. Why not come back where you belong and make a home here for your nipper?"

I simply turn and walk away from him. I don't go back to the tea which a couple of neighbours have very kindly organised. I plead misery as my excuse and the two elderly ladies accept it with compassion. I couldn't endure having to listen to more sympathetic platitudes or further fond remembrances. The dusty carriages and the anonymity of the Metropolitan are the only familiar things I feel that I can cope with.

The last time I saw my mother I had been with Matt.

"Goodbye, Matthew. This has been such a pleasure. God bless you. Good luck."

I picture her standing on the pavement outside the Astoria.

"Goodbye, Rosalind. Goodbye, my darlings. You're going to be so late. But no — it doesn't matter if you're late — just as long as you get there in the end. Take care," she says.

*

Four weeks later Christmas comes. I am glad that none of my memories of Christmas with my mother is of very recent date.

Jane and I spend much of Boxing Day in doing up my

room.

"This was the nicest present you could possibly have given me."

"No," she says, "it needed doing anyway. It was a cheating sort of present." Even while she's on her knees and painting the skirting board, eyes half closed against the constant spiral of tobacco smoke, Rex is draped like a fox fur round her shoulders.

"I wish everyone could cheat on me so gracefully. You've made my Christmas happier than I could ever have believed." (For it had hardly augured well, a few days back, when Congress had finally passed an act on behalf of the alien spouses of U.S. servicemen — expediting their admission into America.) "Thomas is going to love all this," I say, looking at the wallpaper rolls which we'd dashed out to buy, almost on impulse, late on Christmas Eve.

"I sincerely hope so," she replies. "But, my dear, I'm sure it isn't wise to keep on calling him Thomas. What problems ... if Thomas should turn out to be Thomasina!"

"Oh, Jane — he wouldn't dare!"

"That's precisely what I mean."

I laugh at the way she rises to my bait. "No, please don't worry. I would love Thomasina just as much. It's only that I somehow know ..."

"I wish you'd write and tell the father."

"The sod? Can we be talking of the sod?" Today it is I who have provided the gin — though, for the sake of the baby, I am extremely careful to limit my intake.

"The sod has money and he ought to pay."

"But I don't want any part of his money. I don't want his money nor his pity. If I can't have his love — and obviously I can't — the only part of him I want is Tom."

"Pooh! You sound like the heroine of *Back Street* or some Bette Davis weepy. I can see there's nothing for it but just to put my shirt on karma."

It takes me a little while to work this out. "You're talking of reincarnation?"

"And retribution. In his next life he'll experience all the

275

wretchedness he's brought to you in this."

I smile. "Oh, but have you *thought*? What if the buck stops here?"

"Meaning?"

"That in my last existence I might have been the man. That this is the justice I deserve — not Matt."

"Huh!"

The room is finished by New Year — apart from some curtains I am having made and the carpet I'm still looking for. Also I intend to buy one or two pieces of good furniture to replace some of the more shoddy items — nothing to do with Jane, all these expensive acquisitions, but since I've heard from the solicitors that my mother's left me over a thousand pounds I feel I can afford to be a bit extravagant. Eventually I shall move out of Worsley Road and rent a self-contained flat — and the antique rocking chair and Queen Anne chest of drawers, the carpet and the standard lamp, possibly the curtains too, will naturally come with me. This knowledge of the amount of my legacy relieves me of a lot of worry: apart from anything else, it will see me comfortably through the period when I'm having Tom and give me several months at home before I need to find a woman to look after him. (And talking of the will, I don't know how usual this is but I've instructed the solicitors to go to the flat themselves to obtain the pieces of jewellery and other keepsakes so carefully enumerated. Also the knitting.) Bless my mother, whom I was too self-absorbed to realise was even really ill, let alone dying.

My baby is born at noon on the tenth of February 1946; my waters burst at night, after a day of fairly frenzied activity — of giving not simply my bed-sitter but the bathroom and the lavatory and stairs, the landing and the hall and even the front steps, a very thorough clean. People had said that because he was my first he could easily come late. But in fact he arrives pretty much on time.

Yes.

He.

Thomas.

Blond hair and blue eyes just like his daddy. Seven pounds three ounces. I only wish my mother could have seen him.

No, that's not the only thing I wish, of course. I have to keep suppressing thoughts of ... where he might have been born ... and of the different set of circumstances under which he'd then have made his entry into this world ... and of the different set of visitors who would have been coming to see us in the hospital. (But here in Hampstead I have Jane, and the young Australian couple from the floor above me, and some of the girls from Bourne & Hollingsworth, and the curate from Downshire Hill, and they're all of them so kind.) And it's funny to think how, even in those far-off and unfamiliar surroundings, with a different home and nationality and future, Tom would have been exactly this same baby, this identical selfsame baby.

And his mother couldn't have been any prouder of him in America than she is right here in England.

On March 5th I write to Trixie.

" ... so, Trixie, believe me, he really is beautiful — and not just in his looks either. But I won't go on. Let me simply state that Thomas Duncan Cassidy is probably the best baby on earth, just about the most wonderful thing that ever happened to me, and then I'll take mercy on you and shut up for the time being. I return to work in May. When that happens Jane will look after him during the day. There's nobody I'd trust him to more willingly but what if I miss the moment when he starts to crawl or says his first word or pulls off some other equally momentous coup? He looked so pleased with himself this morning when he merely sneezed — a bit surprised for a second but then quite shamelessly proud. I hate to think of everything like this I'm going to lose. But I suppose one has to work — though bother — what a nuisance — why? Before I do go back, however, what about that visit I suggested? At the moment there's an empty room in the house — this would be a good time. Surely your aunt would let you get away. We could moan to our hearts' content about men in general and

American men in particular and of course I'm dying for you to see Tom — though naturally he won't be at his best and I shall never stop telling you how if you'd only come just one week earlier ... So you can see I have lots of jolly treats in store for you. No — seriously. Jane says she can babysit whenever we want to get away — films, shows, shopping, anything. It will be wonderful to see you and we'll have tremendous fun — just make it soon. In the meantime much love and look after yourself, God bless you, Roz."

*

Still no word from Trixie. I wonder if I was clumsy, appearing to gloat a bit over Tommy. Walt's gone and poor Trix may feel she hasn't got a thing.

In any case it doesn't seem she's going to come.

Today Tom and I, we'll take our walk up Rosslyn Hill, stroll as far as the Everyman, look at the stills of whatever picture they've got showing. I don't need any groceries. It's a nice morning: the children playing hopscotch on the pavement, an errand boy whistling as he cycles into Pilgrim's Lane, the delivery man from Pitt's Stores, the shop at which I'm registered, waving to me cheerfully as he passes in his van ... they all add somehow to an atmosphere of holiday — I could almost believe there might be sea just over the rise at the end of one of these peaceful sunlit streets and tell myself that if I meet an ice-cream vendor I might indeed stop him and buy one. I really shan't want to go back to work in four weeks' time — just as the summer is properly getting under way and we could be spending long lazy days on the Heath, with lots of reading for me and lots of kicking and crawling for Tom.

But Trixie? Is there nothing I can do to make things right?

After we've passed a stationer's on Rosslyn Hill it occurs to me at least I could send her a postcard. There's a revolving stand outside the shop and so we turn back and I know that it's ridiculous but as I take each card from the rack I hold it out above the pram. "Now which do you think she'd prefer: a picture of Keats' house, or Kenwood, or the Old Bull and Bush, or Jack Straw's Castle ...?" (I've already told him that when Trixie comes she and I are bound to spend some evenings in the pub. "It's great fun, sweetheart, with everyone standing round the piano and belting out the old songs ... some of the new ones too ... 'Let him go, let him tarry, let him sink or let him swim; he doesn't care for me, nor I don't care for him ...'" Well, Tom's certainly heard that particular one before!) There are some maybe who'd think me crazy carrying on to a mere nine-week-old like this and obviously I must soon rid myself of the habit because later on I shan't want to embarrass him, nor treat him as a little adult, nor appear in the role of the possessive mum seeking to live at secondhand through her overburdened child. But just for the moment, I tell myself ...

Anyway, there's a fellow who comes up to me who clearly doesn't regard me as at all crazy: a sergeant major who's carrying a cheap brown suitcase so carelessly packed that ends of clothing are escaping from under its lid. But it's really the size of his Adam's apple that almost mesmerises me and I just pray he hasn't seen my fascination. The road he wants is somewhere nearby; it sounds familiar but if only I could put my finger on it, I tell him, smiling. I point in the direction where I have a feeling it may be. As I do so I notice that I've still got a postcard in the other hand. But if both my hands are in front of me then neither of them is holding onto the pram. Nor, it further strikes me in a moment of heartstopping clarity, have I yet put on the brake. I whirl around. I see the pram careening down the hill. Down the hill and off the pavement and into the road.

My own scream mingles with the scream of tyres.

21

Forty-four years ago — and yet the echo of that scream reverberates. The old lady stares at me. She looks appalled. Have I gone as pale as she has?

It feels like months since I first came here.

To Worsley Road.

"Forgive me, ma'am," I try to say. "I'm sorry."

It seems the cry just now had come from me.

"I shouldn't have told you," she says.

But she hasn't told me.

Not more than just an outline.

The rest I knew.

"Even for myself," she says, "it seemed to be the end of everything." She pauses for a moment, looking into the future as it might have been. "Tom would have been forty-four by now ... And he was going to be my godson."

"What?"

"I think perhaps you ought to leave." She pushes the startled feline off her lap and rises unsteadily. "I'm sorry. We've both been very much upset. Just give me back the ring and ..."

Ah, yes, the ring. I hold up my hand and stare blankly at the ring. She takes it off my unresisting finger.

"I should never have told you," she repeats.

Her voice, which earlier had struck me as quite deep, almost gravelly, now seems thinner. My God — but how she's aged! I remember how she painted and wallpapered and stood on stepladders and shifted furniture and helped me to unroll my carpet ...

But no. I am still ... Well, evidently I am still very much confused.

I remember seeing a movie with Rick. I remember not only the movie; I remember where we saw it. At a movie house in Hartford ... I remember how the woman had changed in that — grown old and wizened, from having been so young and beautiful — just in the space of several seconds.

It seems that with every minute my past grows more complete. It seems I simply have to summon up the energy; cast off this awful weight of deadness. That's all it requires to make the final breakthrough.

"Perhaps you could come back some other day ... ?"

I still gaze at her in only partial understanding.

"I was saying: I think it's time for you to leave." She tries to urge me to my feet by pulling at my shoulder.

In doing so, she drops the ring.

I pick it up for her; rise slowly from my chair. My limbs feel leaden. "Why did she give it you?"

"She didn't."

"But ... ?"

She says impatiently: "They brought her back here in a state of shock."

"Who did?"

"And then the doctor sedated her ..." Her responses seem a bit off key. Is it her or is it me? "For several hours I sat by the bedside, held her hand. He came back — gave her a second shot — said she wouldn't wake until the following day. He was a fool. I shouldn't have trusted him. Should never have left her. They shouldn't have brought her here in the first place. She woke up in the night ..."

"Yes?"

She looks at me as though I'm not there. Her look seems to go right through me.

"And that's something else that's going to haunt me: always: the way she must have felt when she woke up and found herself to be alone ..."

After a pause her eyes perceptibly refocus. "Somebody found the ring upon the stairs. One of the lodgers."

"But for God's sake," I say. "What happened to her?"

"She disappeared."

"Just disappeared?"

"Walked out of the house that same night. Never came back."

"But people don't just disappear."

"The police said they do. If they want to do so badly enough."

"But she was drugged — a zombie. Wandering aimlessly. How could they not have found her?"

She shakes her head.

"Had she a suitcase?"

"No."

"Nothing?"

"Just her handbag."

"But no clothes?"

"The frock which she'd been put to bed in; the coat I'd spread on top of her for extra warmth."

"And money? What about money?"

"She had a post office account. There was still a fair bit in it."

"Couldn't the police have traced her, then, through that?"

"No."

"But why not?"

"Nor could they trace her through her ration book."

"Excuse me, ma'am — but why in the hell not?"

"Simple. They finally assumed that Cassidy wasn't her real name."

For several seconds I just stare at the old lady. "My God!" Then: "Oh my God."

"She'd always wanted her son to be called Cassidy," she remarks, quite calmly.

"But surely you told them the truth?"

"No."

"No?"

"It was the name she'd been going by for months. There was no reason to suppose she'd now revert. Besides — I decided after a few days to respect her privacy; her right to choose. If she didn't want to come back I didn't mean to force her."

"But she wasn't in a fit state to know what she wanted."

"She didn't want continual reminders of Tom — that much I could be sure of. I telephoned the farm in Suffolk in case she might've gone back there. But I didn't tell them anything; pretended only that I'd lost her new address. Also, I was going to try to get in touch with a friend of hers — she had a friend called Trixie. But as I say. By then I'd decided that Rosalind had the right to self-determination." The old lady's tone has recovered much of its authority. "And, anyhow, if she were dead what difference would it make?"

"Excuse me?"

"Oh, yes. I already thought she might be dead."

"No." I shake my head. "No, ma'am. No."

"I suggested they should drag the Leg-of-Mutton Pond. That's where she often used to go to sit with Tom. But they said it was a costly operation and there wasn't the evidence to warrant it." She pauses. "And it wouldn't have brought her back, either. Would it? So what the hell?"

At last I manage to reply: "No, ma'am. She isn't dead. Rosalind is not dead."

She actually smiles at me — a small smile; touches my wrist for a moment with one arthritic hand. "My dear young man. How can you sound so positive? You don't know anything about it."

"All I do know is: she can't be dead. She can't be. I assure you."

"What nonsense."

"It's instinct, ma'am. Conviction. Not nonsense."

"I just can't make you out, Mr Cassidy."

I wish she could. Then maybe she'd tell me how to do it for myself. "And if she intended only to jump in some pond," I add, "why would she have taken her purse?"

"Forgive me — that's naive."

Then she offers me another gin. "And if you like I could go and make a sandwich." In view of recent events both offers are surprising.

I accept the first, decline the second. After I've fixed the drinks we spend ten minutes looking at some snapshots. (The pictures of the baby show how beautiful he was; Rosalind wasn't exaggerating in what she wrote to Trixie.) There are several of her mother. "I feel that I'd have known her anywhere."

"Yes," she agrees. "There's a strong family resemblance. Even Rosalind's grandmother: change the hairstyle, slim down the face ..."

"Mrs Farnsworth? May I see her room?"

Whatever she may say, her indecision has little to do with any possible objection from the present tenant — who won't be back, I hear, till after six. It has more to do, of course, with her unvoiced fear I could be schizoid. You don't have to be clairvoyant to perceive that.

"But why do you want to see it? I needn't tell you it's completely changed."

Yet we do go up. And there are certain things that won't have changed: the doorknob, the window, the shape of the room, maybe even that maze of cracks upon the ceiling. The wallpaper was hers; so were the curtains; discoloured, faded — but still hers. "What about the bed ...?" At the moment it's unmade but Mrs Farnsworth doesn't seem to notice; and Mr Turnbull need never realise he's had visitors. "Would it have been in that same spot when Rosalind was here?" It fits neatly in an alcove.

She nods. I sit on the edge of it, tentatively. She points out — a tad dryly — that it wouldn't have been the same bed.

"Is there any piece of furniture that would have been the same?"

"Oh, my dear young man. Wait until you're ninety and someone asks you to describe a room when you were half that age. Possibly the chair was here. Possibly the table."

284

Now I go and sit upon the chair, put my hands upon the table. A table small and rickety and badly scarred.

In the middle of the room, beneath a forty-watt bulb. Nearby there's a wireless being played.

> *"It's a grand night for singing,*
> *The clouds are flying high,*
> *And somewhere a bird*
> *Who is bound he'll be heard*
> *Is throwing his heart at the sky ..."*

I'm sitting at the table, hunched into my yellow coat; watching the shadow of the light bulb swing in the draught that blows from door to window. And my hair is stringy, my dress is creased, my whole appearance ... slatternly.

But the room I'm sitting in — it's not the room in Worsley Road.

The light bulb is fly-specked and unshaded; the partly-drawn curtains thin and skimpy, the filthy nets aren't even hanging right. The bed looks as though bedbugs might infest it.

My thoughts revolve around a single topic.

If only I'd stopped to ask Jane if she wanted any shopping. Other mornings I had done so.

If only I hadn't made that extra piece of toast.

(Which was pure greed ... especially with Tom getting so impatient to be taken out.)

Selfish and greedy. No wonder that his father saw right through me.

But then all my life I've been selfish. What about that business with my mother?

I'd known for a long time she'd been ill. Should have known it. For months she'd mentioned little things. If only I'd paused to think about somebody other than myself. Truly — properly — think.

That beggar now ... he'd only asked me for a cup of tea ... oh God the price of just one cup of tea ...

And I'd wanted to give it to him, too. That was the dreadful part. The sun was shining. I'd been feeling happy. I'd even thought about ice cream; just a few minutes earlier I had actually thought about buying an ice cream! And then I'd remembered. I had only a ten-shilling note and a couple of farthings. And I was too mean to part with the one and too embarrassed to offer him the other.

But why hadn't I asked him to wait? I could have changed the money in a shop.

Oh God, just a ten-shilling note and with that I might have bought the life of my child.

And the life of my child's children.

Just a ten-shilling note and with that how many hundreds and thousands of lives ...?

But the sins of the mother.

Shall flatten.

And splatter.

And destroy.

On each of these words I bang my fist down on the table. (Oh, if only I could have been the one to be flattened and splattered and destroyed!) Bang my fist down hard — with intent to make it hurt and bleed; then stare at it, amazed, as though I've just awoken from a trance. I put my arms upon the table — lay my head on top of them — and howl.

"I don't know what to do! I don't know what to do!"

I slide down from my chair — slide down deliberately. I crumple on the floor. I crawl across the carpet.

"My dear, you're ill."

There's an old lady leaning over me.

"I'm going to call the doctor." She puts her trembling hand upon my shoulder.

"Who are you?" I ask.

"My name is Farnsworth. Jane Farnsworth. You've just been ..."

Jane? Jane Farnsworth? But the woman standing here in front of me has wrinkled skin; white hair. How can this possibly be Jane?

The carpet on the floor is worn; in places, threadbare. Even where there's any pile left it's matted with the spillings of countless years of slovenly living. Is this my carpet? My own beautiful carpet that I only had to see to fall in love with? (She's right; I'm obviously not well ... Am I then out of my mind? But I don't want any doctor.) My fingers dig into my prized, once-lovely carpet. My fingers are tanned and strong and have a scattering of hair. These fingers surely can't be mine.

Yet in that case what has become of me?

What am I doing here?

Five minutes later I'm standing at the front door.

"That carpet? Was it hers?"

"The one upstairs?" She doesn't even question how I knew.

But then I just don't get it, ma'am: how could you ever have allowed ...?

She replies as if I'd spoken.

"I sold most of her belongings; gave the money to a charity. But I felt there should be one thing left up there to commemorate her presence ... or her passing. Yes, I forgot the carpet when you asked. I shouldn't have left it in her room, though: an act of vandalism against the very person I loved best in all the world. Are you quite certain you'll be well enough to travel?"

"I'm truly sorry to have put you through all this," I say, dully.

"We could always ring to get a taxi."

"No, ma'am, you've been very kind. I'm fine. Thank you." Only one thing wrong with me, ma'am — even if that one thing does, as it happens, threaten to be terminal.

You see, ma'am ... I'm remembering.

23

I don't know how I get back to Tom's office. Was it by taxi? Or was it by tube or bus or on foot?

And I don't know what time I arrive. It could have been a year since our parting in Grosvenor Square — whereas it's only a week since I first walked up that steep, blue-linoed staircase. I find this quite incredible.

"You're earlier than I expected," says Tom. He sounds preoccupied.

"Why? You told me you'd be through by seven."

"And now it's twenty-to-five."

"You're joking."

I slip off the wristwatch that must have been running down throughout the day. But it's a service that it needs — not a shake. I leave it on a corner of Tom's desk.

"How have things gone?" he asks. "From your expression I'd say you didn't have much joy."

"Joy?"

It occurs to me he isn't looking all that great himself.

"No. You're right. I didn't have much joy."

"But as it turns out," he says, "it doesn't matter."

"Meaning what?"

"Meaning we now know what happened to her."

"And how? Just how do we now know what happened to her?"

His voice is gentle. "I went to St Catherine's. Looked for a death certificate. Found one."

"You can't have."

"I'm sorry, Tex. 1946."

"No. Some mistake. If she'd really killed herself the police would have been in touch with Mrs Farnsworth. She'd been reported missing."

I remember the mix-up in names. "But in any case she isn't dead."

Tom doesn't answer for a moment. "Tex, I didn't mention that she'd killed herself. Who's Mrs Farnsworth? Tell me what you found out."

"Why? You said it doesn't matter."

He fiddles with a paperclip. He's always fiddling with a goddamned paperclip.

"Landlady," I mumble. "Still living at the same address. What I found out ..."

"Yes?"

"... was how her child got killed." I find it difficult to think about; let alone put into words.

"Whose child? Rosalind's?"

"And how she blamed herself for this and ran away from where she'd been secure. How she went to live in squalor, because she thought she needed to be punished." It strikes me that I'm gabbling.

"Where, in squalor?"

"Oh, for Christ's sake. Why's that important?"

"What I mean is, if it was known where she'd gone to, why was she reported missing?"

"Obviously it wasn't. Can't you understand? It wasn't known."

Tom lays aside his paperclip. Emits a sigh.

"Tex, why have you let it get to you like this? Last week you didn't even want to go to Southwold. It was I who had to push. But since then ... Well, since then it seems to have become ..."

"Become what?"

"I don't know ... An obsession."

This time the silence lasts a full minute.

"There are things which I've remembered. Things I wish I hadn't." I give a shrug.

"I see" he says. "I'm sorry." He picks up the paperclip. "Do you want to talk about them?"

"No."

"You don't think it might help?"

A further lengthy silence.

"Things like ... oh, for instance ... like I'm married. We don't care much for one another; not sure we ever did. I remember she wouldn't have children. Partly fear — but

289

partly the sheer inconvenience of it and worry that she'd lose her figure."

But it isn't necessary to elaborate, to burden him with more. I recall a time when she'd thought that she was pregnant: the hysteria, the recriminations; the screaming for abortion. As it turned out, her period had been perhaps a week late — but she'd miscalculated and believed that it was two. Afterwards, no apology. No hint of shame.

I can't go back to this.

"All the same," I say, "I suspect in some ways it may have been my fault rather more than hers."

"In any case, it's not so tragic. People say there's life after divorce."

"And another thing: they claim that if you're born to wealth then money's not important. Untrue. It seems I've always let the dollar sign dictate."

Yet though I can remember this, although I can remember many things, there are still great gaps in my knowledge. For example, I don't yet know my name. I don't yet know the name of my hotel.

"Well, damn it, Tex, you're young. You talk as though it were too late for children or for working out priorities. You talk as though you were an old man."

"And that's the way I feel right now." I give a wan smile. "Perhaps I'm older than I look."

"*The Picture of Dorian Gray*. Now there was a fellow who had trouble with priorities."

"And you know something? I guess I could be nearly as despicable."

*

And I remember a dream. Or, rather, a nightmare. I must have had it often. It's vivid and insistent.

Likewise prophetic — concerning, as it does, a hired detective. Yet he's not at all like Tom. Nor does his office compare with this one. It's shabbier and unwelcoming.

But Rosalind's photo is the same, even if my motive in

290

looking for her has also greatly altered. (It appears I've changed places with my father and merely want to know whether she's happy or whether there's anything that can be done to help.) Nor does the search proceed along the same lines. It's confined to London. A London of some forty years ago.

Yet though the motive and the search are different the outcome's similar: I discover that she's dead.

Flattened beneath a tube train.

Suicide: but not premeditated. She's standing on the edge of a platform. She has no thought of death — well, certainly no more than usual — only of the awfulness of life. But suddenly she sees the train. She doesn't even think. There isn't time enough to think.

Though in my dream I only hear of it in the detective's office, I'm immediately transported back — transported back screaming — to watch the whole thing happen.

*

"But how did she do it, Tom?"

"I don't know."

"*Tell* me."

"Tex, it was forty-four years ago."

"I need to hear."

He sighs.

"When I left St Catherine's I went to the records office of the borough in which it happened. Rather strangely, it was this one, as a matter of fact."

After about ten minutes he makes us both a coffee. "I wish there was something stronger I could offer. Sorry."

"I've got to go now, anyway." Can't manage more than just a sip or two.

"Absolutely no *got to* in any shape or form."

"No, I suppose not. Still ... allow you to get on with other things."

"What will you do? Have something to eat first — naturally. Then why not see a film?"

I nod, abstractedly.

"But — Tom. What was she doing here? In this neighbourhood? She wasn't working any longer at that store."

"What store?"

"Some department store. Bourne and ... Bourne and Something."

"Hollingsworth. Closed down some years ago ... I don't know. She must have found another job."

"No. Too near the one where she'd been happy. Well, yes, that's it, of course. That's why she came back, isn't it? To look at the place where she'd been happy. To look at it just once. To stand somewhere in a doorway and watch them coming out: the people she'd been working with. That's it, of course."

"What film do you think you'll see?"

"No, I'm not in the mood for any movie. I guess I'll head for home."

Suddenly he gets up. "Come on, then. Who am I trying to kid? There's nothing here that's of the least importance."

"No — please don't."

To make it sound less brusque I weakly punch his upper arm. "It's just that somehow I'd prefer to be alone."

"Listen. That's the second brush-off in a single day. I may start to feel rejected."

"You've been good to me, Tom. I'm sorry I've been difficult."

"Hey, what's this? It was just a very feeble joke."

"Sure. I still mean it."

He laughs. "I'm glad you still mean it. And, by the way, 'difficult' I could almost be persuaded to accept. 'Despicable' — never in a month of Sundays."

"Thanks." Then I give him a close hug; a hug which aims to express much more than just my gratitude. "*Au revoir*, Tom. Take care."

"And you, Tex. No — wait — you haven't got your watch on!"

But by now I'm nearly on the next landing.

"Okay," he says. "I'll remember to bring it with me."

24

Out in the street I feel utterly alone. I turn back abruptly, thinking to rejoin him.

A woman comes out of the main door, blocking my retreat. A minute earlier I'd been vaguely aware of her standing at the entrance to the textiles company, trying earnestly to gain admittance. She's thin and wearing a sleeveless dress and sandals. She asks me something which I don't quite catch.

"Excuse me?" It's stupid but it's automatic.

She's already holding out a leaflet; thrusting it towards my hand. She repeats the last part of her question. She has, I think, a Scottish accent.

"... born again?" she asks.

"Oh, Christ." Normally I'd have cottoned on much sooner. "Yes!" I say. "Yes! *Yes*! Just let me be!"

I crumple up her leaflet, toss it down, turn back to the sidewalk. Not the idea of born-again she must have had in mind.

Oxford Street one way — Regent's Park the other. Heat and fumes and traffic; or greenery and water and the chance to think? I head for Oxford Street.

But there I stand irresolute. Left or right? Tottenham Court Road or Oxford Circus? As little point to either.

Bourne & Hollingsworth.

"Bourne and What?" the guy says.

"Large department store. Closed down now. Used to be around here someplace."

"Sorry, mate. Could tell you where John Lewis is."

So next I try a woman more than twice his age. "Yes, dear, you're right — along here somewhere. Terrible how quick you forget. This side of the road though. Perhaps that gentleman selling papers might know. Once got ever such a lovely pair of shoes there."

The news vendor also points me towards Tottenham Court Road. But he's busy and less patient.

A short way further on I'm standing at the kerb, outside a shopping complex called the Plaza. I'm leaning back and peering upwards when a policeman draws level. He's fair and bluff and red-faced from the sun. He has his sleeves rolled up.

"Can you help me, please? I'm looking for Bourne & Hollingsworth."

"Are you indeed, sir? Sorry to have to break it to you. You're about six or seven years too late."

"I know. I'm looking for where it used to be."

"Well, then, you're standing in the right spot. Took up the whole of this block, it did."

"Thank you," I say and he moves on. I stare up again at the shopping complex. After that I turn and look across the road. I experience a brief moment of sickness — even of faintness, almost of dislocation. I'm convinced of it: she'd have been standing in a doorway just opposite.

Except that the doorways then, of course, would all have been different. Or would they, I wonder. How can you tell? To my untutored and unBritish eye this present doorway I'm staring at could so easily have been pre-war. Even its very drabness, its whole air of neglect, speaks of the middle forties.

And my goodness, it suddenly strikes me, rather forcibly, if there is a god he's got to be a pretty fiendish one — because there's a woman over there right now standing in that doorway. Not simply is she standing in that doorway; not simply does she have a real look of Rosalind; she's even — goddamn it — wearing a yellow coat. (I can't remember — did I see in my dream that it was yellow or did Jane Farnsworth tell me? In any case, this is exactly the kind of coat which Rosalind was wearing — even down to the tie belt and single button at the neck. That one, too, had been dirty; in need of a good press.) Yes, you're a cruel god all right. The last thing I need at a time like this is to have tricks played on me.

The one merciful thing, however: at least this stranger isn't going to stay. Hardly have I seen her than she starts moving off in the direction of Oxford Circus. Her walk is the walk of someone who has been utterly cast down by life. Well, lady, I can identify with that; I know exactly how you must be feeling. Briefly my heart goes out to her. I wouldn't have thought this could be possible.

With not even another glance at the plaza I continue on towards Tottenham Court Road. Strange thoughts go through my head. "Don't be so stupid!" I tell myself. I carry on walking.

These thoughts are really crazy; I recognise them as such, truly do recognise them as such, and yet I have to tell myself again: "Don't be so stupid! Don't be such an ass-hole!"

I can't help looking back, though — onto the opposite sidewalk. Now there's only the odd flash of yellow as she gets sucked into the crowd — a strangely colourless crowd, it seems to me, irrelevantly, by comparison. I give myself a mental shake and force myself forward again doggedly. Why, then, do I find my footsteps start to drag? Why, then, half a minute later, am I still using the same argument?

"Have you gone loco? *Loco*? She is dead — idiot! You know she's dead. And even if she were not dead — idiot — she would now be an old woman. You just can't give in to this! *You — just — cannot — give — in — to — this*! For the sake of things like self-respect and even physical health and restoring the proper balance of your mind —"

Then all at once I come to a standstill; someone — I think it is a captain or a major — very nearly collides with me, and apologises. I glance about me at a London that suddenly seems as grey and washed-out as though it were coloured by my own despair. Or desperation.

I say the words out loud.

"Oh, fuck the proper balance of my mind!"

And then, almost before I know it, I have turned and I am running. I am bumping into people; I am weaving through the traffic — the traffic, thankfully, far less dense than usual. I am provoking not just anger but even an actual oath or two. It hardly touches me. I am breathless — sweaty.

Again I catch a glimpse of yellow coat; I see it disappear into the subway. That is the only thing, now, that really does concern me.

In time I too hurl myself into the stormy sea converging on the entrance to the subway. I do my frantic best to penetrate.

Yet in the end I can't get down those narrow steps any faster than anybody else. Why couldn't she have stayed out in the open?

And then I realise. Oh God. I realise. How many minutes since Tom had finished telling me?

The body on the line.

There.

At Oxford Circus.

A realisation, however, which is clearly spurious and which at least is followed by a further moment of lucidity.

You're under stress and you're confused and you're in shock. You're only doing all this for the sake of having something to do; for the sake of having, briefly, a purpose; for the sake of channelling aggression and impotence and fury.

Aren't you?

But all the same I wish I'd got a closer look. I wish she hadn't moved away the very instant I'd laid eyes on her.

"Please let me through! I must get through!"

"You and a million others," says the man in front. He's a labourer with old khaki shirt and a spume of grizzled chest hair. "So take your turn and stop shoving and we'll all get through a lot happier."

When I eventually make it down the steps my sweat goes cold on me. I can't see her at all.

There's a beggar woman on the concourse, holding out her palm to anyone who'll listen. "Price of a cuppa tea, sir? Price of a cuppa tea, lady?" My eye's caught by the splash of yellow thrown across her little group of carrier bags. I know immediately what's happened.

But, oh, God. How on earth — how in the name of heaven — how am I ever going to find her now?

The dress! The dress in the photograph. Black-and-white

in the photograph but I'm well aware that in fact it was wine-coloured. The floral bits were white and ochre.

And I spot her!

In all that milling crowd I actually do spot her.

But she's still a long way from me: on the other side of a barrier and close to one of the moving stairways.

The coat — the dress — it is you, isn't it? It has to be you; it's got to be you. But if only you'd turn round a moment, let me see your face!

The escalator's jampacked.

It's a strikingly long one and yet by the time I get there she's almost at the bottom.

I say it only softly to begin with.

"Rosalind ..."

But then I give it everything I've got.

"Rosalind!"

Yet with all the usual noises of a busy subway how far can one voice hope to carry? Those who do hear turn and stare at me dispassionately. The men look stupid in their stupid trilbies, the women in their horrid headscarves; their senses addled by their stupid cigarette smoke.

"That woman down there! Stop her, will you!" But she has now stepped off the escalator. "Please let me through! It's vital! Somebody's life depends on it!"

People do their best to move over — more embarrassed than anything — but it scarcely helps. Is there another escalator after this? An old guy says there is.

But when I get to it the woman is a long way down.

"*Rosalind!*"

No response.

"That woman's going to kill herself!"

A man calls back to me — an able seaman.

"Where? Which one?"

"That woman in the floral dress! She's ... Oh, Christ."

Again she's just stepped off the escalator. Is wholly out of sight.

But suddenly I know what I must do. The down-escalator and its counterpart run parallel. They share a broad

297

dividing band. I scramble onto it. People gaze at me in fascination. Their smiles, their gasps, their staring eyes don't bother me — I think it's true that since I glimpsed her on the street I've hardly thought about myself.

It's weird, however — the sort of thing that does occur to me ... up here the lighting seems dimmer and for the first time I notice that the escalator steps have wooden slats. I'm struck by the heavy gloss on Rita Hayworth's lips — *Gilda* is back at the New Gallery. Some newsreel theatre is showing the Wembley Cup Final; Shakespeare's birthday celebrations. Certainly, it's odd.

Yet peripheral.

I jump down; turn to the right.

The crowds appear to have thinned a little. But on the platform — which I've entered halfway down its length — people are standing a good half-dozen deep. I see no sign of her.

"Oh, God. Help me!"

I know it's from the left the train will come. Panic-stricken, I hear subterranean rumblings; but these are tubes for other platforms. I thread my way towards the edge of this one — reach it — nervously lean forward and look in both directions. She's over to my right.

Possibly, for the merest instant, I may smile. "Rosalind," I tell myself, "it *is* you."

But then I yell:

"Rosalind! No! Don't! It's me — Matt!"

Yet she still doesn't hear and anyway there's now a roar in the tunnel which just has to be the train for this platform.

"Rosalind! Don't!"

She doesn't hear.

I wave my arms wildly.

She doesn't see.

"That woman in the floral dress! Hold her back! She's going to kill herself!"

Nobody pays me the least attention. The roar in the tunnel is growing tumultuous.

What can I do?

The answer comes with quick storm-centre clarity. You can create a diversion.

Surely no two people ever jumped independently — and during the same minute — in front of the same tube.

"Me," I say. "Not you."

The train is now out of the tunnel: three seconds or less from where I stand.

I close my eyes — and step forward.

*

Darkness.

25

The darkness starts to clear — turns from black to grey — smells like smoke. Smoke that issues from a steam engine.

*

We are about to leave. The whistle has already blown. Probably the small station at Halesworth has seldom been so crowded.

"And believe this, honey. Believe this if you never believe anything again. This time I'll send for you."

"This time?"

Yes; why did I say that? Unaccountably, I shudder. Someone must have walked across my grave.

"I guess I was woolgathering; thinking how crazy I'd go if anything bad ever happened to you ... Oh, honey, please don't cry. I absolutely promise: nothing bad ever *will* happen to you! I just won't let it. I think I'd die for you first."

"Well, if that's supposed to stop me crying it's not wonderful psychology."

"All right, I know I'd die for you first."

"Idiot. Say something heartening, like ... 'See you in three months.'"

"No, that's too long. See you in one-and-a-half. Two at the most. I'll either send for you or come for you or arrange with Harry S. Truman ..." But then we kiss; we cling. The train is now beginning to pull out.

"Please look after yourself," she calls. "I love you so much."

"I should darn well hope you do! I love you too. Enormously."

"What?"

"Always," I shout back. I tap my ring finger. "Always! Always!" And I can see she understands.

I think she calls back.

"Always!"

26

I have a vision of Tom returning to his apartment. "Tex!" he'll call. No answer. But then he'll remember I might have gone to bed.

He'll walk into the sitting room, pour himself a drink; slump into an armchair. After a moment he'll take my watch from his pocket, put it on the coffee table; pick it up again just to admire its slimness.

Still admiring it, he'll idly reach out, flick on the answering machine. After several messages there'll come the one concerning me.

"Hi! Herb Kramer here, from the embassy. Have the gen

you wanted regarding your friend Mr Matthew Cassidy of New Haven, Connecticut. And it all checked out, Tom: just as you gave it me: meat-packing business, older brother who died in '42, Cassidy himself over here from '43 to '45, lieutenant in the United States Air Force, stationed at Boxted, then at Halesworth — both in Suffolk. All spot on. Except one thing. No children. Also ... and here's the heck of a coincidence. Admitted into hospital, in deep coma, last Monday. Condition critical. In fact I've just put through another call, at 3.55pm our time here. Old guy appears to be sinking fast; only an hour or two left, they think — at most. I don't know where in hell this leaves our young amnesiac. Why is life *never* simple? Call me when you can; we'll try to work out some solution."

Tom won't wait for other messages — will turn off the machine. Gaze at my watch in some bewilderment. Get up; gently open the door to the spare room. Stare at the empty bed.

I might have changed my mind, of course — could be at the movies; he'll remember that. I might have decided to go for a long walk. There are several possibilities.

"But no children. That's absurd. Tex, you look so much like him ..." He'll bite his lip an instant. "You look so much like him you could almost *be* him, for heaven's sake!"

He'll come back to his armchair; pour himself another drink; check to see who his remaining callers are.

But none of them is me.

"And Tex. Why did you say *au revoir*?"

At the time it hadn't really sunk in but now it will start to sound less casual. The whole of that last minute will start to sound less casual.

It's not a phrase that Tom has ever used much. His wife, on the other hand, did so continually. "*Au revoir*, my angel, have a nice day!" or "*Au revoir*, darling, hope to return soon!" Indeed, it was so evocative he'd had it written on her gravestone. *Lucy Merrill. 1951 — 1989. Always in my thoughts. Always a part of me. Au revoir.*

Au revoir.

301

Until the next time.

Until we meet again.

He's going to fret about me; I know that. Lie awake at nights worrying. He's going to make inquiries. It will be weeks before he finally accepts the fact I'm gone — ungrudgingly permits me, in Mrs Farnsworth's phrase, the right to self-determination.

She's indeed one of the people he'll see during the course of his inquiries. They'll take to one another. They'll become friends. He'll be nearly like a son to her. Perhaps a godson.

They'll get some weird ideas, the two of them together. (Perhaps it's because she's close to death; perhaps it's just the gin at work — or with Tom, of course, the whisky.)

They'll get a little maudlin. They'll talk about reunion.

In any case, he won't forget me.

Nor will he forget Rosalind.

He'll never sell the watch.